THE FINAL CURTAIN

THE FINAL CURTAIN

PRISCILLA MASTERS

WORLDWIDE®

TORONTO • NEW YORK • LONDON
AMSTERDAM • PARIS • SYDNEY • HAMBURG
STOCKHOLM • ATHENS • TOKYO • MILAN
MADRID • WARSAW • BUDAPEST • AUCKLAND

Recycling programs
for this product may
not exist in your area.

The Final Curtain

A Worldwide Mystery/May 2019

First published by Severn House Publishers Ltd.

ISBN-13: 978-1-335-45539-0

Copyright © 2013 by Priscilla Masters

Printed in U.S.A.

THE FINAL CURTAIN

ONE

SHE'D HALF EXPECTED IT. Some ragging on her first day back after her honeymoon, a trick or a practical joke: a couple of helium balloons here, confetti planted in her locker ready to spill out when she opened it, maybe even a couple of sexy things like a thong or a condom left where she would find them. But even she hadn't anticipated this. Joanna pushed the door to her and Mike Korpanski's office open and there they all were waiting for her, big grins on shiny faces.

He spoke first, his dark eyes warm and welcoming and his voice equally so, rich as treacle, not hiding the fact that he was glad to see her back. 'Welcome home, Jo.'

And it *was* home.

The rest of the team echoed his words: 'Welcome back.' It seemed to bounce at her from the very walls of the room and come straight from their hearts. She felt happiness well up inside her and beamed around at them. 'I'm glad to *be* back.'

'You won't be for long,' Korpanski said darkly. 'Not once your honeymoon happiness has melted away. You'll soon wish you were back in wherever it was.'

She might have known *he* would be the one to bring her back down to earth.

She still grinned at him, her pleasure undented, so far. 'Thanks, Mike.'

'My pleasure, as they say.' But his dark eyes were still sparkling.

They all watched as she flicked on her computer and read what was winking at her from the screen. 'Nice honeymoon?' A raucous message followed underneath along with a fairly explicit activity picture of a couple doing what couples usually did on their honeymoon. She giggled, hand over mouth, then stretched and read the message again, watched by all the other officers who hoped that Detective Inspector Piercy— or Mrs Matthew Levin—would remain in this light and frothy mood.

It was a vain hope. She looked up from the screen. 'No one got any work to do?'

The honeymoon was over.

One by one the other officers melted away, leaving her and Korpanski alone. She tossed a small wooden box on to his desk. It landed with a thud and a soft, dry rattle. He picked it up, studied the picture of a temple dancer with four arms and read the label. 'Tea? Thanks. I'm glad you had time to think of your old work colleagues while you were living it up.'

She smiled across at him. Korpanski and she had started badly, with a frosty and suspicious relationship. But with every case they had moved closer until they were, to the resentment of Mrs Korpanski, bosom pals. 'I got it at the airport when we were coming back. I didn't feel I could return empty-handed.'

'Thanks anyway.' He gave her a sly look. 'So, Jo,' he said, 'how was it? Actually, *where* was it?' Matthew Levin had been secretive about the honeymoon's desti-

nation. Even as Joanna had walked up the aisle she had
not known where it would be—apart from the fact that
it would be somewhere hot and sunny and very beautiful. A tropical honeymoon, Matthew had promised
her, telling her she would need little more than a bikini
and a couple of sarongs. He had spoken no more or less
than the truth. It had been perfect. Korpanski picked
up on her secret smile. 'Did you find out where you
were going before or after you'd boarded the plane?'

'Before—just,' she answered. 'And then only because Matthew was reading a guide book. It sort of
gave the game away. Besides, I had to know from the
check-in queue, destination Colombo and the depar-
ture lounge. He's rather good at keeping secrets, my
husband,' she finished, flushing self-consciously. The
word was still foreign to her.

'So it was…?'

'Sri Lanka. And it was…just wonderful.' She leaned
back in her chair and gazed up at Korpanski, who had
left his desk and was now standing over her, humour
softening his face. 'Close your eyes, Mike,' she said,
'and imagine the most perfect honeymoon. Diving,
sightseeing Buddhist temples, golden sand, beautiful
sea, hot sun, blue whales and dolphins, elephants and
leopards. Mongooses and tropical birds, coconut palms
and mangrove swamps. All simply wonderful—except
for the tsunami alert.'

'What?'

'Yes. There was a tsunami alert but it sort of blew
over. Anyway, it was a wonderful, wonderful honeymoon and the nights were long, hot and balmy.'

Korpanski chuckled. 'OK, Jo, I get the picture. It
does sound fantastic.'

'It was.' She closed her eyes for a moment and re-called Matthew, her husband. Matthew the romantic, his arms around her, his legs wrapped around her, his words, the wonderful romanticism of diving together, pointing out fish and corals, hearing the spout of the blue whales before they dived, riding elephants through the jungle, kissing in dazzling sunshine, sharing break-fast and dinner and simply everything. She opened her eyes. Korpanski was giving her 'a look'.

She sat up. 'What is it?'

'I just wonder if we ought to be calling you Inspec-tor Levin?'

She was back to earth with a bump. 'I don't think so, Mike,' she said sharply. 'Piercy'll do just fine, thank you very much.'

He looked relieved. 'Good,' he said. 'I was a bit worried that...'

'Marriage will change me into a marshmallow? Again, I don't think so, Mike.'

'Thank goodness for that,' he mumbled. He left her desk and returned to his own, switched his computer on and smirked across the room at her. 'I was a bit wor-ried you'd turn soft on me.'

She was tempted to throw something at him but in these days of computers she was lacking a safe mis-sile—a rubber or biro, pencil or notepad. And she couldn't do without her mouse. She tried to give him a withering look instead, which failed completely. He was still laughing, and she joined him. 'I've got mar-ried, Mike,' she said soberly, 'not had a frontal lobot-omy. Anyway, what was all that about, *"You won't be for long"*? What's been going on while I've been away? A spate of burglaries? Jack the Ripper moved into town? Another Doctor Shipman set up in General Practice?'

He shook his head. 'I wish.'

Her eyes narrowed. 'Have you been idling, Korpanski? While the cat was away… Don't tell me Leek's gone law abiding on us? Pur-lease.'

'It has been pretty quiet while you've been away,' he admitted. 'Post-Christmas rush, bad weather. Half the regulars banged up for the festive season and some nasty frosts have kept all the criminals shivering at their fires. There's only really been one thing.'

'Ah-ha. Go on.'

'Some old biddy who lives right out in the moorlands has been ringing us up—sometimes more than once a day—with all sorts of trivial stuff. And I mean really trivial.'

'How trivial?'

'This trivial: an invisible intruder, someone sneaking round the house. She's never actually seen him, she simply *senses* his presence.' Korpanski's scepticism made his face angular and twisted. She could sense his irritation. 'And that's just the beginning,' he continued. 'Her nightdress had been moved off the bed on to a chair. The lavatory seat had been left up when only women live in the house. A window was left open in the kitchen when she's certain she locked it. A dead mouse deliberately planted in the bread bin.'

Joanna's eyes widened. 'You're joking.'

'I wish,' he said. 'She's always saying she's sure *this* time someone will get her and as she does live alone in an isolated location we feel honour bound to at least call. I can just imagine the headlines in the *Leek Post*

& *Times* if something did happen: *Woman found dead after numerous desperate calls to the police.*

Joanna nodded and Korpanski continued in the same, grumbling tone.

'However many times we go out there and find nothing tangible we'll always be blamed if something subsequently goes wrong. If you want my opinion she's barmy, saying someone's outside watching her house, that she's smelt things or heard things, saying she's frightened and demanding we go out there. In the two weeks you've been away we've logged more than fifteen calls from her, Jo.' Desperation was now making his voice hard. 'She needs her own private security force or a psychiatrist. Something, anyway. She's driving us mad. And…' he swivelled around in his chair, '…more importantly, she's taking up time we can't really afford. We can't keep going out there. It's a good half hour's drive each way.'

'Have you ever found any evidence of an intruder?'

Korpanski shook his head. 'Not a bloody thing,' he said. 'And it's a devil of a route, down a muddy old track for a mile or so. It takes at least two hours out of our day, going there and back and taking statements. The place where she lives is remote. Butterfield Farm, it's called.' He said the name with the snort of disdain a country dweller directs at a city person who idealizes the muck and mud of the moorlands. 'There's no one else for miles around. And she lives on her own. Obviously she gets imaginative and twitchy.'

Joanna yawned, bored already. 'Why doesn't she move into the town like most people do when they get a bit older, live alone and are worried about the isolation?'

'We've suggested that,' he said glumly. 'We've even gone so far as to tell her about more suitable places.' He looked aggrieved. 'There's some lovely sheltered accommodation down by the football field but she hasn't taken it up—so far.'

'You say you've found no evidence of an intruder?'

'Not a sausage.'

'Each time?'

Korpanski shook his head.

'Has she a history of mental illness, paranoia? Alzheimer's?'

'Not as far as we know. We had a quick word with her doctor. He says he isn't aware of anything like that. I don't think she's crazy, Jo. Just nervous and a bit over-imaginative.'

Joanna frowned. 'How long has she lived there?'

'Almost ten years.'

'Has she ever called us out *before* these recent episodes?'

'No. Never. We didn't even know she was there. We haven't been there before. Even Timmis and McBrine didn't know it was there—it's so tucked away in its own private little valley. And *they're* patrolling the moorlands all the time,' he said, referring to the two constables. 'It started, quite suddenly, around New Year, when you were setting off on your honeymoon.'

Joanna shot him a look. 'Coincidence, surely,' she said with deliberation.

'Yeah. Well. Since then…' He opened up the file on his computer and Joanna stared down at an impressive list of dates and events involving police attention.

'Mmm,' she said. 'She *has* kept you busy.' What

was the world coming to that they had to deal with this sort of crap?

Korpanski gave an exasperated sigh as he closed the file. 'She's a sixty-year-old incessant time-waster,' he said, but a twinkle lit his eyes as he spoke the next sentence, swivelling around in his chair to watch her face square on and gauge her response to his next sentence. 'Which is why we've elected *you* to be lucky enough to pay the next visit. And in case you worry that you might have to wait a while for the pleasure she's already rung in today. Six o'clock this morning she dialled our number to tell us that she could smell cigarette smoke in the kitchen.'

'I'm supposed to respond to *that*?'

Korpanski didn't even bother replying or concealing his smirk. 'Her name, by the way, is Timony Weeks.'

Joanna's head shot round. 'You're having me on.'

'Ah-ha,' Korpanski responded, shaking his head, his eyes still sparkling with merriment. He was savouring this moment. 'Hand on heart,' he said, suiting his action to the words. 'And to cap it all, she's an ex-child actress. Used to be known as Timony Shore, now Timony Weeks.' He gave a bland smile. 'So off you go, Inspector Piercy, to Butterfield Farm.'

In spite of her irritation Joanna couldn't help smiling. It sounded so pastoral, so quaint.

'It's eight miles away,' Korpanski added. 'Most of it along icy and muddy lanes. I'll give you directions. Your satnav won't find it for you.'

It got better and better. Disgruntled, she picked up her coat from the back of her chair. 'You're right,' she said grumpily. 'It is *not* great to be back.'

Korpanski's grin broadened. 'Told you it wouldn't

take long, didn't I, Jo?' He handed her a piece of paper on which he had written directions. 'Oh.' His tone changed. 'Before you go—there's something else.' Now his expression was wary and more serious. There was something he wasn't looking forward to telling her. And Joanna picked up on this right away.

'What?'

'They've appointed a replacement for Colclough,' he said quietly. 'And it's not good news. At least, not for you.'

'You're really making my day, Mike.'

He was eyeing her with visible trepidation.

'Go on. Shoot.'

'He's from Birmingham. A guy called Gabriel Rush. By all accounts he's a stickler for protocol. Does everything by the book. The officers who've worked underneath him say he takes violent dislikes to people—particularly women officers—who "don't know their place".' DS Korpanski could hardly look at her. 'Doesn't sound like he's going to spoil you rotten. Not like indulgent Arthur.'

It was true. Chief Superintendent Arthur Colclough had made a pet out of Joanna, the first female senior detective he had ever appointed. He had indulged her and sometimes made excuses for her. Even when she had broken the rules she had had a soft fall and had hardly ever been in his bad books. Patently that era was at an end. She'd have to look out in future.

Joanna banged the door behind her.

Korpanski watched the door shiver and sensed that in Leek Police Station sparks would soon be flying. Detective Inspector Joanna Piercy, for all their friendship, was an officer who could be fiery when opposed.

He didn't know who to feel sorrier for: the new chief superintendent or Joanna. Or maybe he should look out for himself, as he would inevitably be the one caught in the crossfire.

TWO

THERE WAS AT least some consolation in being summoned to a remote moorlands house, Joanna reflected as she turned off the Ashbourne road, leaving the town of Leek behind and heading for the vast and empty landscape of the Staffordshire moorlands. She had panoramic views ahead of her, and the sense of limitless emptiness in a landscape that had not changed for centuries. Now, with development protected and even the architecture and materials of the moorlands homes rigidly controlled, it was even less likely to change in the future. She scanned the scene. Undulating hills with craggy stone outcrops, jagged as teeth, isolated farmhouses and the breathtakingly spectacular nature of the landscape made her feel like she was standing at the very top of the world. But even the sense she had of belonging to this wild and raw country did nothing to change her mood, which remained resentful until she had passed the millstone that marked the entrance to the Peak District National Park. She was angry at being sent out on what was most likely a wild goose chase and chuntered loudly to herself: 'Smoke indeed. Bloody rubbish. Sodding waste of time.' She knew she could have pulled rank and sent a junior officer but it would have looked peevish and spoiled. It wasn't her way. And that was why, she reflected, she had gained such respect from her colleagues.

She mucked in. That was what they said about her. Then, quite suddenly, she saw the funny side and chuckled. The party, the celebration and now the let-down.

Using Korpanski's instructions she left the main road and turned down muddy single track lanes, grass sprouting up the middle. Luckily she met very little traffic—two cars and three tractors. The farmers could ride on the frozen earth and complete their winter chore of muck-spreading the frozen fields. As she took in the pale fields bordered by drystone walls, the far-off peaks iced with snow and white ink blots on the grass where the sun had failed to melt it, she found herself contrasting the scene with the Disney-bright paddy fields, lush scenery and scorched sand of Sri Lanka. This was home. It energized her. She opened her car window a fraction to feel the icy blast on her cheek and drew the cold air deep into her lungs. It felt good to be alive. It might be chilly here but she had always preferred the winter in the moorlands when the holidaymakers stayed at home, leaving the countryside to its hardy natives.

Although her spirits had been dampened both by Korpanski's news of Colclough's replacement and the futility of this mission, she could still feel the warmth of the Sri Lankan sun and the thrill of diving on to the reef with Matthew to see the myriads of brilliantly coloured fish which swam through her splayed-out fingers. For a second she almost wished she was back there. And then she truly looked around and reflected: she was lucky to live in such a beautiful part of the country, lucky to work in a job which absorbed her and lucky to be married to a man she loved and who loved her. 'So, Piercy,' she scolded, 'stop whingeing, get this irritating part of the day over and done with and get back to the office.' She glanced at her satnav. Korpanski was right. It didn't even recognize there was a road here. On the tiny screen it looked as though she was traversing a green field. So instead she carried on, following Korpanski's written instructions, and swung left along a stony track, again with feathers of grass sprouting up its middle. She drove gingerly, the car skating across a couple of frozen puddles. She knew she was on the right track when, after a few hundred yards or so, she spotted a plume of smoke drifting out of a chimney far below. She stopped the car for a moment and stared down at the farm with admiration for its symmetry and beauty, but also with a policeman's eyes. It might be in its own private valley, nestling into a tiny hamlet, but this meant it was overlooked from the road. Its position actually meant that rather than being private and secluded it was exposed and vulnerable. It would also be a difficult place to escape from. One road in; the same road out. Steep. In snow this house could easily become a prison rather than a haven. It was beautiful—an unspoilt mellow stone farmhouse, long and low. It had a slate roof which gleamed like old pewter in the wintry sun; its walls were of soft grey limestone which was mined locally, common to properties in this area, and allowed even under the strict Peak District National Park restrictions. The house looked in good condition, well cared for—immaculate, in fact—with none of the tumbledown barns and muddy areas which marked most of the local properties. It was built in an L shape, angled towards the road. Beyond the gate it had a gravelled drive with a small roundabout at its front which was grassed over and raised, bounded by a low stone wall. In the centre of the roundabout was a well.

Not the bijou, twee, suburban garden centre wishing well but what looked like a genuine working well, large and complete with a pitched slate roof, turning handle and bucket. At the side of the house was a huge oak tree, winter-naked now but in spring, summer and autumn it would make this place look even more fantastic. A countryside dream. But Joanna was only too well aware that while it would be a dream in dappled sunshine and daylight, when animals populated the fields and the countryside would seem the ideal place to be, it would be a nightmare through the long winter nights, with no one within shouting—or screaming—distance. The isolation could send someone mad unless they were well adapted to it. Was this what had happened here? Was Mrs Weeks slowly losing her mind, feeling more and more trapped by the remoteness of her home? Added to the location the single-track road in—and out—was steep and stone rough. Even with a four-wheel-drive it would be a challenge to escape, particularly in bad weather. Joanna assessed the incline of the drive with a cyclist's eyes and felt a tightening of her calf muscles. It was easily a one in four. How quickly the Garden of Eden can turn into a prison. It would only take a few centimetres of snow or a heavy fall of rain to wash the stones towards the house. As Joanna studied the property she felt the first stirrings of curiosity about the woman who lived here. If she was so nervous and paranoid why *did* she live here alone? Was she a farmer or smallholder? There was no sign of any animals and the tidiness of the property seemed to contradict that theory. Was she then perhaps a local who had lived all her life in the moorlands and would feel claustrophobic in the town? If this was her profile why had she lived here happily for ten years only to suddenly develop this nervousness and delusion of a stalker? Moorlands folk tended to be prosaic rather than histrionic. They needed to be to be able to survive both physically and mentally.

As she descended into the valley Joanna searched for clues about the owner of Butterfield Farm but found none. The grounds were neat, the gravel freshly raked and free of leaves or debris. Either this was a very energetic sixty-year-old or she had help. And that meant wealth, which didn't come from farming in this area. The moorlands farmers, in general, scratched the poor land and hostile conditions for a living. This was a large and valuable property. She must have made a good living as an actress. Even without a generous acreage, Joanna estimated it would fetch close to a million. But, looking around, if Mrs Weeks did own most of the surrounding land, and probably the entire valley, the property value would be bumped up to nearer two million. This was not the sort of set-up she had expected. It looked too organized, too sane. So, she asked herself, if the call-outs weren't histrionic, the result of an overactive imagination, what were they? They sounded bizarre, but what if they weren't?

Before she had arrived she had assumed that this would be a futile visit. Now? Well, she wasn't so sure. The answer would become clear when she met the woman herself.

Joanna continued gingerly down the track, still asking questions. According to Mike, the call-outs had started in the New Year. Had anything specific happened to trigger paranoia and panic then? Was there anyone in Mrs Weeks' past who might want to frighten her into abandoning the moorlands? Did a neighbour want her land or her house? Or was her initial instinct correct, and Mrs Weeks was deluded, paranoid?

But as the car crunched over the stones and drew nearer to the house, something else bothered her. Anyone who turned in from the road would have a bird's-eye view of the property and its surrounds. And a hundred yards or so back she had noticed a public footpath sign. Here, on the edge of the Peak District, in the Staffordshire moorlands, the footpaths were well used for much of the year. Which meant that although Butterfield Farm was remote, plenty of ramblers would notice it. Underlying Joanna's sense of unease was its isolation and vulnerability, added to the owner's circumstances. If anyone did want to intimidate her there would be no one to come to her aid. There was no good neighbour. She would, in the end, have to rely on the police.

Joanna revised her approach. Normally in cases like this, once the police had decided there was no real threat, they reassured the occupants, quoting low crime statistics as fluently as a politician. Next they would give practical advice, sometimes to update door and window locks, sometimes to secure outbuildings and occasionally to link their burglar alarms to the police station. But here there was still a problem. It would be no use linking Butterfield Farm to the police station. Timony Weeks would continue calling them out on a daily basis, wasting hours of their time. And if there was an emergency it would take the police at least half an hour to reach her. There wasn't a police helicopter for miles. It would have to come from Manchester or Wolverhampton. If there really was a serious problem Timony Weeks would be on her own for some considerable time.

Joanna stopped to open the gate which bore an oval sign, Butterfield Farm, gaily painted with a couple of swallows wheeling around in a sapphire sky, and underneath it a second sign, *Beware of the Bull*. It was an obvious fable—there wasn't an animal in sight—but at least it was a change from *Beware of the Dog*. Or, as Joanna had read worryingly outside one house, *Beware of the Cat!*

With good countryside manners she closed the gate behind her and descended gingerly down the track, avoiding skidding on the icy patches and pulling up outside.

There were two cars parked side by side, a blue Isuzu and a black Qashqai, with garaging room for plenty more. She noted four garage doors, a couple converted from barns, judging by the arches in the brickwork. So Mrs Weeks was not a farmer. Farmers had too many uses for barns to convert them into garages. Close up, the condition of the farm impressed her even more and reinforced her initial instinct that this was the property of either a very wealthy or a very industrious lady. Possibly both. Maybe it was her wealth that was feeding her paranoia. Rich people often suspected someone was about to come along and relieve them of their money and/or possessions. Perhaps this was the simple explanation of the calls to the police. Timony Weeks had so much to steal that she expected someone to rob her. As Joanna wondered she realized something else. Today was as bright and clear as a winter's day can be. There was no pollution in the moorlands. The air was crystal glass, practically ringing in its clarity. The sky was a sheet of perfect azure. The purity in the air comes only in winter, when dust and pollens are ab-

sent and the atmosphere is holding its breath, waiting
for spring to breathe again. But however bright the day,
the house itself was in the shade, which made it appear
colder and darker than its surrounds. It had been built to
peer out on the dark side, facing north-east, which gave
the farm a forbidding and unwelcoming look. Joanna
looked around her and worked out why. The house had
been built with its long angle watching the approach.
She climbed out of the squad car, conscious that she
was treading in the footsteps of almost the entire Leek
police force, including Detective Sergeant Mike Korpanski. Picturing Korpanski's size elevens beating a
march to the front door, she finally chuckled to herself.
It was her turn to meet the old bat.

As soon as Joanna had left the warmth of the car she
felt the raw chill bite her face. It was always a few degrees colder out here than in Leek town centre. Snow
could lie in the moorlands for weeks after it had melted
on St Edward's Street. These lands not only had their
own geography but also their own eco-climate. Global
warming seemed a million miles—or more literally, a
million years—from here. But the strange thing was
that it was even colder down here, in the valley, than
it had been up on the ridge. Unusual again. Normally
people got blasted away by the cold, the wind and frequently the rain, when they were on the top. Valleys
were, in general, where you found shelter—and home-
steads. This was where the farmers would traditionally
build, facing south to scoop up every ounce of warmth,
light and sunshine. But not Butterfield Farm. It had patently been reconstructed in recent years, probably by
its current owner. It faced the wrong direction and, besides, this valley was boggy. Joanna had noticed rushes

sprouting in the surrounding fields, testifying to a high water level. If she was building a house with unlimited funds she would love Butterfield for its situation but she would have drained the valley and angled the house to face south.

Had this simply been designed by someone who did not understand how to make a house suit the land, or had it deliberately been rebuilt at this angle to face the track and keep watch for a lone traveller coming down the road? She stood and studied the farm. Now she understood she realized something else: every window watched her. Then another thought: was she being infected by paranoia too? Joanna wrapped her coat around her, tightened her belt and strode towards the front door. She hunted for either a bell or a knocker, found neither and thumped. As she had suspected from her distant view, Butterfield was a new build, probably rebuilt on the site of an ancient cottage with barns. That was the only way that you could get planning permission out here. So everything, the angle of the house, the watch over the approach and the fact that travellers could not ring or use a knocker, must have been decided by the owner, together with the architect. Why no bell or door knocker?

Had this *never* been either or had they been removed? Was the intention to positively *discourage* strangers from calling in to Butterfield Farm? If so, why?

She only had a minute to reflect before the door was pulled opened by a tall, muscular woman with straggly, greying hair and piercing eyes. She was somewhere in her late sixties, and was wearing baggy dark trousers and a cream polo neck sweater, the sleeves pushed up to display powerful, freckled forearms. She eyed Joanna with suspicion and some hostility.

'Yes?'

'Mrs Weeks?' Joanna asked dubiously. This did not look like the eccentric old bat she'd been imagining on her drive out. Or a retired actress, for that matter.

'No, I'm not,' the woman said flatly. 'She's inside. I'm Diana Tong, her secretary-cum-cleaner-cum-general-dogsbody.'

Joanna felt like retorting that she was also a dogsbody, answering a crappy summons made by a cracked old woman as a 'servant of the public', but she resisted. If the new superintendent was as humourless as Korpanski had warned she'd better be careful. In future there would be no Colclough to make excuses for her, indulge her and haul her out of scrapes. She could not afford to be the teeniest millimetre out of line. And so she gave the woman a bland smile and introduced herself, resisting any sarcasm. At the same time she flashed her ID card and followed Diana Tong inside.

Again, inside Butterfield was tasteful. They had stepped straight into a kitchen, fitted out in yellowed pine with grey granite tops, an island in the centre and gleaming copper pans hanging from steel hooks. The floor was terracotta tiled, the walls painted a buttery cream. A red Aga stood at one end. The image of a farmhouse kitchen was completed with dark beams criss-crossing a white ceiling. Joanna looked around in admiration. Most women would kill for this kitchen. In fact, she would—well, not literally but... Impervious to her admiration, Diana Tong marched straight ahead, Joanna trailing in her wake. They passed through three rooms. Butterfield was a long, low house, one room deep, each room leading into another. They all had low-beamed ceilings and cream-washed walls. The doors were period oak, with thumb latches, and there were plenty of tasteful pieces of antique furniture, oak, mahogany and some walnut, all looking authentic and valuable. Chinese porcelain and Staffordshire figures sparsely distributed gave the rooms an air of quiet, dignified elegance. The walls were dressed with a few pictures that looked like original oils—a couple of portraits of people in period dress and some landscapes with sheep or cows. Lamps illuminated the darker corners with soft warmth and the ambience of shabby chic was completed by Persian silk carpets carelessly thrown around. But Joanna noticed that every single window faced north-east, watching the approach. Each time they moved to another room she was aware of the empty grey lane. Like a castle it guarded its entrance, as though expecting an assault. Beyond the lane were the pale peaks of the moorlands, today capped with snow. The entire place was like a feature in *Period Homes* and further evidence of being out of sync with the vision she had drawn up of a scatty, eccentric sixty-year-old who kept calling out the police in a panic because of strange, almost supernatural events. Joanna had to completely hold back on that assumption. This place was organized and controlled, and none of this was making any sense. Her toes tingled a little as she kept up with the broad back and brisk step of the very businesslike Diana Tong, who finally turned back to say, 'Lovely, isn't it?' She flung her arms out wide. 'This is what money can buy, Inspector Piercy.' Her tone was resentful, her thick eyebrows meeting in the middle in a deep, angry scowl.

Joanna couldn't think of a suitable rejoinder so she

simply nodded and walked behind the 'general dogs-body' into a final smaller room at the end of the house. As they entered a Burmese cat exited snottily past them, tail erect and twitching, as though she was too posh to remain in the room with a mere policewoman. Joanna lifted her eyebrows.

A tiny, bony woman was sitting at a desk, absorbed in a computer screen. She looked up and Joanna's confusion deepened. She looked nothing like the dotty old bat she'd imagined, but a calm woman in her forties, physically no bigger than a child. She was dressed in loose white cotton pyjama pants and a blue silk wrap, something like a smoking dressing gown Noël Coward might have worn. Joanna stared. That was way back in the 1930s. All the same, the woman who was sitting across the room was only missing a long, slim cigarette holder to be cast in a starring role in *Blithe Spirit*. It made the up-to-date computer that she was working on look slightly anachronistic, as though someone in a Jane Austen novel was chatting on a mobile phone.

Again, like the atmosphere from the outside, Joanna had an odd sensation that something here was not adding up.

She cleared her throat and wondered how to begin this. She wanted Timony Weeks to stop this repeated wasting of police time by calling out of police for what appeared to be 'minor incidents' or calling in response to her 'senses'. On the other hand, she owed the woman the benefit of the doubt.

As she waited the woman was busily studying her. Joanna met her gaze. And had another shock. The clothes might be 1930s; Timony Weeks aged sixty. But the face that looked at her was unlined and almost

expressionless, the eyes thickly made-up with heavy
black kohl, false eyelashes firmly and defiantly stuck
on beneath tattooed eyebrows, while her mouth was
plumped up, too big and dominant for the tiny face.
Joanna blinked. The final feeling of a doll's mask was
completed by very thick strawberry-blonde hair cut to
the actress's shoulders and a thick fringe which covered the top half of her face. Only her eyes were untouched by the cosmetic surgeon's attentions. Nothing
they could do about the colour except, perhaps, coloured
contact lenses. At the moment they were faded blue and
regarding her curiously.

Again, Joanna had an odd sense of confusion. The
physiognomy had thrown her. She was not sure of anything about this woman, whether she was sane or mad,
old or young. Her body was as small as a child's but her
eyes were old and shrewd. Joanna studied her further
for clues that would help her fix a label on Timony. Her
arms were thin, the sleeves pushed up to the elbows in
the stuffy atmosphere. The hands were liver-spotted,
sporting large, gaudy rings. Her neck was quite creased.
Joanna raised her eyes to the pale pink lipstick thickly
applied to her mouth, which didn't quite move in time
to her question: 'Who are you?'

'Detective Inspector Joanna Piercy, Leek Police.'

'They haven't sent *you* before.' The voice was undoubtedly old, cracked, harsh and hostile.

'No. I've been away. I've been on my honeymoon,'
she added, still with a sense of unreality at that last
spoken word.

'Honeymoon?' The woman cackled. '*I* should be the
expert on those.' Another cackle. 'I've had enough of

them, haven't I?' The question was rhetorical but the dogsbody smiled politely and nodded in agreement.

'Really?' Joanna was dismissive. She didn't want to hear some long, drawn-out life story. She didn't have the time and she wasn't interested. She simply wanted to put a stop to these frequent calls to the station so they could all get on with their real jobs. Policing, catching criminals and upholding the law. 'I've come in response to your *repeated* reports to the station about intruders on your property and requests for a police presence,' Joanna said briskly, trying to assert her authority. 'In particular, your telephone call today when you claimed you could smell cigarette smoke.' The woman's eyes narrowed with reflected hostility. She'd picked up on Joanna's implied criticism of people who wasted police time. The two stared each other out.

Then Joanna drew out her notebook. 'Would you like to tell me about this latest episode?' She could so easily have inserted the word 'delusional'.

The woman stared at her with chilly dislike. Then she gave a *humph*. 'You'd better sit down, Inspector.' As Joanna looked around for a spare chair she barked, 'Not in here. This is my study. Sacrosanct. The sitting room, Inspector, if you please.'

So Joanna followed Mrs Weeks back into the sitting room and sat on the chintz-covered sofa, notebook in hand. Timony Weeks sat opposite her, crossing her legs, high-heeled mules dangling on the end of her feet with orange painted toenails. The secretary had melted away—wise woman—and Timony was still regarding her with undisguised hostility, which was reflected by the cat. They had disturbed its hideaway on a cushion on the sofa and she had responded with arched back and a glare. Timony Weeks reached out and stroked the animal as it extended its neck and narrowed its sly blue eyes.

'Tuptim,' Timony murmured, then addressed Joanna. 'I'd expected them to send Sergeant Korpanski,' she complained.

Joanna would have liked to have retorted that Sergeant Mike Korpanski had had just about enough of being called out here, but instead she simply smiled and said, 'It was my turn.'

Timony Weeks narrowed her eyes, similar to her cat, and moved her head. She wasn't quite sure how to take this statement. After a brief stare she bowed her head and began to talk, her voice softly modulated and expressive so Joanna could glimpse the actress beneath. 'It was five o'clock this morning,' she said precisely, the words carefully enunciated. 'I was in the kitchen, rinsing out some cups, standing at the sink.' She gave a sour glance towards the door. 'Diana,' her voice was sharp with accusation, 'had left the kettle on the Aga late last night, which had made the room very steamy. The top window had been left open overnight to let the steam out but the glass had some condensation on it, so my vision to the outside was blurred. It was dark but I could see that the floodlights had come on. Obviously I couldn't recognize anyone.'

Joanna listened carefully to every word. So far Timony Weeks was a perfect witness. Logical, clear, precise and concise, giving all the detail that would be asked of her. Even as she was speaking in her soft, coherent voice, Joanna was realizing just how wrong she'd been in her original assumption. This was not a confused and intimidated old woman but someone with a very clear and sequential way of describing events. She was in full possession of her senses. Not *histrionic* but *lucid*. Was she to be believed?

Joanna took careful notice of her choice of words, as Timony continued in a husky voice, 'Through the open window I distinctly smelt cigarette smoke.' She leant forward a little, in mute appeal, hands clasped together. 'Someone, Inspector, was smoking just outside my kitchen window at five o'clock this morning.'

Joanna's thoughts had been tumbling around in her head but this statement was unequivocal, unmistakable. She couldn't ignore it. And yet...

'You've called us out for that?' Joanna couldn't quite keep the exasperation out of her voice.

Timony Weeks licked her lips, suggesting the first sign of nervousness or vulnerability since Joanna had arrived.

Perhaps she was beginning to realize that she might not be believed. 'I know you probably think I'm imagining all this but...' She seemed to be struggling to find the right words to convince Joanna of the veracity of her statement. 'Inspector Piercy,' she said, leaning forward even further. 'My second husband, Sol Brannigan, used to smoke. I never have liked the smell of tobacco so I made him smoke outside.' She smiled, remembering. 'Sol being Sol, a man who did not like being told what to do, resented that one small rule and, as a minor rebellion, he sometimes used to puff away just outside an open window, knowing full well that the smoke would waft in.' Her eyes looked distant for a moment before fixing back on Joanna, the pupils small and earnest as though she was asking her to please believe this. 'So, Inspector, I know *exactly* what it smells like when someone, just outside an open window, is smoking.'

Joanna was silent. Again, this clear and concise account was hardly the paranoid ranting of an elderly lady. 'Who did you think it was?'

Timony appeared to freeze at the question. She did not have an answer off pat—or if she did she wasn't prepared to share it.

Joanna pursued her goal. 'Did you think it might be your second husband? Is he still alive?'

Timony licked dry lips. 'I don't know,' she said dismissively. Joanna tucked the comment away for future consideration.

'Did you actually *see* anyone?'

'No,' Timony said patiently. 'As I have just explained, it wouldn't have been possible. And if I had seen someone I would have given you a description.' Now the blue eyes were fixed on hers with a penetrating sharpness that was disconcerting. 'I have a very sensitive nose,' she continued. 'I can recognize most perfumes at twenty paces.' There was humour in her expression as the stiff face smiled. 'I am surprised that you go for something as traditional as Chanel No. 5 rather than a more contemporary scent.'

Joanna felt like bowing to her theatrical show off. But it was impressive. This was indeed a sensitive nose. Mrs Weeks was sitting on the other side of the room and Joanna was not in the habit of splashing perfume around. She too smiled. 'My husband likes it,' she said. 'His tastes in perfume are...traditional.'

Timony's eyes scrutinized her and Joanna felt uncomfortable, as though she was about to make some other observation, but instead she continued, 'I have an eye for detail too, Inspector. You understand? I remember where things are and where they should remain, considering that I live alone. My attention to detail can be compared with the continuity girl in the film industry. I am very observant and I have a very retentive memory.'

The statements were made in a matter-of-fact manner. Joanna got the picture. This woman was explaining to her that her words should be remembered and relied upon. She sat up a little straighter and began her questions. 'It was dark outside?'

'It was five o'clock this morning.' Timony gave Joanna a haughty look. 'I waited until six before ringing. I had to report it but I imagined the call wouldn't be welcome in the middle of the night.'

Joanna nodded. 'Who's resident on this property?'

'Myself.'

'Doesn't Ms Tong live here?'

'Not bloody likely.' This came from the doorway. 'I have a life, you know. I live in Ashbourne. I come in four days a week. That's enough. And it's Mrs Tong, please.'

Joanna turned her attention to her. 'You live with your family?'

'Not exactly.'

This provoked a derisive snort from Timony Weeks, which both Diana and Joanna ignored as Joanna continued her questioning of the dogsbody.

'And your duties include?'

'More or less everything. Typing, cleaning, shopping, whatever *she* wants.'

'And the grounds? Who manages those?'

Her eyebrows lifted. 'Now there I *do* draw the line.

We have a gardener who looks after the land and his wife does cleaning, ironing, et cetera. They come once a week. Usually Tuesdays, which is one of my days off.'

'Their names?'

'Frank and Millie Rossington. They live in the town.'

'And they come one day a week?'

'Just a morning in the winter and all day through the summer.'

Joanna looked hard at Diana Tong, wondering what her 'take' was on these police call-outs. 'Have *you* ever seen any evidence of an intruder?'

Slowly, and with an apologetic glance at her employer, Diana Tong shook her head. 'Nothing convincing,' she said, looking away.

Which put Joanna two steps back. Was this a charade? Should she even *be* here? Had she been misled by Timony Weeks' apparent lucidity and saneness? She was struggling now. There was just one woman's word and the intruder lights. 'Do either of you smoke?'

Mrs Weeks shook her head while Diana chortled. 'Ah, I see what you're getting at, Inspector. You're trying to… No, of course I don't smoke. And even if I did, I'd hardly be standing outside the kitchen window at five o'clock in the morning having a sly one, would I? Particularly on a Sunday night when I'm not even here on a Sunday, it being another one of my days off.'

'I simply wondered whether you might have dropped a butt outside the window at some other time and Mrs Weeks caught a waft.' She thought again for a moment before addressing both women. 'If someone was outside here, smoking, then I need to ascertain why he or she was here, and whether their motive was malicious. If…' She glanced apologetically at Timony Weeks then looked away. She found it disconcerting to talk to a woman who was sixty but had the undeveloped body of a child and the unlined face of a woman in her forties. 'If…if no one was here then I can return to more pressing police duties.'

Diana gave a soft *huff* from the doorway while Timony simply pressed her lips together in fury and possibly some exasperation.

Joanna felt she must appear to be still searching for an explanation. 'You say,' she said lamely, 'that at five o'clock this morning you were to all intents and purposes alone in the house and you weren't aware that anyone was or could be in the outbuildings?'

'Yes.' Timony was showing signs of impatience at having to repeat her statement.

'This is an isolated house.' Joanna tried to speak conversationally.

Again, an irritated, 'Yes.'

'Excuse me, but you're not—'

Timony's eyes narrowed, challenging Joanna to say *not young*.

Instead Joanna burst out, 'Why live out here all on your own when it's patently making you paranoid, twitchy and nervous?'

'Paranoid?' The word came out like a whipcrack and Joanna immediately regretted her choice. She flapped her hands apologetically. *Oh, no, had she really just accused Mrs Weeks of being mentally unstable?*

'Sorry. I didn't mean…' she said quickly, which provoked a sharp retort from the actress.

'I can live where I please, Inspector,' she said haughtily. There was something both brave and dignified in her response, and also an element of poignancy. 'I will not be frightened into abandoning Butterfield.'

Joanna collected her feelings. 'Mrs Weeks,' she tried, 'who would drive all the way out here merely to make you feel uneasy with simple, silly tricks? Just to blow cigarette smoke in through a window?'

'I don't know,' she said angrily through gritted teeth. 'That's for *you* to find out, Inspector Piercy.'

Joanna bit back her retort. At the back of her mind lay something uncomfortable. Something queasy like the smell of drains in a hot country, or oily black canal water in a sleazy area of a city. Something wasn't right.

She tried again. 'Mrs Weeks,' she said, frowning, recalling the list of trivia her colleagues had been summoned to investigate, 'we can't keep coming out here every time you think you see or hear something out of the ordinary. We've logged more than sixteen calls from you in the last couple of weeks, all of them over very trivial matters.' She tried to rescue the dismissal by making a light comment and smiling. 'You practically need a full-time security guard.'

Timony Weeks' face assumed a mean, challenging look. 'Are you doubting my statements, Inspector?' Her voice was soft as chamois and it fooled neither of the listeners.

'No-o.' Joanna was remembering Korpanski's words about Chief Superintendent Gabriel Rush. It sent an icicle sliding down her spine.

Timony sat up a little straighter. 'But you are refusing to respond to my plea for help.'

Joanna felt like throwing up her hands and saying, *What do you expect me to do?* Instead she looked down at her notebook and took a risk. 'You know the story of the boy who cried wolf?'

Timony Weeks didn't deign to answer, simply pursed her plumped-up lips.

Joanna read from her notes. 'You called us out because the lavatory seat was left up.'

Timony Weeks didn't even blink. 'Two *women* live here, Inspector.'

'What about the gardener?'

'He uses the *outside* toilet. Always. I don't allow him in the house.'

Swallowing a snort, Joanna tried again. 'Well, perhaps his wife, the cleaner...' she suggested. She left stupid but bound to add, 'you have to lift the seat to clean a toilet properly.'

Oh, if Korpanski could hear her. She could imagine his swallowed guffaw and smothered grin.

Timony's response was oddly dignified. 'It was not a day that Millie was here.'

Joanna went through the list of trivial detail followed by trivial detail. 'Music playing, your nightdress unfolded, a feeling that someone was watching the house, a dead mouse in the bread bin. Furniture moved.' She looked up. 'We've never found anything concrete.'

Timony Weeks' face changed. Suddenly she looked vulnerable, a frightened little girl lost. 'I don't know how I can make you believe me,' she said quietly. '*Somebody* is making repeated sorties out here. I sense their presence and their malevolence. They are doing it deliberately to frighten me and to persuade me to leave here.'

'Is that what you think the agenda is?'

Her hands gripped the arm of the sofa. 'I will not be bamboozled into abandoning my Shangri-La.' She looked around her. 'Butterfield is my home. My perfect home.' The crack in her voice gave the words a desperate pathos. 'What has to happen for you to take me seriously, Inspector? Do I have to have a knife sticking out of my back?' Her voice rose hysterically.

Joanna shifted uncomfortably, not only at the melodrama of the demand but also of the graphic image it evoked. It was shocking.

Timony Weeks continued, 'All I'm asking you to do, Inspector, is find out who is playing these silly tricks on me and why they want me to leave here.'

'You really believe that is the motive?'

Timony Weeks stared her out, not answering. Then muttered, as though this was something she been reluctant to admit, 'Possibly not.'

Joanna felt she must press her. 'What other motives can there be?'

But the walls were up now. 'I don't want to go into that right now.'

Patience, Joanna, patience.

But she needed to put a stop to this waste of police time. 'Mrs Weeks,' she said. 'You can't keep summoning us here unless you give us the full facts. Have you any idea who might "have it in" for you, as it were?'

She looked down sentimentally at the cat who lay blissfully unaware of any drama, snoring softly, her thin flanks rising and falling. 'Too many people.'

Again, Joanna was frustrated and practically shouted her questions. 'Who? Why? Why would anyone do this? Surely you can see what nonsense all this is. If somebody really wanted you out they wouldn't keep playing such subtle tricks. They'd do something far more dramatic.'

That pinned the blue eyes to Joanna's face and her hands gripped the arms of the sofa even harder. 'That, Inspector,' she said, 'is what I'm afraid of.'

'Are you talking about *neighbours* who might want your land or the farm—or someone from your past?'

'I don't know. That's for you to find out.'

Joanna felt that she wanted to escape now. 'You have a burglar alarm?'

'Yes.'

'Do you put it on downstairs when you're in bed?'

She nodded. 'Always. I am very security conscious.'

'And the intruder lights?'

'All around the house.'

'It might not be a person,' Joanna suggested. 'They do sometimes come on if there's a fox or a badger roaming.'

'Admittedly,' Timony said in a voice as dry as tinder. 'But neither badgers nor foxes smoke.'

Joanna would like to have pointed out that that was the subjective evidence.

Instead she tried another tack. 'Do you have a relative or friend who could come and stay with you for a while—just while these things are happening?' She looked up. 'Perhaps Mrs Tong?'

'Not really. I'm alone in the world.' The words were spoken with self-pity and sounded more like the lines of a ham actress than a genuine pull on the heart strings. And the glance she shot Joanna from underneath the false eyelashes was unmistakably designed to check on the effect the delivery of those lines had on Detective Inspector Piercy.

Joanna looked around her. Butterfield Farm, if you counted in the land, must be worth well over a million.

And Timony Weeks was alone in the world? Sounded like a good deal for the Inland Revenue if she expired.

Timony met her eyes. She could read exactly what the policewoman was thinking. 'I don't know who to leave my money to,' she said quietly. 'I haven't even bothered to make a will. What's the point?'

'Most people have someone…'

The line was repeated. 'I am alone in the world.'

And it was no more convincing second time around. 'You really ought to make a will,' she responded, feeling more like an advert for a solicitor's than a detective.

Shrewd Timony was back. 'I would if I could decide what to put in it.' She looked down at the liver-spotted hand which rested on the now-purring cat whose nose was up, slyly awake. 'Perhaps I should leave it all to Tuptim,' she said. 'She's probably the only living thing that loves me. And I love her.' She smiled as mischievously as the too-tight face lift would allow. 'She could have a diamond-encrusted collar and her favourite fish dish every day. She could drink champagne-flavoured milk and sit on an ermine cushion.'

The cat yawned, straightened and arched its back then jumped down from the sofa. Timony Weeks watched her go. 'But then maybe not,' she said thoughtfully.

Her eyes moved upwards, towards the doorframe where Mrs Tong had reappeared. Timony shot her an edgy look. 'I couldn't dream of leaving *you* anything, Di,' she said. 'You might be the one to stick the knife between my shoulder blades.'

Diana Tong returned the compliment with interest. 'You wouldn't be worth going to prison for, Timony.'

Timony Weeks was unruffled. 'Quite,' she said.

Joanna listened to the banter passing between the two women and couldn't quite make up her mind about them. It appeared to be a love/hate relationship. In the end she stood up. She wanted out of here. But just in case Chief Superintendent Gabriel Rush took an interest in her recent activities she turned to Timony Weeks one more time. 'I'll ask again—who do you think is behind these events?' *If anyone*, she added mentally.

'Hmm.' Timony Weeks eyed her and Joanna suspected she had picked up on her doubt. She leaned back in the sofa, legs crossed, eyes narrowed, regarding her. 'Do you know, Inspector,' she said laconically, 'I have asked the police to come here more than sixteen times because I felt under threat. You are the first officer to ask me what *I* think. *You* can come again, Inspector Piercy.'

The face gave a stiff, frozen smile which Joanna returned resentfully. She was invited to 'come again'? She cursed under her breath. This was not the outcome she had wanted. And Timony Weeks continued to avoid answering the question. She took a step forward. 'Mrs Weeks,' she said. 'I came here today to try and persuade you to stop calling the police out. I thought you would be someone frail, frightened, vulnerable. I have found the opposite. But I can't, for the life of me, work out what's going on.'

Timony Weeks' mouth tightened. 'Aren't you even going to show me the courtesy of taking a look outside the kitchen window?'

Joanna knew she had no option. Inside she gave a deep sigh. 'Yes. I will take a look outside.' She tried to make it sound as though this had been in her mind from the start.

'Hang on, Tims.' It was Diana Tong who spoke. 'You can't go out there dressed like with that *thing* on. It's freezing outside. You'll catch your death. *I'll* go with the Inspector. *I* know what you saw.' It was kindly said but Joanna wondered if it was meant to give them time alone. Whatever, Timony Weeks acquiesced.

THREE

Joanna followed Diana Tong around to the front of the house and stood outside the kitchen window. Like the rest of the property everything was in order: the path neatly gravelled, the window immaculately painted, the glass polished to reflect the landscape. Although it was a cold day the window was ajar and moved slightly in the breeze, changing the reflection as it shifted.

There *was* a scent. Joanna breathed in and caught the very vaguest tang of stale tobacco. She ran her finger along the window sill. It must have been wiped down recently. There was no mark on her fingertip, no dirt, dust or ash. Next she bent down and studied the gravel. There was some cigarette ash amongst the stones but no butt. That was a shame. She straightened and met Diana Tong's gaze full on. 'Do you smoke, Mrs Tong?'

Diana shook her head with a vaguely mocking smile.

'Does your gardener smoke?'

'A pipe.'

'Window cleaner?'

'Possibly.' She shrugged. 'I really don't know, Inspector, but he doesn't come often in the winter. I don't think he's been here since before Christmas.'

Had the ash been dropped before Christmas? Joanna remembered the weather just after Christmas. There had been heavy rain in the week between Christmas and

New Year, just before her wedding. Better than snow, she had thought, as the wedding had been at the foot of The Roaches, high in the moorlands and prone to being cut off by a snowfall. So the cigarette ash had not lain here for more than three weeks. It would have been washed away. Ergo even if the window cleaner *was* a smoker he was off the hook. Diana Tong's eyes moved in a similar direction and appeared to reach the same conclusion. She cleared her throat as though about to speak but said nothing. Neither needed to point out that far from being an elderly woman's fantasy this pointed to a real and physical presence.

Ash was one thing, Joanna thought as she slipped some into a specimen bag. It was a fairly pointless exercise. Sherlock Holmes might have been able to tell you someone's characteristics from cigarette ash but she, sure as hell, couldn't. Neither could the forensic lab. A butt would have been far more valuable. But then, life was never easy.

She straightened up and faced the woman. 'Mrs Tong,' she said, meeting the other's gaze, 'we've been called out to investigate a string of improbable trivia. Some might consider it wasting police time.' She looked curiously at the woman. 'What do you think?'

Diana Tong pushed a fistful of hair as coarse and grey as steel wool out of her face. She looked a strong woman, both physically and mentally. Her eyes flickered and she did not speak at once but seemed to be considering very carefully what to say and how to say it. 'To understand that question you would need to understand Timony,' she said slowly. Then laughed. 'Timony is not her real name, by the way, but her stage name. She is—was—an actress.'

'What are you trying to tell me? That she's histrionic?'

Diana Tong put her head back and gave an exasperated sigh. 'Why does everybody do this—make assumptions about someone's character by their profession? It's as insulting as if I were to assume you are an unimaginative Plod merely because you are a policeman—or a violin-playing opium fiend because you are a detective. Timony worked very hard to maintain her role as an actress.' She frowned. 'Actresses are not quite what you think but hard-working, professional women. Timony's character makes her vulnerable rather than an imaginative hysteric.' Her face softened. 'We've been together for years. I've been her secretary-cum-wardrobe-mistress-cum agent. And now she is *"in retirement"* I daresay I'll finish up being her nursemaid.' She smiled. 'I admit initially I did think the whole thing was attention-seeking behaviour. Yes, I did. The events were so nebulous and her response, well, yes, a little histrionic. Now I'm not so sure.'

'Have you ever seen any tangible evidence of an intruder?'

Diana Tong looked towards Joanna's evidence bag. 'It's all stuff like that,' she said, shrugging. 'Could be something. Could be nothing. Hard to say and harder to prove.'

Joanna pinned her with a look. 'What's your gut feeling, Mrs Tong?' she asked.

The blunt question threw Diana Tong off balance. 'I—I don't know.'

'In that case you might suggest to Mrs Weeks that she gets herself a dog,' Joanna said, irritated. 'A good guard dog. Something like an Alsatian, a German shepherd. They make excellent guard dogs.'

'She won't get a dog,' Diana Tong said. 'It might not get on with Tuptim.'

'I consider someone's safety more important than the feelings of a cat,' Joanna said sharply. 'And besides, there is an issue of wasting police time.'

'Is that what you think?' There was a mute appeal in the hard grey eyes.

'Wasting police time is currently my primary concern,' Joanna said, 'as it doesn't really appear that Mrs Weeks is in any danger. Even if these little dramas are real and not exaggerated or imagined, there appears no real malice behind them.'

Diana made a face. 'Are you taking her seriously?' There was simple curiosity in her voice.

'Like you,' Joanna said, 'I'm not sure. Certainly nothing serious has happened so far, but...' She looked around her. 'Mrs Weeks is sixty. This is an isolated property. It's as well to be cautious and aware. As I'm here I'll just check the outside doors.'

As she walked around the place there were the odd little questions Joanna wanted to ask. Why did all the windows face north-east? Who had designed Butterfield this way? Why, if she felt threatened, did Timony Weeks cling on to this place with an almost superstitious fervour?

But as it was Joanna did not want to extend the visit by asking what seemed to her to be trivial questions. She wanted to get back to the station and do some real police work.

Every door had the insurance companies' requisite five-lock-security. And they were all intact. There was a good burglar alarm system and plenty of movement-activated floodlights which would drench the property with bright white lights. All was in order and there were no further signs of an intruder.

She entered the house again. This time Diana Tong held back in the kitchen, allowing Joanna to find her own way through. Timony Weeks had returned to her computer and appeared absorbed in her work, almost deliberately ignoring Joanna—which didn't do much for Joanna's rising temper. She waited for a moment then cleared her throat. 'Mrs Weeks,' she said, 'who is it you think is behind these silly little tricks?'

'As I said, I really don't know,' Timony said, still focusing on her computer screen. 'I suppose it could be Sol Brannigan, but I'm not convinced.'

Though Joanna already knew she asked, 'And he is?'

'My second husband—I told you.' She paused. 'My worst and most dangerous husband, actually.' With the last word she swivelled her head and met Joanna's eyes.

Ah, yes, Joanna thought. The husbands: an exclusive but well-populated club.

'What was his full name?'

'Sol.' She hesitated. 'I think his real name was Solomon but everybody always called him Sol. I was married to him for a brief period in the early seventies.'

'That's forty years ago. It seems a bit strange to drag him into this.'

Timony looked irritated at the challenge. 'He was three-quarters of the way to being a gangster.'

'Does he have a criminal record?'

Timony shrugged. 'Probably. I haven't kept up with his criminal activities,' she said haughtily. 'We were only together for eighteen months.'

'Where is he now?'

For the first time Timony looked slightly embarrassed, passing her hand across her face, but it was as if she hadn't heard Joanna's question. She seemed to have her own script and was sticking to it. 'He rang me,' she said, 'eight months, a year ago. He said he needed money.'

'And you sent him some?'

Timony shot a swift, worried look at the doorway. Joanna knew she didn't want her companion to hear her next sentence.

'I put a cheque for five thousand in the post.' She anticipated Joanna's next question.

'An address in Brighton,' she finished quickly. Then added, 'We had no mutual friends so once we'd split up he sort of disappeared from view. I haven't heard from him since I sent the money.'

'Was that the first time you'd sent him money?'

'No. But I told him it would be the last.'

She didn't sound convincing. An easy touch, Joanna thought.

'Has he asked for any more money?'

'Not yet.'

Joanna was getting nowhere. She stood up. There was nothing further to be gained from this interview. She finished up with advice to consider installing CCTV.

Maybe Korpanski was right and the woman was barking, but she doubted she was suffering from anything like Alzheimer's. Joanna couldn't help but feel from their exchanges that she had regressed into some kind of fantasy world, had become the actress again, her words carefully timed, prepared and precisely delivered. Was the entire catalogue of events nothing more than attention-seeking make-believe, or genuine paranoia? Stuck by herself, miles from nowhere, with only Diana for company, her acting days long behind her, had Timony retreated into her own imaginative world? Had she planted the cigarette ash? Joanna was thoughtful as she drove back through the moorlands. One thing bothered her. If all the stories were correct and really had happened, and someone was behind every single one of the call-outs, then whoever it was had somehow gained access inside the property. As the stronger of the two characters she was wondering about Diana Tong and her role. It was an odd situation and a bit outdated, this 'companion' thing. And there was more than a whiff of resentment there. What did Diana really think of Timony? It was clearly a complex relationship. There must be devotion somewhere underneath the façade but it wasn't unusual for two women, thrown together as these two were, to get on each other's nerves. How far would this resentment go? So far as to tease and hint at subtle malice and then deny that anything had happened? She recalled Diana sticking up for her employer when Joanna had dared to suggest she might be histrionic. Something else which wasn't adding up, yet Diana Tong had to be the prime suspect. She was right there, in a perfect position to play tricks on Timony.

But why? Spite? To get even? If she disliked her employer so much why didn't she simply leave? Timony Weeks would miss the strong, practical woman more than Diana would miss her employer, surely?

And then there was Timony Weeks' half-hearted suggestion that a husband she had been married to forty years ago was behind these tricks.

Joanna didn't think so. Sol Brannigan, if he was as

his ex-wife had described him, didn't strike her as the sort to drive all the way up from Brighton, stick around the Staffordshire moorlands and play silly little tricks against his ex-wife. Surely if he wanted money it'd be more in character for him to threaten her, blackmail her or simply demand it. After all, she'd paid up before, though five grand wasn't exactly a fortune for someone with Timony Weeks' obvious wealth.

The whole thing was mad, bizarre and infuriating, so much so that Joanna hardly noticed her surroundings on the way back. The moorlands slipped by unappreciated. She was oblivious to the beauty, panorama, weather and wildness, engrossed in tussling with the problem.

Korpanski was on his way out as she pulled into the last available parking space in the station. She opened her window and he stuck his head in. 'Well?' he asked, grinning. 'Enjoy that, did you?'

She made a face. 'You b—'

He grinned, without bothering to hide his humour. 'So,' he said, 'what did you think?'

'Weird,' she said, 'with that that frozen fish face and odd character. She should be under a psychiatrist.'

'My impression too.'

'But she's worth a lot of money.'

Korpanski nodded.

'How many times have you personally been out there, Mike?'

'Three, maybe four.'

Joanna felt laughter bubble up inside her. 'Well, she's quite taken to you. Maybe you should be the one to go next time.'

That wiped the smile off his face. She didn't mention Timony saying that she was also welcome back.

'What did you make of her?'

He didn't answer straight away but thought about it for a moment, frowning in concentration because he knew Piercy would expect the truth, not some dragged out cliché. 'Bit of everything really, Jo,' he said. 'She seems clear enough about what's happened. She tells her stories well. I mean, they make sense. Maybe she is a bit fanciful. A bit...dramatic. I suppose I just thought she was a bit twitchy, a bit histrionic, highly strung. She was an actress, after all. Attention-seeking. Imaginative.' He was struggling. '*Over*-imaginative. I mean, there's nothing much to go on, is there? Just little things.' He grinned at her mischievously. 'There's hardly a body sitting on her doorstep.'

'Heaven forbid,' she said. 'That is the last thing we want.' Timony's words swam back into her mind. *What do I have to do, Inspector, have a knife sticking out of my back?*

Joanna paused. She recalled the desperation in Timony Weeks' voice, and didn't quite agree with Korpanski's opinion. She might have added another word: *Intuitive.* And another. *Sensitive.*

She tried to put her point across without appearing as though she'd swallowed the woman's stories. 'You know, Mike,' she said, 'this is the sort of case that initially appears to be nothing. And then, just when you're starting to relax about it, something happens. As far as I'm concerned I thought the whole story hung together just that bit too well. Security lights that come on right on cue. Steamy windows. Cigarette Smoke. Memories, a gangster.' It was coming to her now, what had seemed

so unreal about it. 'I could almost hear music floating around the atmosphere. At the time it might have
seemed plausible. But now, it's as though the television
has been switched off. Looking back at it now it's more
obvious what it was.'

Korpanski looked at her questioningly.

'Think of it like this,' she said. 'A film noir script,
rehearsed and revised. And then, just as you despair, in
comes the shadowy villain.' She made a floaty movement of her hands, letting the fingers drift in front of
his face. 'The scary gangster ex-husband hardly visible beyond the sands of time.' She looked up at him.
'How am I doing?'

He put his hand on the car window. 'God,' he said,
his eyes warm, 'I have so missed you.'

It silenced her for a minute. She could do nothing
but ignore the comment, pretend it had not been said.
Then she held up the evidence bag. 'However, I did find
tangible evidence of an intruder.'

Korpanski looked dubious. 'What is it?'

'Some cigarette ash just outside the kitchen window.
Someone *was* outside there, smoking, at some point
fairly recently. Since the heavy rain. Probably in the
last day or two.'

'Could have been the gardener.'

'Been there,' she said. 'I asked. He doesn't smoke.'

'Well, the window cleaner, then.'

'Been there too. He hasn't visited Butterfield since
before Christmas.'

Korpanski shrugged.

'And there's something else,' she said. 'Our smoker
might have been careless enough to drop his ash just

outside the kitchen window, but he wasn't stupid enough to leave his cigarette butt.'

Korpanski's eyes gleamed for a moment. Then he shrugged again. 'So, Jo,' he said. 'Realistically, what are we going to do?'

Joanna sensed, a little like Mrs Weeks must have done with her, that Detective Sergeant Mike Korpanski was beginning to get bored by events at Butterfield Farm.

He patted her on the arm. 'I'm sure there's a perfectly rational explanation for all this. Nothing's going on there, Jo. Mark my words. There's no major crime being planned.' He smiled. 'Just a "B" movie. She'll have a nervous breakdown or something, be admitted to a mental hospital and we'll be off the hook. You'll see.'

She responded dubiously. 'I'm not so sure, Mike. But there's no sign of an intruder inside the property. The doors are all fine. It's more as though she thinks someone's watching her and she wants us to catch whoever it is. Strange. And...'

DS Korpanski waited for her to finish.

'What if it's all true and she's being set up for something?'

Mike had no answer.

'And there's something else, Mike. Did you notice the design of the house? It faces north-east and every single window and door faces the front and looks out towards the drive. Keeps watch. It's a house built by a paranoiac. I had an aunt who was like that. She kept the curtains drawn all day because she was convinced that someone was going to steal the family silver. Not only did she keep the curtains drawn tight but she bought some screens and put them in front. Over the screens she draped woollen blankets. Summer and winter they were in place to stop anyone from looking in.'

'What happened to her?'

'She lay on the floor for three days with a broken hip and died in hospital. She was intestate so most of her valuables ended up with the government and the rest went to a nephew she'd never even seen who lived in New Zealand. That is paranoia for you.'

'Mmm.'

She looked up at the burly DS, realized he was going to make no other response and noted he was wearing a jacket. 'Where are you off to?'

'Going to interview someone who's had a Lexus stolen. There's been a spate of luxury cars nicked round the potteries and here.'

It didn't sound much more interesting than her morning's task. 'Then I suppose I'd better go in and write this up, and I might do some checking up on husband number two. I did suggest that she install CCTV and tried to tell her that we can't keep responding to these calls, but I doubt I'll be any more successful than you've been at discouraging her from picking up the phone.'

'Right ho, Jo. Have fun. See you later.'

She climbed out, locking the door as Korpanski manoeuvred his way out of the car park. A minute later she was sitting at her computer. She had barely finished the report when the desk sergeant knocked on the door.

'We've got another call, from…' he said, tapping his temples with his fingers.

She could feel her temper rising. This was ridiculous. 'I'll take it myself.'

She barely recognized the voice on the other end. The woman she had met earlier had seemed rational, lucid, in command of her emotions. Now she sounded hysterical.

'My husband's watch,' she babbled. 'It was a Rolex Oyster Perpetual. I had it buried with him. On his wrist. He was my first husband. My first love. Gerald.'

'What about this Rolex?' Joanna asked, trying to keep her patience.

'It's here,' she wailed. 'I found it on my bed just now. It has a black crocodile strap and it's here. How can it have come from the grave?'

'Look, Mrs Weeks,' Joanna said patiently. 'If you had your husband's watch buried with him then it is still with him. This must be a similar watch. There isn't only one watch like that in the world. There will almost certainly be a rational explanation for this.'

Her response was angry. 'You just think I'm a hysterical and confused old woman.'

You read my mind, Joanna thought, weary and very bored now. She was not going to make a second journey to Butterfield today. She tried again. 'Mrs Weeks, we simply can't keep coming out to your house. The population of Leek alone is eighteen thousand souls. Include the surrounding moorlands and it takes the number of people that we are responsible for to over twenty thousand people. And then there are the trippers and the tourists and the fact that this is a difficult area to patrol. It's an hour round trip to Butterfield. We simply can't...'

Diana Tong's smooth voice came over the phone. 'I'll stay with her tonight, Inspector, don't you worry.'

'Thank you.' Joanna sighed, put the phone down and logged the call.

I'll stay with her tonight. Don't you worry, Inspector.

Timony Weeks didn't know how lucky she was to have such a friend. Or was she?

FOUR

Monday, January 16, 7.30 p.m.

MATTHEW'S CAR WAS outside when she reached home. She let herself in and immediately smelt flowers. Lilies and roses. She sniffed the air then pushed open the door to the dining room. The table was laid with a white cloth and set with sparkling wine glasses and polished cutlery. In the centre of the table was the source of the scent, a cut-glass vase full of pink roses and creamy pink lilies. She sniffed again. Other smells were coming from the kitchen: onions, bacon, basil. She walked through. Matthew, in a navy-and-white-striped apron over his jeans, was stirring something in a saucepan. Pasta was bubbling vigorously in another. He beamed across at her. 'Good evening, Mrs Levin,' he said with a sweeping mock bow. 'Welcome home. How was your first day back at work?'

'Bloody awful,' she confessed, sitting down, pulling off her shoes and wriggling her stockinged toes. 'But what would I expect after being in the Garden of Eden for a fortnight with you?'

'I see,' he said with mock gravity, affecting a heavy frown. 'Having trouble fitting back into the real world, are you?'

'Yes.' She stood up, put her arms around his neck and met his soft green eyes. 'Can't we sneak off for another honeymoon?' She brushed his lips with her own. 'Is there a law that says you can't have two?'

He looked down at her indulgently and pretended to think about it. 'Not as far as I know, Jo. But you're supposed to be the expert in law, aren't you? If you want my opinion, two honeymoons sound round about twice as good as one. Where would you like to go to next, my lady?'

'Oh, I don't know.' In her heart of hearts she knew there could only really be one honeymoon. That was the whole point of them. She stroked his cheek with her fingers. It was rough and prickly and her fingers made a rasping sound. She kissed his mouth, loving the taste of it, feeling the masculinity of his arms, his back, his shoulders, breathing in the spicy scent. 'Matt,' she said, 'the flowers.' She folded her arms around him even tighter and was unable to resist pulling his leg. 'They are lovely. But...' She gave a mock frown. 'Aren't they the traditional penance for an erring husband?'

He laughed and kissed her very gently on the lips, no more than a brush this time. 'Don't get too used to this treatment, Mrs Levin. It won't happen often.'

'Oh, shame,' she said, slipping her jacket off.

He grinned at her.

She waited until she had showered, they were sitting opposite each other and she had her mouth full of pasta cooked with bacon, cream, onion, garlic, tomatoes and mushrooms. 'De-licious,' she said appreciatively. 'You have my permission to cook this whenever you get the urge. And for your further information I really did have a rubbish day at work. One old biddy is causing absolute havoc calling the police out every day with complete trivia. I think she could take up the entire Leek police force's time. By the time we've written up one report she's back on the blower. Keeps ringing. She's driving us mad. I feel really sorry for Korpanski and the others. They've been plagued by her. I've only been back one day and already I've been out there, and just before I left there was another call.' She raised another forkful of pasta to her mouth. 'I don't know what we're going to do about her. Once the call's logged we've no option but to go.' She thought for a minute then put her fork down and cupped her chin in her palm. 'I suppose, realistically, we'll just have to take longer and longer to respond. Maybe she'll get the hint in the end.' She frowned. 'But, you know what, Matt?'

His mouth was too full of pasta to reply but his eyes encouraged her to respond to her own question.

'She doesn't strike me as confused or muddled. She's one of those face-lifted, in control sort of women. She was an actress and, true to form, has had more than one husband. But she does strike me as sane, if more than a little overdramatic. So what's going on?'

Matthew swallowed and shrugged. 'She's just panicky, I guess.'

'Mmm.' She was unconvinced. 'The call-outs are quite specific in nature,' she continued. 'Things that have been moved, a dead mouse—according to her— deliberately planted in the bread bin. I was summoned today because someone had been smoking outside an open kitchen window at five o'clock in the morning.'

'You're kidding.'

She waved her fork at him then took a sip of wine. 'I am not.'

Matthew's eyebrows were raised but he said nothing, waiting for her to continue. She frowned and met his eyes. 'The odd thing is, Matt, there *was* some fresh cigarette ash outside the window and no one there does smoke, so it all seems reasonable. But this place is miles from anywhere. It's the middle of winter, for goodness' sake—who's going to be standing outside a window puffing smoke into the kitchen? What would be the point? She might even have been asleep and slept right through the whole charade.' She sighed. 'But there is the indisputable evidence of the ash and it hadn't lain there long. The only other explanation is that she or Diana planted it there.'

Now Matthew was frowning too, so she continued, 'I thought I'd got through to her that she shouldn't keep calling us out for nothing but I'd hardly got back to the station when there's another call. This time her late husband's watch has turned up in her bedroom this afternoon in spite of having been buried with him in his coffin.'

Matthew looked incredulous. 'Now that's a trick worthy of Houdini,' he said, grinning.

She nodded in puzzlement and agreement. 'Surely it has to just be a similar watch,' she said. 'Either that or it *wasn't* buried with her nearest and dearest. One or the other.'

Matthew grinned at her indulgently. 'When you've excluded the impossible...' he quoted partially.

'I can only come to the conclusion that in spite of her apparent sanity Timony Weeks is, in fact, losing her marbles. And fairly quickly.'

At the mention of Timony's name Matt looked at her in disbelief. 'You're joking.'

'No. That really is her name.'

Matthew's face was thoughtful. 'Unless these tricks really are being played on her.'

'I really don't know what to think. Anyway, that's not all my bad news.'

'There's more?'

'As well as being haunted by a sixty-year-old lady, apparently a humourless psycho is to replace Colclough.'

'All good news then, Jo.' She was tempted to flick a spoonful of Parmesan cheese at him but knew she wouldn't fancy cleaning it all up later so resisted, merely making a face at him, then reaching across and touching his hand. 'And how about your first day back?' Matthew was a Home Office pathologist, and while his descriptions of his day's work could be gruesome, to Joanna they were invariably fascinating—and a useful education.

'Oh. The usual. Nothing very interesting. Nothing for you. No murders or even a suicide. Just sickness, death and mother nature.'

She eyed him sharply. 'You've come down to earth with a bump too, Matt. We've only been married a couple of weeks.'

He smiled at her. 'We've had our fairy tale, Jo. Now we have to face the real future together.'

She studied him. With his tousled blond hair, stubborn chin, green eyes and lovely grin he was very easy on the eye, as he had been from the time she had first noticed him, when she had met his eyes in the mirror as he had stood behind her, after a particularly unpleasant post-mortem she had attended, and been amused at her squeamishness. Oh, yes. She had noticed him all right. But that angle of his jaw had forewarned her. She and he were two strong characters. There was always going to be a clashing of horns. He was right, though. However turbulent the path ahead might prove they now had to face the real future together.

And that might well be tough. *She* knew she had one vision of their future and *he* another.

She knew he would like to start a family, whereas she…? She could have put it off, perhaps for ever.

As soon as they had finished their meal he stood up. 'I think I'll just give Eloise a ring,' he said, breaking the magic of the evening. 'See how she's getting on.'

Which left her to load the dishwasher and put the pans in to soak.

Tuesday, January 17, 7.30 a.m.

SHE LOOKED OUT of the window to a brightening sky. 'It looks lovely,' she said. 'I wonder if I could risk the bike.'

Matthew came up behind her and wrapped her in his arms. 'No, Jo,' he protested. 'It's too dark. You can't be seen even with lights and a fluorescent jacket. It's too dangerous. And it'll be freezing and slippery.' He nuzzled her neck. 'Wait until the spring, darling.'

But instead of the warm stroke of his fingers on her neck she felt the cold grip of resentment and instead of turning around to kiss him she stayed where she was, staring out of the window at the silver streaks in the sky that heralded the approaching dawn. He was clipping her wings already. She could feel her shoulders bunch up, feel the words line up, ready to say, sharply, that *she* would be the one to make this particular decision, whether she went to work on her bike or in the car. She could feel by the tension in his fingers that Matthew sensed this struggle too and was holding his breath, waiting for her to resolve it. She turned around then and challenged him with a direct stare. His mouth was in a firm line. He said nothing. He was still waiting.

She smiled, somehow feeling that she had gained the high ground here but not quite sure how. 'You're probably right,' she capitulated. Then, 'But I really *must* go out on my bike on Sunday, Matthew, otherwise I'll seize up.'

'Umm,' he said awkwardly.

She just knew what was coming next.

'I meant to talk to you about that,' he said, the words tumbling out too quickly, as though they had been gridlocked in his brain and were frantic to escape. 'I thought it'd be nice to have Eloise over for the day.'

She looked at him, feeling her face and her words freeze. Eloise was Matthew's daughter with whom Joanna had a less than cordial relationship. 'Nice for whom?'

And watched as his eyes grew as cold as her voice. 'Nice for all of us,' he said carefully. 'I thought it would be nice for all of us.'

'Well, it doesn't stop me from going out on my bike, does it, Matt?'

'No, it doesn't.' There was an edge to his voice and she recognized, with a feeling of despair, that the icicles were already forming between them.

'Good,' she said, planning an extra-long route on Sunday whatever the weather. 'Because I can't wait to get on it.'

His eyes flickered. It was no more than that. A simple flicker, a small yellow light in both green irises. But she read it and felt resentful all the way into work.

Did you really think marriage would solve any of your problems, Piercy? she scolded herself as she manoeuvred the car along the road into Leek.

Korpanski's black Ford Focus was already parked up outside the station when she arrived and he was sitting at his desk, his computer switched on. She hung her jacket up on the hook on the back of the door. 'Morning, Mike. Any more calls from our…?'

'Her companion's rung in to say that our friend is going away for a little holiday.'

She sat down and switched her screen on. 'To the funny farm, I hope.'

'She didn't say so but she did ask if we could possibly go out there before they went.'

'What for?'

Korpanski shrugged. 'Search me.'

'Shall we both go?'

He stood up with little enthusiasm.

The wind was up and the chilly atmosphere even penetrated the interior of the car as they drove across the moorlands. 'I'd hate to live out here,' Korpanski said. 'It's so cold and miles from anywhere.' His eyes scanned the barren landscape. 'Nothing to look at.'

'I'd love it,' Joanna responded, her eyes sweeping the panorama, empty apart from a few stray sheep, pale winter grass and drystone walls. 'It's so wild and fantastically bleak and lonely. I'd *love* it,' she said again. 'But it does take a particular sort of person to live out here. They need to be private, self-sufficient.'

Korpanski grinned at her. 'Like you?'

She had missed this idle banter. 'Bugger off, Korpanski,' she said good-naturedly. 'Actually, I wasn't thinking of me but our friend Mrs Weeks. Now she wouldn't have struck me as someone who fitted the profile of a moorland person. She seems much more of a townie. And her clothes and tastes seem to fit that too.' She considered for a minute. 'Plus the fairly obvious and extensive cosmetic surgery.'

Korpanski was smiling. 'Doing a psychological profile, Inspector?'

'Bugger off,' she said again, even milder the second time around. Truth was, she was relieved that her recent married status hadn't altered their relationship. In a way, she reflected, when Korpanski had asked whether he should in future call her Mrs Levin or stick with Piercy he had been asking that very question. What would change? Well, nothing.

As she had done on the previous day they stopped at the ridge to look down on Butterfield Farm and Mike echoed her thoughts. 'For a house that's on its own it's not exactly tucked away, is it? It's easy to overlook from here.'

She turned to face him. 'You're starting to believe her? That there's some maverick, mad stalker out there?'

'Not necessarily but—'

'But what?'

Korpanski's dark eyes scanned the empty panorama. 'Why stay out here if she's so rattled?'

'Because she's stubborn, independent, because she doesn't want to give in to her feelings?'

But she too turned to look at the farmhouse which stood in such isolation, trying to hide inside the valley but only succeeding in drawing attention to itself. 'I don't know, Mike. Maybe she just wants privacy.'

Diana Tong was standing in the doorway, watching them as they drove in. And even before they'd parked they could tell her manner had changed subtly from yesterday. She was less haughty and condescending, stepping towards them as they pulled up and greeting them almost like old friends as they climbed out of the car. 'Inspector, Sergeant. Thank you for coming. Timony and I, well, we think we should do some explaining. Give you some background, you see.'

It was on the tip of Joanna's tongue to say that this trip was possibly yet *another* waste of time but at the same time she was curious. She stayed silent, managing to limit her acerbity to, 'We'd be grateful if you keep it brief and help with the frequent calls your employer's been making. If they continue,' she added darkly, 'we may even be forced to bring a prosecution against her for wasting police time.'

Diana Tong's feathers weren't even ruffled. 'Just hear Timony's story,' she appealed. 'I think you'll find it goes some way towards explaining at least some things,' she replied coolly, holding the door open to allow them to file in.

Timony Weeks was sitting on the sofa looking—frankly—terrified, thinner, older and, if her face had been able to display any emotion, Joanna guessed she would have looked distraught. There was a distinct change from yesterday.

Korpanski said nothing but shot her a swift, puzzled look. It was the look a concerned son might aim towards a parent he has suddenly realized is ageing fast. The watch was lying on Timony's lap. She was looking down at it with an expression of revulsion, her hands and back angled away as though its touch would taint her.

'I had it buried with him,' she said, still looking

down at it rather than at the police. 'It was left on his wrist when he was placed in his coffin. I saw it buckled on, the strap fastened. Gerald loved this watch. It was his favourite thing. He asked to be buried with it—on—his—wrist.' The last few words were spoken in a panicky, hiccupping voice. 'Someone must have...'

Joanna shifted on her feet, wanting to point out that Mrs Weeks' first husband might have loved his watch so much he'd asked to be buried with it strapped around his wrist, but that meant that it was almost certainly not *this* watch. It was a fairly obvious if tacky trick. Unless she had played it on herself. If she hadn't it was indeed a nasty prank. But if someone else was involved it meant that the person who planted this watch must have known of her late husband's wish.

Responding to her unspoken thought without comment Diana Tong passed across a yellowing newspaper cutting. Joanna read it and passed it to Korpanski, who also read it wordlessly then handed it back to her. The headline screamed: *Child Star's Late-Husband's Request.*

Underneath it detailed the whole damned lot, that Gerald Portmann, the late husband of 'child star' Timony Shore, had asked to have his beloved Rolex Oyster (Perpetual *Air-King*) to be strapped to his right wrist and buried with him. It went on to describe the clothes he should also be wearing, and underneath that a perfectly tasteless picture of the dead man in his coffin wearing the (also prescribed) dark pinstriped suit, white shirt and tie, the right sleeves of both jacket and shirt pushed up just enough to expose the shining face and dark strap of the watch in question.

Joanna looked down at the item in Timony's shaking hand. She and Mike exchanged looks and messages. His head gave an almost imperceptible jerk towards the newspaper. She could interpret his comment only too well. *So the whole bloody world knew about it.*

Even so, Joanna tried to put the point over to Timony. 'You can't be sure that this is *his* watch.'

'Oh, but I can. The scratch across the glass.' Staring ahead of her, as though she was a blind person, Timony's fingernail followed a line, a scratch on the watch glass which reached from the top of the one to the bottom of the line which represented four. 'That happened when he had the car accident in which he died,' she explained. 'He was wearing it then too.' Her eyes flicked upwards to meet Joanna's with a mute appeal to be believed. 'He *always* wore it, Inspector. He hardly ever took it off. He just loved it. To him it was the ultimate star status symbol.' Her fingers stroked it and her face looked far away, pillow-deep in memory. Joanna glanced across at Korpanski and could barely resist rolling her eyes. Korpanski, for his part, gave her an innocently bland smile, as though to say, *Well you're the boss, Boss. And I'm just the lackey.* She scowled at him.

'The watch isn't proof of anything,' Joanna said calmly. She wanted to take the item from her but even *she* was a little spooked by the thought of touching a watch which had lain around the wrist of a dead person for…?

'How long ago did your first husband die?'

'Gerald died forty years ago, Inspector,' she said calmly, 'in nineteen seventy-two.'

Joanna's eyes locked on the item. Common sense told her that this could not be the watch that had been strapped to Gerald Portmann's dead wrist. But superstition argued with common sense. Common sense won. She slipped on a pair of gloves and reached out for it.

'May I?'

Timony Weeks handed it over with a tiny shiver of revulsion.

Joanna looked at it. She'd never really seen what all the fuss was about Rolexes but there was something about the feel of it, the elegance and stark cleanness of its dial. Then, using her much-mocked magnifying glass, she peered closer. Embedded around the dial was what looked like soil.

Grave soil?

And the watch itself was ticking, as though it had an unstoppable, malevolent life of its own. A mechanical heart. Had it ticked away in the grave, Edgar Allan Poe like? For a fraction of a second in the room they were all silent, listening to the quiet but insistent tick of the watch. Joanna passed it to Mike, who'd put a glove on his right hand and stretched it out.

Joanna looked back at Timony Weeks. 'Why are you so afraid, Mrs Weeks? What exactly are you afraid of? And if you are that afraid why continue to live out here in this lonely spot?'

Timony Weeks looked at her with her doll-like, expressionless face. 'OK, Inspector,' she said. 'I'll answer all your questions as best I can.' Her voice was quiet, low and husky, but Joanna had the feeling that you could use this voice to create an effect. It could be low and husky, it could also be sexy and strident. Her choice. She continued: 'First of all, why do I stay out here when I am uncomfortable and being hounded?' she began.

Joanna felt on safer ground. This was her beat. 'Well,

it would seem logical, Mrs Weeks, whether these episodes are real or part-imagined, to move into the town.'

Mrs Weeks seemed impervious to Joanna's attempt to bring things down to earth and hurry the interview along. But the detective's displayed impatience did not have the effect of hurrying her through her statement.

'You need to understand about my life,' she said, and again Joanna felt her temper simmer towards boiling point. Bubble, bubble, toil and trouble. She and Korpanski had more than enough work to do. The theft of luxury cars in and around Leek was moving towards epidemic proportions. They simply didn't have the time to listen to a prolonged and drawn-out life history, however eventful that life had been. Child star... And yet, as she glanced across to pick up Korpanski's take on the situation, Joanna could see from his expression of studied indifference and the gleam in his very dark eyes that, like herself, he felt some curiosity towards this strange woman.

Whether Timony picked up on this or not she began the story like an episode of *Listen With Mother*. 'In nineteen sixty,' she began, 'when I was eight years old, I was signed up as a child actress to what would become the biggest...' she smiled to herself, 'I suppose these days you'd call it a soap.' She paused (for maximum effect?) and continued, 'There weren't many TV programmes then and it was one of the few series aimed at...' She paused, and mocked, '"the family". It was called *Butterfield Farm*. It was a huge hit and ran for twelve years. I was the little Shirley Temple in it. I played Lily Butterfield. I was very small for my age. When I was eight I looked about five. I wore tiny nylon dresses, sometimes dungarees. I sang and I danced and I had a mop of curly red hair.' She laughed. 'Not that you could tell it was red. Television then was all in black and white.'

For the first time they saw her really smile with her porcelain teeth. And although her mouth was surgically stiff and swollen, something of the pretty child peeped out from behind the face that had become a tight mask.

She continued, 'The series ran until I was nearly twenty, finally folding in early nineteen seventy-two. I always looked young for my age and the studio managers made sure I stayed even younger. I was on a strict diet and when my breasts began to form they were bandaged up.' Again she smiled but this time her expression was tinged with cynicism and an element of disgust. She looked as though she expected either Joanna or DS Mike Korpanski to interrupt but neither did. They knew they were in for the full version. They were both thinking the same thing—that they may as well sit this one out and then, perhaps, all would be resolved and the call-outs would stop.

After scanning them both, Timony went on: 'These days they're more likely to put fake boobs in the young stars, I suppose. They seem to want kids to look sexually active from the age of eight.' She paused, a shadow straining her face. 'Or even six.' She rubbed her forehead as though it itched. 'Anyway, the show brought its rewards. I was earning in excess of a thousand pounds a week, which was riches in the early sixties.' She smiled, or at least her lips curved upwards. 'Looking at it nowadays, the storylines would seem a bit bland and derivative of American imports, cattle rustling, a lost lamb, a cow that calved.' She humphed, 'With a lot of mooing and groaning. Even a murder. Some poor cowhand was found at the bottom of the well.' Suddenly she looked vague, her forehead struggling to frown. 'I think…' She attempted to retrieve her story with a smile. 'There were so many episodes—one a week every week for twelve years. Along the way I've had five husbands.' She gave a wry smile. 'Not all of them very satisfactory. I'd had two by the time I was twenty-one. My first husband was a lot older than me. He was my screen Daddy on Butterfield.' She smiled at the memory. 'It almost felt incestuous but Gerald was one of the loves of my life. I adored him. Unfortunately he died in a road accident in the States, on the Santa Monica highway. He'd been working on a film out there. I'd been due to join him.' Her finger massaged the area between her eyebrows as though searching for a frown line and failing to find it. 'The movie never happened. I did try the movies later on but I could never settle in the States. Anyway…'

She waved her hands around, crossed her legs and pulled a frown, then continued. 'By the time I was eighteen I'd made enough money and Gerald was wealthy anyway. After Butterfield folded—we shot the last few episodes late in nineteen seventy-one—I didn't really need to earn any more so I had little to do except get married and divorced and make the odd "B" movie. At nineteen I was basically redundant and watched my celebrity fade. A light, first bright, dimming quick.' Showing a tinge of cynicism she looked straight at Joanna. 'Let me tell you how it is, Inspector,' she said, holding up an index finger. 'This is how it happens. At first newspapers, magazines, interviews, opening supermarkets, meeting royalty, cutting ribbons. They were happy days.' She spoke quickly. 'Everyone wanted a little piece of me. And then, poof.' She exploded her hands. 'Suddenly, no one did any more.' She gave a wry smile and looked both bleak and cynical. 'At twenty I was history. You see, I committed the unforgivable sin, Inspector.' She turned her head to encompass Korpanski too. 'Sergeant, I got older. From being the darling of the universe I was thrown out like an old sock with a hole in the toe. You see, no one wanted me to grow up. Ever. My adoring fans couldn't forgive my ageing. They didn't want to know the adult me but preserve my memory in aspic as that sweet little girl.' Again she looked straight at Joanna. 'The only way to keep a little girl a little girl is for that little girl to never grow up. In other words, to die young. Then she remains the child. For ever Timony Shore or Lily Butterfield. Take your pick. Beautiful, sweet little child.' The cynicism in her voice was as toxic as mustard gas.

She paused again, then looked directly at Joanna and then at Mike, as though to satisfy herself that they were listening. 'You have to understand how big and famous I was. There was hardly any family TV in those days, not a great deal of choice, so practically everyone in the UK was tuned into *Butterfield Farm* on a Saturday evening.' She tossed her head. 'I was mobbed everywhere. It was celebrity culture in the early sixties. It brought its pains and gains.' Her face twisted. 'At one point I was threatened—stalked—by a fan who tried to gouge my eyes out as I came out of the studio one evening. I was almost fourteen at the time.' Her finger touched a tiny scar at the edge of her right eyebrow which Joanna would not have noticed unless she had drawn her attention to it in this abstract way. 'After Gerald died I married husband number two, Sol Brannigan, who was as tough as they make them.' Her eyes flickered dangerously at the memory. 'He liked to treat his women rough but he did protect me.'

Joanna recalled that it was Sol Brannigan who had liked to taunt her by smoking just outside her window, and who Timony thought could still possibly be playing tricks.

Timony Weeks leaned forward and appeared to address her next statement to DS Mike Korpanski who was now standing up, his head on one side, looking at her as though he was wondering whether to believe her story and also preparing to leave.

Whether or not Timony Weeks had picked up on the sergeant's scepticism, she carried on with her story anyway. She was now in full flow. 'Robert Weeks, husband number three,' she gave a cheeky smile, 'was already married, to a friend, when he "fell in love" with me.' Her mouth twisted. 'He was a lovely man but after thirteen happy years together he died of cancer.' She gave a rueful smile. 'I like to think that it would have lasted if he'd lived.'

'You've kept the name Weeks.'

Timony's eyes looked shrewd and impressed and then mischievous. 'Yes,' she said. 'I liked the name. It seemed to go rather well with Timony. Besides...I knew it would annoy Carmen.' She stopped speaking for a moment, smiling at her private joke before continuing. 'Adrian McWilliams, number four, was married on the rebound and was a horrible mistake. Violence, alcohol, drugs, gambling—you name it. I was lucky to get rid of him. And then,' another cheeky smile, 'my only foreigner, Rolf Van Eelen, number five.' She snorted. 'A bit of poetic justice here. He walked out on me with one of *my* friends, Trixy, the bitch. I made their life hell until I got used to the fact that marriage really wasn't for me. Then I let them go.' She almost looked shame-faced now. 'So you see, Inspector Piercy and Sergeant Korpanski, I've made a lot of enemies along the way. And not too many friends.' She glanced, almost questioningly, at Diana Tong, who was standing behind the piano, leaning forward slightly, as though to catch every word in a net of attention. Joanna followed the glance and wondered. No softness or reassurance was beamed back from the dogsbody.

Joanna interrupted the reverie. 'Are you trying to tell me that someone from your distant past is trying to exact revenge on you?' she demanded. 'Either an ancient fan who belatedly has decided he or she doesn't want you to grow up or something to do with your multiple marriages and divorces, the feathers you've ruffled?' The words sounded vaguely silly and quite insulting even as she spoke, as though she was ridiculing the entire idea. And this tone did not escape Timony Weeks. She moved her head slightly so she watched Joanna from the corner of her eye.

'We're talking about events that happened years ago,' Joanna pointed out. 'The people involved would be—' She was going to say elderly but Diana Tong cleared her throat very deliberately at that precise moment so Joanna said instead, 'Why wait until now?'

Timony Weeks didn't answer but gave a stiff smile.

Joanna continued, 'Whatever happened in the past, I still don't understand why, if you're nervous, you live out here?'

Cat-like, Timony narrowed her eyes, leaned in close and spoke in a conspiratorial tone. 'I'll tell you why, Inspector.' She flicked her head around to take in Korpanski. 'Sergeant. In a town or a city anyone can come right up to you, unnoticed, and do what they like. That fan that nearly lost me the sight in my eye. He walked right up to me with a pair of scissors in spite of my having four bodyguards surrounding me. He still got to me. Here I can see if someone approaches. I can watch the track. I have fair warning of an intrusion. I have security lights and a burglar alarm.'

But you still think someone's getting to you, Joanna thought and fleetingly reflected on the architecture and design of Butterfield Farm. Timony's words answered some of her questions.

Even Joanna felt spooked by her obvious apprehension. She actually looked around, then caught sight of Korpanski's bland face with its stolid expression, standing like the genie of the lamp, arms folded, thick thighs apart, and she felt ashamed of herself. 'Well, Mrs Weeks,' she said briskly, 'if all these events you've been reporting to the Leek Police really have happened, as you describe, your vigil isn't doing much good, is it?' She glanced down at her notebook. 'Some of the reports are of incidents *inside* the house. The toilet seat left up? The mouse in the bread bin. And now the watch. You're sure all this isn't simply your vivid imagination?' What she had wanted to say was: *an attempt to retrieve your long-lost fame?* But she didn't dare. It was sailing a little too close to the edge. And she couldn't risk doing that. Particularly now with Chief Superintendent Gabriel Rush about to take up his post. So instead she asked, 'You've lived here how long?'

'A little over ten years,' Timony said warily. 'When my last marriage broke up I decided to build in the moorlands. It was one of the few places with the space, you understand.'

'But these little—for want of a better word—tricks have been happening for just over two weeks. Any idea why now?'

Both Timony and Diana shook their heads and looked mystified. There was a pause.

Suddenly Timony Weeks seemed to surface. She looked around her. 'Where's the cat?' she rapped out. 'Where is she? Tuptim? Tuptim?'

Diana spoke lazily from the doorway. 'I'm sorry, Tims, I haven't seen her at all today.'

'Not like her.' Timony swivelled her lizard neck around to stare at her companion. 'Did she have her breakfast?'

'No.'

'Oh.' Timony looked distressed at this. 'Well, now, Inspector, what is it you were saying, that it is all in my imagination?'

Diana Tong, dogsbody, spoke up for her. 'It isn't her imagination, Inspector Piercy. It isn't. I've seen things happen.'

'What things?' It came out sharper than she'd meant, as though she was challenging her, calling her a liar, a stretcher of truth. She had been extremely vague earlier when Joanna had asked her if she'd ever seen any tangible evidence. Joanna's eyes narrowed; she looked from one woman to the other and wondered. They were reading her mind as precisely as a stage psychic. She glanced at Korpanski. His face twitched as though he was swallowing a smile. He actually put a hand in front of his mouth. Joanna scowled at him.

'Things in the wrong places,' Diana said irritably.

Then, turning to her employer, 'Oh, what's the use, Tims? No one believes you—or me.'

Unexpectedly a tear rolled down Timony's cheek. 'Please believe me,' she begged. 'Please. I know something—someone—is out there and wishes to harm me.'

'I'm sorry,' Joanna said. 'I'm really sorry. We have all your calls logged but there's no hard evidence.'

'What about the watch?'

Joanna wanted to ask: how can you be sure it's his watch? Back would come the response. From the scratch. So, if it is, is it possible you might have been mistaken about burying it with your husband? Were you, perhaps, tempted to retain it? As a keepsake?

She said none of these things but picked up her statement solidly. 'No break-ins, nothing stolen. No assault.' She felt she needed to say something more. 'If anything it is, possibly, a mischievous neighbour. Nothing more worrying than that.'

'But I'm frightened, Inspector.'

Joanna was adversely affected by the 'little-girl-lost' voice. High-pitched and squeaky with just the right amount of cracking. She must have been a really great actress in her time.

'We can't go out to every person who feels frightened,' Joanna said in exasperation, getting ready to leave. 'All I can suggest is that you move to somewhere less remote. What about sheltered housing or a gated estate, somewhere secure? There are a few places going up here in Leek, old mills being converted into luxury flats. You'd be much safer there, Mrs Weeks. And happier.'

'But I've explained,' Timony said frostily.

'I understand you have a holiday booked?'

'We go next week to a favourite hotel of ours in Devon,' Diana said. 'We've stayed there before. It's rather lovely and has a pool.'

Joanna turned to Diana Tong. 'Is it possible you could stay here until then?'

'No.' Said flatly and without much sympathy.

Joanna looked at Mike for help. And he stepped right in with his size elevens. 'You say money is no object, Ms Weeks. Have you thought of hiring private security?'

'It's Mrs,' she snapped at him. 'Weeks is my married name. Shore was my...' she hesitated, '...stage name. And I'm *still* legally married.'

'Well, what about your husband then?' Korpanski was still trying. Hard.

'Chance'd be a fine thing,' she snapped. 'I don't think Rolf would come and act as nursemaid to me. He has Trixy.' Her face became vinegary.

'Children?' Korpanski tried next. You had to hand it to Mike, Joanna thought. He really was trying very hard.

'Child stars don't have children,' Timony said haughtily.

'Not even when the child stars grow up?' Joanna asked.

'Especially not then.'

Joanna looked at Mike. Neither knew how to proceed.

Timony Weeks made one more appeal. 'Can't you get it into your heads? Someone is out there trying hard to get at me,' she said, as though stating an indisputable fact. 'I can go away for a holiday but I will always have to return here, to Butterfield. If you can't find out what's

going on and who is victimizing me this trouble will
not go away, it will escalate. Do you understand?' Her
tiny shoulders bunched together. She looked unhappy.
'You have to solve this before something dreadful happens.' She looked at the watch, still held by Detective
Sergeant Mike Korpanski.

'We'll take the watch in for forensic examination,'
Joanna said.

Timony said nothing but simply stared.

Joanna left feeling frustrated. She kept turning
around as they drove back up the track. Timony Weeks
was watching them through the window. She looked
fragile and vulnerable. Joanna turned around in her
seat and took the car all the way up the lane to join the
road. Something was bothering her about the whole
situation. It wasn't just the way Butterfield seemed to
lie in permanent shadow on the brightest of winter's
days or even the way the place nestled in its hamlet,
almost as though it expected the hills to protect it, or
even the fact that it was all too easy for anyone to spy
on this isolated property. No. It was the story about the
deranged fan who had tried to gouge little Lily Butterfield's eye out in spite of there being four bodyguards
surrounding her.

She was quiet on the way home but Mike wasn't.
He was whistling tunelessly under his breath. And the
sound irritated her. 'Stop whistling,' she said. 'I can't
hear myself think.'

'Sorry. Can't get the tune out of my head.'

'What tune? There isn't a tune. Just noise.'

He looked at her. 'I think it's Ding Dong Bell,' he
said apologetically. 'Can't think what's set that off.'

She looked at him sharply. 'It's the well.' The words

were out before she'd thought about it. She looked at him. 'I hope the damned cat hasn't fallen down the well,' she said. 'That'd really set her off.' Then she muttered to herself, 'Nursery rhymes, children's programmes that went off the air forty years ago. A Burmese cat with a strange name. A house that sits and watches for a stranger to call, practical jokes, a dead man's watch. I don't know what the police force is coming to,' she grumbled.

FIVE

THEY'D ARRIVED BACK at the station. 'Right,' Joanna said, feeling a sudden burst of energy as though she'd just drunk three large cans of Red Bull. 'You make the coffee, Mike. I'll run a search about *Butterfield Farm*, the TV series.'

'I don't know what you think you'll find looking at a kids' TV thing from back in the sixties,' Korpanski grumbled, but headed out through the door towards the coffee machine anyway. He was still chuntering when he returned with a couple of cappuccinos. A posh new coffee machine had recently been installed in the station and it was well used by the staff. No Styrofoam cups any more but thick cardboard mugs with corrugated aprons to stop their fingers from getting burned. Joanna took a big sip as they both peered into the Google search, Joanna reading aloud, *'Butterfield Farm. Shown 1960–1972. The story of a saccharine rural Derbyshire family who milked cows, survived blizzards and power cuts, lost animals but usually found them again. It was mainly filmed in and around Buxton and in the Manchester studio. The most dramatic storyline was in 1965 with some cattle rustling. It was a deliberate attempt by the BBC to encourage family viewing of English rather than American series. Undoubted star of the show was Timony Weeks, who played Lily Butterfield, daughter of the household. With engaging sweetness, a mane of red hair and looking much younger than her years, she simpered and lisped her way through episode after episode. The public interest in her increased when she married her screen father in 1969, when she was just seventeen and he was fifty-six.*

'Nothing here about a murder,' Joanna observed. 'It sounds a bit too much like family viewing for a story line like that, particularly in the early sixties when family viewing meant just that. Mum, Dad and children all sitting round the one TV.' She'd seen the old movies: black and white, tiled fireplaces, coal fires and the cheery voice of the commentator.

'So do you think Timony is mistaken about the cowhand found at the bottom of the well?' Korpanski queried. 'She did seem a bit vague about it.'

'I wonder.' Joanna looked again, frowning into the screen. 'It clearly says here that the most dramatic storyline was about cattle rustling. Nothing about a murder or a body down the well.' She smirked. 'Mind you, dead cowhand beats cattle rustling any day, eh, Korpanski? She did appear dubious, didn't she? And yet specific. Could she be blurring fact with fiction, I wonder? What if it wasn't part of the storyline of *Butterfield Farm* but something that really happened?'

'Seems a bit far-fetched to me.'

'The whole bloody lot's far-fetched. Let's just look through police files for murders in Derbyshire between nineteen sixty and nineteen seventy-two and see if there's anything that appears similar.' She swivelled around in her chair. 'I wonder. Fact or fiction?'

'Something in her head, more like,' Korpanski said. 'A figment of her over-excitable imagination and sense of drama. I'm sure she's exaggerating events.'

'Probably. Look, we'll just have a quick check then get on with something real. OK?'

'Couldn't agree more.' Korpanski felt he'd be relieved to move away from this to something concrete.

It was an easy task on the PNC 2 which rumbled into life. They found plenty of tragedies, climbing accidents, road accidents, a death in custody which had caused quite a stir, a couple of unexplained disappearances. But nothing even remotely like Timony's story of a body down a well. 'So,' Joanna agreed wearily, 'looks like you were right and it was something in her head. But that would suggest she *is* crazy.'

'We-ell?' Korpanski challenged. 'Would you give her a certificate of sanity?'

Joanna laughed and shook her head. For a few minutes she sat and thought. Everything screamed at her that Timony Weeks was not quite sane. And yet... Her toes were tingling with something. She had the oddest feeling that she was sliding into some parallel world, where fact and fiction merged and blurred and altered until they were so distorted it was impossible to tell what was true and what was false.

'Perhaps we should run a check on Sol Brannigan,' she said.

'That seems a better idea,' Korpanski said heartily.

'OK, you do that.' She stood up. 'I'm going to have a quick word with Colclough.'

'Whatever for?'

She gave him a cheeky grin. 'He just might remember something about the series. He's that sort of age.'

As she left, out of the corner of her eye, she saw Korpanski roll his towards the ceiling. She could guess what he was thinking, that this case had been bad news from the start and that she shouldn't waste any more time and energy on it. Trouble was, she agreed with him.

Colclough was in good humour. Very good humour. She could tell that from the way his eyes twinkled when he looked at her. 'Piercy,' he said warmly. 'Sit yourself down, my dear.'

From anyone else that would have sounded patronizing but from Colclough she could almost forgive him anything. With dismay she acknowledged that she was going to miss him like thunder every time she encountered Chief Superintendent Gabriel Rush.

'Not long to go now,' he said cheerfully. 'We're planning to spend the summer in Cyprus. Looking forward to it. Little Catherine will join us for the school holidays.'

Catherine was his adored granddaughter.

'I'll miss you, sir,' she said impulsively.

He leaned across the desk and patted her shoulder with a soft, bouncing hand. 'We all have to move on, Piercy,' he said. 'And I'm sure Chief Superintendent Rush will be an excellent successor. He's a very able man, you know.'

How she disliked that word: able.

He looked at her reproachfully. 'Surely you don't begrudge me a bit of laziness? I've been lucky to have escaped early retirement, you know. I've served my time and enjoyed myself, seen all the changes the government—and the criminals—can dream up. I'm ready to go, truth be told. Now what brings you in here? Purely to commiserate with me?'

'No, sir. I wanted your advice.'

'Go on.' His eyes were sharp, bright, shrewd and

alert. He might be ready to retire but he would miss the challenge of 'the chase'.

'It's about the lady who's been calling us out to Butterfield Farm,' she said.

'Ah, yes. She's proving to be a bit of a nuisance, isn't she? What have we logged up? Fifteen calls, is it?'

'More than that, sir.'

'Bit of a frequent caller, eh? Want to know how to deal with her?'

'Not exactly, sir.' She drew in a deep breath. 'Today, when Sergeant Korpanski and I went to Butterfield Farm, in response to an invitation, she started telling us about her days as a child actress in the early sixties.'

'Oh, yes? What was she in then?'

'That's it. *Butterfield Farm.*'

'What's her name?'

'Timony Weeks, sir.'

He leaned back, steepled his fingers together and half closed his eyes. 'Timony Weeks,' he mused. 'Timony Shore, you mean. *Butterfield Farm.* Of course. I wondered why the name Timony sounded so familiar. Saturday evenings, BBC.' He chuckled. 'There only was the one then. Seven thirty till eight thirty it was on. My sister lived for it. She must have watched every single episode right from the start.' His long grey eyebrows moved together. 'No video recorders then, Piercy, or iPlayers. No downloads and computer games. Half the street didn't even have a telly. All the kids used to come to us. We used to have a bottle of Corona and some plain crisps with the salt in blue wraps. And we'd sit there, cross-legged, on the floor. Of course, my brother and I preferred *The Lone Ranger.* Much more exciting. We'd sit on the back of the sofa and have shootouts. And my dad preferred *Dixon of Dock Green*. But the girls—they just loved *Butterfield Farm*. For me all those cows and pinnies was a bit much. It was sickly sweet. Totally unrealistic. Very girly. But TV was TV, Piercy.' His eyebrows met in the middle as he threw out the challenge.

'Yes, sir.'

His eyes flicked open suddenly. 'So?'

'Mrs Weeks mentioned a murder in the plot but she didn't seem very sure.'

Colclough frowned. 'I don't remember a murder. Not in Butterfield. It was all about milking cows and making patchwork quilts, as far as I remember. Some jam got burnt and a lamb was born in a snow storm, poor little thing. It was touch and go for the entire episode.' His face crinkled in amusement. 'Great drama. But Butterfield being Butterfield there was never any doubt that the lamb would be all right. And so it was. A cow wandered into the road and nearly got hit by a tractor and a bull terrorized some ramblers. But a murder? No. Doesn't sound like Butterfield to me, though there was some cattle rustling in one episode that we found very exciting. In the end it was a neighbouring farmer who took some cows. They didn't exactly have a shootout but they did come to blows on market day. But no, I don't remember a murder.' He thought for a minute. 'Tell you what, Piercy, you go and see my sister. She's got a much better memory than me for detail. She'll know.'

'She wouldn't mind?'

Colclough gave a loud guffaw. 'Mind? She'll love to reminisce. You'll have more of a job keeping her quiet and getting away. She's a widow, lives on her own— quite a chatterbox, you know. Elizabeth Gantry's her name, married a guy called Bob Gantry. Nice bloke.

He died a few years ago. Heart trouble. Poor old Lizzie. Lonely ever since.'

'Do you have her address and a telephone number, sir? I should give her warning that I'm coming.'

And so on that Tuesday afternoon, just as the sun sank behind the sharp crags of The Roaches, speckled by a few flurries of snowflakes, Joanna found herself outside a smart semi on the Buxton road out of Leek. It was almost one of the last houses in the town before the road climbed and climbed towards The Roaches and The Winking Man, a craggy outcrop in the shape of a man's profile, which watched the bleak and empty scenery of the moorland without comment, except to wink at you as you passed.

As she rang the bell she smothered a smile. Colclough's sister? Things didn't get weirder than that. She wondered if Elizabeth Gantry had the same bulldog jowls as her 'little brother'. Or if she had the same beneficent attitude towards people.

She looked around her. The place was neat and clean, the drive swept, the hedge clipped. Windows were polished and the paintwork fresh. The place had an air of brisk, efficient activity. In the drive stood a clean and polished four-year-old blue Ford Focus.

Colclough's sister opened the door to her first knock. She beamed at Joanna, a plump and smart-looking woman who looked much younger than her sixty-two years. Joanna looked for some family resemblance and found it in the perceptive twinkling eyes.

'So you're the famous Detective Inspector Piercy,' she said in fine humour, pumping Joanna's hand in a bone-cracking shake. 'I'm so glad to meet you at last. I've heard a lot about you from my brother.'

Joanna smiled, already warming towards her.

Elizabeth rattled on. 'He thinks the world of you, you know. You're going to miss him when he finally retires.'

Like thunder.

Aloud Joanna said, 'I certainly will.'

'He rang and said he thought I might be able to help you with an enquiry. I'm completely intrigued. Let me make you a coffee and you can tell me how.'

She bustled off into the kitchen and Joanna wandered into a neatly pristine sitting room strewn with framed photographs and dominated by a tall shelf of books. Joanna glanced along the shelves at the titles. It was an eclectic mix. Novels, ancient and modern, books on sewing and embroidery, *Lyles Antiques Guide*, books on nursing and midwifery, tropical diseases and gardening, as well as a peppering of bestsellers. When Elizabeth Gantry, née Colclough, returned with a tray of tea (in bone china mugs, Joanna noted with interest) she saw Joanna studying the titles. 'I do like my books,' she said, with the enthusiasm that she shared with her brother. 'Trouble is I can't bear to throw any of them away. Some of those I haven't opened for years. But they make me feel comfortable. A home isn't a home unless it has a few shelves of books, is it?'

Joanna nodded.

Elizabeth Gantry set the tray down. 'Now do tell me how I can help you, Inspector Piercy, before I burst with curiosity.'

'My name is Joanna. Please call me that, Mrs Gantry.'

The blue eyes were still sparkling. 'I will, if you'll call me Elizabeth.'

Joanna nodded again, aware that she must tread carefully. 'Elizabeth' might be Colclough's big sister but that did not give her the right to information that only the police were privy to. She was still the general public.

'I wanted to ask you about the TV series *Butterfield Farm*,' Joanna said carefully, 'which was on in the sixties.'

Elizabeth's blue eyes widened. 'And now I'm even more intrigued. What on earth can a forty-year-old television series have to do with you today?'

'One of the actresses in it lives near here and has been involved in a number of incidents.'

Elizabeth Gantry's eyes were wide open. 'Who?' she breathed.

'She was a young girl then. Only eight years old when the show began. I understand she played the part of Lily Butterfield, the youngest daughter.'

'Oh,' Elizabeth gasped. 'Not Timony Shore? My idol. I so wanted to be Lily Butterfield. She was so beautiful. Beautiful red hair that curled right down to her waist.'

Joanna contrasted that with the bright, dyed mane of today.

'But I thought TV…?'

'You're quite right, Inspector. TV *was* black and white but you could tell that Lily Butterfield had the most beautiful red hair. There were often pictures of her in the magazines. She was quite a celebrity. And she always wore spotless white pinnies and little white socks. It was on all through my childhood from when I was about ten. I loved *Butterfield Farm*. And particularly Lily. She could ride a horse like a cowboy and was really brave. In one episode there was a savage dog and she confronted him, soothing him with her words, until he licked her hand. She was all heart too. Kind to ani-

mals. In another episode there was a wounded fox. And
the master of the hunt, a big bully of a man, was there
on his tall horse brandishing a whip, and Lily stood her
ground fearlessly, told him to go away and persuaded
her daddy to take the fox to the vet's. She was my heroine, Inspector. Not only beautiful but brave. I was dev-
astated when she took some time off for...' she smiled,
'exhaustion.' She did a sudden double take. 'And you
tell me she lives near here?'

'Not in Leek, out in the Staffordshire Moorlands. In
a farm that's all on its own, named Butterfield. After
the series, I expect.'

Elizabeth nodded, then opened her mouth to speak
again. This could go on for a very long time. Joanna
interrupted quickly. 'Was there an episode where there
was a murder?'

Elizabeth looked startled. 'A murder? Oh, no. There
was never a murder.' She thought for a moment. 'Oh,
no. Not murder. That wouldn't have been its style. In
the early sixties people wanted to protect their children
from reality. Whether it was the war or whatever, there
was almost a conspiracy to protect children from un-
pleasantness.' She frowned. 'It's funny. I've never really thought why things were as they were then but for
certain they were different from today where parents
appear to want the children—particularly daughters—
to look, well, like...' She couldn't quite say the word.
She gave Joanna an apologetic smile. 'Well, grown up.
Parents then wanted to keep their children children for
ever.' She gave an abstracted smile. 'There was one episode where someone tried to steal some money and another when a cat was stuck down a well but one of Lily's

brothers, Sean, rescued it. Like most of my friends I was madly in love with Sean. He was a dish.'

Joanna smothered a smile at the outdated slang.

Elizabeth continued, 'That episode was so exciting. He lowered himself down into the well and picked the cat up. The episode ended with the cat licking its way through a saucer of cream.' She began to hum a tune.

Ding dong, Joanna thought. She tried a long shot. 'Was the cat a Burmese?'

'Oh, no.' Colclough's sister looked puzzled at the question. 'Just an ordinary tabby. A mouse-catcher. Nothing posh like a Burmese.'

So much for instinct.

'The boys all liked the cattle rustling bits, particularly when Farmer Butterfield pushed the thief, an unpleasant rival called Amos Jones, backwards right into a cowpat that had been dropped by one of the very cows he'd been trying to steal. Everyone was roaring with laughter, particularly Arthur.'

Joanna giggled at the image of Arthur, in short trousers, chuckling at this very appropriate punishment. Poetic justice, indeed.

'Was there, at any time, any trouble towards Timony?'

'There was,' Colclough's sister said. 'You've probably heard about that mad man. He got right up to her, actually attacked her with a pair of scissors. He was sent to prison or a mental hospital or somewhere. It was horrible. Poor girl. She was only in her early teens. She had some time off after that. I wondered if she'd ever come back. I think it really frightened her. But apart from that one isolated incident, everyone else just adored her.'

If her stories are true, someone doesn't any more, Joanna thought.

'While she was away hundreds of people sent her cards and flowers and presents. I believe,' Elizabeth continued, now well into her memories, 'that Timony herself has, subsequently, had quite an eventful life.'

'Yes.' The words, *eventful life*, set Joanna thinking. If there was someone behind these minor occurrences surely the key was more likely to lie in her subsequently dramatic life rather than in her long-ago career as a child star? On the other hand, if these call-outs had no basis in fact but were the product of paranoia and an overactive imagination, the origin might well be the assault in her past. In which case, Timony Weeks needed not the police force but a counsellor.

She stood up. Elizabeth did too, blushing a fierce red. 'I don't suppose...' she began awkwardly. Wringing her hands, she said, 'Could you? I mean, you wouldn't get me Timony Shore's autograph, would you? It'd mean so much to me.' The words tumbled out in an embarrassed rush.

The request embarrassed Joanna almost as much as Colclough's sister but she nodded. 'I'll try,' she said.

'Thank you. Thank you very much. I would so appreciate it.'

She thanked Elizabeth Gantry for her help but at the door she hesitated. 'Do you know anything more about Timony?'

Colclough's sister was unabashed at this exposure of her idol worship. 'Lots. I followed her life and career for years. Right up until it folded. I was twenty-two by then. She had a very eventful life, my dear. Several husbands. There was a whiff of scandal about her, you know. Not surprising when you think how famous and beautiful she was. She married her screen father,

Joab Butterfield, but I believe he died abroad, only a few years after they'd married.' She frowned. 'In tragic circumstances.'

'A car accident,' Joanna filled in, 'in the States.'

Elizabeth Gantry nodded. 'And then there was this business with the "crazed fan", as the newspapers called him. She went missing for quite a few months after that. Of course, the family kept talking about her on the show.'

'Did they make up a storyline to cover her absence?'

'Something about an aunt having broken her leg so saintly Lily acted as nursemaid.'

Joanna smiled.

'I was really worried that she wouldn't come back—not ever. I think I even wrote in to the BBC.'

'And?' Joanna prompted curiously.

'They wrote back thanking me for my concern and saying that she would be on screen again as soon as she was better, but that she'd been terribly upset by the assault and the subsequent court case.' She caught herself up sharply. 'Is that what's happening now? Is that why you're involved—another stalker?'

I hope not!

'We don't know. It's possible. We're not sure whether Mrs Weeks is being a little imaginative or whether something really is going on. If there is it doesn't appear to be too serious. Do you remember anything else?'

Elizabeth was obviously trying to scrape something—anything—else up. Her eyes brightened. 'When her first husband died it was in all the papers that she buried him wearing his best pinstriped suit and a Rolex watch. What do you think of that?'

What *did* Joanna think of that? She wasn't quite sure,

except that it gave her a very creepy feeling. Which compounded as Elizabeth spoke her next sentence. 'I said to Arthur that it must be worth thousands—I hoped someone didn't dig him up and nick it.' She gave a cackle of laughter. Joanna did not join in.

'Is there anything else, Elizabeth?'

'No-oo, I don't think so.' She looked disappointed. 'Well,' she said brightly. 'I could go on all day about Butterfield. But somehow…' again the eyes sparkled with mischief, 'I don't think you've got all day to listen.'

'No.' But through the reminiscences Joanna was seeing a faint glimmer of light. 'Do you know anything about Timony's illness? What sort of illness was it? Mental illness?'

Elizabeth Gantry's frown deepened and she looked thoughtful. 'I don't know,' she said with some surprise. 'The press wasn't as intrusive then as it is now. I don't think the details were ever released. She simply vanished from view for a few months. That's all I know. The public understanding was that she was traumatized by the assault. And, as I said, that was the line the BBC put out.'

'When was this?'

'Sometime in the mid-sixties.'

'So Timony was fourteen?'

'I think she was only thirteen.' She hesitated. 'She seemed different when she came back.'

'In what way?'

'Her manner. Before she had seemed to fizz. She always jumping up and down, screeching with excitement over something or other. When she came back she seemed older, not quite so excitable. I don't know.' She smiled. 'Maybe it was I who had got older.'

'Yes. Maybe. Elizabeth,' Joanna finished slowly, 'if I think of any other questions I want to ask would you mind if I came back?'

'Not at all. I'd be delighted. I'll get my scrapbook out ready next time.'

Privately Joanna hoped that this would not be necessary and that she had heard the last of Timony Weeks' eventful life. She wanted to get back to real-life policing. Real crimes—not imagined ones. And if Timony did call them out again next time she would like some hard evidence. Fag ash was just that little bit too insubstantial.

They shook hands and Joanna left.

When she arrived back at the station Korpanski handed her a sheet of paper. How easy it is to find out anything about a person, particularly when they have a criminal record. Here it was. Name, address, car registration number, mobile phone number, credit card details and police criminal record. Sol Brannigan had served time and was currently out. Joanna read on. He appeared to have had a penchant for Grievous Bodily Harm x 3 and Armed Robbery x 2. He had married Timony while out on bail for the first of these charges and served a few prison sentences—never quite as long as they ought to have been. But he had never killed anyone and it appeared he had a few advantages which would have stood him in good stead with judge and jury. He was intelligent, had a silver tongue and appealing manner and, with his ill-gotten gains, could usually afford good counsel. Usually the excuses dreamed up by the accused are so lame as to need running blades but Brannigan had not done the 'just passing' one or pretended he had simply 'found' the stolen goods. Oh, no, his stories were full of people who could hardly be traced but were often tracked down to some Eastern bloc country. He had covered his paper trail, vaporized witnesses—except the ones who poured doubt on the prosecution, used tortuous methods of banking and managed cash flow so the juries were foxed. Hence the light sentences. Nothing could be *proved beyond reasonable doubt*. Brannigan had been convicted on, in the judges' words, 'the strongest suspicion' and 'unavoidable conclusion'. But in the jurors' minds the little seeds of doubt had been sown, ready to sprout like weeds in the cracks of a pavement.

So Brannigan was clever and he came over well in the courtroom.

He was also… Joanna studied the mugshot…very good-looking, in an Italian style. Black hair and dark eyes, whose power stared out of the photograph, and full, mocking lips.

There was the confidence of a man who had organized crime propping him up.

Joanna read the pages through a couple of times, then said, 'Thanks, Mike. He looks a nasty and dangerous piece of work.'

Korpanski shifted the observation into a question. 'So can you really see him travelling all the way up to Staffordshire just to play those stupid tricks on his ex-wife?'

She looked at the face again and shook her head. 'He's certainly clever and devious enough, but no. He's more likely to ring her every now and again when he's a bit short of money. She's helped him before; why would he take her refusal seriously now? But he hasn't even been in contact recently.'

'He'd ring her, like he's done in the past, if he had money problems.'

She came to a decision. 'My feeling exactly. We do nothing further, Mike. No more investigations or questions. We drop the case.'

Korpanski's response was a huge grin. 'You know what,' he said, 'I just might take Fran out to the Belgian Bar to celebrate.'

Even though it was now dark outside she felt lighter too for having made a decision.

And yet...

It might be only seven o'clock but it was densely dark outside, the street lamps shining fuzzy orange, and she could feel the cold even in the car with the heater turned full up. But she decided to take the road home through the moorlands, knowing it was the road which would take her along the ridge above Butterfield Farm.

For one last time, she told herself.

Maybe it was Colclough's sister's obvious heroine worship of the ex-star but she was still curious about Timony Weeks. It was possible that the months away from the set had been spent in a mental hospital. Maybe she had had a nervous breakdown. She wished plenty of things: that the well did not sit quite so prominently in the front of the house, because it conjured up an image of something—or someone—falling down it. Even if it was only a cat. She wished too that the house had not been named after a long-defunct soap. For some stupid reason she even wished that the cat with the snooty disposition and the exotic name had not been missing. And she wished too that Timony had not mentioned a murder which everyone else appeared to have forgotten. Certainly Diana seemed to know nothing about it.

It was still and starry as she reached the top of the ridge and looked down on the house. There were a few outside lights on but otherwise no sign of life at all around the property. If Timony was inside she must have all the curtains tightly drawn. Joanna couldn't even see how many cars were in the drive—if any. She opened the car window to listen and heard music being played very faintly. A strumming Spanish guitar, a little like the signature tune of a Western. It sounded strange and foreign floating on the still night air. Then she froze, for a moment, because she heard a shriek. She waited and heard it again, an agonized, animal sound. And then a fox trotted towards her and Joanna turned for home.

SIX

Wednesday, January 18, 8.30 a.m.

THE MINUTE SHE walked inside the station Joanna knew something was up. There was an air of puzzled tension that was foreign to the normally calm and friendly place. Today everyone looked fed up and apprehensive. Tense, eyes looking elsewhere. Avoiding hers.

She tried the desk sergeant first but he merely looked even gloomier than the rest, didn't respond to her question of whether everything was all right, except to jerk his head towards her office.

Korpanski's face was no different from the others. He was sitting at his desk, staring at the floor, his shoulders bowed. He didn't even look up when she entered, which was a very bad sign. There was something even he was not looking forward to telling her. She fixed him with a direct stare, forcing him to meet her eyes. 'Are *you* going to tell me what's the matter with everyone?'

He groaned as she hung her coat up, then gave a big sigh. 'Chief Superintendent Rush has decided to make a visit here,' he said, 'prior to his taking up the post next month.'

'Oh, great.' She sighed, sharing everyone else's gloom. Then she dropped into her chair and switched her computer on. 'Just great. Bugger all interesting going on in Leek and he decides to pay a visit. With the government cutbacks we'll probably be closed down and become a six-hour-a-day satellite from Stoke.'

Korpanski half turned in his chair. 'Well, there *was* a hit and run last night,' he tried hopefully.

'Fatal?'

He shook his head and peered into the screen. 'Cuts and bruises. *And* we've identified the van driver through CCTV.'

'As I said, bugger all going on.' She leaned forward on her elbows. 'When did Leek get so law abiding?'

Korpanski frowned. 'You seem a bit out of sorts for someone who's just got back off her honeymoon, married to the man of her dreams.'

'And who has the daughter of her nightmares coming for...' Joanna affected a high-pitched, silly little girl's voice, 'lunch on Sunday.'

Korpanski's frown deepened. 'If you marry a guy you take on his family, Joanna.'

She scowled into her computer screen. 'Don't preach to me, Mike. *No one* can take on the Devil's child.' She logged on with heavy, thumping fingers, banging the keys so hard they practically complained.

Korpanski tried to make light of it. 'If she's the Devil's child then Matthew must be the Devil.'

She would have pointed out that fifty per cent of Eloise Levin would surely be her mother but the truth was that when their marriage had finally broken up, Jane Levin had melted away like an actor exiting a scene. She had simply vanished and now was remarried with another family, presumably happily. So she was wrong-footed and unable to do anything but glare at her colleague.

He continued, 'Well, you knew what Eloise was like

before you married him. It isn't as though he's suddenly thrust her on you. You knew she was tricky and hostile.'

She didn't respond. All of a sudden something very weighty and tired had come over her, as though she had a long and wearisome journey both behind and ahead of her. She dropped her forehead into her fingertips and rubbed at her hairline. 'Well, I've got Eloise to look forward to and now I've got Chief Superintendent Rush joining the party...'

The words died in her mouth. A tall, thin man in his late thirties, with a spike of red hair, pale skin and a hard, straight scar for a mouth, was standing in the doorway, watching her. 'Inspector Piercy, I presume,' he said, stepping forward, lips pressed together tightly. 'I've been *so* looking forward to meeting you.'

Like hell. It was written all over his face.

'You must be Chief Superintendent Rush.' She forced a smile on to her lips, knowing it would not reach her eyes. Then she stood up and extended her hand.

He shook it and nodded. Obviously a man of few words. Then he swivelled his head around in a sharp, angular movement. 'And DS Korpanski?' Mike was treated to another tight smile.

Joanna searched his face for a single line that hinted at humour—and found none.

Great.

His eyes were a pale, cold icy blue, hardly human as they peered at her. 'Oh, and congratulations, Piercy, on your recent marriage.' Spoken in a voice not a degree above freezing.

She responded equally frostily. 'Thank you, sir.'

'I shall talk to you both later,' he said, still standing in the middle of the room.

The three of them stood awkwardly until they were saved by the telephone bell which dropped nicely into the silence.

Joanna picked up the receiver, hoping Rush wouldn't hear the relief in her voice at the interruption. 'Yes?'

The desk sergeant's stolid voice broke in. 'Sorry to disturb you, ma'am, but I've got Mrs Weeks on the phone again. She, umm, sounds a bit upset.'

Rush was listening in. Antennae quivering.

'Put her through.' Her heart was sinking. This was one case which definitely didn't show her or the Leek Force in a good light. 'DI Piercy,' she said tightly, wishing Rush would just go away. She would prefer him not to hear this conversation.

She hardly recognized the voice on the other end. Timony Weeks was screaming, hysterically, down the line. 'Tuptim,' she wailed. 'Tuptim. My cat,' she wailed.

Great, Joanna thought. *The traditional crappy call-out of the fire brigade.* She said a prayer: *Don't say it's stuck up a tree, please, Mrs Weeks. Or down the well.*

And even she could hear the irritation in her voice as she asked, 'What about your cat, Mrs Weeks?'

It was Diana Tong who took over the phone and even her normally controlled voice shook. 'Someone appears not to like cats, Inspector. It's been strung up on the front door.'

Joanna was shocked. 'What?'

'It's hanging there.' Diana's voice was breaking.

Joanna hadn't liked the snooty moggy but this was horrible. She gave Mike a swift glance then spoke into the phone. 'Don't touch anything, Mrs Tong,' she said. 'We'll be out there as soon as possible.'

Rush was standing motionless, eyebrows raised,

waiting for an explanation which Joanna was forced to give.

'This is a sixty-year-old lady,' she explained. 'An ex-actress who has been repeatedly calling us out for minor occurrences.' She paused. 'So far. Some of these might have been in her imagination but she's convinced someone is threatening her. She lives alone in an isolated house on the moorlands and was a well-known actress in a sixties soap. More than forty years ago she was quite seriously assaulted by a fan. She also has an ex-husband who is a convicted criminal. Yesterday we were called out because she was convinced her dead husband's watch, which was buried with him, had turned up on her bed. Today—this.'

'What?'

'She has a pedigree cat which she's extremely fond of. It has been missing for a day or two. Apparently it's turned up dead, hanging from her front door.' She didn't need to spell out that this was an escalation of events, but Chief Superintendent Rush appeared to feel *he* needed to say it, eyebrows flexed. 'It appears then that something really *is* very wrong.'

'Yes, sir.' But Rush was still eyeing her, waiting, she supposed, for her 'take' on the incident.

She gave it to him—as best she could. 'It may just be some local person who's playing tricks,' she said, 'or it may be something connected with her colourful past. Anyway, the sooner we get out there and take a look around, the better. I'm sure you agree.' Korpanski was already on his feet, apparently as eager to escape as she was. 'We should get over there right away,' she finished apologetically, as she slipped her arms into the sleeves of her coat.

Rush gave her a tight smile and a nod and Joanna breathed a tiny prayer of thanks to Mrs Timony Weeks as she followed Korpanski out of the room.

As he manoeuvred the car out of the tight parking lot she turned to him, screwing up her face. 'He's just as bad as I thought he'd be,' she said grumpily. 'If not worse.'

Korpanski took his eyes off the road to grin at her. 'Go on,' he teased, 'I can see you two being the best of friends.'

'Sod off.'

Korpanski simply laughed out loud. A rich, throaty, masculine bellow, then sang in his deep, gravelly voice, 'There may be troubles ahead. But while there's music and moonlight...' He resorted to humming the rest of the tune until he got to, 'Let's face the music and dance.'

She couldn't help herself laughing. 'I won't disagree with any of that. So what do you think about *this* call-out?'

'Sounds a bit more serious this time, doesn't it?'

She nodded, wishing she hadn't even thought that she would like some more tangible evidence than cigarette ash, then tried to put the brakes on. 'Let's just wait and see exactly what *has* happened.'

Almost through force of habit they stopped on the ridge and looked down on Butterfield Farm. It looked calm and peaceful in the winter sunshine, though the property itself was, as always, in the shade. But it was hard to imagine anything as brutal or cruel happening here as the murder of a much-loved pet and the deliberate act of hanging it from the front door. Joanna stared. It was Beatrix Potter land, surely? There couldn't be a more idyllic spot than here. Even Korpanski mur-

mured something about it being 'pretty perfect'. But if
this truly had happened someone else must have looked
down on it, as they were now, but with malicious intent.
That person had not wanted to admire it, but to spoil
it and intimidate its inhabitants. So was this mischief-
maker even now creeping around the place? Looking
as they were at its stone roof and neat surround, busily planning another crime? Joanna scanned the entire
panorama of pale and empty fields superstitiously. She
could see nothing untoward, no one skulking. In fact,
nothing at all out of the ordinary.

But she was well aware that if the assault on the cat
had happened as described it was a disturbing turn in
events. And someone was behind it.

Korpanski let out the handbrake and as they descended the track and neared the farm Joanna found
herself wondering: what next? Where is this all going
to lead? Where will it end?

They pulled into the yard, parking next to an elderly,
mud-spattered Volvo. 'The gardener and his wife,' Joanna observed. It looked appropriate, a sturdy rural
vehicle.

'Rossington,' Korpanski agreed. 'Frank and Millie.'

Diana Tong must have been watching for them. She
hurried out of a side door as they pulled up. 'This is
dreadful,' she said, her face pale and shocked and her
hands clasped together. 'Dreadful. Poor Tuptim. She
was there when I came in this morning. Why anyone…
Such a cruel thing.' She snatched a breathy sob. 'How
could…?'

'Let's have a look, shall we?' It was Korpanski who
spoke while Joanna watched Mrs Tong with interest.
There were times when she appeared resentful towards

her employer. Angry, even. But now all this had apparently melted away. Because she had finally got her revenge?

Diana Tong led them around to the front door and Joanna stood and stared. She would never have harmed any animal although she wouldn't have described herself as an 'animal lover'. But this? It was enough to turn your stomach. God only knew what the poor animal had suffered. A loop of rope was nailed to the door from which the cat dangled, head lolling, eyes dulled blue glass, tail hanging down like a rat's, looking somehow larger and yet less important in death than in life. It was horrible and cruel. There was simply no point to it. Joanna felt angry. This had been done purely to upset Timony Weeks.

But a tiny whisper insinuated something else. *This had achieved something. This was irrefutable evidence. Her stories would be believed now, her call-outs treated with priority.*

Joanna argued with herself, while her eyes absorbed the scene: Timony Weeks had adored this cat. She had stroked and caressed it as a child, or perhaps even a lover. Many people do substitute an animal contact for a human one. Maybe, after so many failed marriages, Timony had joined these ranks.

She couldn't have done this.

The cat's tail hung down almost to the floor, its paws dangling limply. The scene had been set to extract maximum horror. And the effect had obviously worked. At the foot of the door was a pool of fresh vomit. Joanna eyed Diana Tong. 'Poor Timony,' she said. 'She just threw up and then fainted.'

Korpanski's eyes were on the vomit. 'So no DNA there then,' he muttered, disappointed.

Whether the animal had been alive or dead when it had been pinned to the door was uncertain. Joanna's guess was that the animal had already been dead or surely the poor creature would have struggled, and there were no scratch marks on the woodwork. Blood trickled from its mouth, so her guess was that the cat had been strung up straight after it had been killed. Probably strangled with the rope. At her side Korpanski was standing still, frowning. She knew her sergeant. Something was going on in that blunt instrument of a brain of his.

Joanna drew out her mobile phone. No bloody signal. Of course, they were in a remote valley. Without a word Diana Tong handed her the house phone and Joanna summoned the police photographer and forensics. The sight of the dead cat had triggered a memory of a lecture she had heard a while ago. The point of the lecture had been to alert the police to sadistic assaults on animals. They were, it had been claimed, often the first signs of abnormality a psychopath displayed. The next target, the lecturer had pointed out, could well be human. She looked up to see Diana Tong watching her and knew she was thinking along the same lines: what fate was planned for Timony Weeks? What was the reason for this cruel warning? For almost three weeks now there had been taunts and hints, half-revealed glimpses of something hiding behind the curtain. Now the pointless psychological jokes had escalated into a very real threat. What effect would it have? They followed Diana Tong inside.

Timony Weeks sat, shrunken as a mummy, wrapped up in a blanket, shivering, on the sofa. No Noël Coward costume today. She looked tiny in her white towelling dressing gown and she was shaking with shock. Mike, watching from the doorway, looked like a powerful bodyguard. There was something almost biblical about his stance and threat. Joanna sat down next to the actress, waiting for a moment before speaking to Timony in a gentle voice, as though speaking to the inner Timony, the child actress who lived inside this sixty-year-old's body.

'I'm sorry about your cat,' she said. 'I have sent for a photographer and a team of forensic evidence collectors.'

Timony Weeks said nothing; neither did she look up.

Joanna pressed on. 'We will do everything we can to find out who committed this cruel act.'

Timony Weeks still said nothing. Apart from the shaking there was no other movement. Head and body did not respond. It was as though she could not hear. All the same, Joanna continued, 'This signifies an escalation in events which worries me.'

Timony Weeks' head cranked around so her eyes stared straight into Joanna's face. Her lips were dry as cracked leather and her face looked as if it was struggling against the facelift to burst out with some emotion. She mumbled something which Joanna did not quite catch the first time around.

'Sorry?'

'In what way, *worries* you?'

Joanna was reluctant to relay the contents of the forensic lecture she had attended. But all the same, 'I'm worried about...'

'You believe me now? That this person means me harm?'

'I think it's possible, Mrs Weeks. I think it's time for us to take a look at all this more thoroughly.'

With a further effort Timony lifted her head to stare straight ahead. 'I told you there was something bad behind all this, didn't I? I knew that something was very wrong. The atmosphere here…' She scanned the room and looked out of the window, towards the empty lane and the ridge beyond before it rested on the rocky tors of The Roaches. 'It was all wrong. I knew something awful would happen, Inspector. I was just waiting for it.' She bent her head so she was almost touching Joanna's hand. She smelt of rose water and lavender. It was an old-fashioned, pleasant smell, nostalgic, sweet and suitable.

'You did,' Joanna agreed. 'So we need to know who and why. I could do with some names, Mrs Weeks, a place from where to start our investigations. Think. Who could wish you harm, apart from Sol? Could it be to do with Butterfield Farm? Is there someone who wants you out of here? A neighbour, someone who wants the land? It is a lovely property.'

But at the back of her mind other things were niggling her as she tried to put the jigsaw together. Who could have known about the Rolex watch? Anyone. Colclough's sister had known. It had been in all the papers. Timony Shore's life had been played out in public. So what about some of the other little menaces? The smell of cigarette smoke. Was it pure coincidence that it had reminded her of an unhappy previous relationship?

'You don't understand.' Mrs Weeks was regaining some of her spirit. 'This isn't about Butterfield Farm. It isn't about property or money. This is personal. It's about me.'

Joanna glanced across at Korpanski. What did he make of this? she wondered. But he wasn't looking at her. His eyes were fixed on the woman as though he, too, was puzzling this one out. Even Diana Tong appeared to be holding her breath, watching, motionless, intrigued as to what answers could be forthcoming.

Timony Weeks seemed to be distracted by some mental image in the far distance. 'There is something there,' she said. 'Some guilt. When I write my... It lies at the back of my mind, like an oil slick, something I am responsible for. I have flashbacks,' she said in her throaty voice. 'They stem from my days—years—in the Butterfield series. I seem to have different memories.' Her eyes looked questioningly at Joanna, as though she might be able to interpret these flashbacks, then she cleared her throat, puzzled. 'But surely it was a happy time?' It was a statement that sounded like a wondering question.

Timony continued, 'Then sometimes I am not sure. I think some things must have been...different from how I recall them. Something determined to push into my mind; the sunshine of my past is hidden by a cloud. And yet when I try to push the cloud away and remember whatever lies behind it, it slips away downstream, laughing at me as it goes. Certain things trigger these memories—the tricks that have been played. But how can anyone know what's buried so deep in my mind that even I struggle to remember it? When I smell smoke when none of us here smokes, or see the toilet seat left up as though a man had just used it, or I hear certain music playing softly which evokes half a memory. When I find the watch that was buried with my long-dead husband or the burglar alarm goes off at three o'clock in the morning, startling me out of a dream or a nightmare.' She met Joanna's eyes. 'I can't even answer that bit, whether it was a dream or a nightmare. But when these things happen it seems to awake a monster that had been long dormant. Do you understand, Inspector?'

'I'm not sure I do,' Joanna said, knowing that her blunt honesty would risk Mrs Weeks' trust but unable to even try to deceive her. Timony Weeks was smart enough to sense when the truth was being told. And if she thought the detective was even trying to pretend Joanna would be the one to lose status.

'Well, this…all these…events are something to do with that.' She fumbled for the words. 'Those ghouls and goblins that peep at me from behind the curtain. When I turn to look all I see is a ripple of cloth, and feel the air rush of a billowing curtain. I know they are there but I cannot see them. I cannot put my hand on them. Possibly I never will because they are insubstantial. Perhaps none of this exists outside my imagination.'

Joanna was stunned by Timony's frank admission. At last, were they getting to the truth? Was Timony Weeks mad after all? A schizophrenic, deluded, living in two different worlds? But if she was telling the truth, what were these long-suppressed memories threatening to rise to the surface? And why would someone want her to remember? With Rush peering over her shoulder she could not afford to be investigating the delusions of a mad woman. He'd soon have her back on sergeant's pay.

Timony's frightened eyes peeped out of her flawless, featureless face. 'I believe,' she said, 'that something happened. I seem to remember horrible things. Something dark and threatening.'

'Do you mean the fan who assaulted you?'

'No. No. I see and remember that clearly. I see his hand, the flash of the blade, blood trickling down my face. I see the bodyguards throw him to the floor—too late. No, Inspector, it isn't that. It is these grey, wraith-like memories. I think I remember things—like someone dying horribly on the set. Most times I think it must have been part of the storyline—the cowhand dying down the well. But I've watched most of the episodes a couple of times and I can't remember ever seeing anything about a murder.' She paused. 'So then I start worrying. If it wasn't part of the plot where *did* it come from? Why do I have this feeling of panic, of power-lessness? I'm not imaginative enough to have dreamed the whole thing up. I was just an actress, speaking lines that were written for me. And I was a child. How could there have been anything in a family soap that would give me this horrid feeling? Why should I feel perma-nently frightened?' Her eyes appealed to Joanna for the truth, an explanation.

It was something Joanna could not give. 'What exactly *do* you remember?'

The question made Timony Weeks angry. 'For good-ness' sake,' she said. 'Have you been listening to a word I've said? I can't tell you. Things flit in and out.'

'What things?' Joanna tried to be patient.

'A man's face,' Timony said. 'He's looking up at me. He's appealing for something. He's moving away from me. I know he is going to die. That's all. That's it. End of story.'

Not exactly a story. More a fragment of a story.

'Why do you say a murder then? It could be a cliff

rescue or an accident—a car down an embankment. Something like that.'

'No,' Timony said flatly.

'Why not? How can you be so sure?'

'Because I'm glad he's there. I know he's going to die and I don't care.'

'You think you killed him?' It sounded like a fairly typical bad dream to Joanna and Mike gave a tiny, almost imperceptible, agreeing nod.

Timony was staring into space.

Joanna tried again. 'Why do you feel glad?'

'Because he won't be able to hurt me any more.'

'Hurt you? How? Who?'

It was no good. Timony's eyes were drifting away. Joanna wondered whether she had been dosed up with a sedative. She needed something more concrete to move this case on. 'Do you recognize the man?'

'Not sure.'

'Do you remember *anything* about him?'

That pulled Timony up short. 'He's unwashed. He smells. He has dark hair. He wishes me harm. I have to stop him doing something.' She frowned. 'Or...'

'Or what?'

But nothing came. 'Age?'

'I don't know. Twenty...thirty...forty?'

'And you're still sure it wasn't part of the storyline?' Joanna looked up at Korpanski and caught the twitch of his mouth.

It would be just like her to be looking into a murder that happened in a soap forty years ago.

'Part of the storyline?' Timony frowned. 'I don't know. I don't think so.' Her voice changed. 'I don't know for sure,' she said. 'I only remember that there was a period...' She looked up with panic in her eyes, as though she thought she'd said too much. 'I'm not sure I know what's real any more,' she said, looking at Diana Tong for support. 'I only seem to remember that there was a time,' she said, 'when there were police around.'

This was concrete. Police kept records. At least, real police did. Actors probably didn't. If the police were real they should be able to find out something.

'Was it the same time as when the fan went for you?'

Timony simply shrugged. Out of the window Joanna could see the police van slowly descending the track. Forensics was here. She stood up.

She heard them banging on the side door, went to answer it and started to direct their operations. At the same time she took the opportunity to speak to Mike privately. 'Well,' she said, eyebrows raised, 'mad, bad or intuitive? What on earth are we up against?' Korpanski was frowning as his eyes scanned the door with its grisly decoration and the forensic team's methodical approach to the scene. 'Someone did that,' he said. 'Knowing how much store she put by it I'd say it's like doing that to a child. That cat was her pet—she loved it. Whoever did that wanted to hurt her, upset her, frighten her. I know only two things, Jo. It really happened and she didn't do it.'

SEVEN

JOANNA WAS THOUGHTFUL as Mike drove them back to the station. The killing of the cat, though horrible and an obvious attempt to upset its owner, was not, as far as the police were concerned, even factoring in the plethora of recent call-outs, going to be a big enough case to attract major resources. But if it was the portent of a more serious crime, ignoring it could prove to be a big mistake. And one which she had no doubt that Chief Superintendent Gabriel Rush would take pleasure in noting. So she decided she would not turn it into a major investigation, but she would make sure that all the evidence of the assault on Tuptim was preserved as meticulously as if it was part of a murder investigation.

Having reached a decision she looked across at Korpanski. 'So, who do you think did this?'

'Someone either doesn't like cats or they've got a grudge against our child actress,' he said gruffly, keeping his eyes on the road. 'Maybe they resent the fact that the child star has grown up.'

'State the obvious, Mike, why don't you?'

He simply grinned across at her, completely unruffled by her manner. 'All right,' he said, 'what I really think is it could be anyone who doesn't much like her, from our dear Mrs Tong to the bloody gardener or one of the farmers from hereabouts.'

She glanced at him sharply. 'Aren't you ignoring Timony's famous and high-profile past?'

Without waiting for a response she continued, 'You don't think it's someone connected with Butterfield—the soap? You think her stories of a dead person down the well are untrue, either made up or a figment of her imagination?'

Korpanski shrugged. 'I'm keeping an open mind, Joanna, but wherever this nightmare of someone dying came from it didn't come from the TV series.' He looked across at her. 'I think we're all agreed on that. It wouldn't have fitted in, would it?'

'No,' she said dubiously. But what bothered her was that Timony had portrayed the scene just a little bit too graphically, as something she had actually seen, as real as though it had just happened. Added to that was the fact that the scene had embedded in her subconscious rather than in her conscious memory. Perhaps it was nothing more than that—a dream. She continued thinking aloud. 'I don't believe in ghosts, Mike. Ghosts didn't murder that cat.' She glanced across at him, frowning. 'Maybe you're right. Looking at it objectively it is much more likely that these recent events are coming from someone who's close to her now. The TV series was too many years ago. Most of her fellow actors would be in their sixties, at least. It would be a bit unlikely for them to start playing these tricks after all this time. Why wait until now? What would be the point?' She screwed her face up. 'What does someone hope to *achieve* by this? That's what I don't understand. What is the bloody point?'

Korpanski had no answer so she carried on. 'The only likely outcome is that Timony ups sticks and leaves

Butterfield. I can't think of anyone who'd want that. It wouldn't benefit a single soul.'

'Except, maybe, the neighbouring farmers.'

'Hmm.' Joanna was unimpressed by this.

Struggling through the roadworks that seemed to bedevil Leek, they'd finally reached the station. Korpanski swung the car into an empty parking space, switched the engine off, turned around and challenged her. 'So what do we do next?'

She shared her decision. 'We'll hang on to the forensic evidence and run it through the labs if anything else happens. No one is going to fund a load of fingerprint stuff and DNA analysis on the killing of a cat. The last thing I want is Rush arriving here and straightaway taking the piss out of me for wasting police resources on finding the Hanger of Cats.' She formed her fingers into claws and wriggled them in front of Korpanski's eyes. He couldn't help himself smiling and gave a little chuckle. 'And for now?'

'We'll ask Timmis and McBrine to keep an eye on Butterfield. It won't be hard for them, the place being so visible from the road.'

Police constables Josh Timmis and Saul McBrine made up the Moorland Patrol. Based in Leek but covering a huge area of largely empty moorland, isolated farms and craggy outcrops such as The Roaches, their day-to-day work consisted of rescuing overambitious climbers and sorting out road traffic incidents caused by drivers who assumed that the Highway Code didn't apply up here. And then there were the minor offences: littering, heath fires and the results of extreme weather conditions, whiteouts and blizzards, torrential rain and the occasional mud slip. They were kept fairly but not too busy. Josh Timmis was both a bloodhound (persistent) and a terrier (he never let go). Thorough and honest, he had watched the moorlands for years. Saul McBrine had recently married his long-term girlfriend, Josie, and rumour had it that Josie McBrine was expecting their first child.

While Timmis was short and wiry, McBrine was tall and lanky. They were firm friends and enjoyed working together, usually. Luckily this Wednesday lunchtime they were in the station together rather than out on patrol, and at 2 p.m. were listening to Joanna and Mike's accounts of recent events.

'Have there been any other attacks on animals in the area?'

Timmis shook his head. 'Not that we've heard.'

'No one been spotted brandishing a knife?'

'No.' Timmis was frowning. 'I know that place,' he said, 'though I've never called in there. It always looks deserted—apart from an elderly couple who drive over once a week.'

'Haven't you seen Mrs Weeks herself? Skinny, dyed red hair, wears sort of theatrical clothes,' Mike asked bluntly.

'No.'

'How long has the house been there?'

''Bout ten years, I suppose. There was a tumbledown cottage there. Old shepherd's place. It was demolished and Butterfield was built on the site. They'd never have got planning permission otherwise. You know how tight the moorland planning department is,' Timmis volunteered. He was obviously spokesman today. 'You want us to visit?'

'No.' Joanna shook her head. 'Nothing too obvious

but keep an eye on the place. And keep a log, will you, of who comes and goes? There is a sort of secretary-cum-companion called Diana Tong. She's tall and well built, straggly grey hair and generally wears trousers. They have two cars, a blue Isuzu and a black Qashqai. The elderly couple you've seen are the Rossingtons, Frank and Millie, home help and gardener. They have an ancient Volvo estate, dark green. I understand they come once a week, for a full day in the summer and a morning in the winter. Any other cars are visitors which Timony Weeks tells me they rarely have so considering recent events any strangers would be noteworthy. Do you know who owns the surrounding land?'

McBrine took over. 'There's a couple of farmers got land borderin' on Butterfield,' he said. 'To the north-west is a guy called John Reeves. He's a decent, honest sort of chap but an 'opeless farmer. How he's kept going over the last few years I don't know. In fact, I've heard that he's *not* keepin' his head above water but is sinkin' fast with major money worries.'

'Right. And the other one?'

'Tom Brassington owns the land to the south-east. He's a sticky one. Hard to work out,' McBrine said. 'Wouldn't you agree, Josh?'

His colleague nodded. 'I think he's a bit on the fiddle. Nothing major, just insurance scams, animals lost, a cow struck by lightning, that sort of thing, you know? He's a bit sharp. Kind of bitter. Goes on a bit about the tough life of farmers, you know. Feels the world owes him a living just because he's a farmer.' He finished the sentence in a sing-song voice that made Joanna think that he had heard this phrase once too often.

'Plenty of people like that about,' McBrine concurred. 'The rest of the land is owned by the Peak District National Park.'

'There was one episode a few years back,' Timmis said slowly. 'Never really came to anything but it seems he took a pot shot at a guy whose dog was chasing after some of his pregnant animals.'

This sounded a bit more like it. 'Was the guy injured?'

'No. Shaken up. He made a complaint but no one could prove anything.'

'Surely there was some evidence?'

'Plenty of shotgun pellets lying around but it didn't prove anything. Brassington said he often shot at rabbits so there would be plenty of shotgun pellets lying around. The case was dropped. There was never a chance of it going anywhere.'

Joanna met Mike's eyes. This sounded a bit more promising, though it didn't really fit the profile. Brassington sounded too much of a blunt instrument. Not subtle enough to have played the minor tricks. The murder of the cat and the display of her body, however, sounded more like his style. Perhaps it was a lead.

'OK. Talk to the two farmers,' Joanna requested. 'Keep an eye on them, particularly Brassington. See if you can pick anything up.'

'Such as?'

'General stuff, their attitude towards Butterfield and its inhabitants, anything. If they had nothing to do with the cat business maybe they saw something or have heard a rumour.'

Joanna gave them one of her very best smiles. 'Look, you two, this is hardly going to be a major investigation, is it? A cat hanged, even if it was a snooty Burmese named Tuptim. I wonder where she got the name from,' she mused. Korpanski and the two moorland patrol officers simply shrugged, uninterested. Surely it could have nothing to do with this minor investigation?

'OK, then?' McBrine asked. They were anxious to return to their native moors.

'Yeah. Thanks.'

When they'd gone Korpanski gave Joanna one of his looks. Stubborn, pugnacious and above all, curious. 'So, what are we going to do now?'

'*You* are going to do a bit of digging into Diana Tong's past,' Joanna said, 'while *I* am going to speak to James Freeman.'

'Who the hell is he?'

Joanna tapped her computer screen. '*He*, Sergeant Michael Korpanski, *is* or *was* the producer of Butterfield Farm. He's now in his eighties, has all his marbles and a website devoted to his work, mainly, of course, the long-standing series, which was, apparently, his greatest success. I have emailed him outlining events and he has just emailed me back. He lives in Knightsbridge and I have set up a video link and am about to interview him.' She couldn't resist a smirk, which Korpanski bounced right back.

'So how much time *are* we going to spend on this case, Jo? The case of the mad woman and a dead cat?'

'We'll keep it on the back burner,' she responded, 'but I'm not dropping it. I'll have a word with Fask later and see what forensics he's got on the cat's corpse and the door, et cetera. I can't see Rush authorizing a ton of expensive tests on a cat's demise but if things do escalate further at least we'll be ready for them.' To her sergeant, who could be a superstitious being, the phrase, flippantly uttered, sounded like a temptation to the fates.

She settled back in her chair and focused on the screen. James Freeman, she decided, as she looked at the image displayed in front of her, was one of those lucky people who never age. They never become frail or weak; they don't lose their hair, their teeth or the use of their legs. Their voices remain firm and strong and their memories crystal clear. He was a delight to interview, with an impish sense of humour and a frank honesty that endeared him to her from the start.

'Timony Shore,' he mused. 'Such a long time ago. What does she look like now?'

'Well, umm.'

Freeman burst out laughing. 'No. Stop. Don't tell me.' He put his hand up. 'Let *me* tell you. She's had a facelift, liposuction, dyed her hair and had her teeth veneered and she's still as skinny as they come.'

He was so near the truth that Joanna couldn't smother the giggle that escaped her lips. She put her hand up to her mouth.

'So,' he said, smiling. 'I'm right so far. Now what's she been up to that has the police on her back?'

'She appears to have been subjected to some harassment,' Joanna said cautiously.

'Not for the first time,' Freeman responded cheerily. 'She was the star of the show. And subsequently had a bag-load of odd letters; some woman kept writing to her claiming she was her long-lost sister, and she had lots of proposals for when she came of age, but the worst time was with a sort of crazed fan who followed her for months. We had to get security for her because he would wait for her to leave the studio after rehearsals. One night, unfortunately, he got close enough to lunge at her with a pair of scissors. She had a nasty scar which we could write into the script. We simply had her fall off a hay cart but she very nearly lost an eye. And that *would* have been a problem for the Butterfield scriptwriting team. And besides, it would have made her rather...' His eyes flicked to the side and he licked his lips, realizing he should stop short of being politically incorrect to a policewoman. 'Well, let's just say she wouldn't have looked quite so pretty.'

'I'm sure.' Joanna was a little shocked. But then she supposed that this was the way you thought about things when you were the producer of a major TV series. Heartlessly practical, your actors turned into commodities. Dehumanized. So now, far from envying their glamorous lifestyle she almost pitied them.

'We put a Band-Aid over her brow to draw attention to the wound and then put make up over the scar.' His eyes twinkled at Joanna. 'She was a valuable asset to the studio. Even the tumble off the hay cart had to be done by her screen double. We couldn't have had Timony really falling off a cart. That would have stopped production for months the way she used to go on. But because of Lily's stage presence, the gentle but determined way she defended animals, always hugging horses and freeing cats from traps, protecting foxes from the hunt and so on, she had quite a following, you know.' He smiled. 'She was a sort of early Animal Rights Campaigner. She really milked it,' Freeman said. 'Kept having fainting fits and being sick. She's quite histrionic, you know.'

Joanna nodded in agreement, half forgetting that Freeman would pick up on it. He looked amused. 'In the end we had to give her six months off to recover.'

'And how did you write *that* into the script? Or did you use a screen double during her absence?'

For the first time Freeman looked unsure of himself. 'Well, you know, I think…'

Think? Joanna thought. *But you produced the whole thing. To lose a star of the show for six months is a big deal.*

'We had a distant aunt break her leg,' Freeman said awkwardly. 'Saintly Timony went to look after her.' He gave a lopsided grin. 'She had a terrific postbag for that one, fans begging her to return.' He smiled into the screen. 'We did a lovely scene,' he said. You know the bit in *The Railway Children*, when Bobby wanders down to the station and meets her father?'

Joanna nodded. *Everyone* knows that scene. Even now, years after her own father's death, it still had the power to jerk unexpected tears out of her.

'Steam train, father alights, walking towards camera, face nicely obscured by the steam.' His grin broadened. 'I swear they got that scene straight from Butterfield. Only it wasn't Roberta, it was Lily returning to Butterfield. Wrung tears out of grown men, according to the postbag.'

'What year was that?'

'I don't know.' Freeman blew out a breath. 'About 'sixty-six or 'sixty-seven. A few years before the famous film. Somewhere around then, anyway,' he said airily. 'Luckily Timony always looked young for her age so although she was almost fourteen Lily Butterfield would only have been about twelve. The fans sent her lots of cards urging her to return.'

'And was Timony Weeks saintly in real life?'

Freeman smiled and shrugged. It was obvious he had

not been in the habit of analysing his child protégée's personality. He had simply wanted her to deliver her lines. 'Who knows,' he said carelessly. 'The actor and the part they play frequently merge. As far as I know she was fond of animals but I didn't read anything in the newspapers about her really chinning up to the master of the hunt or nursing a sick aunt. She was a bit more self-centred than that.'

'And the cast? They were close?'

'Too bloody close,' Freeman grumbled. 'There were all sorts of things going on. Affairs, petty jealousies, little factions. It's the same in any long-standing production. They get too close. Like a family. And then the quarrels break out. People take sides.'

'And, of course, Timony eventually married her stage father.'

A shadow crossed Freeman's face. 'Gerald.' He smiled. 'Far too old for her really. She was only just seventeen when they married. He was in his fifties. I think he had to marry her to...' His voice trailed away and all of a sudden Joanna caught something in Freeman's eyes. He had said something he shouldn't. He wavered and hesitated, his head moving, his face frozen into tension, eyes warily wondering whether she had picked up on his faux pas. He looked uncomfortable and sucked in a sharp and worried breath. His eyes had dropped from hers. He regretted that last sentence.

'Sorry,' he mumbled. 'Out of turn. Fact was she did adore him. And he her.'

Too late. Joanna had absorbed the statement and would remember it. *He had to marry her to...* Normally that meant that the bride was pregnant and the shotgun wedding took place so the infant would not be born a bastard. But there had never been mention of a child. In fact, Timony had said categorically that she did not have children.

She kept digging. 'What did you mean by that?'

He blustered his answer. 'I suspect they were already having sex.'

'Timony was of age,' she pointed out.

'Quite.' But his eyes still looked shifty.

Joanna probed. 'Timony was eight when Butterfield first hit the scene?'

'Yes.' He appeared uncomfortable, squirming in his seat.

'How exactly did that work?'

'How do you mean?'

'Her parents…?'

'Were thrilled at the opportunity for their daughter.'

'They didn't mind handing her over to you?'

'No. No. As long as we had an adult responsible for her. Sandra McMullen was the wardrobe mistress. She became a mother figure to little Timony. Took her under her wing. She had a house near the studio so Timony lived there with her. The whole thing worked perfectly.'

Joanna chewed this over for a moment. It all sounded neat. As neat as a lie. She licked her lips. 'I want to ask you something more specific,' Joanna said, 'about an event that may or may not have taken place. Timony has mentioned a storyline about someone dying horribly. Perhaps sliding down somewhere. I got the impression it was a man who had slipped down a bank or fallen and died and she was looking down on him. Maybe he'd fallen down the well? She said she was glad because he wouldn't be able to hurt her any more. Does this sound like one of your storylines?'

'Not on the Butterfield set,' Freeman said. 'Wouldn't
have worked. Too scary by half for all those early sixties kids.' Equilibrium restored now, he gave a little
laugh. 'Besides, if anyone had hurt Lily Butterfield
there would have been outrage. Oh, no. She must be
thinking of some other part she played. She did quite
a bit of stage and screen work after Butterfield folded.'

'Why did it fold?'

Freeman leaned back in his chair and thought for
a moment. 'The easy answer,' he said, 'is that ratings
went down and new dramas came along, but the real
explanation is that the audience simply outgrew it. The
kids that came later had different tastes. They wanted
something else. Westerns, *Doctor Who*. Audiences were
falling so the BBC pulled the plug. And to be honest,
we'd run out of steam. Our storylines were looking
stale and our ideas had all been tried before. There's
only so much mileage you can get out of any series,
in my opinion, unless you change radically. This was
about country life, a farm, a family. To be honest, when
it was decided in '72 that it would be our last series, I
wasn't sorry. To use a modern phrase, Butterfield was
past its sell-by date.'

'Right. Well, thank you. One more thing. Mr Freeman, Timony has been subjected to a series of rather
teasing, mischievous events, the latest of which is that
someone has killed her cat and strung her body up on
her front door. Can you think of anything or anyone
that might have given rise to these?'

'No. She was always popular with the other members of the cast.'

'What about the attack by the fan?'

'It's over forty years ago. He was a schizophrenic,

poor chap, suffering from delusions, and ended up a long-term patient in a mental hospital, I believe. Probably dead by now.'

Joanna agreed. Mentally she had discounted the 'crazed fan' of so many years ago, apart from the fact that he might not be the only fan who was crazy and obsessed. It was one of the real costs of fame. She fished around. 'The parts she took up after her work on Butterfield?'

'Nothing as high profile,' Freeman said, 'or as long running. She did a few stage productions for which she was overpaid and some minor screen parts for which she was also overpaid. She learnt the spoiled brat approach early in life.' He gave a calm smile.

'Is there anything else that might…' She smiled at him, knowing she was mocking herself, '…help us with our enquiries.'

He returned the smile with twinkling eyes. The self-effacement hadn't escaped him. 'Not that I can think of, Inspector Piercy.' He paused. 'It must be something to do with her current life. I can't believe there's any connection to her role as Lily Butterfield.' He frowned. 'This is nothing too serious, is it?' He too was fishing. 'I mean, she's not in any danger, is she?'

'Well, the business about her cat has upset her.'

'Ye-es. I am sorry to hear that,' Freeman said. 'Very sorry. Give her my regards when you speak to her.'

'I will.'

The interview was finished.

AT 4 P.M. Mark Fask called in to the station. He had once been a scenes of crime officer in the police force. But a few years ago the decision had been made that this was a job for a civilian. So Fask had promptly left the Force, picking up his pension on the way, and formed his own company. It was very successful. Fask was familiar with the laws of admissible evidence and his former colleagues almost always engaged his firm to glean the specimens from numerous crime scenes. It hadn't escaped Joanna's notice that the former officer, whose car had previously been a Skoda, was now driving a top of the range BMW. Success indeed.

Fask was a stocky man with pale skin, thick curling hair and dark brown eyes. 'I've bagged up the cat,' he said cheerfully. 'I'll pop it in the deep freeze and keep a hold of it for a bit.'

'What about the rope used to hang it?'

'There's a coil of it in one of the outhouses,' Fask said. 'It's been cut with a serrated knife. Apart from that there's nothing much to get from it.'

'Any fingerprints on the door?'

Fask shook his head. 'None apart from the ones that should be there.'

'Anything else?'

'Not so far. Poor animal looks as though it had its neck broken before it was strung up. The head was loose. Rope was knotted real tight around its neck. I've preserved the knot. Nice cat too. Seal point Burmese, if I'm not very much mistaken. I suppose that's why they called it Tuptim.'

'What?'

'Tuptim. Burmese name.'

'Is it?' Joanna felt stupid.

'Haven't you seen *Anna and the King of Siam*?'

'Years ago.'

'Don't you remember the Burmese girl who was

given to him as a bride? Fell in love with Lun Tha, the man who brought her to Siam.'

'Vaguely. So that's where she got the name from.'

'Yes.'

'Well, you've answered one question at least.' *The least important one*, she could have added but didn't.

Fask grinned. 'Glad to be of service, Jo. And the cat, by the way, would have been worth a few hundred pounds.'

'Really? You're a mine of information, Mark. I didn't realize you knew so much about cats—or the films industry.'

He looked abashed. 'Pub quizzes,' he explained.

'Did you get anything else from around the scene?'

'Not a lot.'

'Do you know where the cat was killed?'

'Probably in the big barn. That's where the rope was. There's a saucer of water there. My guess is that the cat was lured in and—'

'Do you have a time frame?'

'Well, Mrs Tong says she stayed at Butterfield overnight as Mrs Weeks was getting increasingly twitchy about being there on her own. Apparently Tuptim liked to roam during the night, went in and out as she pleased through the cat flap. She was found at seven this morning and last seen late Monday evening, they think, so the usual rules. Somewhere between those two times. She was pretty stiff and cold by the time I got to her so my guess is late last night.'

Joanna nodded. 'Anything else that might help, Mark?'

'Not really.'

He left and Joanna remained with a feeling of dissatisfaction. Korpanski was busy in another room so she was on her own.

She spent the afternoon on the computer and downloaded a couple of episodes of Butterfield Farm. There was no doubt about it—Timony Weeks had been a beauty. Not a great actress, that was obvious. She hammed her lines a couple of times, relied too much on a helpless look for a wide spectrum of emotions: fear, grief, happiness, guilt and confusion. All were created by a widening of the eyes and a slight parting of the lips. The episode Joanna was looking at had been shown in 1963 when Timony would have been eleven. She looked younger, more like eight. But however poor the acting had been and the frequent fluffing of lines, even Joanna could recognize that Timony Weeks had had an undeniable screen presence: long, thick hair which she tossed around to great effect and huge, vulnerable eyes which looked beseechingly into the camera. They were enough to melt the hardest of hearts. Added to that was a mouth that trembled every single time she looked at a wounded animal—which was roughly four times per episode. And the check shirts and denim dungarees which she wore around the farm were very 'cutesy' while the nylon dresses, hair ribbons, white ankle socks and sandals that she wore into town were undeniably dainty. Watching episodes of the series Joanna soon realized that Timony Weeks had stolen the show with her winsome ways. She had two older brothers, Keith and Sean, great muscular monkeys of men who guarded and protected her at every step and in turn she rewarded them with her sweet smile, a flash of *those eyes* and occasionally a quick, embarrassed kiss on their rough male cheeks. And then there was

David, a younger brother who seemed to have no purpose at all in the series and no part to play except to be
cuddled and comforted by his soft-hearted sister, Lily.

Gerald, who played Joab Butterfield, her screen father, looked old enough to be her grandfather rather than
her father. The part he played was taciturn and dignified in dungarees whereas May, her screen mother, was
a troubled, fretting scold with permanent scowl lines
scoring her forehead. Joanna looked closer at Gerald.
At a guess he would 'scrub up' very nicely. He was
tall and thin, and could have been distinguished-looking in a suit rather than denim. He had a proud, erect
posture and thick grey hair. In spite of his age and the
part he was playing, Joanna caught a frisson of attraction between the screen stars and felt uncomfortable
when Timony climbed on to his lap, threw her arms
around him and gave 'Daddy' his goodnight kiss. Joanna watched a couple of episodes but soon got bored
with the sickly sweetness of the storylines, the stilted
acting and disjointed conversations. Freeman and the
BBC had been right to pull the plug, probably a few
years too late, and bow out. It wouldn't have passed
muster for today's more sophisticated dramas like *East-
Enders* or *Coronation Street*. She switched off and sat,
thinking, for a while. She knew she was missing something and central to that conviction was the certainty
that it was all to do with Lily Butterfield, or Timony
Shore. She rubbed her forehead, closed her eyes and
tried to picture what it was that was disturbing her.

She longed to talk this over with Matthew but wasn't
sure she could find the right words. The events were
so nebulous and insubstantial. It was all about feeling

and impressions, instincts and ideas. Even the business about the watch seemed insubstantial.

All except the killing of the cat. That was real enough.

As SHE DROVE home that evening her mind kept returning to the puzzle of events at Butterfield Farm. Something was troubling her. It lay at the back of her mind, an oily, green sludge which she could feel in her brain. She was conscious of it all the time. The urge to talk the case over with Matthew strengthened with every mile she drew nearer to Waterfall Cottage. But when she reached the lane and their home she realized that Matthew was not there. There was no sign of his car and the cottage was in darkness. She sat outside for a while, disappointed. It was not late. Only seven o'clock, but this was unusual. A first, in fact. As a pathologist Matthew did not have to go on calls and emergency stuff. He was generally home around six. She decided she would ring him on his mobile once she'd gone inside and lit the woodburner.

He answered on the second ring. 'Hi, Jo.'

'I'm home,' she said, 'and you're not.'

'Oh. Sorry. I forgot to mention it. There's a lecture tonight. It's on tissue sampling and toxicology. I promised Eloise I'd take her. There's a dinner afterwards, Jo, so I'll be quite late and won't need a meal. I'm so sorry. I simply forgot to tell you.' His voice was in the stage whisper of someone about to enter a lecture theatre and surrounded by people he did not want listening in.

Her mouth dropped open. This was a first. Not only was it a first but she suspected it would not be the last. It wasn't a problem but Miss Eloise being involved was rubbing salt into an open wound. She could just picture the girl's snide little comment.

'Tightening up the apron strings, Daddy? Being scolded for staying out late?'

Joanna glowered. She doubted this situation would have arisen *before* they were married. Was he already taking her for granted? Had marriage given Matthew Levin, her very new husband, a confidence he had lost when he had dissolved his marriage to Jane and resumed his affair with DI Joanna Piercy?

'OK, Matt,' she managed, in a friendly tone, unwilling for Miss Eloise to score any points at all, 'I'll maybe see you later.'

Piss him, she thought when the call was ended. *Piss him*. She needn't have headed home so fast. She could have stayed on at the station, caught up with the backlog that had accumulated during her honeymoon. Or she could have gone out for a drink with Korpanski like the good old days. Instead, like the good wife she was, she had hurried home, hoping to talk to Matthew about children's TV in the 1960s. She blew out a heavy sigh. She felt foolish.

Oh, well.

She poured herself a glass of chilled rosé wine and switched the computer on. This case was intriguing her, pulling her in. Behind the interest, she knew, was her degree in psychology. What makes people think and do the things they do? What influences behaviour and social attitudes? The why and wherefores. And the subject that interested her over all others and which she had done her thesis in: why is a particular era in history the one that produces the Beatles or Hitler, Elvis Presley, Martin Luther King, Tony Blair, Margaret Thatcher?

These people all had one thing in common. They had come along at a time when a certain sector of people had needed them. So…could she apply this to a TV series? She believed so. She used this skill to look into children in the early sixties, found Butterfield Farm on the Internet, settled back and began to watch another episode.

This one was from 1965 and began with the strumming guitar music which was becoming familiar to her. It was the sort of rhythmic sound that she might have associated with an old Western. Relaxed. Easy. As she watched the credits rolled up. Timony Shore was the fourth name. And the action began.

It started in the kitchen, with Lily holding a tiny lamb and burying her face in it, weeping. She wrapped the lamb in a blanket and sat near the stove, cradling it, her hair falling over her face and the animal. Then she set it down and went to fetch a feeding bottle which presumably contained milk. It was boat shaped, with a teat on the end. The lamb simply moved its head away and flopped down. Even Joanna felt a bit cheated. Surely it was not going to die?

Then, as she watched, a young man swaggered in. One of the monkeys. Lily's brother, Sean. Joanna smiled. The one that Colclough's sister had labelled a 'dish'. There was certainly a raw sexuality about him. He took the lamb from her and began to rub its fur vigorously. He was stocky, with thick, curling hair and powerful, hairy forearms, shirt sleeves rolled up to expose a tattoo. Joanna peered at it. A tattoo of a tractor? She put her hand over her mouth, giggling. As she watched, Sean stuck the teat into the lamb's mouth and, as he stroked its fur, the lamb began to suck greedily while Timony watched, eyes wide open. How old was she? Thirteen going on eight. The acting was ham. And Colclough and his sister had been right. It was sickly sweet. And yet, for all that, Joanna had to admit that it did tug at the heart strings. Even she was moved by the plight of the lamb and the little girl.

You cry, Piercy, she warned herself, *and you'll have to stop watching.* And then she wondered. What was it about these corny stories that could have such an effect?

She watched the next scene, Sean Butterfield handing the lamb, milk bottle and teat very carefully across to his little sister. How old was Sean? she wondered. At a guess nineteen, twenty.

As the action moved outside Joanna was stunned to realize how closely Timony Weeks had recreated Butterfield Farm. This was no coincidence. She must have copied the place deliberately. Even down to the well at the front, complete with rack and bucket. Of course, everything else was different—old-fashioned lumpy tractors, some Shire horses clopping over cobbles, a Rayburn rather than an *Aga* in the kitchen. But it sent a shiver down Joanna's spine as she watched the action, which lasted an hour without any breaks.

She assumed that Butterfield had been recreated because it had been a period of happiness and success for Timony. It was an unusual but hardly unique scenario. But what the hell did all this have to do with recent events?

She switched the computer off and sat, staring into the darkness, wondering. When Timony Weeks had her holiday with Mrs Tong, would Butterfield Farm once again be a happy hunting ground? Was that what she wanted? No answers, no explanation? No more bother?

No. Something wasn't right here. If she was honest

with herself she did want to understand what and why all this had happened. It was preferable to silence and nothing. She wanted to know.

EIGHT

Thursday, January 19, 8 a.m.

As JOANNA DROVE to the station, she was anticipating another summons from Timony Weeks. She felt the apprehension crawl up the back of her neck the nearer she got
to the town, which was even more congested than usual
because protestors were trying to save a roundabout.

What next? she thought, as she fumed in the grid-
lock.

She was dreading the next call—partly because she
didn't have a handle on the woman or the events, but
partly because she had a feeling of impending doom.
Things that had happened so long ago could surely have
no bearing on recent events? But riding on the back of
this was the unpleasant picture of the cat, Tuptim. So
elegant and superior in life, with its twitching tail and
arrogant posture, but so pathetic in death. Just a cat. A
moggie. It was a bit like celebrity, she thought, drum-
ming her fingers on the steering wheel. Alive they were
sportsmen or millionaires, models and royalty. But dead
they would all eventually be just corpses, their fame
and fortune nothing but memories and photographs.

Joanna frowned. These thoughts were too morbid.

But if events were to escalate further what would or
could happen next? At the back of her mind, irrational
or not, was the image of a mad person stalking a celeb-

rity, waiting for his opportunity, then fighting his way through bodyguards, trying to gouge Timony's eyes out with a pair of scissors. And judging by the proximity of the scar to Timony's eye, he had come bloody close. Half a centimetre to the right and he would have succeeded. What would have happened to her career then? She had been just a child—almost fourteen years old in years, about ten in appearance and possibly even younger in her mind.

Finally she broke through the traffic, parked up and entered the station. Joanna eyed the desk sergeant, who simply grinned at her, wished her a *very* good morning and added nothing more. She hovered, waiting, but he simply looked at her, still smiling, and added nothing to his greeting. She almost, *almost* asked him if there was any word from Butterfield Farm but said nothing except to return his greeting.

Mike breezed in at 8.10 a.m., raised his eyebrows at her in question and when he got no response except a shrug, sat down and swivelled his chair around to face her. 'No summons up to Butterfield?'

'Not so far,' she said. 'What have you got for me, Mike?'

He grinned. 'Plenty.'

'You went over there yesterday afternoon?'

He nodded. 'Got Mrs Tong all to myself. Madam Timony was busy with her memoirs.'

'That'll be an interesting read.' Joanna stored the information away. It could prove useful. 'Go on,' she prompted. 'Stop teasing.'

'Diana Tong,' he began, 'is a very interesting and intriguing character.'

'I'm sure.'

'She's been with Timony since nineteen sixty-four. She was her secretary, teacher, wardrobe mistress, chauffeur, bodyguard and friend. She's seen her through marriages and divorces, tragedies and periods of happiness. Good times and bad times. You name it, she's been part of it. The production company employed her as a companion just before the fan attacked Timony. Timony had had a few odd letters and there was a suspicion that she was being stalked. Of course, it turned out that Dariel, the fan who assaulted her, had been following her for a while, so Diana was part bodyguard as well as everything else. When she called herself a dogsbody she was speaking the truth. She's done everything. Even acted as agent. Got her bookings and parts after Butterfield folded, sorted out travel arrangements. The list goes on and on.'

'Did you get the impression that she was fond of her?'

'It really is a sort of love/hate relationship. I think part of her admires her. She's done so much.' He made a face. 'And Timony needs her. In fact, they both need each other.'

'Symbiosis,' Joanna murmured.

Korpanski nodded. 'And she's paid very well. She did say that.'

Joanna nodded. 'Did she say whether she was aware of any violent behaviour on set?'

'No. Nothing happened, as far as she knows.'

'Anything else? Did you get the impression she had any idea who was behind all these little tricks?'

'That's the strange thing—she thought it was Timony herself, until the cigarette smoke. Turns out she thought Timony was playing around because she wanted to get back into the public eye, gain some sympathy so she'd make a lot of money from her memoirs. At the moment she's writing them but having trouble getting a publisher interested. They all say she's old news, that she should have written them fifty years ago.' He grinned. 'Bit unkind, I thought.'

'But probably true.'

'Mmm.'

'Diana said that when the cat was killed she knew it wasn't Timony. She said that Timony adored Tuptim and she couldn't have killed her.'

'Right, but the fact remains that until then she really thought Timony was doing all this to herself? And ringing the police? Just to get attention?' Even though Joanna had thought the same she found it hard to stomach that someone so close to the soap star could entertain such a thought. Despite their unusual relationship, Diana was supposed to be Timony's friend. Was this why she hadn't said anything until now, when she was sure Timony was innocent?

Korpanski nodded, sucked in a deep breath and blew it out. 'I know it's hard to believe, Jo,' he said.

'But why would she do it? Just to rekindle public interest in her and ensure a book deal?' She folded her arms sceptically. 'It's a bit weak. It's not like she's in desperate need of the money.'

'It isn't just that, Jo. A part's coming up in a new drama. She believes it was made for her. It's set in and around Buxton so isn't even that far from her home. More importantly, James Freeman is producing it.'

'He didn't mention it.' Then she remembered Freeman's comments about Timony's appearance and she doubted whether he was about to throw a part her way.

'So if Timony couldn't have hurt the cat, who is Diana's second big suspect?'

'She doesn't have one.'

'No one else in the picture?'

'No.'

'You mean to tell me that *no one* from Timony's past would try getting their own back for some malicious slight years ago?'

'I tried that tack, Jo,' Korpanski said indignantly, 'but she wasn't biting. Just said the past was the past and to leave it there.'

'So what next?'

'I guess we wait for the next call,' Korpanski suggested.

Joanna sighed but she had no better ideas.

ALL MORNING JOANNA struggled to concentrate on other matters. Each time the telephone rang she jumped, convinced it would be Timony. And each time it was somebody else. About something else. Joanna found it hard to concentrate and she could tell that Korpanski was plain fidgety. She wanted to go out in the fresh air and stop phone watching but was too apprehensive and expectant, not wanting to miss anything. Joanna rubbed her hand across her forehead. This was too much. She was being drawn more and more into the situation. She didn't know whether she wanted Timony to phone or not to phone. And each time she closed her eyes the image of Butterfield Farm seemed pasted to the inside of her eyelids.

At 4 p.m., Korpanski spoke. 'This is the first day she hasn't rung for three weeks,' he said. 'It's spooky.'

By 5 p.m. Joanna was anxious. The silence now

seemed ominous. What was happening out there? She dialled Butterfield, got Diana Tong's cool voice on the other end and was assured that all was peaceful. She replaced the receiver with a sense of anticlimax.

Was that to be it?

Friday came and there were no more calls.

By Friday afternoon Joanna couldn't bear it any more. It felt like unfinished business. Just because the events appeared to have ceased it didn't answer any of her questions. She drove out to Butterfield, banged on the door and waited for Diana Tong to open it. It seemed to take an age. It was apparently beneath Timony's dignity to open the door herself. 'Sorry,' Diana said without a note of remorse. 'I was upstairs, packing. We've decided to bring our holiday forward.' She gave a disarming smile. 'I suppose it's Timony you want to see? Your sergeant gave me a pretty thorough grilling the other day.'

Joanna smothered a grin. She could well imagine. 'Thank you, yes, if I could speak to Mrs Weeks that would be good. I'm sure Sergeant Korpanski has asked you all the relevant questions.'

'Then I'll lead on.' There was a note of mockery in Diana Tong's voice, as though she was nursing a secret and it would take more than Korpanski's blunt instrument to wheedle it out of her.

Timony was sitting in the study where Joanna had first seen her. She looked comfortable at her desk, tapping on a laptop, absorbed in her work. By her side was a pad of notes and on the floor a lever-arch box full of newspaper cuttings. She looked up as Joanna entered and Joanna was struck by how wan and haunted she looked. Frail, fragile and very vulnerable. Timony might blag that she didn't believe in ghosts but she had to believe in haunting, surely? One only had to look at the dark shadows underneath the eyes to be convinced that something here was terribly wrong. When Joanna had first met the actress she had been struck by how thin she was. Now she looked skeletal. And unwell. Her face was chalk pale. No amount of make-up and plastic surgery could hide this. She gave Joanna a quizzical glance. 'We haven't rung you,' she said simply, then, speaking over her shoulder, she checked, 'have we, Diana?'

'No. There's nothing to report.' The companion gave a watery smile. 'All quiet on the Western Front.'

Timony gave Joanna a straight, challenging stare. 'So why are you here? You and your colleagues have spent enough time telling me off for calling you out. And now you've come without me asking.'

'After the cat business I was a little worried.' Then Joanna lied. 'This is on my way home so I thought I'd pop in.'

'Where do you live?' Diana Tong rapped out the question like gunfire.

'Waterfall,' Joanna responded coolly. 'Right in the village.'

This elicited a retort from Diana Tong. 'That's not a village,' she chortled. 'Just a pub, a church, stocks for the villains, a couple of cottages and no bloody waterfall.'

'I live in one of the cottages,' Joanna responded tightly.

Diana Tong's eyes bored into hers. 'It's a bit of a detour, isn't it?'

'I prefer the scenic route.'

Diana Tong stared pointedly out of the window at the grey, uninspiring sky. 'What you really mean is that Butterfield isn't on your way home at all.' Diana Tong gave Joanna a hard stare and leaned towards her, her words hostile. 'What you mean to say is that the cat business has, at last, worried you.'

Slowly Joanna nodded.

'Well, let's hope this little incident's over then,' Diana said tartly.

'And that from now on you'll be left alone,' Joanna agreed.

The two women looked at each other then Diana spoke up. 'We're both exhausted with all the tension,' she said. 'We'll be going to Devon on Tuesday. Traffic's too heavy down the M5 on a Monday.' She paused. 'We may even stay down a little longer than planned.'

'That would seem a good idea,' Joanna responded. 'We'll do what we can to keep an eye on the place and I take it the Rossingtons will…'

'Continue to come in once a week,' Diana Tong inserted coolly.

Joanna still felt she was missing something. She took a step towards the door then stopped. 'Has anyone ever tried to extort money out of you?'

Timony looked a little shocked at the idea. 'No,' she protested.

'I take it you are quite wealthy?'

A smug nod confirmed that.

'But you say no one has tried to blackmail you?'

'I said not.' Timony sounded quite firm and very slightly cross at having the question put to her a second time.

Joanna turned. 'So what do you think is the real purpose of it all?'

The two women gave a swift exchange of glances, but neither even tried to answer the question. Instead they treated Joanna's question as rhetorical, simply shrugging and saying nothing.

And Joanna left, again with the feeling that none of this was right.

This time Matthew was home when she reached Waterfall Cottage. In fact, he was using their table to prepare a talk using PowerPoint, but looked up as she came in. 'Hi, you. I have an idea. Why don't we eat at the Red Lion tonight? I could murder a sirloin steak.' He glanced at the computer screen. 'For getting on so well with this I can treat myself to a pint or two of real ale; you can have a nice glass of wine and then we can stagger home.' He eyed her. 'And make mad passionate love. What say you?'

'You're on,' she said, laughing because his face looked so eager, so happy, so animated. 'That's an offer I can't refuse but first I'd better get changed.'

'Good. I can finish my presentation on traumatic amputation.' He looked up at her. 'Don't worry,' he said. 'The next slide's only a thumb.'

She rumpled his hair and rested her arm on his shoulders, breathing him in. All people have a scent. Matthew was fastidious to always shower at the mortuary before he came home and the mortuary itself had an excellent air exchange system, but in spite of his using deodorants and aftershave his own personal scent invariably held the faintest tang of formaldehyde.

She had a quick shower and came down in a short

black skirt, black tights, high-heeled shoes and a scarlet jacket.

Matthew looked appreciatively at her. 'Nice,' he said and she beamed at him. This marriage business, she thought, felt good. But she felt bound to add words of warning.

Enjoy the détente, Piercy, she said to herself. *While it lasts*. Because nothing lasts for ever.

But for tonight she would party.

They had a great evening at the pub. The pair who ran it were lively and friendly and the food was locally sourced and home cooked. A few residents of Waterfall were present and a half-hearted game of darts resulted. No one really cared who won. As the usual banter took place Joanna noticed a couple sitting in the corner kept glancing over. Eventually the man crossed the floor and stood in front of their table. 'Inspector Piercy, aren't you?' He had a strong moorlands accent.

'Off duty,' Joanna responded.

'Arrgh, I know that. You're investigatin' the strange goings on at Butterfield, I think?'

With an apologetic glance at Matthew, who hated her work to intrude on their private life, Joanna answered, 'Yes, I am. Do you know anything about them?'

'Not exactly.' He put his hand on the table. It was begrimed with years of working the land and quite beyond ever being clean. He would go to his grave with Staffordshire soil ingrained in his skin. 'I'm John Reeves,' he said. 'A neighbour of Mrs Weeks and Mrs Tong.'

'And can you shed any light on events?'

Reeves didn't answer directly. 'I 'eard 'er cat were killed,' he said gruffly.

Ah, so that was what had flushed out Farmer Reeves,

whose wife was glancing over, a mite irritated by her husband's defection.

Joanna nodded.

'I can't 'elp you,' Farmer Reeves said, 'except to tell you that there 'as bin another car there on occasion. I've seen it.'

'What sort of car?' Joanna's heart missed a beat. 'Can you remember the number?'

Farmer Reeves shook his head. 'Too far away,' he said. 'But it were a silver Mercedes.'

Of which there are probably half a million in this country, Joanna thought.

Still, it was a start.

'You wouldn't know which model?' Too hopeful. He shook his head.

'Can you remember when you saw the car?'

'It were during the bad frost,' Farmer Reeves said, unable to resist adding a word of explanation. ''Cos of the frost I couldn't get the tractor over the field so I were muck spreadin'.' He paused for a moment, then said, 'So that would have been two weeks ago.'

'How many times have you seen that car?'

She could almost have predicted his answer.

'Couldn't tell you that.'

'If you do see it again,' Joanna said, 'would you try and get the number plate, please?' She fished a card out of her bag. 'And contact me?'

'Sure will, Inspector.' And with a show of good manners and a swift glance at Matthew, he added, 'Sorry. Hope I haven't spoiled your meal.'

Matthew was at his most charming. 'Not a bit of it, Mr Reeves.'

Joanna merely smiled.

When Farmer Reeves had returned to his table Matthew asked very softly, 'Are all your witnesses so informative and helpful?'

She laughed. 'Mostly. At least,' she added more truthfully, 'they try to be.'

The evening passed pleasantly and they headed back to Waterfall Cottage, arm in arm. It was a night of marital harmony. Joanna hoped for plenty more.

NINE

Sunday, January 22, 8 a.m.

SHE COULD HEAR the rain even as she lay in bed. Thundering down on the roof, splashing from the gutters, pouring into the drains. And she knew that Matthew could hear it too. But, wisely, he knew better than to draw attention to it. He knew that any comment he made on this sad weather would be read by her as an attempt to put her off her bike ride. She lay still, warm, dry and content, snuggling under the duvet and coiling her legs around her husband, feeling the musculature of his torso, which made her just a little bit frisky. She felt his chest move up and down, his arm tighten around her, and drew in a deep breath. So why leave this and go out there, just to get drenched and freezing and make a point? She closed her eyes and breathed in the bedroom air with its whisper of chill through the crack of the open window; neither of them could sleep with the window tight shut. She lay still and reflected. Why did she have to do this, create difficulties? She knew better than most that it is practically impossible to keep your hands and feet warm on a blustery, soaking bike ride. It was January, for goodness' sake. It would be unpleasant—not fun. So why do it? She almost said it out loud: Why, Piercy? Why do you always have to set yourself these challenges? She cleared her throat and dared Matthew to speak. Wisely he continued to fake sleep and by extraordinary discipline kept his breathing regular and deep.

She sat up. Delay the moment. 'Coffee?' she asked idly.

It didn't deceive her husband for a minute. He lay back against the pillow, biting in the smile that was already blooming on his face. She knew exactly what he was thinking. He was daring her to chicken out. 'Thanks,' he said, mock sleepy. 'I'd love one.' He finished the sentence with a theatrical yawn.

She drew back the curtains and stared out of the window. The weather was every bit as nasty as she'd anticipated. The rain was streaming down the pane in lively little rivulets. Already she could practically *feel* the icy water dripping from her cycling helmet and trickling down the back of her neck. She tilted her head back and scrunched her shoulders as though to stop it. She put out a hand and touched the glass. Even this side of double-glazing felt ice-cold to her exploratory touch. It was a day to stay indoors. For the sensible. She smiled. She'd never been accused of that. Besides...

She'd *said* she was going on her bike and that was exactly what she was going to do. She'd spent most of Saturday hunched up over either computer or telephone and felt she needed to move. And she did not want to waste another day.

Matthew was watching her lazily from the bed, a half smile on his lips. If he knew what *she* was thinking she also knew exactly what *he* was thinking. That she didn't want to go on a bike ride at all. But he knew once she'd said she would go she would keep to her word. And so she would ride—whatever the weather. Besides, she wanted to avoid Eloise for as long as possible. And a bike ride followed by a long hot bath would keep her out of his daughter's way for a while.

Joanna was tempted to turn around and tell Matthew off for smirking so obviously and spying on her from underneath half-closed eyes but decided it would appear childish. So she went downstairs, boiled the kettle, filled the cafetière with the aptly named *Lazy Sunday*, and returned with a tray of milk and two mugs. Nothing is as good as the scent of fresh coffee to get you out of bed in the morning. She handed him one, drank hers quickly and, before she could change her mind, tugged on a pair of cycling shorts, tucked her hair underneath a Beanie, cleaned her teeth, put on a slick of lip gloss and left the bedroom without another word. Downstairs she zipped herself into a waterproof, strapped on her helmet and closed the door behind her, letting herself out into the blast of particularly foul weather.

As she wheeled her bike around the side of Waterfall Cottage she hoped that the rain had looked and sounded worse from the inside than it was on the outside, but it proved to be a vain and over-optimistic hope. She was quickly drenched and the wind was spiteful, seeming to find any gaps in her clothing to freeze her body core temperature. The cold and the drops stung her face, and even by the time she'd rounded the front of the cottage her feet and hands were already wet and cold. They would get wetter and colder. But she could ignore it when she felt the familiar pull on her legs as she rode through the village, passing the Red Lion pub on her right and descending the hill, the wind screaming behind her, like a pursuing banshee. She closed her eyes for a minute, hearing the noise of the weather and savouring the challenge. Just for the briefest of moments she was sheltered from the wind. Bliss.

Matthew and Eloise would start the lunch and they'd have a fine old time chatting about immunology and bacteria, radiology and cells. Eloise the medical student and Matthew the pathologist always had plenty to talk about. Whereas she… Joanna grinned to herself, checked for traffic behind her and swung out to her right, to the road that opened out on the ridge that overlooked Butterfield Farm. She had other fish to fry.

The farm was barely visible through the filter of the weather. But she could make out the 'L' shape of the house and the well at the front. She peered through the lashing rain. And had a shock. The black Qashqai was there but the Isuzu was gone. And in its place was a Mercedes, gleaming silver in the rain. She swung her leg over the bike, stood on the ridge and looked down, wondering whose car it was. She ran through the alternatives in her mind. It was perfectly possible that Diana Tong had a second car and this was it. Or that the silver Merc had been sheltering in one of the garages all the time. But she quickly disregarded both these theories. None of the officers conducting the enquiries had mentioned a third car.

Joanna tried to think things through logically. Today was a Sunday—not one of Diana Tong's usual days at Butterfield; the missing Isuzu was probably hers. Neither was it the gardener or his wife's day at the farm. So who was the visitor? It looked as though Timony was alone in the house with the driver of the silver Mercedes.

The rain continued to lash down, blurring her view, but the place looked peaceful enough. Not the scene of some great drama. Smoke was blasting out of the chimney. Inside the logs must be roaring in the wood burner. It all looked normal. So it probably was. Why shouldn't Timony have a visitor? She must have some friends from her soap star days. But although Joanna could easily explain a strange car standing outside Butterfield, she still felt curious enough to act. She could almost hear Korpanski's grunt of disapproval over the cacophony of the warring wind and rain. Feeling more like an amateur sleuth than a detective inspector she wheeled her bike slowly down the edge of the track, keeping her eye on the car and watching out for any of the doors opening. But until she got fifty yards from the house there was no sign of anyone. Then the front door opened. Which put her in a quandary. It would seem intrusive to be seen sneaking up on the place, though she could justify it by saying she was simply doing her job. Surveillance. On a bike? On balance she didn't fancy explaining her presence at all so she moved back quickly, out of sight, behind a bush, dropping her bike to the ground behind the wall, and watched curiously as someone emerged from the front door.

It was a man who looked in his forties, smartly dressed in a dark suit, a huge brolly held over his head. Insurance rep, Joanna decided. Then smiled. Maybe Timony had taken out life insurance on the cat? But there was something stiff and reserved in Timony's manner, holding back from the man as they took their leave of one another. They didn't shake hands but stood well apart. Like strangers. Over the weather Joanna couldn't hear a word of what they were saying but their manner looked formal. Almost hostile. Guarded in their interaction, as though neither quite trusted the other.

Definitely wary. Joanna had the sense that something was very wrong in this encounter. There was something uncomfortable about it. Then the wind gusted across the scene, the man climbed into his car and drove slowly up the track, passing Joanna without seeing her. She made a note of the number. She would check up on it on Monday. She glanced back at Butterfield.

Although the weather was foul, instead of going straight back into the house Timony was standing, apparently oblivious to the weather, watching the car ascend the track as though she wanted to check that the driver was leaving the property. There was something bleak in her manner; her shoulders drooped and she passed a hand across her eyes as though wiping back tears. Joanna could almost feel the anguish. She wondered whether to call in on her, say she was passing and check whether anything was wrong. The unexpected visit might tell her who Timony's awkward visitor was. Then she stopped herself. She wasn't a nursemaid but a policewoman who had spent the last week (her first fresh from honeymoon) pandering to a histrionic retired actress whose cat had regrettably met a violent death. Even so, she waited until Timony had disappeared behind the door. She didn't want the actress to see her. In her years in the Force Joanna had learned that when it came to them the public had double standards. While Timony Weeks would have no problem calling the police out on a daily basis, an uninvited attendance from police would be perceived as police intrusion. Harassment, even. Joanna gave a deep sigh as she turned her bike around and cycled back up to the top of the track, turning towards home and bending her head against the weather, which was promising to be more docile now.

Like a lion tamed into submission, it had lost its rage. She offered up the prayer that the week ahead would be similarly tame and that Timony and her pal would head off for Devon on Tuesday and the whole thing would be over, the stalker, or whoever it was, tired of their game. Her questions would have to remain unanswered.

But as she cycled along the ridge she had the feeling that this was perhaps too optimistic. The murder of the cat was no game. It had been vicious and the display of its body calculated to cause maximum distress.

As she gave her final battle against wind and rain her mind tracked elsewhere. Timony Weeks had said they didn't have many guests. *Many*, no. *Any* was a different matter. There was probably a perfectly rational explanation. Why shouldn't Timony have a visitor? No reason at all. There was nothing suspicious in it. Joanna knew she was doing what Matthew occasionally accused her of—looking at events with a suspicious policeman's mind. She arrived back at Waterfall Cottage an hour and a half later, thoroughly cold and wet, but, annoyingly, with curiosity still burning inside her. She wanted to know who the owner of the Mercedes was and what he was doing at Butterfield Farm. Why had Timony seemed so uncomfortable in her visitor's presence? Or, again, had she read something in the woman's behaviour that simply wasn't there? Had the angry weather misled her? She gave a little smile. The answers would likely be banal, but she couldn't stop herself from asking the questions.

Rounding the corner towards Waterfall Cottage, she saw Eloise's blue Suzuki parked outside. *Great*, she thought as she wheeled her bike around the back and into the shed, giving it a cursory wipe with a towel.

She pushed the door open. And was met by the appetizing smell of a Sunday roast, but the kitchen was empty. She took her shoes off and walked through. Matthew and Eloise were sitting at the dining table, poring over some books. A scatter of papers covered the surface and Eloise was frowning and looking very disgruntled. 'I just don't get it, Dad,' she was saying.

Neither looked up as she entered. Matthew, in a dark blue sweater, jeans and slippers, was leaning back in his chair, his hands clasped behind his head and his face looked calm and pleasant. He was always happy sharing this love of medicine with his daughter. 'It is a tough one,' he admitted. 'The classifications of pulmonary fibrosis are a bugger but you don't need to worry about them just yet. That's tertiary consultant stuff, Eloise. Years in the future.'

She was not mollified. 'It pisses me off when I don't understand something,' she said petulantly.

Then, as though on cue, they both 'noticed' her. Matthew grinned across. 'Nice bike ride, Jo?' he asked smugly.

Eloise simply raised her eyebrows in greeting.

Joanna took off her sodden Beanie and shook her hair out. Raindrops scattered. And then the three of them laughed. 'It was bloody horrible,' Joanna confessed. 'But I feel better for doing it. I'll just jump in the bath and then sort out lunch.'

Matthew's eyes were warm as he looked at her. Even Eloise managed an almost smile but soon bent her head back over her books again.

After a scalding hot soak, Joanna rather enjoyed herself cooking the lunch, peeling the veg, crisping the roast potatoes, stirring the gravy as she listened to *Clas-*

sic FM and finally serving the roast beef meal up with a bottle of blood-warm claret. And everyone appreciated her apple pie. With vanilla custard.

She smiled to herself. Then looked up to see Eloise watching her, amusement making her features less sharp. 'Bit domesticated, isn't it, Joanna?' she challenged, 'All this?'

'I can do domesticated,' Joanna responded, trying not to rise to the bait. The fact was she did enjoy cooking. It was just that she didn't always have the time.

But Eloise persisted. 'So is this the new you?' Perhaps it was only Joanna who heard the mockery in the girl's voice.

'No,' she replied testily.

'Oh.' Eloise batted her fine blue eyes in her father's direction and Matthew gave her an indulgent smile.

They loaded the dishwasher together, tidied the kitchen then spent part of the afternoon playing *Trivial Pursuit*, but it wasn't long before Matthew and Eloise gravitated back to the dining room table, so Joanna went on the computer and watched another couple of episodes of Butterfield Farm. This time she was struck more by the relationship between the two older brothers and their pretty little sister.

Sean, in particular, seemed very protective of Timony, but occasionally he would have an angry look about him, as though he had a bad temper. There was a lot of flexing of muscles. Even Keith, the oldest brother, seemed wary of Sean. His eyes frequently flitted towards him almost whenever he said something that might annoy him. It was Sean who was the obvious pin-up of the series. Joanna could well understand Elizabeth Gantry's passion for *the dish*. In fact, Joanna was surprised that it hadn't been Sean that Timony had married. He was much nearer her in age. So why had she married Gerald or 'Joab', the patriarch? The man, in spite of being well preserved, was unmistakably in his fifties. It was hard to believe that they had married. It seemed incongruous. The age gap must be more than thirty years. On set he appeared more paternal than predatory. There were a lot of shots of him working or driving a tractor, but there were also many scenes when he was doing little but watching everyone and always with that faintly wary expression in his eyes. Once or twice, when the camera was panning around, Joab Butterfield looked disturbed. Worried. And, partly due to the lack of acting skills on show, Joanna sensed that this was not part of the script or action but a very real sense of concern which mixed oddly with the bland and flowery soap. This sense of unease permeated through the two episodes from the mid-sixties that she watched.

The concern seemed mainly centred on Timony, the artlessly pretty star of the show. It even extended to May, whose gaze was also mainly focused on her screen daughter. And the screen 'parents' concern seemed to intensify in the scenes where Sean was comforting his little 'sister' over the latest animal tragedy. There were a few shots where all the actors seemed to be looking at some sweet thing that Timony was doing—trying to bake a birthday cake, feeding a lamb, looking for a lost calf. The possibilities were endless. But Gerald's expression was different from the others'. Of course, Joanna had to remind herself that in the later instalments, post 1969, the 'child' Gerald was watching was his real-life wife, but this look of worry made his face seem older and the relationship even less appropriate. Sometimes he looked pensive, as though worried about what would become of Timony. This look sat inconsistently on the face of a moorlands farmer. And yet they were wealthy, successful and he could have had no premonition that he would die within three years of taking his wedding vows. Occasionally the look extended to Sean, but these times it was less worry and more anger.

Joanna watched, absorbed in this play behind a play being acted out in front of her. Joab's concerns were for two people, she decided. Timony and Sean. Once or twice he made involuntary movements with his hands when the two were on set, as though to intervene.

It was intriguing. She kept watching. Keith, the older son, and David, the youngest, didn't seem to cause their father the same anxiety as the turbulent Sean. In fact, David Butterfield had virtually no part to play apart from looking wide-eyed and a little puzzled by more or less everything. And as for May, his stage wife, Joab hardly seemed to notice her. The couple rarely spoke to each other and never touched. There were no kisses and no holding hands. No affection at all. They were the least emotive and the most stiff on set. Joanna wasn't surprised there were no bedroom scenes in this family show, but they did appear an exceptionally detached couple. What had been going on behind the scenes at *Butterfield Farm*?

TEN

THERE FOLLOWED MORE than a fortnight's peace. The Leek Police Force breathed a sigh of relief and continued with their other, slightly more mundane work. There was plenty to keep them occupied. Drugs had started appearing in one of the secondary schools, and the entire Force wanted to find the source. Some of them had children of their own there, which made the case even more poignant and the feelings ran high. Trouble was, in the drugs business, finding a dealer was like cutting off the head of the Hydra. Others simply opened up shop. It could seem like a lose/lose situation, that you were never going to win the battle. But they still needed to try. What worried them all was a youngster trying to have a bit of adventure and losing their life for it.

Joanna and Mike, in particular, were involved in tracking down the dealers and the sources, which meant long hours talking to chemists. Most drugs had a chemical 'fingerprint' which could be traced back to their original sources. But Joanna hadn't been able to get Timony Weeks and her peculiar problems out of her mind, and had run a check on the silver Merc. It belonged to an accountant from Monmouth, which didn't ring any alarm bells. Maybe he specialized in 'entertainment law'. The vet had confirmed Mark Fask's findings—that poor old Tuptim had had her neck wrung before being pinned to the pretty front door of Butterfield Farm. Timmis and McBrine hadn't been idle either. They'd spoken to the two farmers whose land was adjacent to Timony, and also to Frank and Millie Rossington, the couple who did the garden and the housework. None of them could shed any light on the cat's fate. Joanna typed out a detailed report and filed it on her computer. She had a feeling that when Timony Weeks and Diana Tong returned from their holiday things just might blow up again. She hoped not but wanted to be prepared for it. And so, like a guilty conscience, the bizarre events at Butterfield stayed at the back of her mind to fill any idle moments.

They were just getting used to this new state of affairs when on a Friday evening in February the whole thing blew apart, and the case turned into something completely different.

Friday, February 10, 6 p.m.

JOANNA WAS JUST thinking of packing up for the day and heading home. She slightly hoped that she and Matthew would go into Leek for a curry. She could almost smell it already and taste the sharp spices against her palate. She was salivating in anticipation. Instead…the phone rang and it was an apologetic desk sergeant. He might have guessed she had been planning her evening.

'Sorry, Inspector.' Everyone in the station knew she hated being called ma'am. Joanna or Inspector was how she liked to be addressed. And in general they stuck to it.

'What is it, Alderley?'

'I thought you'd want to know that a Mrs Rossington has just rung reporting a break-in at Butterfield Farm.'

For a moment Joanna couldn't think what a Mrs Rossington had to do with Butterfield Farm. Then she remembered: Timony Weeks' cleaning lady, Millie, other half of Frank. 'Is she still on the line?'

'Yes. I told her to hang on.'

'Put her through, will you.' Already she was wondering, *what now?*

Millie Rossington's voice was querulous as she spoke. 'There's been a break-in here,' she said. 'Frank and I were passing and we thought as we hadn't been in this week we'd better just check that everything was all right. As we drove up we could see the kitchen window was broken. I looked through and there was glass all over the floor. I know you police like everything kept just so but we had to come in to use the phone as our mobiles don't work here. We've been ever so careful not to touch anything. We thought we'd better not spoil the evidence.' There was an element of self-satisfaction in her voice. She was patting herself on her shoulder for her forensic awareness.

Joanna gave a mental, *Thank you, CSI.* 'Good,' she said, coat already half slipped on. 'Stay where you are, Mrs Rossington. I'll be over right away.'

Korpanski had already left for the evening so instead she took PC Phil Scott and WPC Dawn Critchlow, making a call to the SOCOs as she left. It was, after all, a crime scene for at least the second time. The question was, how serious was this crime? A petty burglar, realizing the place was empty? Or was there a connection with the strange events that had disturbed the two women since the new year? Did someone know that the house would be empty? She filled the two officers in on some sketchy detail as she drove along the nar-

row moorlands roads. It was pitch black now, the few
blinks of light coming from the isolated farmsteads.
The rest of the moorland was an inky black canvas. It
was exactly this sort of night, crystal clear and frosty,
that can make you feel that pollution is a million miles
away and pity the people who live in cities, forced to
inhale dirtier air. It even tasted different out here. It was
like comparing spring water with tap water.

Dawn Critchlow didn't appreciate the icy blast in
her face, so reluctantly Joanna had to keep the window closed and shut out the sharp magic of the night.

'Sounds an odd case,' Dawn commented prosaically.

Joanna smiled at her. 'You don't know how odd,' she
said. 'I couldn't begin to tell you.' She wouldn't know
where—or when—to start. In nineteen sixty when a
child star was born or at any other of the points when
Timony Weeks' life had mimicked a TV soap?

Phil Scott blew out a puffing breath. 'Don't know
what the Force is comin' to,' he said grumpily. 'Sometimes I wonder. Half the day you're cooped up in a
speed wagon tryin' to catch the unwary motorist and
the rest of the time you're lookin' into Who Killed The
Cat?' He ran his fingers through his hair. 'It's not what
I joined up to, ma'am, findin' out who's left the toilet
seat up.'

Joanna ignored the *ma'am*. 'Well it looks like a burglary this time,' she said. 'That suit you better, Scott?'

'Yeah. S'pose so.'

The three of them chuckled as they turned down the
track that led to the farm.

Like the beam from a lighthouse the lights of Butterfield guided them in across the dark sea, descending
into the trough of the valley. The elderly Volvo, silhou-

etted in the drive, faced them, and behind that the Isuzu. They must have gone on holiday in the Qashqai. Phil Scott gave a low whistle as the floodlights flicked on in response to their arrival, turning night into day with their white intensity. 'What a lovely place. So this is what a part in the soaps earns you?' He started chuckling. 'Maybe I should have been an actor.'

Dawn Critchlow poked him in his expanding belly. 'With that?' But Joanna was distracted by his words. 'I'm not absolutely sure,' she said dubiously, 'where her money came from. She's had a few husbands, at least one of whom was wealthy. I think in the end it's been a combination of a successful career and marrying men with a bit of dosh.' She looked thoughtfully at the large and beautiful house. 'She certainly is worth a bob or two. It must be worth a million. Maybe two.'

Scott responded with another impressed whistle.

The Volvo faced out of the drive, ready to leave. The Rossingtons had obviously simply meant to glance around, not to stay, as Millie had intimated. The car wasn't even parked straight but slewed at an angle. They were peering out through the broken window as they pulled up. Most of the lights were on, as though they'd been so spooked they had lit every corner of Butterfield Farm.

Already Joanna was beginning question the situation. Why had they called to check on the property in the dark when it would have been so much easier to come by day, in the light? Butterfield wasn't on the road to anywhere so how could they say they had just been passing? The single track lane, down from the road, led nowhere else—only here. Two simple questions. What, she wondered, were the answers? Like most cases simple, pointless lies often covered up some not quite so pure motive.

As they reached the house the front door was opened.

'You go round the side,' Joanna said to Phil Scott. 'Keep an eye open for tyre tracks. Dawn and I will check out the house.'

She'd been right about the Rossingtons. They were goggle-eyed at being party to a real-life crime and, now the police had arrived, they were loving every minute of it. Barely concealing their excitement they led the officers through to the kitchen. The blast of freezing air hit them even before they reached the room. Inside the curtains billowed gently, wafting in the chill. Shards of glass peppered the floor. They trod carefully.

Phil Scott spoke to them through the window. 'Whoever it was has used quite a bit of force,' he said. 'They've splintered the frame as well.'

'Any sign of what they used?'

Scott searched around with his flashlight. 'Ah ha,' he said and held up a sledgehammer.

Joanna peered at it. 'Probably found it in one of the barns. Well, bag it up in case our burglar forgot to wear gloves.'

'Gotcha.' Scott grinned and carried on inspecting the outside of the property, his flashlight making pools of light dance around the yard in the dark corners the security lights couldn't reach.

Meanwhile, Dawn Critchlow was checking out the other downstairs rooms while Joanna studied the burglar's point of entry. There was a clear boot print on the inside window sill, and another on the draining board. The SOCOs would have something to work on. She took a good look around then spoke to the Rossingtons. 'Why did you call in so late?'

They looked guilty. 'We'd promised we'd look in at least once a week and we hadn't been near.' It was an explanation of sorts.

'Have you had time to look around and make a note of what's missing?'

Millie Rossington answered for both of them, Frank standing at her side, silent and frowning. 'I did have a quick look around,' Millie said, still with the same eagerness in her voice. 'The drawers in the dressing table have been pulled out. That's where Mrs Weeks kept her jewellery. But I don't really know what jewels she had. Some boxes have been thrown on the floor which I suppose contained stuff, but how valuable and what it was I don't know. I never looked inside,' she finished primly.

'Is anything else gone?'

'Her study has been turned upside down. Maybe they thought she kept money there. It's in a right mess, papers scattered all over the floor, but I don't know if anything has been taken. I feel awful, Inspector,' she confided. 'I should have come in the week to check up on things but with Mrs Weeks being away there didn't seem a lot of point. So I can't even tell you *when* it happened.'

'In the last couple of days, I think,' Joanna said, looking around. 'We've had a couple of heavy storms in the last week and a bit of snow but yesterday and today have been dry but cold. There isn't much sign of rain in here so I'd plump for in the last forty-eight hours.'

Apart from the glass on the floor the kitchen was untouched. Cupboards and drawers were closed. The room had simply been a mode of entry. Nothing more.

But the study was a different matter. Millie Rossington had been right. There had been a thorough search here. Papers were strewn all over the floor. Drawers were pulled out, their contents emptied. Books had been pulled down from the shelves and lay where they'd fallen. The computer was tipped over, the screen on its face on the floor.

Joanna turned to Millie Rossington. 'Did she keep money here?'

The cleaning woman looked flustered. 'I don't know,' she said, eyes flickering towards her husband who still stood, mute and watchful. 'I don't think Mrs Weeks kept a lot of money around the house. She paid us by standing order. I never saw her with any cash.'

'Hmm.' Joanna's mind was busy and, as she glanced at Dawn, she could see the same scepticism in the WPC's dark eyes.

They all trooped upstairs next. The burglars must have been in the property for some time. All the bedrooms had been disturbed, drawers pulled out, contents strewn all over the floor, wardrobe doors opened, even clothes, still on their hangers, flung around. Everywhere had a sense of urgency and disruption. Joanna had seen this many times before. It was an all too familiar scene. She knew the ways of burglars. Always in a hurry. In a hurry to get in, find the 'loot' and make their escape before someone found them. And that sense of urgency now permeated the entire house. She could almost hear the heavy breathing, the shouts, the flinging around of someone's personal possessions. They wandered through. The three bathrooms were the only spaces left untouched.

Joanna came to a decision. 'We'll need the SOCOs

here and Mrs Weeks will have to come back from her holiday and tell us exactly what's missing,' she said. 'Have we got a contact number for her?'

'I have,' Millie said. 'Shall I ring her now?'

'Why not?'

'Do *you* want to speak to her?'

'I'd better.'

Millie Rossington took a small notebook from her pocket, studied the entries, then slowly began to dial. The other end was picked up almost immediately and there followed a three-sided conversation, Timony Weeks' shrill voice piercing the air, Diana Tong's deep voice in the background and Millie Rossington doing her best to play things down and put some calm into the scene.

'They haven't done a lot of damage.'

Shrill shouts from Timony.

'It won't take me any time to clear it up, only the police want to know what's missing, Mrs Weeks.'

More shrill barks down the line and Millie continued with her soothing voice. 'They're going to send a scenes of crime team round and they'll take fingerprints and get any *evidence*.' (She spoke the word with great deliberation.)

Millie's reassurance didn't do a lot of good. From where she stood Joanna could hear the muted tones of Timony down the phone, hysterical and sobbing. In the end the phone was handed to Diana Tong, who sounded shaken but a great deal calmer, and Joanna took the phone from Millie Rossington's hands, which were still shaking with excitement, she suspected, rather than anxiety.

'It's DI Piercy here,' she said. 'We need you to come

back. We need to know what's been taken. And, of course, the property is currently unsecured.'

'We'll stay.' Frank Rossington had spoken at last. 'Till they come back.'

'That would be helpful,' Joanna admitted.

Diana's sensible voice came on the line again. 'We'll head back within the hour.'

'You're in…?'

'North Devon. It'll take us a few hours to get back to Butterfield but we'll leave straight away.'

'Just one question, Mrs Tong. There's no burglar alarm here?'

'What would be the point?' Diana Tong asked coolly. 'Who would hear it?'

Heaven help her, Joanna thought as she spoke again. 'You could have them connected to the police station.'

Diana's response was a snort. 'Four false alarms and you're disconnected.'

She was right. 'I'll call over in the morning,' Joanna said, 'and we'll get the scenes of crime team to pick up any evidence. They'll be along in the morning too.'

She handed the phone back to Millie Rossington, who agreed with her husband's offer. Perhaps they had guilty consciences about neglecting their employer's property. 'We'll be here, Mrs Tong,' she said, reassurance oozing out of every pore. 'We'll stay and wait for your return.' It seemed a good idea.

ELEVEN

Saturday, February 11, 8 a.m.

MATTHEW WAS NONE too pleased when she told him she had work to do. They had had the curry the night before but a few hours later than planned. He grumbled for a bit as she climbed out of bed, then said, 'What time do you think you'll finish?'

She took in the discontent on his face and responded with false brightness. 'I expect to be busy for most of the morning. I'm sorry.' She tried out her charm, sat down beside him and stroked his cheek, smiling at him and waiting for him to return it. She breathed in the spicy tang of his aftershave, felt the muscles in his arms tighten. She could feel his mood change and gave him a broad smile with more than a hint of flirtation. 'But I should be free this afternoon.'

'Good,' he said. 'Then we can go for a walk.'

'Perfect.' She kissed the last vestiges of grumpiness away from his mouth and felt it curve into a smile. Matthew didn't usually sulk for long.

Even as she opened the front door of Waterfall Cottage to let herself out and walked down the path to her car, she realized that it was a good day for a winter's walk. It was bright, crisp and not quite so cold as it had been lately. Spring whispered to reassure the countryside that it would return and melt the winter blues away. Soon. Soon.

The drive out to Butterfield was pure pleasure today, the air laundered clean by last night's frost. She only wished she had been on her bike. Apart from the odd slippery patch where the sun had not beamed it was a perfect day for a hard ride followed by a long wallow in a hot bath, scented and oiled.

The farm itself looked Beatrix Potter-esque, peaceful nestling in the valley. It hardly looked like the scene of a crime—even a minor one. This scene seemed a million miles away from sordid city theft, doors kicked in and television sets lugged down three flights of stairs, screaming police cars and deafening burglar alarms.

The three cars stood neatly side by side, the elderly Volvo looking even more ancient and scruffy when sandwiched between the sparkling Isuzu and the Qashqai. The Rossingtons must have kept to their word and stayed the night, or else returned to Butterfield very early this morning. Joanna switched the engine off and sat for a while, thinking.

Nothing about this case felt quite real: the people involved, the incidents. She almost felt, particularly with the farm deliberately mimicking the TV series, that even Butterfield itself was part of a deliberate illusion, a manufactured scenario. Joanna felt like a bit player, someone who had been written in to one of the more dramatic episodes of the soap rather than in real life. For the first time in her life she felt like a puppet, carried along and controlled by others—if not her body then her mind. She still wondered. Was all this about Timony being attention-seeking, wishing to return to the days when she had been *star of the show, pet of the people*?

Did she hanker after fame? Were these little tricks simply a way of getting her headlines back, to draw the public's attention and sympathy towards her once again and increase the value of her memoirs? Was she *using* the police to earn an extra half million or so? *Poor Timony, victim of a secret stalker.* It certainly had a ring to it but even the local paper had not, so far, been interested in running the story. Maybe now, with the burglary... But that would draw the wrong sort of attention, not from the book-buying public but the criminal fraternity. The stupid thing was that Joanna couldn't work it out for herself. Here she was, a detective of some years' experience and a psychology graduate to boot, and she didn't have a bloody clue whether Timony Weeks had invented these events and was using the police for her own ends. Deep down she felt uneasy, particularly by Timony's claim of 'grey, wraithlike' memories from her past attempting to surface. Could these somehow be linked to recent events? Was she really the victim of a sinister and secretive prankster? If so, where would they stop? *When* would they stop? These are the worst sorts of cases for the police. A murder and you could dive right in with all the resources you needed at your elbow. But this? Sheer frustration. Or was she looking into this too deeply, almost willing events to escalate further? She didn't know. But, as she chewed over recent goings-on, Joanna had to admit the story of Gerald Portmann's watch had a particularly pleasing ring to it. Even she could have penned the accompanying headlines. *Dead Man's Watch Found In Star's Bedroom!* And the lines underneath telling of the fact that the watch had been buried in Gerald's coffin only to magically reappear forty years later certainly had an Edgar

Allan Poe-esque ring to them. *The Pit and the Pendulum* or *The Fall of the House of Usher* or *The Premature Burial*. Take your pick.

And now there was the burglary. A simple enough crime, a broken window, probably valuables stolen. But this was completely different. Far more tangible, less reliant on Timony's testimony, particularly as she had been away at the time and not even been the one to discover it. That had been left to the humble Millie Rossington. But surely this was about gain rather than malice.

Even now Joanna was wondering… Was it possible that Timony Weeks and Diana Tong had not been in Devon earlier in the week but actually had been here, setting the scene for yet another dramatic event? That would make Diana Tong a colluder rather than victim/dogsbody. Somehow Joanna didn't think so. But the very fact that she was questioning in such minute detail made Joanna aware of how doubtful she was of every single 'fact' she had been fed.

She climbed out of the car, locked it and walked the few steps to the door. The truth was the only sort of person she could imagine hanging around Butterfield Farm to play these silly tricks was a histrionic and slightly mad actress. And the obvious answer to that was Timony. Joanna knew that it wasn't fair to assign a character simply because of a profession, but there was a powerful argument to support this theory. There would be no gain for anyone else. Joanna updated that statement. Now there *would* be gain. If jewellery had been stolen it would be worth something. It still didn't exclude Timony. She owned it anyway but there was bound to be an insurance payout. And so the theories and counter theories went round and round in Joanna's head.

She was just wondering again about Diana Tong's role in all this when she opened the door herself. And as Joanna looked at the calm and competent face she found it hard to believe that Mrs Tong would enjoy this drama. In fact, if anything, she looked slightly bored with it all. 'Good morning, Inspector,' she said. It looked as though the Rossingtons were just leaving. As Joanna faced Diana Tong they were emerging from the front door, saying their farewells to a stony-faced companion and an embarrassingly effusive Timony Weeks, who gave the odd noisy sob and hugged her cleaning woman. A quick glance at the Rossingtons' faces told Joanna that they were acutely embarrassed at this show of emotion. Frank hurried past her, head down.

Joanna watched them scuttle away like impatient crabs, climb into their car and drive off. As the Volvo moved up the track it passed the white SOCO van coming down. Things were moving forward.

Once the greetings and introductions were over it was time for business and Joanna became focused. 'I'd prefer it if you didn't tidy up just yet,' she said to the two women. 'The police photographer will want to take some pictures and the less you disturb the scene the more evidence we can collect and the greater chance we have of securing a conviction.'

Again, she appealed, 'You still don't have *any* idea who's behind this?'

Both women shook their heads. 'If we had,' Diana Tong said sharply and reprovingly, folding her arms, 'we would have told you long ago. We're fed up with all this attention. We don't want you coming out here all the time.' She finished with a bitter, 'We're perfectly aware that you resent it. We just want a quiet life.'

As do we all, Joanna thought, recalling the temptation of staying in bed with Matthew that morning.

Timony butted in peevishly. 'Diana's right,' she said, hands wafting in the air in dramatic appeal. 'All I want is to finish my memoirs and have a peaceful life out here.' She upped the drama and uttered her next lines in a deep drone. 'Alone with my memories, my *good* memories. That's all. Is it too much to ask?' Her eyes flickered upwards. Towards the heavens. Maybe they'd taught her that move in RADA but it seemed over the top in the Staffordshire moorlands.

'Apparently, yes,' Joanna said, slightly irritated by the woman and her expansive, arm-waving gestures. 'It is too much to ask.' She was wondering why she had a growing feeling of dislike towards her. Was it because something about her was insincere? Not just the falseness of the patently obvious plastic surgery or the stary eyes, not the plumped-up lips or even her overdramatic manner. It was the words she spoke and the emotions she pretended to feel. Maybe, she thought with a flash of clarity, it was the disparity between facial expression, or rather the lack of it, and the words she spoke, although with the surgery that couldn't be helped. Joanna looked at her closely. And caught something else. Something much more authentic. Flickering eyes, a quivering of the lips. Something real underneath the facade? So what was it? Fright?

But a second later Timony Weeks, actress, looked not vulnerable but amused. So Joanna was left to wonder whether it had been real terror she had seen in the woman's eyes. And to ask herself, once again, the question that refused to go away—was it all an act?

Diana Tong was watching, her face impassive, hands and body perfectly still, in stark contrast to her employer. Joanna analysed the atmosphere between them. She believed they were both perfectly aware of her scepticism and irritation. But did they care? Not really. As she and Diana Tong exchanged glances she wondered about the exact nature of her role. *Why* did she bury herself out here, devote her life to one woman she didn't seem to particularly like? Was she incredibly well paid? Was she here out of love for the actress, a sort of starstruck desire to be close, to be touched by celebrity and fame even though it was forty years out of date? Was she a sort of...fan? What exactly was the relationship between the two women—two women isolated in this lovely but very private world that they had carefully built up around them? It fascinated Joanna. But looking into Diana's bland face told her nothing. If Timony Weeks was flamboyant in her display of emotions, Diana Tong was the diametric opposite. Her emotions were buried so deep they were invisible. She was impossible to read. And lastly, Joanna wondered, why didn't she live here? She might want to escape Timony from time to time but it would have saved so much money. She was practically always here anyway.

Joanna was glad that Mark Fask had arrived and was already brushing aluminium fingerprint dust on the kitchen window frame. 'Nothing so far,' he responded to Joanna's unasked question. 'Nothing on the outside frames. Whoever it was must have worn gloves.' He grinned cheerfully at the two women. 'I'll want some specimens of yours,' he said, nodding at them, 'just to exclude them, you see.'

'Have you had a chance to look through and see what's missing?' Joanna addressed the question to Timony.

'Surprisingly little.' It was Diana's cool voice which answered.

Timony spoke up then. 'Some jewellery,' she said. 'I had a few really good pieces that Gerald had given me. A diamond necklace. Some lovely sapphires and an emerald and diamond brooch. A ruby bracelet, some rings and a watch. I have photographs,' she said helpfully, 'and the insurance documents.'

'Good,' both Fask and Joanna said in unison.

Timony was obviously trying to be helpful. 'I'll be able to make a proper list.'

'Thank you.'

As Mark came in through the front door Joanna followed him. 'Is this the work of a local burglar?'

'Could be.' But he was frowning. 'I'm not really sure. Things have been a bit quiet on that front since we banged up the Jellicoes last year. But there's always the odd chancer who'll have a go at these isolated country properties. Someone from Stoke or on a crime holiday from Liverpool or more likely Manchester. And they generally do quite well out of these raids.' He made a face. 'There's always stuff lying around. And this house, for all its isolation, is so easy to spy on from the road.'

'You noticed that too.'

Fask nodded.

'So you think it could have been an opportunistic burglary?'

'Possibly. And then there's the footpath.'

She almost laughed. 'Come on,' she said. 'People don't do a burglary halfway round their hike, then put the swag in their rucksacks.'

He grinned at her. 'I agree; it's unlikely. But…' He held up an index finger. 'The footpath does pass near the house. A hiker could easily have made a note of Butterfield then come back in the car.'

Joanna pursued her point. 'But surely this must be someone local—even to be out here.'

'More than likely,' he agreed in his ponderous way. 'But I'm keeping an open mind. Things are often not quite what they appear to be.'

'Tell me about it,' Joanna muttered. 'But there is one other thing. If the pieces they took are valuable they'll turn up on the open market, won't they?'

'If they're distinctive it's even more important that I track them down before they get broken up into individual gems and the gold, platinum and silver melted down. There are so many outlets these days for precious metals. Once that's done we'd have no hope of identifying any of the pieces, and that means you and I would be unlikely to secure a conviction. You know, Jo, most times it's the jewellery that leads us back to the criminal. All the collection of forensic evidence does is to link their presence to here in a court of law. The weak point is the Fence.' He grinned and made a joke of his own. 'More of a hurdle, really.'

'OK. You carry on. I'll have a word with them.'

The two women were huddled together on the sofa when Joanna re-entered the sitting room. They stopped speaking the moment they saw her. But they looked furtive, as though they had been discussing something they didn't want her to hear. In fact, they looked guilty, almost as though they had committed the burglary themselves. What on earth were they plotting? Joanna wondered as she smiled another hello with a twitch of her shoulders towards the scuffle throughout the house—the SOCOs doing their job. Was this an insurance scam? Joanna was tired of these cat and mouse games. She felt awkward.

'I'll be leaving now,' she said. 'Mr Fask will continue collecting evidence. Have you anything to add?'

Both women shook their heads.

'So if you can let me have the full list of missing property as soon as possible as well as any photographs and receipts I can circulate the details.'

As she left Joanna still couldn't shake off the feeling that Timony Weeks and her hard-faced companion were using her.

She glanced at her watch. 1.30 p.m. Matthew would be pleased. She hadn't stayed out late. And the day was as inviting as possible, clear, clean and frosty. They had a couple of hours' walking time before dark. And then she would cook for him. She could write up the report on the burglary first thing Monday morning.

Matthew was indeed pleased her work hadn't taken up the entire day. As she let herself in he put his finger over her lips. 'Not a word about work, Jo,' he pleaded. 'And no more watching any more of that dreadfully stilted programme. The word Butterfield,' he said, laughing in her face, 'is *verboten*.' She looked at the even teeth, the expression of merriment, this great way he had of loving her, teasing her, mocking and disciplining her all at the same time.

His face was full of happiness.

She giggled and said, 'So what shall we do with the afternoon?'

His eyes gleamed. 'I've got a couple of ideas,' he said. 'One of which is a little walk round the town and then over to Leekbrook. We can end up in the Belgian Bar and then stagger back home.'

'Matthew,' she said. 'It sounds perfect. One minute and I'll get changed.'

TWELVE

Monday, February 13, 8.30 a.m.

POLICE OFFICERS' REPORTS are meant to be factual, not stories full of ideas and conjecture. They are not supposed to display prejudices or preconceived ideas. Joanna had read the guidelines over and over again. Yet it was hard to keep her personal feelings out of the report on the break-in at Butterfield Farm.

She struggled to find words which did not reveal her instincts about the break-in and the persona involved. She had three goes at it but when she reread the report she thought how bland and uninspired it was. It didn't describe any of the flavour of the woman who lived alone in Butterfield Farm. It could have been any burglary on anyone, anywhere. Yet this was the police force the public demanded, free of prejudice or instinct, not influenced by chance sayings and accidental findings. Back to Plod, she thought resentfully, and away from Frost and Taggart. What the public wanted was a police force grey and unimaginative. OK, she thought. Let them have it.

She glanced through her emails. The forensic reports were, so far, disappointing. The burglars had left little usable trace evidence, no fingerprints, hair or anything else that could have led the Law straight back to the perpetrator. The footprints had proved to be Reebok

ZigActives, size nines. A popular shoe and a common size. Not much help there either and there was nothing in the footprints that marked them out, no gouge out of the sole, no unusual wear pattern. It was disheartening. More of a surprise and possibly a vital piece of evidence was the value and distinctiveness of the jewellery Timony had listed as stolen. There were eight pieces in all. A diamond necklace alone was valued at £5,000, an emerald and diamond brooch at £2,000. The entire value of the pieces came to a little over £20,000. Joanna stared at the list. Maybe these pieces would solve this part of the puzzle. As Fask had said, they were distinctive Art Deco—right up until the moment they were broken up into bits. She was disinclined to return to Butterfield but knew she should be assuring a sceptical Diana Tong that they were doing all they could to recover the property. It wasn't strictly the truth. The truth was that she was stuck. What they had done was circulate the photographs of the missing pieces. Now all they could do was sit back and hope that they had a lucky break, because she was right out of ideas. Timony had rung yesterday and put up a reward of £2,000 which, considering the alleged value of the pieces, struck Joanna as overgenerous, but even as she'd spoken she'd sensed that she didn't have much faith in its bearing fruit anyway—whatever the size of the reward. And by now Mike was thoroughly bored by the whole affair, which didn't help. He was much more interested in the gang of car thieves who were targeting top-of-the-range cars, Lexuses, Audis and Jaguars in particular. The tip-off was that they were being doctored somewhere in Manchester, engines re-identified and numbers obliterated. But two of the cars had tracker systems. One had been disabled by the thieves; the other had not been under the bonnet or in any of the usual places but behind the dashboard. So the net was closing in and Korpanski was getting caught up in the action. He was so happy he was humming as he arrived at work. Joanna could read his mind. This was real detective policing. Not pandering to some weirdo. She'd lost her buddy.

Tuesday, February 14, 8 a.m.

IT BEING VALENTINE'S DAY, Matthew had woken her early with a huge bunch of long-stemmed red roses and a very sentimental card which had a simple message. YOU, it said in giant letters, ARE MY LIFE.

She had stared at it, then at his face, which held love, hope and sentiment in equal amounts. She handed him her Valentine's Day card and knew it wouldn't measure up to his. A simple Happy Valentine To My Husband, against a black background and a shiny red heart. She'd felt an idiot buying it. 'I'll cook for you tonight,' she said and made a mental note to pick up a couple of fillet steaks and some salad.

But reading through the report a second time had rekindled her interest in Butterfield Farm, and reminded her of her wet and cold bike ride and Sunday's visitor. Perhaps she should look a little closer at Stuart Renshaw, accountant, date of birth January 21, 1966—maybe even ask some of the local force to visit him at his address in Monmouth. She scanned down the few further details. There was no criminal record apart from a speeding fine in 2008. Now she was involved in an investigation into a burglary as well as the killing of the cat she decided she could afford to take a risk. She dialled the number which she now knew from memory. As luck would have it, it was Timony herself who answered the phone in a soft, rather tentative voice. 'Hello?'

'It's Detective Inspector Piercy here.'

Any normal mortal who has been subjected to a series of events such as Timony had and then been relieved of some jewellery would at least have got curious at this contact, asked whether she had any news, caught the villains or recovered some of her possessions. Not Timony. She merely said, 'Yes?' in a guarded and suspicious tone.

'In response to the publicity generated by the jewellery theft,' she said, tongue in cheek, 'some walkers have reported seeing a silver Mercedes at Butterfield on the twenty-second of January.' She hesitated to allow her statement to sink in. 'I've checked and it isn't either of your cars.'

'Oh.' Timony's tone was even more guarded.

'We wondered if it might have some connection with the burglary,' Joanna said. 'Perhaps the thieves were...' police jargon wouldn't go amiss here, '...casing the joint.'

'Oh?'

'We have the registration number of the vehicle and have checked it out,' Joanna continued.

There was silence on the other end.

'It seems it belongs to a Stuart Renshaw.'

If the visitor was bona fide this was Timony's chance, but she did not respond. 'Do you know someone of that name? Is he a friend of yours? He's an accountant who comes from Monmouth.'

'I don't think so.' Timony sounded very hesitant.

Surely either you know or you don't, Joanna thought,

but didn't press the matter. 'He isn't someone you know?'

Timony gave a delicate laugh. 'Wait a minute,' she said. 'I do remember now. I know who he is. He's the... the son of a friend,' she came up with impressively quickly. And then as her story gathered detail, she added, 'He's done a bit of accountancy work for me. He was in the area and thought he'd pop by.'

'Oh, there we are then,' Joanna said. 'Not a suspect at all. Well, that's helpful.'

There was an awkward silence before Timony made an attempt to shut the conversation down. 'Was there anything else, Inspector?'

'No. Not at the moment. Thank you.' She couldn't resist adding, 'Oh dear—a dead end.'

There was no response on the other end of the line.

Joanna put the phone down thoughtfully, still uncertain what she'd learnt from the brief phone conversation. Should she follow this lead up or drop it? She glanced across at Korpanski. His chin was jutting out, his eyes drinking in the screen of his computer. He was making little thrusting movements with his head—a sure sign of excitement. He was completely absorbed. In a world of fast cars, exciting chases and every officer's favourite word. Arrests. On the screen she could see registration numbers of cars. No chance he would want to break off his investigation. Then she looked at the mountain of work ahead of her. Crimes generated nothing but paperwork, it seemed. Audits and number crunching, a whole ton of stuff fed to successive governments to prove that they were doing a great job on law and order and thus should be re-elected and re-elected. But as Joanna started filling in the online forms and paper versions she knew the heart was being drained out of policing. She'd loved the job so much she wanted it to return to the exciting life it had been. But for now Butterfield would have to sit on the back burner, behind other, more important crimes that were targeted for attention. This month's included car crime and drugs to minors. Maybe next month it would be burglary and then they could concentrate on retrieving Timony's jewellery.

But something happened that felt as strange as a stormy sea suddenly gone millpond calm.

Just like the fortnight before the burglary, the daily contacts stopped and as the days went by there were few developments, except that a ruby and opal ring that fitted the description had turned up at a London Antiques Fair, only to be denied by Timony as being hers. Timmis and McBrine called round to Butterfield a couple of times and reported that the farm was quiet and that there had been no further disturbances. Perhaps Timony was too busy with her memoirs to be ringing the police.

In those interim days only one thing happened to draw her attention back to Butterfield Farm. It seemed puzzling but insignificant. Roderick Beeston, the vet, rang her up on the twenty-third. After a brief preamble he came to the point. 'Fask asked me if I'd take a peek at your Burmese who met such a miserable end.' He forestalled her. 'Don't worry,' he said, 'I won't be billing you for the PM. I just did it out of interest really. I don't know if this fits in with your case,' he continued, 'but I ran a few toxicology tests on Tuptim.'

For a moment Joanna struggled to remember who exactly Tuptim was. Then she remembered. The cat. 'Go on,' she said. Surely as everything in this case was so puzzling one more twist couldn't make it more baffling?

'The cat was drugged,' he said, puzzled. 'Heavily. She would have been stuporous at the time of her, umm...' He struggled to find the right word and, as is so often when it is a struggle, found the wrong one. 'Demise,' he finally came up with.

'What was she drugged with?'

'A barbiturate. Plenty of it, too. She wouldn't have known a thing. She was practically anaesthetized.'

When Joanna didn't comment, he added: 'Don't know where this fits into your case, Jo, but it was a totally unexpected finding, I can tell you. I thought I'd better let you know.'

'Yes, thanks.'

After a bit more chit chat—Beeston was curious about the newly appointed chief superintendent—he rang off.

Leaving Joanna staring at her desk. Where did this fit in?

Wednesday, February 29, 11.30 a.m.

IT WAS THE first warm day of the year, sunny as the South of Spain, the temperatures equalling the Algarve thanks to the wind which breathed softly and warmly up over the entire British Isles. Taking advantage of such a beautiful day was a pair of hikers who had decided to explore part of the Staffordshire moorlands. And the route took them right past Butterfield Farm. Roger and Betsy Faulkener were a successful couple from London who had recently bought a holiday cottage in nearby Hartington, one of the prettiest villages around. They'd got up early that morning, had a hearty cooked full English breakfast and packed their ruck-sacks with ham and tomato sandwiches and a vacuum flask. It should have been a perfect day.

But as the farm they passed looked so pretty, quiet and the water well looked so picturesque, they made a mistake. They decided that their picnic spot should be just there, sitting on the step of the well, using the stone wall to support their backs. Strictly speaking, they knew perfectly well that they were off the footpath but the step made a comfortable seat, leaning against the wall, and most times no one really minded trespassers pro-vided they took their litter home. The worst that could happen, they decided, was a hostile wave of a walking stick and a snarl from a dog. Or so they thought.

They were halfway through their picnic when Roger Faulkener remarked to his wife that there was a strange smell in the vicinity. Was it possibly the stagnant water in the well, he wondered, or had an unfortunate animal fallen down and drowned, and with the advent of the unseasonably warm weather its body was now slowly decaying? They both peered over the rim to investigate. It was a very deep well; they could not see the bottom, only an oily black sheen which looked ominous. But the smell now was overpowering. And unmistakable. Something was rotting down there. Roger found his torch and shone it down. He picked up what looked like the top of a head with red hair, something which was still and only moved with the gentle swell of the water. He took a step back. 'I can't be sure,' he said in a shaky voice, 'but I think there might be a person down there.'

'What?'

Betsy took the torch from him and shone it down.

There definitely was *something* there. And to her it looked like human hair. 'If we're wrong I'm going to feel a right fool,' Roger said.

They glanced across the yard at the farmhouse. It looked still and abandoned, one car outside. 'Do you think we should…?' But neither of them was anxious to knock up the inhabitants and ask if they knew about the body down their well. The words sounded too melodramatic and unreal. Besides… They looked at each other. For all they knew…

And suddenly the isolation of the spot had caught up with them so they were uneasy.

Roger pulled out his mobile phone. 'Damn,' he said. 'No signal.'

They looked again at the pretty farmhouse, packed up their sandwiches and without communicating walked quickly back up the track until Roger had a service signal on his mobile.

'We could be wrong,' Betsy said just before he dialled. 'It could have been a—oh, I don't know, an old rug someone's thrown down.'

'We'll let the police sort out what it is,' Roger said sensibly and dialled 999. Something he'd been dying to do all his life, but the opportunity had never presented itself.

Until now.

Joanna listened to the desk sergeant's words and made her decision. For once she would not go haring round there. The sensible approach was to find out whether PCs Timmis and McBrine were in the vicinity. Luckily they weren't far away when the call came. They looked at one another and wondered. They'd been keeping an eye on the place ever since the first incidents had been reported back in January. They'd dropped by and introduced themselves to the inhabitants and left their contact details. They'd done drive-bys a couple of times a week, checked the comings and goings of the occupants and generally done good community police work. Their surveillance had been escalated following the burglary but they had never seen anything suspicious. No one from Butterfield had ever rung them. So gradually the two moorlands police had loosened their watchfulness, but the burglary had worried them. Although the entrance had been clumsy the thieves must have known that the occupant was away and that meant they had staked out the place. Was this the beginning of what the press called a crime spree? It looked that way.

Butterfield wasn't the sort of property that was usually targeted by a casual thief. It was too isolated, with only one way in and one way out. Too easy for the police to block an exit if a nosey passer-by happened to see them. And it was overlooked from the road. But if there was a gang targeting isolated country properties they'd be back if they weren't caught. If not to this property then to others in the area. Which affected them. This was their patch. And so they were wary. In the end both Josh Timmis and Saul McBrine, chewing through their sandwiches, sitting in the car and keeping an eye on the farm, had failed to decide which it was— amateur or professional. But they had agreed that only someone with local knowledge would have known that Timony Weeks kept jewellery at the farm. So when the hikers' story was relayed to them they listened with interest, turned the blue light on and screamed along the moorlands road.

Saul McBrine eyed his colleague, unable to resist a

smile. 'Nasty smell,' he said, 'coming from the well?' They exchanged amused glances. This was typical of the sort of panic call that came from Butterfield Farm.

Josh Timmis was already thinking. 'The well's not even on the walking track, is it? It's more than a hundred metres away. So what were they doing near enough to pick up a bad smell?' He pondered for a moment. 'They shouldn't have been on the property. They could have fallen in.' They both found this so hilariously funny that they chuckled intermittently all the way along the road.

The two hikers were waiting for them at the top of the track, sitting on a drystone wall, apparently not feeling cold and looking expectantly in their direction as the squad car slid to a halt. They were easily identifiable in their khaki shorts, huge boots and rucksacks, and worried expressions. They had waited at the top, the officers surmised, not wanting, apparently, to descend back into the valley. They were unmistakably of the breed of hardy hikers who frequented the moorlands most of the year round, but even they had been spooked. As they drew close the man held up a large mitten to stop them.

Josh McBrine rolled down the window. 'Mr and Mrs Faulkener?' This drew vigorous nods from the pair of them.

Timmis made an attempt to bring normality to the scene. 'Now what's this you think you've seen?'

'We can't be sure,' Betsy said, more dubious now than she had been initially, 'but we think there's something down the well.'

'It looked like a person,' her husband put in. 'The top of a head. I could see hair. Red, or maybe gingery.'

McBrine was alert. He watched carefully as Betsy Faulkener wrinkled her nose up and said, 'And it stinks. Awful. Awful.' She flapped her mittens in front of her nose as though to waft away the recalled smell.

'OK. Let's take a look, shall we? Want a ride?' Saul McBrine threw open the back door and the hikers scrambled in. Josh Timmis swivelled round in his seat. 'Better just clear it with the owner.'

'I don't think anyone's in.' Roger Faulkener spoke guiltily, his trespassing conscience pricked. McBrine glanced at him sharply in the rear-view mirror. The man was flushed with embarrassment. He could guess why. They hadn't knocked on the owner's door not only because they were trespassers but also because they had been frightened they would be alerting an axe-wielding murderer. He smothered a smile. In his opinion people watched too many of these horror movies. All the same, it was a good job they didn't know about the batty, hysterical woman who really lived there. That would have spooked them even more. And, of course, city dwellers—he took in the posh and little-used hiking gear, the big polished boots and expensive, Alpine mittens—were always uneasy in this underpopulated environment, however much they tried to pretend they liked it in 'The Wilds'. Well, well, well. He eyed the man. 'Londoners, are you?'

It was Betsy who answered for both of them. 'Yes,' she said, adding proudly, 'but we've bought a holiday cottage in Hartington.'

Thought so.

But McBrine said nothing. They'd reached the farm.

Josh Timmis banged on the front door. At first it appeared that the farm was deserted.

Then the door was pulled abruptly open by Diana Tong, who looked at the four of them with patent disapproval. 'Yes?' she said.

'These people,' McBrine managed, 'thought they saw something down your well.'

Diana's eyebrows were raised and she asked the obvious question. 'What were they doing peering down the well?'

Roger Faulkener stepped forward. 'We're really sorry,' he said. 'It looked so pretty.'

'And it's such a lovely day,' Betsy put in.

Her husband glanced at her, annoyed, and finished his defence. 'We thought we'd have a picnic sitting on the step.'

Diana Tong gave him a sideways look then said matter-of-factly, 'Well, then, we'd better have a look down the well, hadn't we.' She stepped outside, closing the door behind her.

Timmis and McBrine approached with caution. Ten yards away they caught the scent too; years of working in the police force had taught them both to recognize the stench of putrefaction. Whenever there was a world catastrophe they knew why everyone wore a mask. Whether it was 9/11, To-hoku, Sebrenica or a tiny Indian Ocean island affected by the 2004 tsunami, the stench was the same. They also knew that no mask in the world kept the smell from entering your nose, your mouth, your nasal passages, down into a heaving stomach and back up into your brain to surface and be recalled every single time you smelt *that smell* again. It was strong and pungent enough to draw vultures and carrion crows from five miles away, and disgusting enough to make police officers vomit. It was the stench of death which embedded itself in the memory. PC Timmis's police issue torch was more powerful than Roger Faulkener's. But like the hiker he peered right into the depths of the water and he, too, saw something that looked like luxuriant red hair.

Behind him, Diana Tong gasped.

THIRTEEN

Wednesday, February 29, 3 p.m.

IT TOOK AGES to get the police diver out. Diana Tong had
left them to inform Timony what was happening while
Timmis and McBrine had rung Joanna to inform *her*
what was going on. The Faulkeners hung around, partly
out of excitement and curiosity, but also because they
were uncertain whether they *could* go. And so the four
of them had spent an uncomfortable few hours sitting
around the kitchen table, the unwelcome guests of a
tight-lipped Diana Tong and an increasingly hysterical Timony whose odd, jerky movements and strange
throaty noises made them all think she was already having a breakdown. None of them referred to *whatever
was down the well*, though when they met each other's
eyes they knew that they all shared the same nightmare
and that the divers would pull out... It was too horrible
to contemplate. But none of them actually voiced their
fears. They skated around the subject like profession-
als, weaving and ducking away from the issue. It was
as though by not referring to it they could pretend it did
not exist, that nothing was down there and that whoever
or whatever it was would simply disappear. Vaporize.

Resentment and possibly worry stiffening her demeanour even more, Diana Tong poured them all a
second and then a third cup of tea without asking any-

one if they actually wanted one. It was only by putting their hands over their cups that the Faulkners avoided a fourth cup. The silence was broken only by the cheerful wail of the kettle as it reached the boil on the Aga. No one tended to it straight away. The paralysis apparently extended even to Diana Tong. And Timony Weeks was motionless apart from the tremor which vibrated her hands. So the kitchen became increasingly hot and steamy as the kettle boiled away, furiously demanding attention and not getting it. In the end Diana Tong's gaze swivelled towards it and she made another pot of tea, but no one would have another cup. After all that tea Betsy Faulkener wanted to go to the loo but she felt embarrassed to ask where it was. Besides, there was some safety in numbers, some measure of comfort in the fact that they were all together, even in this hot and humid kitchen. She and Roger both wanted to escape the embarrassing comradeship but didn't quite dare. Most of all, Betsy didn't want to be separated from Roger, who was the only person here that she really trusted, apart from the two policemen, who were sitting a little apart from the others, watching the proceedings with a wooden stare at each of them in turn, followed by a cynical twist of the lips and a silent exchange of views. While Roger simply stared back when they looked at him, Betsy had the horrid feeling that they could see right through her, even to the bulging bladder, but that they would still interpret her discomfort as guilt. She took a sneaky glance at the two women, the tiny, fragile-looking Mrs Weeks with the tough-looking woman who seemed like her minder. They were odd enough. Then when she recalled *the thing* floating in the black water she decided that she didn't want to be led along the corridor by either of them to locate the toilet. In spite of the idyllic location and luxurious interior of the farm there was a disturbing atmosphere here. So Betsy ignored the protestations of her bladder and crossed her legs. Roger stood up, restless, and she joined him. They both felt the need to escape the claustrophobia of the room and finally wandered around the outside of the farmhouse, trying to forget why they were here and playing the fantasy game of: if they sold their Fulham flat and their newly acquired holiday cottage they could afford to live here and somehow stretch the distance to their jobs, which were both in central London. They felt more comfortable out here than in the kitchen, back in their laced-up, muddy boots and fleeces, even though when the wind shifted direction, wafting the scent towards them, they were reminded why their walk had been cut short. At least out here they could talk normally. Inside, after the usual chat about jobs and how lovely and unspoilt the Staffordshire moorlands were, the conversation had dried up to an awkward, desiccated silence. But after twenty minutes they'd grown cold and returned to the kitchen.

Just as things were getting really embarrassing a white van with a pink stripe appeared at the top of the track and started to descend slowly, scraping to a halt outside the front door. Once the introductions were over the diver squinted at the dark patch that broke up the oily surface, sniffed the air, joked that he wouldn't need his deep-sea diving equipment today and started tugging on his wet suit. There followed a long delay while an elaborate but presumably safe system of ropes and pulleys was set up by his buddy and he could be lowered into the well to retrieve whatever was down there.

PCs Timmis and McBrine watched curiously. Working high up in the moorlands meant that this was only their second encounter with the Police Diving Unit. Their first had been when a girl had been found floating face down in the Mermaid's Pool, which had proved not to be bottomless but nevertheless was no less sinister for all that. Roger and Betsy clung to each other as though they were about to be parted on the Titanic but watched the events with unblinking fascination while Diana and Timony stood back in the doorway, looking as though they might dart inside any moment and bolt the door behind them if anything nasty came up. The clunking and clinking started up and the diver was lowered.

There was some splashing and the silky sound of oily water moving around, then a rush of water as something was drawn up.

It was red, hairy, dripping, and landed with a soft *splosh* on the plastic sheet, laid down to receive whatever was in the well. Then the diver went back down again and something much bigger and even more foul-smelling was pulled out, water pouring from its putrefying body. That, too, was laid on the sheet of plastic.

They all stared, unable to comprehend or make any sense of what their eyes were registering.

It was PC Josh Timmis who broke the silence with an embarrassed chuckle. 'Call me a country bumpkin,' he said slowly, 'if you like. But that,' he indicated the larger item, 'looks like a dead badger to me. And as for that…' He touched the second item with the toe of his police issue policeman's boot. 'I'm no fashion expert but it looks like a wig.'

Betsy was tempted to laugh. This was a joke. They'd

been taken in by this? She put her hand over her mouth and giggled. Then she looked back at the two women.

It might be a joke to her but it wasn't to Mrs Weeks, who was shrinking away from the sodden red hair, her eyes wide and staring as though it truly was a person's head. Then Betsy Faulkner realized something else. The wig was exactly the same style, length and colour as Timony Weeks' hair. She looked from one to the other and realized why the woman was bordering on hysterical.

A few minutes later the diver was cranked back up. 'No worries,' he said, unable to resist a smirk. 'Nothing more there. No dirty deeds. Just a badger.'

'Fallen into the well?' Roger Faulkner stepped forward. 'Isn't that a bit odd?'

'Suppose it is,' the diver acceded grudgingly. 'But these things 'appen.'

'And the wig?' Roger persisted.

'Someone must have got tired of it.'

Timmis and McBrine were arguing amongst themselves who should be the one to report back to Detective Inspector Piercy, who had already been tried enough by this place.

The diver's mate couldn't resist it. 'Ding Dong Bell,' he said loudly to everyone's annoyance.

Timmis and McBrine were still in a bad mood and couldn't resist muttering to each other that they'd known this would prove to be nothing—again. Basically they'd been 'had' and were cross with themselves. But most of all with these two infuriating women.

'Hardly the crime of the century,' Saul McBrine grumbled, feeling particularly exposed, but his colleague who had sharp eyes and bloodhound tenacity had, like Betsy Faulkener, made the connection between the dripping wig and Timony Weeks. Rather than draw attention to it he squirrelled the knowledge away. Then he looked closer at the bloated corpse of the badger. Holding a scarf over his nose and mouth he moved nearer. 'Looks more like roadkill to me,' he said. 'Think I'll take that along to the vet.' He paused. 'Just to make sure.'

His colleague looked puzzled. 'Sure of what?'

'Use your noddle,' Timmis said softly so no one else could hear. 'Why would you put a dead badger down a well right in front of a house? They're just left by the road or picked up by a badger's charity. Not this,' he said.

'Yeah, but what does it matter?'

'I just want to be sure that the badger was dead when he was dropped into the well.'

His mate looked sceptical.

'All I do know,' Timmis muttered, 'is that it does matter. Someone is playing silly buggers both with those two.' He indicated the two women in the doorway. 'And with us.'

Timony was watching the proceedings frozen in horror, eyes wide, hands in front of her face, covering her nose and mouth as though to block the smell of the rotting corpse and perhaps to suppress any scream. As the bloated body was sealed in a body bag she shrank back. 'First Tuptim,' she said to Diana, 'then this. Next it'll be me.'

'Nonsense, don't be ridiculous,' Diana said in her usual matter-of-fact voice, but she too looked shaken. 'The policeman must be wrong,' she said, quickly searching for a better explanation. 'The badger must have been injured, crawled down the track and fallen in,' she said. 'Poor thing was looking for somewhere to lick its wounds and lost its footing. That's all.'

'And if you believe that...' Timony said scornfully.

It was a few hours before everyone had left the two inhabitants of Butterfield alone. The two hikers had cadged a lift back into Leek in the police car. It was late now and starting to get dark. They'd lost their appetite for a moorlands hike anyway and didn't fancy finishing their walk so McBrine took pity on them and dropped them off in Hartington. They were subdued all the way back, sitting hand in hand in the back of the police car without exchanging a word. Neither of them could decide whether they felt silly for having raised the alarm, or good citizens. Certainly they were disappointed that it had not turned out to be the manhunt they had expected. They were puzzled about the redheaded wig and upset to have seen the badger in such an advanced stage of decay. Timmis, too, was quiet all the way back to the station. 'Think I'll just have a word with Inspector Piercy,' he muttered thoughtfully when they turned into the station car park.

He was concise in his report but Joanna's eyes were serious as she listened to all that he said. 'So,' she said briskly. 'Another false alarm. Another trick.'

Timmis simply waited for her to make a decision, glad it wasn't his job. 'OK,' she said finally, 'I'll authorize a post-mortem but you do realize whatever the result is it won't prove anything. It is just a badger.'

Though he didn't quite agree with her Timmis nodded and made a last attempt to put his point over. 'I realize that, Inspector,' he said, 'but putting all the facts together, the odd occurrences that, let's face it, we've all taken with a pinch of salt, then the burglary and the business about the cat and now this. *Something's* going on out there. I'm sure. I don't pretend to know quite what it is but something is very, very wrong.' Joanna listened carefully to her junior officer, noting the concern in his face. She liked working with colleagues like this, whether senior or junior to her: people who enjoyed their work, worked hard at it, were willing to go out on a limb and take chances, people who had ideas and weren't afraid to act on them. People with intelligence and curiosity. It was what you needed. She smiled to herself. That and a good dollop of intuition.

She assured him she had heard his comments and would be thinking about how to act next. He left looking a little less troubled.

When PC Josh Timmis had left the room she waited for Mike Korpanski to return to the office and spent an hour holed up with him, listening to his opinions too. It was hard to get him to focus on anything but the luxury cars but he was listening, his dark eyes thoughtful, his brow furrowed. Finally he spoke. 'There's a lot going on here, Jo,' he said. 'Loads of stuff from the past. Who knows if there's a stalker or something? People are odd when it comes to fame. Even years later.' He looked up. 'Someone's out to rattle her, at the very least.'

'And if they're just going to keep playing silly games we probably don't need to take it all too seriously. But if it becomes more serious than a burglary we're going to wish we'd stepped in a bit sooner. Listened a bit harder.'

It was exactly what Joanna was scared of, but she was utterly powerless. What next? she wondered.

FOURTEEN

Friday, March 2, 2 p.m.

SHE DIDN'T HAVE long to wait to find out. Lunchtime brought a phone call from Roderick Beeston. 'You're investigating a very odd case here, Joanna,' he said accusingly, as though she was personally responsible. 'First a pretty nasty thing that happened to that poor cat,' he said, 'and now Brock the badger.'

'And what exactly did happen to Brock the badger?'

'Probably run over,' he said. 'I didn't do a full post-mortem.' He chuckled. 'I didn't think your budget would stretch to it. Especially with Chief Superintendent Rush about to *hop on your tail*. Or is it *breathe down your neck*?'

'Don't remind me,' she said darkly. 'I'm trying not to think about it.'

Even Beeston the jaunty couldn't think up a suitable response to that. He continued with his report. 'I did do some X-rays, though. His back leg and a couple of ribs were broken. Brock wouldn't have been able to walk very far.'

'He wasn't…'

'Alive when he was dropped in the well? Thankfully, no. There was no water in his lungs. No. Poor chap— not that the average dairy or beef farmer would agree with me. They're very hot on the badger being responsible for most of the bovine TB. But Brock had probably been dead for a couple of days before he floated to the top of the well and began to stink quite so badly.' She could sense he was smiling. 'Good job the weather's been so cold,' he said. 'Otherwise the stink could have been terrible. They're big animals. Take ages to decompose and they'd have looked for ages to find the source of the smell.'

'Quite. So what was the point…?'

'Exactly what I've been asking myself,' Beeston said. 'Left under a hedge his corpse would have rotted away and been subject to predation. To put it down a well is plain odd. I can only think it was to intimidate the ladies who live at the farm. Someone must want them out of there.'

On the other end of the line Joanna was frowning. 'But why?'

'If I'm thinking of the right place,' Beeston said, 'it is a rather splendid house and in a beautiful location.'

'Beautiful and splendid enough to play so many odd dirty tricks for?'

Beeston hesitated. When his response came it was smooth and predictable. 'Luckily it isn't my job to solve your cases, Joanna,' he said, 'only to feed you the salient facts. There is one other explanation.'

'Go on.'

'Well, it is just possible that someone simply ran him over and disposed of the body down the well.'

'It isn't a criminal offence to run over a badger,' Joanna pointed out. 'It wouldn't make sense to do that.'

Beeston paused then chuckled. 'None of it makes sense,' he said, adding, 'the bill will be sent to you as usual.'

Joanna smiled.

The day Roderick Beeston forgot his vet's bill would be the day the Polar ice caps melted. He was a meticulous businessman.

Her mood was sober when she'd thanked the vet and put the phone down. Things were escalating but she wasn't sure in which direction. She was still worried about where it would all end. What had initially appeared like histrionics had developed into assaults on animals and a burglary. What next? She had the horrid feeling that she knew but it was as though she was watching it on television, powerless to change the future. As though she was in a nightmare and could merely watch without any ability to participate.

All she knew was that this wasn't over yet. This very real drama unfolding in front of her had snagged her, so instead of being able to give other 'more important' cases her full attention she was constantly being drawn back, yet again, towards Butterfield Farm. She sighed as she emailed Beeston's bills to the accounts manager. She might be able to wangle the badger one, pretending she'd wondered if it had TB, but she sensed that Chief Superintendent Rush would sniff this out as a red herring. He was no fool.

She was going to get this one wrong however cunningly she played it. And just when Rush was about to take up his post. It gave her a sinking feeling.

Korpanski was not at all keen on abandoning his luxury car case, even temporarily, to visit Butterfield again. It was obviously the last place on earth he wanted to visit and he was progressing well in his investigation. He'd homed in on a large garage in Manchester which had extensive workshops at its rear. This, he believed, was where the cars were 'processed' and made 'clean' for resale. He scowled at her, tore his eyes very slowly and reluctantly from his computer screen and gave a deep, heart-rending sigh so Joanna took pity on him, let him off the hook and took DS Hannah Beardmore instead. She couldn't deprive Korpanski of his moment of triumph. So she patted his broad shoulders, resisted the temptation to ruffle the black hair and left him to it.

Anyway, she liked working with DS Hannah Beardmore. The soft voice and gentle nature of the DS would be a welcome change from Korpanski's fiery questions. Even considering the assaults on the animals he'd made it quite clear he found her interest prurient, claiming it had become an obsession, her questions irrelevant and repetitive, her interest in the sixties soap odd, and the repeated visits a complete overreaction to a handful of happenings and the animals' sad fates. But the drum beat constantly in Joanna's mind was, *What next? What next? What next?* Where do the roots of all this attention lie? Who is the intended victim here, what is the intended outcome? As the events compounded was something more serious lurking around the corner, something she could and should prevent? And the main question: who was behind it?

There was desperation in Diana Tong's eyes as she pulled the door open even before they had had a chance to knock. She must have been watching the lane, perhaps sensing that someone from Leek Police would visit today. 'We tried,' she said softly. 'We did try to escape, get away. But we were pulled back by the burglary.' Her eyes skittered around the garden, rested a while on the tape that fluttered around the well. 'We just had to return.' She put her face close to Joanna's. 'I am not a fanciful woman, Inspector,' she said, her mouth quivering slightly, 'but I have a feeling that a trap is being set. There is an atmosphere of evil around here, enveloping Butterfield in a poisonous smog. Someone is…' She frowned and thought but she couldn't find the words. 'And they will win. You understand? They—will—win.' She stood back, flat against the door. 'You'd better come in,' she said.

Joanna had the feeling that Timony had taken or been given a tranquillizer. Either that or she had drowned her sorrows in alcohol. Or maybe a bit of both. 'Finished,' she said without further explanation. Her speech was slurred, her laptop on her desk. She was rubbing her temples and staring down at the screen. As she registered Joanna's arrival her eyes were bloodshot and her gait, when she rose to greet them, was unsteady. She must have realized that Joanna was looking at her with suspicion and cognition because she quickly apologized for her state. 'I'm so sorry,' she said. 'I'm so upset. First Tuptim and now this.' Her tears started to flow and she reached for a tissue. 'Tuptim was my child,' she said finally. 'My family. The only thing that loved me. My beautiful, beautiful pet.'

Diana Tong hovered in the background, still looking anxious but adding nothing. Joanna might have expected her to intervene, contradict her employer's statement, assure Timony that she would always have her. But of course, the relationship between the two women was much more complicated than that. Diana was watching Timony with a look of despair, as though she were a hopeless case, as though she did not know quite what to do with her.

Joanna stopped herself from saying that she could

always get another cat to love her. Even she, who was no cat lover, realized that this would appear as insensitive as telling a woman who has just miscarried that she can always have another baby. The comparison caused her heart to skip an extra beat as she recalled her own miscarriage a few years ago.

Hannah Beardmore was already sitting with her arm around the actress, soothing her with words, the equivalent of 'There, there.' Given the sensitivity of the situation Joanna was extra glad that she had brought the DS rather than Korpanski. He would have contributed precisely zero sympathy. This was exactly what was needed here, a little bit of kindness.

'It was only a badger that was down your well,' she said. 'He was almost certainly already dead when his body was deposited there.'

No reaction from either woman. No *by whom*?

She continued. 'And the other was a wig.' She fixed her gaze on Timony Weeks' head. 'Red hair,' she said. 'Just like...'

For the first time ever Timony Weeks looked embarrassed. 'Sometimes,' she began, swallowed, and spoke again, 'if I don't get to a hairdresser...'

'What she's trying to say,' Diana snapped, 'is that she sometimes wears a wig when her hair's a mess. It belonged to her.'

Behind her Joanna heard a tiny snort. She didn't turn around and meet her sergeant's eyes or she would have joined her. Instead she drew in a deep breath. 'When we've checked that it doesn't hold any significant forensic evidence we'll return it to you,' she said.

Timony was shaking her head. 'No, don't,' she said. 'I don't want it back.'

Joanna should have pointed out that it was her property, and that she should sign a disclaimer if she didn't want it returned, but she desisted.

Diana still watched from the doorway. No offer of tea or coffee. But Joanna sensed that her attention was not focused on either her or DS Hannah Beardmore. All her attention was concentrated on her friend, her employer. She was looking at her with such a look of pity as would have melted a granite heart. Joanna watched and realized that she actually knew very little about these women's personal history besides the essential facts. What glued them together? Diana Tong had another house, lived elsewhere, *was* or *had been* married. Family? All she knew about Timony was in the public domain. She could have gathered it all from a newspaper over the years. But Diana Tong was a closed book.

A secret. Maybe it was time to find out a little more.

She decided to start at the beginning, even if that meant covering some of the details Mike had already gleaned when he'd interviewed Diana. 'How long have you two been together?' She dropped the question into the room and wondered why Diana Tong's face looked at her now with respect, as though she had been wondering when the police would get around to asking these pertinent questions. She made no reference to her conversation with Mike.

'Years,' she said, entering the room now and, with a quick glance at Timony, sitting down on the sofa. *At ease.* 'I was Timony's wardrobe mistress from the mid-sixties. I had been...' She looked a little sheepish. 'I'd been quite a fan of Butterfield Farm from when it started. In nineteen sixty-four they were looking for someone to take over as Timony's guardian and I was lucky enough to get my dream job.' She smiled. 'Timony interviewed me herself and we hit it off right away. From then on I was her wardrobe mistress, personal secretary and sometimes bodyguard.'

'You were there when the fan assaulted her?'

There was a quick look between the two women, as though each was checking her story against the other's. 'I wasn't there that night,' Diana said carefully. 'Timony had another escort to and from the studio as well as a chauffeur, so she didn't really need me. I wasn't there,' she said firmly.

'You were there at the time of her first marriage,' Joanna proceeded conversationally, 'to Gerald?' Joanna was aware that DS Beardmore was taking all this down in note form.

Timony's face grew sentimental. 'Gerald,' she said, 'was my first real love.'

Joanna watched her carefully. True? Or false? She directed her next question to Diana Tong.

'And what did you think of Gerald?'

Diana Tong was startled by the question. She had not expected this. Her eyes looked a little panicked. Then she quickly recovered herself. 'He was,' she said, 'a perfect gentleman.'

Timony looked pleased with the answer.

Joanna was not so sure. 'Two of Timony's husbands are still alive,' she continued. 'We wondered whether…'

'Possibly three,' Diana corrected.

'Remind me,' Joanna said. 'Husband number two?'

'Sol Brannigan,' Timony inserted. 'We were hardly together.' A quick glance at Diana for confirmation. 'Were we? I don't know why he married me. For a bet, I sometimes thought. He began so charming, so attentive, and ended up completely not caring. He also stole from me,' she sighed, 'to fund his gambling habit, I suppose, which doesn't excuse his thieving.' She lay back on the sofa, arms outstretched. 'I was glad to see the back of him, truth be known.' Her *young* face looked tired. 'He frightened me. I never could prove it but I always believed that some of the money he splashed around was the proceeds of organized crime. I told you he was a gangster. I knew for a fact that he had guns in our house during the brief time we were together. Strange people used to call at odd times of the day or night. And always I would be ordered out of the room. They threatened me never to listen at the door or pick up the phone during a conversation and eavesdrop. I felt very threatened and it was something he enjoyed.' She half closed her eyes. 'He loved having power over people.' Her eyes flicked wide open as though she was baring her soul. 'If you want my opinion these…tricks… and the cruelty towards Tuptim fit in with his character all too well. He liked to irritate and intimidate me. Blowing cigarette smoke into the kitchen was typical of Sol.' She paused. Smiled. 'And then along came Robert Weeks. So unfortunate he was actually married to my friend, Carmen.' She gave a wicked smile. 'But then I'm not the sort to let another woman stand in my way. *He* fell in love with *me*,' she said, as though trying to convince her audience to believe this story. 'Robert Weeks. Absolutely lovely. *Gorgeous-looking*. Terrific actor. He'd hoped eventually to be a director. We married in '77 and were happy. We had almost thirteen good years together but, cruelly, cancer took him from me.' Her words might be clichéd theatre but Joanna had no doubt at all that the sorrow behind Robert

Weeks' death was genuine. Then Timony's face broke
into a mischievous smile. 'Carmen never forgave me,'
she said. 'She turned up at his funeral, made an awful
song and dance about things. She had to be taken out.
Such an embarrassment.'

'Is Carmen Weeks still alive?'

Timony shrugged. 'I don't know,' she said. 'The
last I heard she was living in Dubai.' Her expression
changed. 'I told you, Inspector, I'm not a good person
when bad things happen to me. And I'm definitely not
good on my own. I married on the rebound the following year. Another mistake. Adrian MacWilliam was a
lot younger than me.'

Mentally Joanna was compiling a list of potential
'perps'. So far it contained two fairly unlikely persona, Sol Brannigan and Carmen Weeks. 'Go on,' she
prompted.

'When Robert died I was desperate not to be alone
but I knew within a month that Adrian was a big mistake. He was a drinker.' Her mouth tightened, became
almost prim.

'Is Adrian still alive?'

Timony shrugged. 'Haven't a clue,' she said, 'but I
would think so. He would only be in his early fifties.'

Joanna glanced across the room at Diana Tong. 'Do
you know?'

Mrs Tong was patently surprised at the question. It
startled her. 'No,' she said bluntly. 'Should I?'

'He might be,' Timony interspersed, 'although he
was a drunk. And they don't tend to live such very long
lives, do they?'

'I suppose not. That is if they don't mend their ways,'
Joanna said. 'And then there was Mr Van Eelen.'

'Another mistake.' She gave a sudden radiant smile. 'I have had an eventful life, haven't I, Inspector?'

No one could disagree with this statement. Joanna nodded, as did Hannah Beardmore.

'I've made enemies.'

Joanna nodded again, warily.

And Timony suddenly burst out: 'What do I have to do to convince you? I know there is a threat, Inspector. I want you to find out where it's coming from and do something about it. Stop it, please.'

'But I don't know where to look,' Joanna said, exasperated. 'I've asked repeatedly who you think might be behind this, and for any information or clues you might have. All I get is vague answers. I need your help.'

Both women sat stony-faced, silent.

Joanna appealed to Diana Tong. 'Was an arrest made of the fan who went for her?'

'I believe he went to Broadmoor. He was insane.

'And his name was Dariel,' she confirmed.

'Yes,' Timony put in, shuddering. 'Paul Dariel. Look, I really don't want to have to remember all this. He stalked and threatened me for years. I was just a child, thrust into the limelight, living in an artificial world created by a television series. I was thirteen years old when he started but my mental age was much, much younger.' Her face assumed an odd, faraway look. 'I'm beginning to realize that now. Emotionally I really was Lily, the little girl who lived at Butterfield Farm with her mummy, daddy and her brothers. When, all of a sudden, I am catapulted from a Disney view of the world into a Tarantino or a Kubrick, I was, emotionally, unable to deal with it. It was horrible. The studio didn't seem interested in my mental state.' She looked across

at her friend sentimentally. 'If I hadn't had Diana I don't
know what would have happened. Just to keep me working the studio had assured me that they didn't take the
threat seriously and I think that provoked Dariel. I didn't
have the skills to convince them how frightened I was.
I was just a child.' She dropped her hands into her lap.
'Completely naive. It is only now, as I have been writing
my memoirs and reliving the times, that I see just how
simple I was. How I saw things in my own way, without understanding.' Timony half smiled. 'You mustn't
forget, Inspector, that all this was a very long time ago.
Dariel himself would now be in his sixties. He may still
be in Broadmoor. He may even be dead.'

Joanna nodded. She could easily find out about Paul
Dariel. 'So five years after you broke up with Adrian
MacWilliam you married Rolf Van Eelen.'

Timony lost the anxious, distraught look and appeared mischievous again. 'Ah, the lovely Rolf. A toy
boy,' she said, not without affection. 'I was forty-eight.
He was thirty-one and gorgeous. A hotel porter.' She
chuckled. 'Not stupid, but uneducated. I really should
have known better, shouldn't I? He just loved the fame,
the attention, the money, the jet-setting lifestyle. He
loved all that. Trouble was he didn't love me.'

Joanna smiled in sympathy. Hannah Beardmore was
looking completely fascinated. Goggle-eyed, her mouth
slightly open, she looked like a star-struck fan herself.
The story of Timony Weeks' life was a long way from
her own moorlands background, her husband's infidel-
ity and the subsequent battle scars.

'And you're still…' Joanna asked the actress delicately.

There was a twinkle in her eyes as she replied. 'Yes.

Still legally married. Never bothered with a divorce. Every now and then Rolf is in contact, tries to touch me for some money, like Sol. Sometimes I send it, sometimes I don't. Depends how I feel. I told you he went off with a sort of friend of mine, Trixy. Good name for her, though I'd have spelt it differently. Glamorous blonde with no breasts—at least, not real ones. An actress who'd been married to a very wealthy financier who conveniently died not two years after they'd been married.'

'Are they still together?'

'Far as I know.'

'And where was he when you last heard from him?'

'Appropriately enough, Marbella,' Timony said with a snort. 'But that was a few years ago now. I haven't heard anything for two or three years.'

'Has he ever threatened you if you don't give him money?'

'Gracious, no,' Timony said with another snort. 'For all his faults Rolf was not an evil character, not like Sol. He was not a bully and certainly not violent. He would wheedle stuff out of you. He was greedy. And boy, did he like the women. He had an extraordinary appetite for them.' She gave a secretive smile. 'And I don't mean just sexually, Inspector. He just loved women's company. Any age, blondes, brunettes, redheads, old, young, fat, thin, tall, short. He just liked women.' Her eyebrows moved up a difficult fraction of an inch. 'Particularly rich ones in expensive clothes, smelling of expensive perfume, high maintenance and generous with their assets.' She laughed. 'He was born to be a gigolo, that one.'

'Mmm,' Joanna said. 'Should I be interested?'

'Unfortunately, probably not,' Timony said. 'None of these mind games is in his character.'

'And then there is this long-lost sister who also stalked you for years. Freeman mentioned her.'

Timony sat up, wary.

'Did you, in fact, have a sister?'

'No.'

'So…?'

'It went on for years, from the early sixties. Letters. All made up. The woman was a fantasist. She was always trying to meet up with me. She was a creepy one. Sent me photographs of my "family". MY family!' For the first time Timony seemed angry.

'Did you ever find out who she really was?'

'No.'

'What did she want out of you?'

'For us to be together, loving sisters, that sort of thing.' She grimaced and continued. 'It was quite scary, you know, not knowing who she was. She could have been anyone. And I never knew where or how the next approach would be. There were telephone calls that went dead when I answered, tears and threats down the phone, presents I didn't want, cheap stuff.'

'Similar to what's happening to you now,' Joanna observed. 'Edgy practical jokes.'

'Yes, except…' Timony frowned. 'Except that these seem more subtle. Cleverer. And more sinister. I knew what my "sister" wanted. Money. Love, affection, an acknowledgement of our supposed relationship. With this I don't know what this person wants.' Her small fist beat the palm of her hand. 'My life or my sanity, I suspect.'

Joanna frowned. The interview was quickly descending into the usual melodrama.

'You can't imagine how famous I was,' Timony said, her eyes bulging. 'I was like Liz Taylor or Sophia Loren. People wanted a piece of me.' She leaned forward. 'Have you seen any of it? It's available in DVD.'

'I've seen a couple of episodes,' Joanna said, awkward that she couldn't honestly claim to have either enjoyed it or been impressed by it. So she fixed on a smile. Timony looked pleased anyway and Joanna proceeded towards the point of her reference.

'It seems to me that you've deliberately recreated Butterfield Farm here, even down to the well.'

'The well was already here, Inspector,' Timony said severely. 'It belonged to the cottage that was here before. It was its water source.'

'But the farm itself is a faithful copy,' Joanna persisted.

'Yes.' Timony appeared to feel the need to defend her actions. 'My childhood was special and wonderful. I was happy then. When I was settling for my autumn days it was natural to want to return to those memories.' But Joanna detected a glimmer of uncertainty, as though she was trying to convince herself. Had Timony remembered something from her past?

'Quite so.' Joanna avoided mention of the fact that all the windows faced north-east keeping watch over the approach.

She had one more avenue she wanted to explore. 'I suppose,' she said slowly, 'that it's possible the two farmers whose land borders yours might want you out of here?'

'Why ever would they?' Timony looked genuinely surprised at the suggestion. 'I don't own much land

and they couldn't afford Butterfield.' There was hint of snobbishness about her. 'It would be out of their league.'

Joanna rose. She hadn't really learnt anything that would help either explain or put an end to the events surrounding Butterfield Farm.

She had one last request. 'I wonder,' she said awkwardly. 'Would you mind?'

Timony looked up, puzzled.

'My chief superintendent's sister is a fan of yours. I wonder…would you mind signing an autograph for her?'

With a practised hand Timony fished a photograph out of the drawer, turned it over and looked up. 'What's her name?'

FIFTEEN

Wednesday, March 14, 8 a.m.

'SHE'S BEEN SHOT.'

Sergeant Alderley did a quick double take. 'Sorry?'

'She's been shot,' the female voice repeated, distressed and irritated.

'Sorry, ma'am, who is it speaking?'

The voice got angrier and louder. 'I'd have thought you'd have recognized *my* bloody voice by now.'

Unfortunately Sergeant Alderley did—only too well. 'Who's been shot, Mrs Tong?' He paused. 'It *is* Mrs Tong, isn't it?'

'Ye-es.' The voice cracked with emotion. 'I blame myself. I left her late last night at Butterfield because I needed to go home. But when I woke this morning I had a dreadful feeling. I tried to ring her first thing but there was no answer so I came round straight away. I thought she was asleep at first. Maybe just tired. I tried to wake her. And then I realized.' She gulped. 'She's dead. Please, please, please send someone round. Now.' There was a quick gasp of a sob. 'Please come. Hurry.' She was panicking now, falling off the edge. In freefall, a scream only microseconds away.

'Are you sure she's dead? Shall I call an ambulance?'

Diana Tong was quickly regaining her composure.

'She's dead, poor lamb. But please, do hurry. I'm frightened.'

Alderley's finger was already on the button, his mind working furiously to make sense of this latest development. She's *been* shot, she'd said. Not she's shot herself. *Been* shot could only mean one thing. Timony Weeks had been murdered. The stalker had finally got to her. The thought sobered him up quickly as he took stock of the situation. There had been the teasing threats, the gentle reminding of her vulnerability, the intimidation. And now this. 'Are there signs of a break-in?'

'I—I haven't looked around. I came straight upstairs. Please hurry.'

The hairs on the back of Alderley's neck began to prickle. 'Is it possible someone is still in the property?'

'It's possible.' There was a stiff, sudden pause as Diana Tong considered the possibility. 'At least…'

Alderley could imagine her glancing behind her, looking over one shoulder then the other. Checking around the room, seeing her own face palely reflected in the mirror. Another face behind it? But he had something else to consider. 'You say she's been shot. You're absolutely sure she's dead?'

'I—I think so.'

'Do you know where to look for a carotid pulse, Mrs Tong?'

'Yes.'

'I'll stay on the line. See if you can feel it.'

There was silence. Alderley heard footsteps padding across a thick carpet, each step a muffled tread. Then—

'I can't feel a pulse.' She snatched in a sob. 'She feels cool.'

'And she's not breathing?'

'No.' Another noisy gulp. 'I'm quite sure she's dead.'

'Right. Listen carefully.'

'Yes.'

He could hear her nervousness bouncing off the walls, a frightened voice in an empty room in an isolated house, empty apart from a corpse. Alderley could practically feel the mounting terror and was glad he wasn't there. Knowing the location of Butterfield Farm, he was aware that she couldn't exactly 'pop' next door and wait for the emergency services over a cup of hot, sweet tea with the neighbours. He felt chilled. 'I want you to leave the house,' he instructed. 'Get into your car and drive to the top of the track.' He was all too familiar with the geography of the place from descriptions the officers had fed him after their numerous wasted attendances. 'We'll send someone round straightaway with an ambulance.'

He felt he should add some more practical advice to focus her mind, keep her thinking rationally. 'Don't touch anything. Don't disturb anything or move anything. Someone will be with you as soon as possible.' Alderley was shaken himself. He felt a measure of responsibility. He'd spoken to both women, living and dead, on numerous occasions. He knew just how much of a nuisance the pair of them had been. He'd managed to put them off once or twice. Now he felt guilty for the dismissal that must have come across.

'OK.' She was recovering herself. 'Thank you.'

'Right you are.'

Alderley quickly called for an ambulance, then looked at his watch: 8.05 a.m. His problem was the word *shot*. The police had a rigid protocol for everything, particularly incidents where firearms were involved. Luckily for him, because of the number of shotgun licences held by farmers both Timmis and McBrine had both been through firearms training. And they were due in any moment now. Should he summon them? He was in a quandary. Then the door opened and Detective Inspector Piercy walked right in. An answer to his prayers.

'Good morning.' Joanna gave Alderley a wide smile until she realized he wasn't returning it. Her face stiffened.

'Mrs Tong's just rang,' he said. 'She says Mrs Weeks has been shot.'

There is a moment when catastrophe flaps towards you on big ugly, black wings. You hear its harsh caw and hope it is a nightmare and that you will soon wake up, your head burrowed into a soft pillow but then it flaps its filthy feathers and gory beak right into your face. There would be no relieved waking moment because this was no nightmare but reality. The worst had happened. She half closed her eyes, gave a tiny shake of her head as though to block it out. 'What?'

Alderley didn't need to repeat his information but he did anyway.

'Timony Weeks is dead?'

'According to Mrs Tong.'

Then she picked up. 'Shot, you say?'

'Timmis and McBrine are due in.' Right on cue, the pair arrived. Alderley briefed them and Joanna gave a nod of consent. She'd broken the rules once and got away with it under Chief Superintendent Arthur Colclough's indulgent eye. She couldn't afford the same mistake again, particularly with Rush taking over. The two officers fastened their Kevlar jackets and prepared to leave in the armed response vehicle.

'OK. Good, so far. Have you called an ambulance just in case?' Both knew it was a forlorn hope. From what Diana had said, Timony was dead.

'Yes, ma'am.'

'Is anyone else is on their way?'

'I thought Hesketh-Brown. He's been on nights, ma'am.' Alderley knew she would excuse the forbidden epithet—if she'd even heard it.

'Anyone else around?'

'Jason, ma'am.' This time he did correct himself. 'Inspector.'

Joanna couldn't stop herself from smiling. Jason (bright) Spark. With his carroty hair, prominent ears, bouncy enthusiasm and boundless energy. What would they do without these willing specials who were so keen to join the Force that they gave up their time for nothing? Nothing except the feathery promise that one day there *might* be a vacancy so one day they would be true and proper, fully paid up, real live coppers. Unlike many in the Force Joanna had respect for these ambitious and generous wannabe policemen. 'Don't bother Hesketh-Brown,' she said to Sergeant Alderley. 'Let him get home. He has enough broken nights with little Tanya. We'll take Jason. And he'd better be kitted out with a bulletproof vest. Is Korpanski in yet?'

Mike swaggered in, grinning from ear to ear, only stopping when he saw Joanna and Alderley's faces, their expressions mirrored. After years in the Force he could read the signs only too well. 'What's up?'

'Have a guess,' she said slowly. 'Butterfield.'

Korpanski began with a, 'Not ag...' then searched her face and drew in a long, deep breath. 'I'll drive,' he said.

It was a measure of how well Sergeant Mike Korpanski knew his inspector that he didn't ask what was happening or whether he really needed to be there. He simply pulled his car keys out of his jacket pocket and trotted by her side, Jason following so terrier-close he nipped their heels a time or two.

Ahead of them they could hear the police siren of the armed response vehicle, driven crazily through the moorland, as alien a sound as a burst of Hawaiian *Aloha* music.

As Korpanski drove Joanna filled him in on the little detail she knew. His face was initially grim, then worried. He knew the implications as well as she did. Unusually, in this murder case, they had been involved well *before* the crime. And it didn't take much imagination to anticipate the recriminations—that good policing would have prevented this tragedy. Mike chewed over the knowledge as he drove fast, blue light and siren carving the way through the early morning traffic.

When they arrived Timmis and McBrine had already entered the house, checked there was no hidden gunman and, with their weapons, returned to the ARV. It stood at the gate, its blue light still strobing, brightening up the dingy panorama. The ambulance was behind them, its blue light shining impatiently into the car's interior. Ahead of them the door was open, exposing a bright interior. Mike Korpanski did a spectacular handbrake skid right in front. Diana Tong had walked ahead of them back down along the track to the farm. She met them in the hall with an unhappy, accusatory look. Her face was haggard, the features sunk so she looked ten years older than at their last encounter. 'I told you. I warned you,' she said bitterly, her hand gripping Joanna's arm

so hard it would surely bruise. 'I *knew* something bad
would happen. It's been building up. Getting worse. I
could *feel* it inching closer. *We* could sense that…' she
paused, 'even if you couldn't.' Her eyes were wide and
staring. 'I know I was sceptical at first but even after
poor Tuptim was murdered you still didn't believe us.
You just thought we were making the whole thing up.
Lying. A pair of histrionic old bags. And now?' There
was something uncontrolled in her features. A sort of
mania. 'Now it's happened, Inspector.' Her gaze went
from Joanna to Mike Korpanski's stolid and reassur-
ing figure before sliding over Jason Spark as though
wondering who the hell he was. 'All our nightmares
manifested,' she said, her face uncomfortably close to
Joanna's. Joanna gritted her teeth. She'd expected this.
'So who do you think is behind this, Mrs Tong?' she
asked coolly. 'You haven't given us any idea of either
motive or perpetrator. We've had no constructive help
from either of you—only a series of minor and repeated
call-outs.' She changed her voice. 'The scent of smoke,
the toilet seat left up, a watch magicked from a grave, a
dead mouse, a dead cat. A dead badger. People supposedly watching you, things moved, things turning up.'

'There was the cat,' Diana Tong cut in. 'If nothing
before that had warned you surely that should have?
And the burglary.' Her voice was furious. 'Did you
think we imagined that? And then Timony's wig,' she
said tightly, but grief almost turning the words into a
wail. 'Down the well with a dead animal. Did you not
think these were warnings, Inspector? Warnings.' She
drew breath—at last. 'Well,' she said, in a tone half
of triumph and half of resignation, 'now you can see.
Come and have a look for yourself. At the damage.' She

led the way up the oak staircase, each step a hollow sound, turning back only once to accuse Joanna again. 'You should have prevented this. You should have protected her.' Joanna blew her cheeks out, giving a half smile of encouragement to Jason Spark, who was still, puppy-like, at her heels. She didn't want him to be put off joining the force by this altercation. He may as well get used to the public's complaints. They were becoming ever more common.

The paramedics were standing respectfully back from the bed, hands folded in front of them, their contribution over—not that it had ever begun. They watched silently as Joanna and Mike entered. One of them gave her a slow nod of recognition; the other had queasy eyes fixed on the central figure on the king-sized bed, queen of the tableau. Joanna looked down with pity. Timony Weeks looked so tiny, the duvet folded down to her waist. She must have been shot while asleep. She lay on her back, pools of blood staining her pink silk nightdress, one small bullet hole torn through the silk, a neat black scorch mark ringing the wound.

Joanna was no weapons expert but even she knew that the gun must have been held right up against the material. There was one such mark to her chest and another to her head—a neat, red *bindi* in the centre of her forehead and a stream of dried blood which meandered across it, passing her eyelid, down her cheek, towards her ear. It was—it had been—a neat execution with, at a guess, a small bore gun, probably a pistol. There were pools of blood beneath her on sheets which were quite unruffled, her head looking comfortable on the pillow. Her eyes were not quite shut so she looked as though she might be peeping out from beneath her lids.

Her mouth had dropped open, in a round 'O' of surprise. Or perhaps she hadn't woken but had slept right through and the open mouth was a snore. She looked young, even younger than in real life, girlish almost, small as a child and definitely dead. Without a doubt. Joanna looked around her. The bedroom was neat, clean and ordered apart from the stained figure in the centre. There was a pleasant but not overpowering scent of a sweet floral perfume which overlay the equally sweet and sickly scent of fresh blood which, like putrefaction, is instantly identifiable. The paramedics shifted their weight. Korpanski was standing still as a statue. Jason Sparks' mouth was open, his eyes round and fixed on Timony Weeks. And Joanna had the strangest sensation of complete unreality—that Timony Weeks was playing her final and most famous part.

They heard steps bounding up the stairs and a second later Mark Fask was peering around the doorway. 'Got a doctor coming, have we?' he asked, businesslike. Then adding as though to justify his matter-of-fact words, 'We'll need to get her certified and the coroner's permission before we can move her. Then we can get started.' He spoke with a certain amount of relish for the job ahead of him. Diana Tong put her hand to her mouth but Joanna would have sworn the word *ghoul* had already escaped her lips.

'Alderley's been dealing with it,' she responded to the SOCO. 'He'll have contacted someone. They'll be on their way over, though there isn't much room for doubt here. Even I can tell you she's dead all right. And unless anyone can spot the weapon and work out how she managed both the chest and the head wound we'll be looking at murder with a firearm, probably a handgun.'

Korpanski's eyes flickered in her direction, a nod of agreement, while Jason Sparks' face went red with excitement.

Fask practically rubbed his hands together. 'Right. OK. We'll be getting a move on downstairs then.'

In spite of the stillness of the central character in the opulent bedroom, Joanna knew there was a lot of work to be done here. Fask was right. The sooner they got started the better. 'Fine,' she said. 'Take Jason with you. Give him some instruction on the preservation of crime scenes and basic evidence collection, will you?' Sparks' face lit up like a high-voltage lamp. He was thrilled. It was a reward for all his hard, unstinting work. He trotted at the SOCO's heels. Joanna listened to them clop down the stairs then looked across at Mike. She knew that his brain, like hers, would already be filing through the list of potential suspects. It was a long enough list. Ex-husbands x 3, crazy fan, long-lost sister, jealous colleague, covetous neighbours. And then there was...' Her gaze swivelled around to Diana Tong, who stood, paralysed, in the doorway, fingers combing through her hair in a gesture of panic while her eyes darted around the room, evaluating. Unless she was a better actress than her mistress, this was, surely, nothing to do with her? She looked grief-struck. Genuinely. Her mouth was working, her face stricken. Two deep lines of sorrow scored either side of her mouth, which sagged miserably. Her eyelids looked heavy and two frown lines corrugated her forehead. Heartbroken. Bereft, as though anticipating the bleakness of her life ahead.

Joanna eyed her for a minute or two then went downstairs to don a forensic paper suit, snap on a pair of latex gloves, paper overshoes and finally the hat. It was a most unbecoming outfit which billowed out unflatteringly over her rear. No policewoman in such a suit would ever dare to ask the, *'Does my bum look big in this?'* question. There was only one truthful answer.

But at least no one wearing this uniform could sully a crime scene with so much as a stray hair. So, like most unbecoming outfits, it was…practical. Suitably garbed, Joanna returned to the bedroom and continued looking around for anything that might help, Korpanski mirroring both her clothes and her actions. They looked like a pair of spacemen wading around the scene. A photographer was already recording it before anything was disturbed.

Through the bedroom was a surprisingly spacious bathroom, so pure white it dazzled the eyes like a snow scene on a bright day. Lit by overhead high-voltage spotlights, it was as clinical as an operating theatre. It smelt of bleach, which added to the surgical ambience. Joanna opened the mirrored bathroom cabinet. Inside was the usual paraphernalia of cosmetics, toiletries and cotton Q tips plus, more interestingly, a half-empty bottle of Temazepam. She eyed it and mentally added it to the list of items she wanted Fask to brush his fingerprint dust over.

She returned to the bedroom and pulled open the top drawer of the chest of drawers. Amazingly, it held even more boxes of jewellery. The burglars had obviously missed these. So even after the burglary Timony had not wanted for adornment. Joanna opened the nearest one and found a pearl necklace in an antique, satin-lined box, a New Bond Street jeweller's name in gold lettering. She eyed it thoughtfully. Since Matthew had given her the briefest of lectures on pearls when he had presented her with her beautiful black pearl engagement ring, she knew enough about them to know that the irregularity and slight difference between their colour meant that these were genuine 1930s South Sea pearls. Not freshwater farmed or 'cultured' but the real McCoy, dived for and matched up to form this lovely three-strand necklace. Two cream-coloured strands either side of a strand of the palest pink. They were beautiful.

She returned them to the box. They were probably 1930s and must be worth a few hundred pounds. They weren't terribly distinctive so would be easily saleable. So far it appeared that the motive had not been a second robbery.

Korpanski was watching her and she knew from the look in his deep, dark eyes that his thoughts were tracking along the same path as hers. They had worked together on so many cases they could read each other's minds.

Why had Timony been murdered? They looked around them for an answer, at the luxurious bedroom, at the diminutive body in the bed and at the concerned companion. Then at the walls which were hung with press photographs, heavily posed, of the cast of Butterfield Farm. *The Happiest Family in the World*, was the strapline. Fact or Fiction? Joanna wandered around the room, looking at the pictures, wondering if these held the explanation.

Amusingly there were even a series of wedding pictures: the first of a child bride and her paternalistic father figure, his arms protectively around her, more tightly than you would expect in such an image. Why had she needed protection? The walls didn't answer. Joanna moved on. Some of the photographs came with corresponding newspaper headlines: *Timony Shore Marries Again*. And yet, as Joanna moved closer to take a look around the walls, she could sense that DS Mike Korpanski was focusing on the picture of her first nuptials, the one picture where she looked particularly vulnerable and frightened.

'What was she frightened of?' She sensed Korpanski was speaking to himself rather than directing the question at her. She stepped back. Had Timony Weeks spent her entire life being frightened, feeling threatened?

Joanna reflected that in all the call-outs when Timony really had seemed frightened, she had never seriously indicated any idea as to who was behind all this. Even her early suggestion of Sol had sounded weak. The threat had been nebulous, a cloud which hovered over her rather than one particular person. And that had communicated to the police, sowing the seed that her fear might not be real but imagined. Joanna frowned, met Korpanski's eyes again and saw his face twist into an equally frustrated scowl. They both knew that even with Timony's murder they were no nearer an explanation or an understanding. They were nowhere.

She watched Fask brush the surfaces with grey fingerprint powder. And so the work began. Perhaps this time it would lead somewhere. It *had* to lead somewhere.

Matthew turned up half an hour later. She heard him talking to Fask downstairs and looked over the bannisters to see him being handed the obligatory white forensic paper suit. Not even Matthew could look smart in that. She met him at the top of the stairs and, in spite of the circumstances, was unable to keep her grin away, a grin which was both welcoming and intimate as she queried his presence. 'How come *you're* here, Matt?'

His eyes were warm. Soft moss green. 'Well,' he said, crinkling them with his grin, 'I knew this was your case, so when the call came in I volunteered.'

'I'm so glad you are here,' she said softly. 'Although there probably isn't much doubt about the cause of death I haven't a clue why the crime was committed or by whom.'

His eyes twinkled. 'So, cause of death, Jo?'

'Well, she was shot twice—once in the head and the other in the chest. I thought that might…'

Matthew nodded and looked towards the room. 'She was in bed when…?'

'Yes.'

'Asleep?'

'She doesn't appear to have moved,' Joanna replied cautiously. She knew Matthew's work, had watched his thorough and structured approach ever since she had first met him. This meticulous method of working had been one of the things that had attracted her to him. He checked everything, took nothing for granted, and questioned even his own findings more than once.

'So, I'm about to meet your actress,' he said, snapping on the pair of Latex gloves.

'You are,' she said and led him into the bedroom. Korpanski nodded a hello. There had always been a guarded relationship between the two men. They skirted each other as warily as a couple of wrestlers who had just entered the fray.

Matthew's eyes took in the scene 360 degrees and she knew his memory would be as accurate as a photograph. He looked last at the still, small figure in the bed. Drew back the covers and touched the blood, dried as stiff as starch, with his index fingertip. He nodded then pulled out a thermometer. 'Give us a hand, Jo.'

Reluctantly she helped roll Timony Weeks over. She had never quite lost her aversion to dead bodies but Matthew, as a pathologist, was oblivious. He regarded them as a string of clues. Which, she supposed, was what Timony was—to him. Not a person but a collection of evidence which he would painstakingly tease out of her inert body. He didn't so much dehumanize them as detach them from the living person they had once been. But then he never had met Timony Weeks alive.

He read the thermometer. Picked up a limb and dropped it again, glanced at his watch, took an ambient temperature reading then looked up with a grin. 'Some time in the night? Will that do you?'

Matthew was well aware of the conflict between the police, who would like an exact time of death, down to the very minute, to help their enquiries, and the pathologist, who knew just what an inexact science estimating the time of death was. She raised her eyebrows and he continued, 'It's ten now. She's probably been dead for eight or so hours. There's some rigor mortis in the jaw but it hasn't really spread. I would doubt it was earlier than midnight and certainly not later than six this morning. I'm really sorry, Jo.' His face was warm and friendly, lit by an impish grin. 'I'd love to say five past midnight last night or whatever but you know I'd be sticking my neck out too far.'

She nodded and looked down, pondering the still figure and the story behind her intimidation and now murder. She almost wondered whether they would ever know the truth. She doubted herself, however much evidence Matthew extracted from the post-mortem. The police photographer was, even now, photographing the scene, but would those photographs ever be perused by a jury? Would an accused stand in the dock?

Matthew continued making his notes. 'By the way,' he said, 'I suspect she'd had a heavy dose of barbiturates so didn't know anything about this. I'll do some toxicology and stuff. But that's my instinct.'

'Thank you, Matt.' She was so tempted to kiss him. Why not? He was her husband.

But Korpanski was standing by and Matthew was starting to pack his equipment away. 'Get her down to the morgue, Jo.' He gave another swift glance at his watch. 'I might even be able to fit her in this afternoon. I'll have a word with the coroner.'

As she watched his long legs skitter down the stairs, two at a time, Joanna was suddenly aware that a) he was her husband, b) he was very attractive and c) how many cases they had now worked on together. She vividly remembered the first, an old lady bludgeoned to death, the work of a half-crazed cocaine addict who didn't even remember the crime when he had been charged. The woman had been small and frail and in her nineties. It had been an ignominious death for a much-loved great-grandmother for a profit of exactly £7.80. Both the post-mortem and the crime itself had upset her so much she had felt nauseous and had moved to the sink, hoping no one would notice her weakness. And then, embarrassingly, in the mirror over the sink, she had caught Matthew Levin's merry green eyes laughing at her. The rest, as they say, was history. A long and complicated one at that.

She caught up with him downstairs as he was just

about to leave. 'Jo?' he queried. And then he must have caught a hint of the conflict she was struggling with. 'Hey,' he said, bending down and kissing her very lightly on the cheek. 'It isn't your fault, you know. You couldn't have known it would come to this.'

She was relieved that he understood some of what she was going through. 'I know but—I feel involved; in some way I do feel responsible.' She met his eyes. 'If I'd done this or that differently. Maybe listened a bit harder.' She frowned. 'I worry I'll never know who's responsible. And now there's this ghastly Superintendent Rush who's bound to rub in everything I do wrong.'

'Hey,' Matthew said again, 'come on. Be fair. Give the man a chance. You don't know he's that bad.'

'His reputation goes before him,' she said grumpily. 'And it's bad all right.' She made a face. 'Believe me, Matt,' she said, meeting his eyes, looking for more reassurance.

'OK.' He patted her arm. 'Maybe he is. I'll see you later. Do you want to attend the PM?'

'I don't know.' She managed a watery smile. 'Yes and no. I feel I knew her.'

'OK.' He started finding a number on his mobile. Joanna knew he would be ringing the coroner, moving things forward without delay. Matthew could be a very impatient man. She let him carry on with his call and climbed the stairs again. Korpanski was standing at the bedroom door conferring with two uniformed police.

She stood for a moment looking down on the bed. 'She's so small, isn't she, Mike? Quite tiny. Fragile. Vulnerable.' And all of a sudden something welled up inside her, something more like anger and frustration than grief. 'Why didn't you leave here?' Joanna appealed to her corpse. 'Why didn't you go away after the burglary? Why did you stay?'

'What, leave and give in to it?' Joanna jumped at Diana Tong's harsh voice behind her.

She moved away from the bed and studied the companion's face. Hard, inscrutable, hostile, unreadable and unfathomable. Something was troubling her that was even deeper than the murder of a friend and employer. Joanna regarded her without speaking, feeling that Diana held some answers. Answers that she might well not share.

Diana Tong was oblivious to Joanna's feelings. She was gazing at something to the side of the bed. Joanna followed the line of her gaze. At the side of the bed, on a small cabinet, a photograph was propped up. It was a publicity photograph, similar to the one she had signed yesterday for Elizabeth Gantry. Unmistakably Timony, probably in the early days of Butterfield: white ankle socks, gingham dirndl skirt, a tumble of red hair. And she was surrounded by her film family. Father, brothers, mother. All giving toothpaste grins. She would have picked it up but there was no fingerprint dust on it. Yet.

Diana Tong had moved right into the room and was now behind her. Her face was sad, her hands clasped together. And something struck Joanna. Timony Weeks was a stage name. She remembered Diana's early words to her: *Timony is not her real name, by the way, but her stage name.* She turned and faced Diana Tong. 'Who is she?' Joanna asked. 'Who is she really? Who is Timony Weeks? We don't even know who she really is, do we? But you do.'

SIXTEEN

DIANA TONG'S ENTIRE body seemed to sag.

'I wondered when you'd get around to that,' she said quietly.

Joanna tilted her head at Korpanski. He took the hint. She wanted to be alone with Diana Tong.

'Shall we go into the sitting room?'

Diana nodded.

When they had settled down Joanna asked her curiously, 'Whatever's wrong with someone knowing your origins?'

Diana heaved a great sigh. 'Maybe it doesn't seem to matter so much these days,' she said, 'but in the early sixties there was a lot of snobbery about. Particularly amongst the BBC lot.' A faint smile crossed her face. 'Have you ever *listened* to the BBC announcers from that era? I mean, *really* listened?'

'Are you trying to tell that Timony's background was lower class?'

Diana shook her head. Her skin looked lined and old, parchment white, thin and white as silk. Worse,' she said. 'Her father was…' She began again. 'Her father… What I'm trying to say is that her…' Her voice trailed off.

Joanna waited, wondering what on earth was so hard to reveal that Mrs Tong could hardly say it.

'Timony's real name was Dorothy Hook,' she said

at last. 'She was from Balsall Heath, Birmingham. If you know Birmingham,' she continued, 'you'll know that Balsall Heath is not one of the wealthier areas. And in the fifties and sixties it was considered a slum.' She looked up sadly. 'The old back-to-backs, you know?'

Joanna nodded. The practice of building houses bordered on three sides, sharing backyards, was one which had largely been cleared from the UK, although she couldn't see what Diana was getting at. Still... *Does this have something to do with Timony's death?* She tried to listen patiently, without interrupting.

'Poor old Mary Hook.' Diana looked up. 'Dorothy's mother. She had a hard time of it. There isn't a nice way to say this,' she said, looking up, 'but Hugo Hook spent some time in prison. He was a burglar who used force. Timony was in a school play and a scout from the TV company saw her. The rest,' she said with a smile, 'is history. Naturally, when Timony was given the part Mary was thrilled at the thought that her daughter would be away from all that. It's quite possible that money was involved but Mary did make Freeman promise that Dorothy—or Timony, if you prefer—was properly taken care of. The trouble was that as far as the production company was concerned the last thing they wanted was for pretty, innocent little Lily Butterfield to be associated with slums and the daughter of a convicted burglar. A violent burglar, at that. It would have done the series harm so it was suppressed.' She looked up. 'Successfully.'

Joanna was fascinated. To be able to reinvent your past sounded like magic to her. Timony could shed her mother, her sister. And her violent father. 'So,' she said, 'new name, new identity.'

Diana nodded. 'But she lost her family. She was vulnerable.'

'I see.' And she did. There had been no one to represent the interests of an eight-year-old girl. She suddenly cottoned on. 'And the sister who repeatedly wrote to her? Was she real?'

'There *was* a sister. Dead now. Her name was Kathleen.'

'And Timony's mother is, I assume, also dead.'

Diana nodded carefully.

Something struck Joanna. 'Was all this going to come out in her autobiography?'

Diana Tong blinked then nodded. 'Yes.'

Joanna stood up. 'We'll talk again,' she said. 'But for now I have work to do.'

Diana Tong bowed her head and nodded.

Wednesday, March 14, midday.

AS SHE AND KORPANSKI, along with another twenty or so other officers, started setting up a major incident room in one of the barns, she was painfully aware of all that had gone wrong. It was almost as though Chief Superintendent Gabriel Rush was already conducting an enquiry, telling her she should have probed more when the call-outs escalated, taken more notice after the cat incident, delved further into Timony Weeks' real history and, in particular, the assault, even though it had been years ago, which had scarred her and almost cost her her sight. She could practically hear him speaking quietly and without drama into her ear with his clipped, public school accent. She knew he would take great delight in her mistakes. Hah, she wanted to say. *Easy in retrospect. If I'd known she was going to get bloody well shot I'd have taken a bit more notice. What about all the other 'more important' crimes on my desk?* She knew that at the beginning Timony Weeks had appeared a rather histrionic sixty-year-old woman. All the same she could still imagine Rush focusing on all the questions she *should* have asked and hadn't. More detail on the husbands who were still alive. And in all probability Rolf Van Eelen would prove to be her legal heir. So there was a motive. A few million constituted a very real motive for murder.

But what about the fan who *had* tried to kill her, the only person who appeared to have wished the child star real harm? Joanna considered this possibility but was tempted to reject it. That had been the frenzied attack of a madman. Not intelligent, structured intimidation, almost a warning of what was to come, followed by a cold-blooded execution. There was no sign of emotion in the death of Timony Weeks. It hadn't been a jab with a pair of scissors but two accurate shots which had ensured her death. No, for her money she should have pursued Rolf Van Eelen, husband number five; at least found out where he was, asked a few questions about his financial situation. Did he need money? How badly? Of course, he could be purely avaricious but murder was a hell of a risk to take. And what about the woman who had claimed she was Timony's long-lost sister? Who was *she* really? Had the pursuit continued?

Sol Brannigan. Had they been wrong to discount him so readily?

There were the two farmers who were, geographically, in the running as suspects but she judged them both incapable of the more subtle psychological bullying.

And then there was the wild card. Who was Stuart Renshaw? A bona-fide accountant? Son of a friend? Or was there something or someone else that she was missing?

Joanna had to admit: she'd done a very half-hearted job of investigating either Timony Weeks' past life or the more recent complaints. Now she wished she'd spent more time in Butterfield Farm, walked around, looked more carefully and with more insight at the pictures of Timony in her various stages of life, with her multiples of husbands, and listened more carefully to her stories; delved further into her histronics, the supposed blurring of fact and fiction, to seek out the truth. She had heard the tales of a child growing up under the glare of celebrity, and in her day Timony Weeks had been as famous as Cheryl Cole or Kristen Stewart were today. Now it was too late.

Followed by Diana Tong, who was now silent, Joanna wandered around Butterfield, from room to room, realizing that the rooms were set out like a stage set. But even observing the house she couldn't connect the Timony Weeks she had known with someone whose father had been in prison and had spent her early years in abject poverty, living in what had, even then, been classed as a slum. Usually Joanna could detect accents. Most people give their roots away in a tone or a phrase, their pronunciation of one or two giveaway words. But stage school and elocution lessons had eradicated any sign or sound of a regional twang. Her mother appeared to have signed her daughter away, believing that to escape from poverty was an answer to her prayers without considering what really lay ahead for the child. What sort of mother had she been to give her up so completely to a TV set? Back came the answer. A mother who was naive.

So did Timony have any living relatives? Now that it was too late Joanna wished very much that she had done more, had at least glimpsed the real child who lay behind the manufactured fantasy figure.

Diana Tong observed her activities without comment. But her lips seemed to press together tighter and Joanna had the impression that the companion was not only grieving but uneasy. As she walked past her Diana opened her mouth as though to say something but her eyes slid away and she didn't speak, merely frowned and gave a slight shake of her head.

Eventually Joanna and Mike holed up in the barn, ineffectively heated now by electric radiators; much of the heat seemed to soar into the rafters. They might be cold but the barns were, like the rest of Butterfield, immaculately clean, with no hay and not even the faintest scent of an animal. Joanna had never been in such a sanitized barn. The team gathered around her on makeshift benches and she wrote names on a whiteboard, trying to focus the enquiry, fully aware that she could be accused of 'shutting the stable door'.

What else was she to do?

She addressed the entire room but in reality she had already decided which teams to allocate and where. 'Find out all you can about the dead woman, both as Dorothy Hook and Timony Weeks.' She walked across the barn floor and deliberately shut the door. It was possible that when the story broke there would be a prurient interest out of proportion to the secluded life

Timony Weeks had adopted in the past few years. The first name she wrote was: *Diana Tong.*

She turned around and addressed DC Hesketh-Brown. 'Danny, you and Hannah just keep an eye on her, will you? I can't think of any obvious motive she might have for setting up recent events and I certainly can't imagine her killing the cat in such a cruel way, but it has to be said, she's the one on the spot.' She turned back to the board. 'Bridget, you and Phil Scott look into the ex-husbands, will you?' Again she wrote three names on the board, bracketing them together:

Adrian MacWilliam, Sol Brannigan and *Rolf Van Eelen.* 'I've picked Sol out because Timony herself said he was a nasty piece of work, and we know he's been in prison for grievous bodily harm and armed robbery. Adrian MacWilliam—well, no reason really, except that he was her husband.' She turned back to the board. 'Rolf Van Eelen is probably the only one with a real motive. He is almost certainly Timony's legal beneficiary if she died intestate and they were never divorced. See if you can track these down then speak to her solicitor and find out more exactly how much money Timony Weeks had and who gets it. And while you're at it you might search out Carmen Weeks, last heard of in Dubai, and see if it still rankles that Timony stole her husband.' Bridget Anderton and Phil Scott nodded and smiled.

'Korpanski, Mike,' she appealed, as she wrote another name on the board: *long-lost sister.* 'According to Diana, Timony or Dorothy Hook had a sister, Kathleen, who has died. Just look into her, will you, please?' She knew he was far more interested in the luxury cars which were vanishing from around the area than the death of the actress. But he raised his eyebrows and smiled. He would not let her down. 'Take Jason with you and look into this. Alan, you take WPC Critchlow and find out about the *fan* who assaulted Ms Weeks, Paul Dariel. See if you can try to make contact with him.' She gave them all a smile of encouragement then spoke to PC Paul Ruthin, a relative newcomer to the Moorlands. 'I'd like you to look into the wild card, *Stuart Renshaw.* I just wonder about him.'

Beneath that she wrote, *John Reeves* and *Tom Brassington*, then addressed PCs Timmis and McBrine. 'You two may as well stay in the moorlands and look into the two farmers whose land borders Butterfield. I'll be honest,' she continued, 'I can't really see either of them having much to do with this but check it out anyway. And while you're at it you might have another word with the Faulkeners. Just dig around and see if there was any reason why a pair of hikers ended up trespassing on this particular property.' She scanned the room, smiled and finished the briefing. 'And in case you're wondering what *I'm* going to get up to, I'm going to do a spot of reading.' She risked a joke. 'No, I don't mean the latest bestseller from Peter Lovesey, though I have to say I'm tempted.' There was a titter around the room. They all knew her predilection for crime fiction. 'I'm going to take a look through Timony Weeks' autobiography and see if there's anything there that gives us a hint. Let's meet back here, shall we say tomorrow morning, eight o'clock. Any questions?'

There was a general shaking of heads so she thanked them and dismissed them.

Korpanski had stayed behind but she didn't know why. She assumed it would be to grumble because he had been pulled off the case of the high-profile cars.

'Mike?' she queried, knowing he was disgruntled, if not fully understanding why. Later, when she analysed it, she realized his dissatisfaction was, in a way, predictable. Korpanski was a realist, a pragmatist who dealt only in concrete facts, disliked ideas and fantasy. Particularly hunches. He wanted reality. This was the very worst case he could have been asked to work on.

'We didn't even know her name,' he grumbled. 'Only her stage name.' His neck was red with anger. 'Bloody woman, I wish she'd never moved to the moorlands. Or at least,' he conceded, 'if she did have to move here that when the threats started she'd moved herself out again.'

Her head jerked around. Unwittingly Detective Sergeant Mike Korpanski had put his finger on something. 'You have a point,' she said. 'Why did she come *here* in the first place and then stubbornly stay if she was so unnerved by the attention?'

'Didn't she say something about feeling more comfortable in a remote location than in a city?'

'It seemed a pretty weak excuse to me,' Joanna said. 'But if it was true there are plenty of other remote locations. She didn't have to stay here but she was determined to.'

'She didn't,' Mike agreed, his anger cooling as they discussed the case, 'but she'd recreated her Shangri-La here, in the moorlands. She'd have had to start all over again, get planning permission in the green belt, which can be difficult to obtain. And it seems that she didn't want just any old house. She wanted to recreate Butterfield Farm. She was lucky to get planning permission for it here. She would probably have had no end of trouble in another rural location.'

Joanna nodded slowly, starting to see things from another angle. She hadn't been able to leave, to abandon this recreation of a happier life. She had been prisoner to the illusion she had created.

Korpanski looked straight into her eyes. 'There's something else that's struck me, Jo,' he said. 'These practical jokes obviously unsettled her. So why didn't Diana Tong move in with her permanently?'

'She needed something, somewhere of her own. Timony would have swallowed her up whole,' Joanna responded, but knowing she had had similar thoughts. 'Though she did seem to spend most of her time there anyway.'

'Hmm,' Mike said, turned around and spotted Jason hovering near the door. 'Well, I'd better be off. Come on, Sparks.'

Joanna felt restless watching the officers depart to their allocated tasks and, on leaving the barn, seeing the forensic teams scour the property in their slow, methodical way. She wandered up to the house with an overwhelming feeling that it was Timony's past which had resulted in her murder. The pranks had been a warning and, when not heeded, she had died. Someone had been trying to tell her something, to warn her of what might happen if she didn't comply. What were those dark memories threatening to surface? If Timony had read the messages she had not heeded them. And Joanna did not understand them. Comply with what?

Where better to look for the answer to that than in her own story of her life? She met Diana Tong, stony-faced, in the hallway. 'Timony's memoirs,' Joanna said, stepping towards the study. 'I'm going to take a look.'

'Whatever for?' Diana Tong looked genuinely puzzled. Joanna decided she was sick of giving reasons, of being dictated to, of having her strings pulled by others. 'I don't need to give you a reason, Mrs Tong,' she said flatly. 'Butterfield is now a major crime scene and her book may hold some clues.'

And so Diana Tong pressed back against the wall and Joanna passed her, feeling the companion's resentment hot and angry. She didn't care.

She reached the study and switched on the computer. No password, she noted. Open to anyone. She copied *My Memoirs* on to a USB stick and took it back to the barn, like a lion hoarding its kill. She moved the heater closer, inserted the memory stick into her own computer. And read.

At two thirty Matthew rang to see if she intended being present at the post-mortem. She looked through the windows as he spoke. Butterfield was a hive of activity and the teams were working equally hard, some on the telephone, others on their computers, and still others had left the area to pursue their suspects. They would all be following up their initial leads but they could do without her for a while. And the post-mortem of a murder victim necessitated a police presence—if only to validate the samples. She asked Matthew to wait for her to arrive, told Mike he would be in charge for the next few hours and drove the thirteen miles towards the mortuary in Stoke. Mark Fask would meet her there.

The mortuary in Newcastle-under-Lyme was an unprepossessing building, small and square with little to announce its function apart from an unobtrusive board. It was as though it wanted no one to notice it. Which was reasonable, Joanna decided, given its purpose. She slid her Honda into the parking space next to Matthew's BMW.

He was already gowned up in his scrubs and looked anxious to begin. In the mortuary he always wore an air of slight impatience, as though he wanted to get on with things quickly. He was frowning as he stood back and waited for her to fasten a gown on over her own clothes. Though Joanna had attended scores of post-mortems she still had the usual feeling of apprehension. The truth was she hated them. Although she was acutely aware that they were necessary they seemed to her to be the final insult to the victim—even their inner organs and most private secrets would be exposed, under the arc light. All the way through, from the jud-dud of the Stryker saw and the clumsy stitching of the attendants whose job it was to stuff the organs back into their cavities, they still made her feel slightly sick, though she had never repeated her first performance in this very mortuary. They all watched in silence as the attendant did the initial weigh-ins of measurements and observations. Matthew stood back, eagle-eyed, his hands clasped. He moved once and that was to check the video camera was set up properly. He made a brief introduction, name, persons present and then slowly ran the camera over the body. Timony Weeks, or Dorothy Hook, was finally fully exposed.

She looked even thinner naked. As tiny as a child and bony too. Joanna was struck by her physical vulnerability. Even she was unprepared for the feeling of pity she felt for this woman in death, who had appeared so irritatingly strange in life.

Matthew's attention was now on the X-rays he had taken to help him locate the final positions of the bullets. When he moved back over to the body he began, with a probe, to follow the trajectory of the two bullet holes, taking careful measurements to ascertain the calibre of the firearm. Then he began excising the tissue around them, moving in with the probe until he found the bullets. These were removed with a pair of long, angled forceps ready for the ballistics department. Hopefully, at some point, they would have a weapon to compare them with. The rest of the post-mortem was routine. Apart from the attentions of a cosmetic surgeon Timony, it appeared, had been in good health.

Half an hour later Matthew was giving her his findings. 'The head wound was inflicted first,' he said. 'There is slightly more contusion and bleeding there. Immediately after that, I would guess, she was shot in the heart. The head wound entered the frontal lobe of the brain, ricocheted against the cranium and lodged in the top of the spine. The heart assault was similarly deadly. It entered the left ventricle and lodged in the thoracic spine. Death would have been virtually instantaneous.' He was looking down at Timony as he related his findings. 'Nothing else of note really. She was in very good shape, some of it thanks to surgery.' He looked across at her. 'Some clumsy, most very skilled, particularly the very enthusiastic face lift. Oh,' he added as an afterthought, 'and she had had a child at some point.'

'What?' News indeed, when Timony had categorically denied it.

'Yes,' he said defensively. 'You can't mistake it, Jo. The cervix changes shape.'

'You're sure?'

Matthew looked affronted. 'Yes, I am sure.'

He could not know how many things this altered.

'When?'

'I don't know that,' he said, still a bit peeved. 'Probably in her teens.'

'But there's been no mention of a child.' She thought for a minute. 'There *is* no child.'

He grinned at her and gave the smallest twitch of his shoulders. 'Can't help that,' he said, 'but she had had a pregnancy and a vaginal delivery. I've seen the episiotomy scar. That means,' he said, eyeing her, 'that she went into labour. I can't know if the child lived or died but she did definitely give birth.'

Joanna digested this little snicket of information, then, 'Anything else?'

'We-ell, looking at the X-rays...' He crossed the room to the computer screen to study the image, which even she could see was displaying an easily recognizable forearm. Radius and ulnar. 'There is this...' He traced a faint mark on one of the bones. Joanna peered but could not interpret the point he was making. It looked like a thickening. 'What is it?'

'Ossification,' he said, 'of an old—a very old—fracture of the right radius. Probably done when she was around ten. Possibly a greenstick. Not set very well, I'm afraid.'

'Why would that be?'

'It wasn't set properly. I would assume that she didn't receive medical attention.'

'Why might *that* be?'

Matthew shrugged. 'Who knows? Perhaps she didn't think it was that bad. A greenstick isn't a complete break but a partial snap. Or...'

'Yes?'

'It was probably done years ago. She might have been just a kid.'

But at the age of ten Timony had been a 'studio kid'.
Pampered and observed all the time.

'What would it mean?'

Matthew was busy scrubbing his hands. 'You mean
as far as a deformity is concerned?'

She nodded.

'Very slight. She might have had trouble writing—
unless she was left handed.'

Joanna tried to remember and failed. People use both
hands on a computer keyboard. 'Is this likely to have
any bearing on her…?'

Matthew's eyes gleamed mischievously as he slipped
out of his rubber apron. 'I'm just the simple pathologist,
Jo,' he said. 'You're the clever police woman. I just report the facts. It's you who must draw the conclusions.'

She could have thrown a pillow at him—if one had
been to hand. As it was she made do with scolding him.
'Matthew Levin,' she said severely, tempted to wag a
finger at him. 'You can be the most irritating.' His smile
was far too warm for her to continue. She substituted
the scolding with a giggle, then asked, 'Anything else?'

'No. As I said: she was in great shape for someone
starting her sixties. No atheroma. No nasty holes in the
brain. She had the body of a healthy fifty-year-old.' His
expression changed. 'She would probably have lived
for years.'

'Instead…' There was no need to finish the sentence.
She smiled at him. 'Thank you, Matt.'

'My pleasure, my lady,' he said, sweeping a mock
bow. She watched him, feeling his good humour leak
into her psyche. His boyish enthusiasm for his work
endeared him to her. He could never know how much.

'You've taken some toxicology samples?'

He grinned again. 'You don't have to remind me of my job, Joanna,' he said gently.

'No. What about the cosmetic surgery? Before I go just run me through it.'

'Hmm,' was his response. 'We-ell, as you probably guessed, a whole heap of stuff, some done years ago. They don't use these breast implants any more. Far too synthetic-looking and they've capsulated anyway, and the work on her abdomen is quite crude. It's almost butchery. Cheap stuff. Not done in the States or Harley Street, at a guess, but one of the provincial centres. Teeth.' He inserted a gloved finger into the mouth. 'All veneered. Done more recently. An expensive job this time. At a guess none of this has any bearing on her murder.'

'OK.' She took a last glance at the still figure. 'I'll get back to Butterfield then. See you later, Matt.' He merely grinned at her and raised his hand.

As SHE DROVE OUT through the city of Stoke on the A53, passing through Endon and Stockton Brook, she reflected. In the old days she would have called in the station and informed Chief Superintendent Arthur Colclough of events, filled him in on the lines of enquiry they were pursuing and anything else that might have a bearing on this major investigation. But these were not the old days. Rumour had it that Chief Superintendent Gabriel Rush was to start on April 1. Not only a Sunday but April Fools' Day, she thought, as she took the congested road through the town passing the roundabout, which was currently the subject of furious debate to the citizens of Leek who were resisting change. They wanted their dear and unique town to stay exactly the same. There had been a few noisy demonstrations and one or two of the more impassioned demonstrators had camped on the roundabout, but so far the police had not been involved and certainly not DI Joanna Piercy. She drove past the station, continuing through the town and out the other side to take the Ashbourne road towards the Peak District and eventually Butterfield Farm.

The minute she passed the millstone and entered the Moorlands she was aware of her environment. It was as though the purity of the atmosphere seeped into her car. It was a crisp, clear day, as clean and fresh as any winter's day can be, cleansed by a sharp overnight frost and the blessing of a cool winter's sun all day. Sheep wandered around baaing aimlessly, the winter wool heavy on their backs. They looked perfect against the snowy hills, like a painting by Hunt or Morland. But when she reached the ridge which overlooked the farm and looked down she decided that no one could be deceived into thinking that *this* was a tranquil place. As the light of the dying winter sky, slate grey with a tinge of pewter, began to fade, lamps were being switched on all over the house. And outside stood a car park full of vehicles: forensic vans, police cars, private cars. Arc lights illuminated the front of the house like an urban factory besieged by burglars. It was unmistakably the centre of great drama. A rogue thought entered her mind. *Timony would so have loved this.*

Joanna parked in the yard and walked into the barn, brightly lit, the warmth from the heaters at last making the temperature bearable. In fact, she felt as cosy as a cow. She sniffed. The barns had obviously not held animals for a long time and the place was swept as clean as a kitchen. But now she did catch an underlying scent of long-ago cattle, of a dairy, of milk and cow feed and cow dung too that made it both authentic and comfortable. Probably the scent lingered from the cottage long ago, soaked into the stones and the fabric of the site. She couldn't imagine Timony doing any milking herself. She sat down at a makeshift desk, slid the USB stick into the computer and opened the file, *My Story*. She began to read and was absorbed. An hour later she was nibbling her thumbnail and staring into nothing.

She heard the door opening—and closing, looked up to see Korpanski watching her. 'Jo?' he asked uncertainly.

She looked up and gave a half smile. 'This is the oddest autobiography I've ever read,' she said. 'Timony Weeks must have been a schizophrenic. It's almost as though it was written by two people.'

'How so?' He hunkered down beside her, focused too on the computer screen.

'Well, look at this. *"I was born in a Midlands town of working-class parents. This is what they told me, that my mother and father were ambitious for their pretty daughter and enrolled me in a stage school."'*

'So?' Korpanski looked puzzled.

'For a start, it's not strictly the truth. She was spotted in an ordinary school play. And then it tells you nothing. No specific place, no names, no details. Not even her date of birth.'

Mike still looked puzzled so she explained. 'I mean, as an autobiography it's terrible. It doesn't tell you *anything*.'

'Had she already been paid for it? A what do you call it, had an "advance"?'

'I don't think so. I'll check with Diana Tong. But more worryingly, Mike...'

Korpanski's spine stiffened as he regarded her,

'...it's the bits later on in the book. Look at this. Nineteen sixty-five. She would have been about thirteen years old. *"Filming all day. It was tiring as I was supposed to be looking after a baby lamb, covering it with my coat. But it kept running away. I was running after it but I couldn't catch it up. I ended up falling over in the muddy field and dirtying my pinafore. The wardrobe mistress..."'* Joanna met Mike's eyes. Underneath, in italics, was written,

'"*Right in front of everybody Sandra pulled my knickers down and smacked me really hard, told me I was nothing but a spoilt brat and a nuisance. That she hated me. I ran to Gerald and he told me not to worry, that he'd look after me. I LOVE GERALD.*"'

Korpanski frowned. 'Thirteen years old?'

Joanna nodded. 'This, presumably, is Sandra McMullen, with whom she lived and who had the daily care of her.'

Korpanski was silent so Joanna continued. 'There's worse,' she said.

Korpanski's shoulders twitched. 'Not sure I want to hear it, Jo. Does it have any bearing on her murder?'

'Don't know,' she answered simply. 'I only know that some of these actions taken against a child would be considered abusive nowadays.'

'Her parents?'

'Father in prison. There's no mention of her mother; apparently access visits were discouraged or indeed any contact at all. It appears that both Sandra McMullen and James Freeman acted *in loco parentis*.'

'And then Gerald marries her when she's seventeen? Seems a bit incestuous to me.'

'And to me.'

'Does she mention any threats or coercion?'

'It's odd, Mike, but it's almost as though she operates on two levels—the sweet, public image of Butterfield and this darker, unsavoury undercurrent.'

'Is that possible?'

'I've read something,' Joanna screwed up her face. 'Some article I read some time ago. I think they called it Replacement Memory Syndrome.'

Korpanski waited.

'It describes a certain psyche which replaces unpleasant memories with a sort of fairy-tale story. As an actress Timony Weeks would have been an ideal subject for that. Writing her memoirs was a potentially dangerous experience for her. It was unleashing a beast. It's possible that even she doubted these events could possibly be true. She must have tried desperately to bury the bad bits but each time she went back to the book they bubbled up again. No wonder she was confused about the difference between fantasy and reality.'

Korpanski suddenly twigged. 'So might that be a reason for someone wanting to *suppress* the memoirs?'

She nodded.

Korpanski ventured further. 'Stop their publication?' He paused, watching the expression on her face. 'Try and frighten her into submission?'

'I think you're getting there, Mike.'

'I think *we're* getting there.'

They looked at each other. So naturally attuned, voicing the next logical question was unnecessary.

Who?

'I've left someone off the list,' Joanna said. 'Freeman, the producer of Butterfield Farm. He may be elderly now but he would still want to guard his reputation, wouldn't he?'

'Suppose so,' Korpanski agreed.

She looked at her watch. It was five o'clock. 'I'll be talking to Diana Tong again in a minute,' she said. 'Want to join me?'

'Wild horses wouldn't keep me away, Joanna.'

She put a hand on his arm. 'There were a couple of things,' she said, 'that came up in the post-mortem.'

'Go on.'

'At some point she'd had a child.'

'What? Was Matthew sure?'

She nodded. 'And it had gone full term. She'd given birth. It wasn't a miscarriage.'

'But she said…'

'I know what she *said*, Mike, but the evidence was there. And,' she continued, 'she'd broken her right arm at some point. Matthew thought that it had probably happened when she was about ten but it looks as though she didn't receive medical attention.'

'It doesn't make sense,' Korpanski said.

She waited for him to draw his own conclusions. And he did, his face grim. 'So she was both neglected *and* abused.'

'It would appear so.'

'Crikey,' he said. 'Her autobiography would have been a hot potato.'

'Exactly. Shall we?'

They crossed the icy yard and entered the house, found Diana Tong sitting on the sofa, quite still. Logs were burning in the grate, giving out a sweet, smoky scent. As they opened the door a billow of smoke puffed into the room adding to the hazy look. After the chill of the outside and the half warmth of the barn the room was warm and the woodsmoke welcome. At a guess Diana had been sitting, without moving, for some time. She moved her head stiffly as they entered.

Joanna murmured more polite condolences before she and Mike settled themselves into the two adjacent armchairs and opened up the questions. 'For now, Mrs Tong,' she said, contrasting the careless appearance of the companion with her erstwhile employer's carefully manicured public image. How must it feel always to be the ugly sister, second fiddle, the understudy instead of the star? 'We'll just stick to the facts. There's a lot you haven't told me, isn't there?'

The companion's lips tightened and she said nothing. Joanna gave Mike a quick glance. This was going to be a long haul. She leaned forward. 'You don't mind if we record this?' Mrs Tong looked as though she would love to have refused the request. As it was she contented herself with a very negative-looking shrug. Joanna glanced across at Korpanski, who was sitting in the adjacent chair, his thighs apart, watching eagle-eyed. She was glad he was there and looked forward to his feedback later. She knew she could trust him not to interrupt unless it was called for and she also knew that he wouldn't betray by look, words or gesture the information she had just fed him.

'You were born in…?'

'Nineteen forty-four.' She seemed to feel that something extra was called for. 'I was eight years older than Timony.' Her mouth twisted but it didn't look anything like a smile. 'Twenty when I began working for and with her.'

'And you joined the staff of Butterfield Farm in?'

'Nineteen sixty-four.' Again, she seemed to think that she should add something so said, uncomfortably, in her gruff voice and without apology, 'I was a school-leaver. Not very academic. More practical.'

Joanna nodded. 'What exactly did you join Butterfield as?'

'Sorry?'

'What was your title?'

'I—I didn't really have one. I was a sort of gofer.'

'But as regards Timony? You were employed to look after Timony?'

'Well, ye-es.'

'And it worked?' Joanna prompted.

'Obviously,' she retorted stiffly, 'otherwise I wouldn't still be here, would I?'

'I suppose not.'

'We became friends, I suppose. Naturally we became close.'

'Was it you who was encouraging her to write about her experiences?'

'Not really. But—' Here she stopped herself abruptly.

'But…' Joanna prompted her gently.

'Timony lived a lavish lifestyle,' Diana said. 'And her series ended a long time ago. They didn't pay that much in the sixties.'

'But Timony told me there was plenty of money left. She told me she was worth a few million.'

Diana's response was a wry smile. 'I'd have thought you would have realized that Timony was a fantasist.'

Joanna gave Korpanski a swift look.

'Her divorces didn't come cheap either. Bloody scumbags took her to the cleaners.'

'Which particular scumbags do you mean?'

'Brannigan, MacWilliam and Rolf. The damned lot of them,' she said. 'Timony was a soft touch. Even Rolf, that toad. What I'm saying is that there wasn't that much money left.' Diana spoke reluctantly, every word dragged out of her as though it pulled at her flesh. 'So she approached some publishers to see if they were interested. Initially they weren't and then they were.' Something in Diana Tong looked proud. 'She decided to reject the offers of a ghost writer and write it all herself. I could tell the publishers were a bit sceptical. Actresses, particularly child stars, aren't known for their writing skills. Anyway, they said they'd take a look when she'd finished. They warned her it wouldn't be quite as easy as she thought but she got on with it. They'd promised her a "generous" advance on delivery and acceptance of the manuscript. I assume the word acceptance meant if it was publishable and there was a market.' She attempted an explanation. 'The grey brigade, you know. There's a lot of nostalgia for the sixties. The publishers thought there would be a demand providing it gave away enough secrets.' She smiled and looked directly at DS Mike Korpanski, who did not return the smile but beetled his eyebrows together as though evaluating her 'story'. His eyes were dark enough to be unfathomable and after a moment or two Diana Tong looked away. Joanna watched his face and wondered what he was making of all this. She'd know later. Korpanski wasn't one for concealing his feelings.

Diana Tong absorbed the snub with a toss of her head. 'It's always hard,' she insisted, 'to know what to buy the over-sixties as presents for Christmas and birthdays. They have everything. What they want is nostalgia. They want their past back. And so you give it to them as a book or a DVD. You give them back their memories of when they were young.'

Joanna nodded. 'I've been reading bits of it,' she said. 'I'm not sure her readers would be expecting some of those "secrets"'.

Diana Tong sat so still it was as though she was frozen into a solid block of ice. Joanna knew why. She was wondering what bits the detective had read. Joanna returned a bland smile. Diana Tong cleared her throat, licked her lips. 'The trouble was,' she said slowly, 'the publishers made it clear that they wanted what they called "the dirt".' Her gaze drifted upwards to stare into Joanna's face as though trying to convey a message without actually speaking the words. She licked her lips again and ploughed on. 'They didn't want some bland, jolly sixties thing, all hair ribbons and pretty frocks.'

'Let me get this quite clear,' Joanna said slowly so there could be no mistake about her question. 'Are you saying that Timony might have…'

'Embellished her story? I suspect so, though I haven't read all of it.'

'But you've read most of it?'

Oddly enough, Diana Tong didn't appear to know how to answer this. She opened her mouth. Nothing came out.

Joanna took note and changed the course of the questions. 'You are married, Mrs Tong?'

Diana did not like the question and tried to fend it off with one word. 'Briefly.'

'Your husband's name was…?'

'Colin. Colin Tong. We weren't married for long. Less than a year.'

'And when you joined the cast in nineteen sixty-four you say you were twenty and Timony nearly thirteen.'

Diana Tong nodded warily, obviously anticipating an awkward question.

'So you were there when she was assaulted.'

'I've already told you, I wasn't with her that night.'

Joanna smiled. 'So you have. I understand that after the assault she took some time off.'

'Naturally.' Even this silky answer was guarded.

'Her parents didn't keep in touch?'

'I don't think so. It was better they severed contact. It was discouraged.'

Funny, Joanna thought. It would be the exact opposite in today's climate.

Father in prison + living in a slum + morphs into a successful actress = Great Story.

Diana seemed to think she needed to say something more. 'I really have no idea whether her mother attempted to make contact and was discouraged by the studio or if she simply let her go,' she said. 'Why don't you ask James Freeman? He'd know. All I know is I never met her parents.'

'Why exactly *were* you taken on?' Korpanski put in.

Diana Tong looked astonished by the question. She tilted her head on one side and regarded Mike Korpanski who returned her gaze steadily.

'I don't understand, Sergeant,' Diana said.

'Well. When she was younger, eight, when she first joined the set, Sandra McMullen looked after her, didn't she?'

Joanna knew he was thinking about the broken arm.

And Diana Tong understood. 'Sandra left,' she said, 'I took her place.'

'As?'

'You mean was I engaged as a chaperone?'

Joanna nodded.

Diana Tong seemed to have to think about her response to this one. She drew in her breath. 'No. I was engaged more as a companion,' she said, 'and general dogsbody.'

And here you've stayed for nearly fifty years, Joanna thought. She wanted to ask so much more, more about the 'long-lost sister', about the fan, about the multiple marriages, about relationships between cast members, about the 'secrets' which Timony had supposedly embellished. But she decided to hold back. She didn't want to antagonize the companion.

Keep something up your sleeve, Piercy, and better to have a card up it than just a handkerchief. She smiled. It had been one of her father's favourite sayings.

So instead of pursuing the subject she veered off towards the practicalities. 'Will you be dealing with her funeral arrangements?'

'Yes.'

'You realize we'll have to wait for the coroner to release the body?'

'Yes.'

'Had she *no* family?'

'Not that I know of. None that she was in touch with.' But her words were said dismissively, without conviction, her eyes flickering along the floor. Diana Tong was considering her situation. Joanna waited, watched her face for clues and wondered whether she was about to volunteer some information but after a pause, Diana looked up and met her gaze with a steady stare. And Joanna knew she was going no further. Not today, at least.

Well, two could play at that game. In return she would suppress the fact that the post-mortem had revealed that Timony had had a child.

Tit for tat.

SEVENTEEN

Thursday, March 15, 8.30 a.m.

JOANNA SCANNED THE ROOM. This was how she liked her officers: awake, alert and, above all, eager. All except Hesketh-Brown, who looked a little bleary-eyed and was doing his best to disguise a yawn as a cough. She could forgive him. He had a little baby, Tanya, who had the habit of keeping Danny and Betsy, his wife, up for much of the night. Lately he had looked permanently tired. But studying the others' expressions she knew they would work doggedly and keep working until they'd got right to the bottom of this.

She turned to the whiteboard and began briskly. 'So, we'll begin with you, Bridget and Phil. I think you were going to tackle the two ex-husbands and Rolf Van Eelen, as well as speak to Mrs Weeks' solicitor about her will.'

Phil spoke up for both of them. He'd always been keen to join the plain-clothes branch and had only recently moved to the detective force from uniformed. Joanna smothered a smile. The newly created Detective Constable Scott was still intent on proving himself and self-conscious enough to blush like a virgin when addressing his colleagues.

He cleared his throat, looked around to make sure he had everyone's attention, and began. 'We spoke to Mrs Weeks' solicitor,' he said, 'a Mr Claude Drake from Battersea. As Timony died intestate and she had no other close relatives he's confirmed that Mr Rolf Van Eelen will be cited as her next of kin. There'll be nobody to contest it so he'll probably get everything as they were never divorced.' He grinned. 'There's not quite as much as Mr Van Eelen might have hoped. Apart from the farmhouse Mrs Weeks didn't have a lot of assets. In fact she might have struggled to hang on to the farmhouse. According to Mr Drake she wasn't exactly careful with her money. And then—his words not mine—there were Mrs Tong's wages to be paid.'

Joanna felt her expression change. She had not asked about or considered the companion's wages.

'Did he say how much Mrs Tong was paid?'

'Forty thousand a year plus expenses. But he did add that for that Mrs Tong practically gave up her life.'

'I see. And the farmhouse—how much is it reckoned to be worth?'

'Well, naturally, being a solicitor rather than an estate agent he thought that large country properties in this area, with not enough land to viably farm, would probably fetch well under a million. Still…' He'd found the confidence now to grin at his fellow officers. '*I* wouldn't mind it.'

There were a few nods of agreement around the room and Phil Scott looked pleased with himself.

WPC Bridget Anderton spoke next. 'Mr Drake said that he'd tried to persuade Mrs Weeks many times to make a will but she was superstitious and was convinced that it would, somehow or other, hasten her death. He couldn't make her see that this was nonsense.' A few people in the room nodded. It fitted in with their opinion of Timony Weeks, a superstitious woman, who wanted to drink from the eternal fountain of youth. Bridget Anderton continued, 'Mr Drake also pointed out to her that if she died intestate a considerable sum of money might well go somewhere she wouldn't want— also that the government would take a substantial cut.'

'Did he actually point out to her that Mr Van Eelen would inherit?'

Bridget shook her head. 'She assured him that they were divorced so he'd assumed that the lot would go to the State or to some distant relative. Not to Van Eelen.'

It was another of Timony Weeks' idiosyncrasies. She had lied about Van Eelen. They weren't divorced at all but still married.

'So when did he find out that they were still legally married?'

'Apparently Mrs Tong told him. She rang him yesterday evening.'

Joanna's toes began to prickle. 'And did *she* know that Timony had died intestate?'

'Apparently not. She rang him to ask about the terms of Timony's will.'

It got murkier. Joanna wondered if Diana Tong, faithful companion, had expected *a little something* in return for her doglike fidelity.

'Right,' Joanna said. 'Does the solicitor have a current address for the lucky Mr Van Eelen who has just won life's lottery?' She smiled. 'Maybe not quite a Rollover but a Win all the same.'

There were a few chuckles around the room.

'Not a current address, Joanna. The last one he has is a Marbella address, but he said he'd find out where he was now within twenty-four hours.'

Bridget smirked. 'Somehow I think the idea of inheriting money will soon flush Van Eelen out, waving a flag. Over here. Over here.' She shimmied her hand in a suitable action.

Joanna smiled at her in agreement. 'Yep. Money's a great magnet for finding folk. And Sol Brannigan?'

'No luck there, sorry.' Phil Scott gave a tentative grin. 'We'll keep on it though.'

'Did you try the last known address in Brighton?'

'He left there six months ago and left no forwarding address.'

'And what about Mr MacWilliam?'

'Died last week of alcohol-induced cirrhosis of the liver.'

So that let him off the hook.

'There's a warning to us all,' Korpanski muttered darkly at her shoulder. He was already looking irritated with his shadow, Jason, who was bouncing at his side with eagerness.

She turned towards them both. 'Did *you* get anywhere yesterday evening?'

Korpanski had secreted Jason in the corner of the barn where they had surfed the Internet for details of Timony's stalker.

'The long-lost sister?' Joanna prompted. 'I don't mean the one that died, Kathleen, I mean the one that stalked her.'

'One and the same,' Korpanski said, frowning, as though he didn't quite believe it.

'What?' It wasn't the response she had been expecting.

'We found some stuff on the Internet and looked in the police files.' Korpanski winked at Jason Spark, who beamed back. 'Then we made a couple of phone calls and had a quick word with our mutual friend, Mrs Tong.' His grin was bordering on cheeky but she didn't care.

'Go on.'

'It was *Kathleen* who wrote to her from the time her sister left home until the time of her death.'

'I don't understand. If she really was her sister why not acknowledge her?'

'I can only think that Timony's humble roots were an embarrassment to her.'

'But they were in regular correspondence?'

Korpanski nodded.

'Mrs Tong offered nothing about all this.' She looked at him.

There was something about Korpanski's face. Deliberately bland. But his eyes were gleaming. Joanna could have punched him in frustration. He was keeping something else up his sleeve.

'Kathleen Muriel Hook,' he recited. 'Born in nineteen thirty-nine. Married nineteen sixty to a Tom Renshaw.'

'Renshaw?' Joanna repeated. 'I don't suppose…?'

Korpanski gave an irritating and, in Joanna's opinion, slightly smug, smile. 'They have one son.'

'Stuart,' Joanna supplied. 'So she's kept in touch with her nephew.'

Korpanski prompted Jason with a nod. 'Born in nineteen sixty-six,' Jason said importantly. He had been dying to give this one out. 'And he was adopted.'

'Timony would only have been fourteen years old.' Jason nodded.

'And she would only have been thirteen when she got pregnant. The father?'

Jason shrugged. 'Anybody's guess.'

Joanna wondered who it was. The obvious choice was Gerald. That was her first response. Then she remembered the clip of film she had seen of Sean Butterfield, aka Malcolm Hadleigh. The way he had sat little Lily on his lap, the way his hand had strayed over her knee, the creepy way he had gripped her arm.

She needed to read more of those memoirs. Perhaps all this legwork would then prove unnecessary. All she had to do was to read that book from beginning to end. But would it actually tell her who had killed its author? She shook herself. The rest of the officers were ready and eager to report their findings.

'OK,' she said. 'So let's move on. Well done, Mike and Jason.'

Special Constable Sparks blushed orange to match his hair while Korpanski grinned a slightly sheepish smile. But his eyes were dark and friendly and for a brief moment she felt the glow of their friendship and camaraderie like a sudden burst of sunshine on a dull day.

She broke away and turned to Danny Hesketh-Brown, who was still yawning. 'You want a coffee?'

He nodded gratefully.

'OK, we'll have a short break and then you can give us your report.'

There was a buzz in the air as they queued up at the drinks machine and filled their cups. While they were drinking Joanna wandered across to the board which held a photograph of Timony Weeks in happier days. It was a wedding photograph taken from the house of her and Van Eelen, the date below 2000. She was beaming into the camera, wearing a short white dress and fresh flowers in her Titian hair which tumbled down her back. It was undoubtedly her most striking feature. And certainly not a wig—not then. She looked lovely. Twelve years ago, at the age of forty-eight, Timony Weeks had been a beautiful woman. The facelift and Botox had frozen her in time but had left her with a strange disparity between her real and apparent age. Even the most skilled scalpel-wielder cannot completely disguise the ravages of time.

Joanna turned her scrutiny to Van Eelen. He was big and blond, with a slightly pudgy face which made him look bloated and dissolute. He also looked calculating and, looking at the body language, Timony rumpling his sleeve as she clutched at his arm, gazing up at him adoringly while he stood, confident. From the body language a few hours into the union Joanna surmised that Van Eelen, Timony's brand-new husband, was rejecting the contact, his smile aimed not at his new wife but straight into the camera lens. On Timony's left was a smiling woman, a little younger than her, wearing a raspberry cocktail dress and similar flowers in her hair. Presumably this was the bridesmaid. Joanna unpinned the picture and looked on the back. *Me, Rolf and Trixy.* So Van Eelen had absconded with the bridesmaid. What a cliché! She looked a sharp-featured, conniving sort of woman. As Joanna studied her smirking face one could almost imagine that she already *knew* she would end up with the bridegroom. However, Van Eelen had not actually divorced Timony and married her, which might have been laziness on his part or it might have been optimism that Timony would die and he would inherit her money.

But that was all changed now. Timony had a son.

Adoption by her sister might have displaced him as her child but he was still her nephew, therefore her next of kin. No wonder Timony had not wanted to publicly acknowledge her sister. Kathleen had held the key to a less-than-savoury period in her little sister's life. Joanna wondered, for a while, which one of Butterfield's star cast had been Stuart Renshaw's father. Whoever he was, he should have gone to prison. Timony had been under-age. Whoever had had sex with her, the scandal would have meant the end of his career, possibly the end of the series. Butterfield exposed, not as an idyllic, beautiful and safe place for a child to grow up but somewhere where a child was coerced into having underage sex, persuaded to marry a man old enough to be her grand-father and exposed and humiliated by the very people who were supposed to protect and care for her. But-terfield was not a beautiful place but sordid and ugly.

The officers filed back, a couple reeking of ciga-rette smoke, a few still nursing mugs of coffee. Joanna was very reflective as she returned to the front of the room. Now that she knew more about the actress she felt slightly guilty at the abrupt way she had dealt with her. But she also wished that Timony had been more honest. Perhaps found the courage to face up to her demons?

'OK, Danny,' she said to Hesketh-Brown, revived by the coffee. 'How did you and Hannah get on with Mrs Tong?'

'She wasn't amazingly helpful and she didn't give us anything we didn't already know.'

'What was your impression of her?'

'Hard to work out,' Hannah said, frowning. 'She and Mrs Weeks have been together for years but I really wasn't sure how fond she was of her.'

'Did you pick up on any particular animosity or resentment?'

'No. It seemed more like a grudging admiration, the sort of fond respect you might have for someone you knew very well.'

'Did she appear very upset by the murder?'

'Upset, yes. Very, no.'

'What I'm getting at is could you imagine her shooting her friend?'

They both shook their heads.

'Can you think of any *reason* Diana would want her dead?'

Hannah considered the question before answering, shaking her head very slowly. 'Not that I can imagine. Unless she thought she'd inherit some money.'

It seemed to be a weak motive.

'Did she talk about her Butterfield days?'

'A bit. She obviously felt great nostalgic affection for those days.'

'Mmm.' Joanna frowned, chewing over the word nostalgic. 'I don't suppose she offered any explanation as to who shot Timony or who's been playing these tricks?' Something was gnawing into her mind like a rat through a corpse. It released the same stench. Something rotten.

'She just kept claiming it must be Dariel,' Hesketh-Brown added wearily. 'She said he was the only person who had ever wished Timony harm.'

'Maybe she's right,' Joanna said. 'Maybe it was Dariel.' She considered this for less than a second before rejecting this too. Too much time had passed from his first attack.

Alan King and Dawn Critchlow shifted on their feet but said nothing. Their turn would come.

Joanna resumed her questions, still searching for something. 'Did you get a chance to speak to the Rossingtons too?'

'They weren't a lot of help either,' Hannah said, obviously feeling that they had drawn the short straw in the investigation. 'They seem to come in, do their work and don't—didn't—interact much with either Timony or Diana. They don't appear to have much opinion about anything.'

'Oh, dear.'

So that was that.

DC Alan King and WPC Dawn Critchlow came next. It was obvious from their brisk demeanour that they did have something to contribute.

Alan King spoke first. 'We tracked Paul Dariel down to a Care in the Community Hostel in Manchester,' he said. 'The person in charge said he's quiet and withdrawn, very thoughtful and intuitive. She said he's on medication and isn't a danger to anyone now. He's in his late sixties but looked well. She said we'd be perfectly safe so we saw him alone.'

'Did he tell you why he attacked Timony?'

'He said that, as a youngster, he was obsessed with her.'

'Any particular reason?'

'He said it was because of her purity and innocence.' King's eyebrows rose. 'Those were his exact words.' he said. 'Then one day he sensed she'd lost it. She was just *pretending* to be innocent but it was all fake. She had become a whore.' He looked apologetic. 'His words,' he said quickly.

'Strong sentiment,' Joanna said. 'Go on.'

'He said her deceit made him mad. He *knew* she'd lost her purity. Worse,' he said, 'he also sensed that she was pregnant.'

Joanna held her hand up. 'Wait a minute,' she said. 'Timony was attacked when?'

'November, nineteen sixty-five.'

'And Stuart was born?'

Jason Spark supplied the answer. 'Late January, nineteen sixty-six.'

'So Timony was six months pregnant when Dariel attacked her.' She thought for a moment, remembering. Lily Butterfield had been stick-thin. A six-month pregnancy would have been visible to an obsessive fan. And a little obscene—a child who was about to produce a child?

DC Alan King continued, 'He said he was enraged.'

'With her?'

King nodded.

'And that was why he attacked her?'

'Yes. He called her his fallen angel. In the aftermath he was arrested. It was a very high-profile case. Subsequently he tried to hang himself in his cell. The verdict was that he was of unsound mind and he was detained under a section of the Mental Health Act, considered a risk both to himself and to the general public. He was finally released in nineteen ninety and has committed no further offences.'

'Does he still feel angry with Timony?'

Both officers shook their heads.

'Has he made any effort to contact her since being let out of a secure unit?'

Again, the answer provoked shakes of the head.

'Does he know where she lives?'

'No.' King answered for both of them.

So could she let him off the hook? Had the verdict been correct? Was Dariel no longer a danger to the general public and Timony Weeks in particular? She wished she felt more convinced.

She aimed a questioning glance in Korpanski's direction and raised her eyebrows. He simply nodded and smiled. And she made her decision. For now, rightly or wrongly, she would focus the investigation elsewhere.

'Right. Ruthin. You spoke to Stuart Renshaw?'

'I rang his office,' PC Paul Ruthin said, 'and spoke to him.' He looked uncomfortable. 'Mr Renshaw *said* that he was acting for Mrs Weeks, managing some of her affairs.'

'That might be true,' Joanna said coolly. 'I take it he didn't think to mention that she was also his aunt?'

Ruthin shook his head. 'No, Inspector,' he said. 'He didn't. He just said he was acting for her in a professional capacity which could have no bearing on her murder. He said he couldn't help us but would be happy to cooperate in any way he could.'

'Hmmm,' Joanna said dubiously, her eyes narrowing. 'I'll bet.' She was only too aware that Timony had deceived her about Renshaw.

The son of a friend? That had been her statement. Oh, no. Much closer to home.

The case would have been so much easier had Timony only been honest with them about her entire past. Maybe if she had she would still be alive. But none of this was taking her any nearer unmasking the killer.

She moved on. 'And did you have any luck tracking down any of the stolen jewellery?'

'None of it's turned up yet,' Paul Ruthin said. 'I've pasted a notice out to jewellers, checked eBay and spoken to one or two people who can give me information about fences for stolen goods,' he said. 'Most of the pieces were distinctive and one of the local dealers in antique jewellery told me those pieces might have already been broken up or melted down. There are a few places who will take precious metals and even stones, no questions asked. Just stuff them in a Jiffy bag.' He looked apologetic. 'Sorry, but these days, with the economic downturn, it's not uncommon for people to raid their jewellery boxes.'

Joanna nodded and tried to suppress her growing irritation. So many factors were making this investigation difficult.

She turned next to Timmis and McBrine. 'You were looking into the two farmers and our Happy Hikers. Have you got anything to add?'

They blew out their cheeks, unconsciously mirroring her own frustration. 'No. Both the farmers say they don't know anything about Mrs Weeks, that they aren't interested in the property at all, not even in the land, and they can't help us in any way, because...' He grinned at his fellow officers and quoted the farmers' words verbatim and in a broad Staffordshire accent, *'"We know nowt."'*

'What about our happy hikers, Roger and Helen Faulkener?'

'They've gone back to London but we managed to contact them on their mobiles. They can't help us either.'

'Did you ask them why they chose that particular spot to have their picnic?'

'Just because they thought it looked a nice place to

stop.' Saul McBrine paused, frowning. 'Mrs Faulkener, Helen, said it reminded her of somewhere in a film.'

'How right she is. OK.' She addressed the entire room. 'Well done. I think in spite of all the blind alleys we are getting somewhere. It's just a bit slow. There are still some good lines of enquiry and plenty of work to do.' She smiled encouragingly round the room, looking at each face in turn, trying to instil confidence in them. 'Keep at it. We'll meet again in the morning.'

She turned to her side. 'Mike, I want you to do something for me. I want to pursue two other lines of enquiry, but low profile. Get in touch with James Freeman, the producer. I want to interview him again myself. Face-to-face this time. And the other person I want to speak to is the guy that played Lily Butterfield's older brother, Sean. What was his real name—Malcolm?'

'Hadleigh,' Korpanski supplied, a little surprised. 'Malcolm Hadleigh.'

'Track him down, Mike. I *will* get to the bottom of this.'

Korpanski frowned. 'By "this" I take it you mean Mrs Weeks' murder?'

'Which surely has its roots in her abuse as a child? Someone didn't want the truth to come out.'

Korpanski looked sceptical. 'This many years later? What could it possibly matter?'

'I think, to someone, it does.'

'OK.' Korpanski sounded dubious. 'So why haven't they destroyed Timony's manuscript? Broken the computer, lost the backup files?'

'It's not that easy these days, Mike. She had Cloud Cover. Anyone could access those files as long as they

had her code. Every word as she wrote it became in-
destructible.'

He blinked. 'And you? What are you going to do?'

She patted his muscular shoulder. 'I'll be busy. Don't
you worry.'

The officers filed out and Joanna sat at a table and
read a little more of Timony Weeks' autobiography.
She'd got to the end of 1964 and wasn't surprised that
events were sounding much more complicated.

*Sean has been really nice to me lately. He told me
only yesterday that I'd improved. He's started flirting
with me, saying things like I was getting more beautiful every day. I just giggled at first. And then he told
me as we were brother and sister we could...* The writing stopped. And then it was as though Timony's current voice cut in. Baldly, she stated, *I can't say. I won't
say. Even now, years later, I cannot write it down. I
know now that what he said was nonsense. What he
did was evil.*

*I reflect now, so many years later: how many people
watching that wonderful, beautiful series, supposed to
portray a perfect, happy family, had any idea of what
was really going on behind the scenes? That I was
abused in one way or another from the day I arrived
on set. I'd always thought that the studio picked me because I was pretty or showed talent. That was not true.
They picked me for two reasons. One: I was completely
innocent. Like raw pastry they could do as they liked
with me. Flatten me, roll me out, cook me till I was hard
and when I became stale they could just throw me out.
And the second reason I was fit for purpose was that
my family were quite happy to abandon me. This meant*

*that the studio could do as they liked with me because
I had no one to run to—except my sister...*

Joanna stared into the distance, shocked by Timony's
naivety and vulnerability then which had been exploited,
and her venomous insight now.

She continued reading, still wondering what bearing
these words and the story behind them had on its author's murder. But now she had confidence. She would
understand all this in the end. It was just so much more
complicated than she had initially realized. She continued scanning the words and knew, without a doubt, that
this book would be a bestseller. But a cruel exposure to
anyone who had watched and loved Butterfield Farm.
Like Colclough's sister, Elizabeth Gantry.

1965.

*Sean has been funny with me for a month or so,
sometimes looking as though he wants to hurt me. He's
always been a bit cruel. Even on set he'll pinch my arm
hard enough to bruise me. He pushed me over once
when I was about ten and I hurt my arm very badly. It
felt terrible. I cried and cried it hurt so much. Ever since
then I've been a bit frightened of my 'big brother'. He
has a nasty streak to him all right. He loves to humili-
ate me. At times I think he wants to kiss me. At other
times I think he would be more likely to kill me. Bang
bang. He says his lines in a nasty, mocking way and
when this distracts me so I forget my own lines and get
everyone angry he just laughs. I can't work him out.
And he loves this. It puts him in the driving seat, right
there in full control.*

There were a few empty pages where nothing was
written and then in April there was another entry.

Sean asked me what I would be doing later, after re-

hearsals. I told him Diana and I were going to the pictures. He asked if he could come instead of Diana so I told her I didn't want her to come. That I was going with someone else. But I didn't tell her that someone else was Sean.

We didn't go to the pictures that night. Instead we went back to his flat. He talked to me first, telling me what he wanted me to do, as though he was the director and we were in rehearsals.

'Let's pretend it's just a scene,' he said. 'You're about to have a bath.'

When I said no, I didn't want to have a bath, he grabbed my shoulder. 'It isn't real,' he said, sounding as though he was laughing at my stupidity. 'It's just a scene.'

I didn't want to but I didn't want to appear a silly little girl any more either.

Joanna read through the account, feeling vicious, as many people do, towards a person who assaults a child. But then she looked around her and thought a little deeper. Timony hadn't really been a child, except in the eyes of the law. She had been a stunted adult and would remain so for the rest of her life. She had kept her secret well until now. And Joanna's policeman's nose, which Matthew laughingly told her actually twitched when she was on to something, sniffed out that this was the reason why Timony Weeks had had to die. Bang, bang. One shot in the head, another in the heart.

She continued reading. Timony had finished the chapter and moved on seven months. It was an account of Dariel's assault. *I hadn't been well. I'd been feeling very sick and my stomach was swelling. Diana was looking at me in a very odd way, as though something was very much the matter. I found her uncomfortable company so I avoided being with her as much as possible. I often told her to stay at home when I went for rehearsals.*

Joanna frowned. It appeared that, if her theory about Stuart Renshaw's identity was right, Timony was writing some very selective memoirs indeed. Some bits in, others out. For example, when was she going to pen in her pregnancy? Where was Freeman in all this, the producer who was supposed to be *in loco parentis*? And how much of this was actually true? Diana had suggested Timony might have dramatized events in her life to spice up her memoirs or maybe, even, to invite sympathy. Or was Diana herself to be believed? Might she have an ulterior motive for casting doubt on Timony's memories?

It was in November 1965. I was coming out of the studio after some late rehearsals when a young man came towards me. He looked quite nice. He was smiling and had lovely blue eyes. I smiled back. I thought he wanted my autograph so I asked my bodyguard for a pen. He was fishing in his pocket for it when I felt something hit my face. Then something warm ran down my cheek. I put my hand up and it came away smeared with blood. The man was still looking at me, still smiling. I screamed and my bodyguard grabbed him but I was bleeding and screaming and terrified. Some blood must have trickled into my eye because I couldn't see. I thought I would be blind. I don't know why he did it. He said I was evil. He said lots of things but I don't know why he wanted to blind me. It made me frightened but Gerald comforted me and then Malcolm did.

Joanna frowned. Years later she had an explanation—of sorts.

I heard later that the person who'd attacked me was someone called Paul Dariel and that he was crazy, telling lies about me. I took a few months off from filming after that.

So that was how they had covered Timony's pregnancy up, by calling Dariel crazy and avoiding a public court case. The assault had been opportune. While the nation's sweetheart crept off to give birth and dispose of the child they had had the perfect excuse.

Further on she read: *'I feel so guilty. So neglectful. Responsible. They told me I had led him on but I didn't know what I was doing. He told me it was all my fault.'*

The voice was pathetic, childish, vulnerable and naïve, but Joanna was puzzled. Whom did she mean? Who had told her, so cruelly, that the assaults, whether from Dariel or members of the Butterfield cast, were all her fault? Who was it she was supposed to have 'led on?' And who had spun this monstrous lie? Gerald or Sean Butterfield? Or someone else, someone so far faceless? There were bits missing and bits out of place and the rest was all jumbled up.

Joanna sat and puzzled over the words then left the barn and slowly walked back towards the house. The door was unlocked and she walked in and found Diana Tong, on the floor of the sitting room, surrounded by a scatter of photographs.

She looked up when Joanna entered but said nothing. Joanna sat down and picked up a couple of the pictures. Names and dates were pencilled in on the back. *Me—on set.*

She turned it over. Timony, aged about eight, looking about six, leaning precociously forward, big bow in her hair, short nylon dress, hands clasped together, head coquettishly to one side, smiling into the camera. Joanna stared at it for a while, reflecting what a strange childhood Timony Weeks had had. Abandoned by her parents, the darling of the country throughout her childhood and into her teens. Behind the scenes abused and belittled, scolded and scorned. Multiple marriages which, if Joanna remembered from her psychology degree, usually meant someone desperately seeking an idyllic, perfect love. Desperately trying to cling on to her youth, cosmetic surgery for the physical ageing and five marriages to preserve the illusion of still being the nation's pet. But a pet is constrained and has to live by the rules of her master—in this case the general public. And when a pet is beyond his or her usefulness he or she can be taken to the vet's and 'put down'. Joanna met Diana's calm grey eyes and sensed a communication that Timony's death had been fitting, the final act in a play. A death as theatrical as her life. The last scene.

She looked again at the companion. Diana Tong would be a woman who would do 'the necessary'. Whatever needed to be done she would do. It was as simple as that.

Wordlessly she leafed through more of the photographs. Gawky teenager, smartly suited in Crimplene, wearing clothes too old for her, white gloves, pillbox hat, standing with a tight-lipped smile into the camera. The wedding photograph of a very, very young Timony clutching the arm of Gerald. Joanna peered closer. He was wearing the Rolex watch on his wrist. The one which had been buried with him? Or the one which had turned up here a few weeks ago? Were they one and the same? Who knew?

She smiled to herself. Even if Colclough had not been

about to be replaced by Chief Superintendent Gabriel Rush she knew she would never get permission to exhume Gerald's body purely on the pretext of checking whether he was still wearing his Rolex watch.

She picked up another wedding photograph. Sean Butterfield, aka Malcolm Hadleigh, stood proudly, legs apart, hips thrust testosterone forward. Gerald's best man. Hadleigh was keeping a wary eye on Timony, glance sliding surreptitiously to his side. Joanna studied the bride's face under a magnifying glass. Her head was facing forwards as though if she did not hold it rigidly it would swing around to Hadleigh. Joanna sat back and thought. So who was Stuart Renshaw's father? DNA would prove the point quickly enough. It was very possible that Timony had borne Hadleigh's child three years before this picture was taken, way before she had been of marriageable age. It was also possible that Renshaw's father was someone else. Joanna looked for clues at the other members of the wedding group. May Butterfield, Lily's mother, was watching, a little detached from the others, a slightly sour expression on her face. She looked as though she wanted no part in this. Keith and David were lined up but also looking as though they were playing no part in the proceedings, as though they too, wanted to detach themselves from this particular scene. No—the magic triangle existed between Timony, Gerald and Sean. Magic triangle? Joanna questioned her phrase. If it was magic it was black magic. There was nothing good about this. Behind Timony stood a tall, bulky woman who glared into the camera as though she resented being there. Joanna looked up and saw the same angry glare in Diana Tong's face. She smiled. The dogsbody hadn't changed much. But she was waiting for Joanna to see something else. She looked back at the photograph. In the place where Timony's father should have stood was a tall, thin man with a hooked nose. He had thick grey hair, eagle eyes and a hooked nose.

'James Freeman,' Diana said. 'Producer.' Then, quietly, 'There's somewhere you should visit.'

EIGHTEEN

Friday, March 16, 11 a.m.

AND SO ON the following morning Joanna found herself driving along a small lane in Worcestershire, turning into a farm entrance and standing on the hallowed turf of what had once been the real Butterfield Farm. One sign remained: a battered piece of wood with its name painted on still attached to a five bar gate. Joanna parked up and stood, leaning over it, staring, her mind's eye seeing what it must have been like.

The approach was a tarmac drive, weeds sprouting up the middle. There were muddy puddles dotted here and there and the grass was unkempt, almost obscuring the way. There were nettles and brambles. It spoke of years of decay and neglect. Hard to think that it once would have been a hive of bustling activity and glamour.

As the gate was padlocked she climbed over, glad she was sensibly dressed in jeans, low-heeled boots and a skiing jacket, thick gloves keeping her hands warm and dry as she crunched up the drive.

Years ago, it must have been, the real Butterfield had clearly been burnt down almost to the ground. Nothing was left now but a shell, a few piles of discarded bricks. The roof had long ago fallen in, leaving the interior open to the elements. Elders sprouted here and there, nature reclaiming its own. There were large clumps of nettles and the usual detritus of dereliction: rusting cans, a vague stink of stale urine, a few MacDonald's and KFC's Styrofoam boxes and a pile of broken beer bottles. It was a forlorn, depressing place now. Whatever its glamorous past no one loved it now. It had been abandoned rather than rebuilt. Half a mile up the road Joanna had passed another sign for Butterfield Farm. It was the most modern of bungalows, solar panels on the roof, triple glazing to the windows. She assumed that it was the rebuild and this was the wreck. After the fire the farmer must have abandoned Butterfield to its fate and replaced it with something much more practical. She searched around, wondering if she would find any sign at all of Butterfield's past, but she found nothing. Not even an ancient clapper board or a rusting lipstick. Not a piece of sodden paper holding a line of script or a scrap of material from a costume. She would have liked to have found a piece of Timony's hair ribbon or a piece of shoe leather; something concrete to prove to her that Butterfield really had existed. But standing here, on a cold day, without even a hint of sunshine, it was easier to believe that it never had existed in reality but was all fantasy, something that only existed inside the wooden box of an old-fashioned television. It was not real at all. It never had been.

So what did you expect, Piercy? she muttered. *It was fifty years ago.*

She turned away, glad she had come alone, without Korpanski. She could just imagine his groan at another wasted morning. But she wished she had gleaned *something* from the visit. The atmosphere here was oppressive. Depressing. There was finality about this obliteration. It wasn't just decay. It was more as though it never had been. Well, there was no chance of Butterfield being resurrected, she thought, except it had been. Not here but elsewhere, it had been faithfully copied in the Staffordshire Moorlands. Had this Butterfield been deliberately torched, she wondered, when it had been superseded? Had its destruction been the result of a simple accident? Or deliberate arson? Had someone wanted to cover up what had happened here? Why had it been *so* neglected when it had once been the epicentre of an iconic series of the sixties? It could have been turned into a tourist attraction. But instead it had been left to ruin, as though it was ashamed of its past and wanted to forget it. Perhaps there was *nothing* to be learned here because there was nothing of its past left here. She looked around and wondered how many times the actors had stood in this exact spot, replaying scene after scene while Freeman shouted, 'Cut', and, 'Let's do that scene again'. While the wardrobe mistress fretted over costumes, the animal trainers fussed over their charges, the continuity team and the rest produced what today appeared a heavily dated and rather stilted soap. It must have been so different in those far-off days. Joanna closed her eyes and pictured it as it would have been then, bustling with people and animals, the farmhouse itself pristine, grass and drives manicured as she had seen on the television. Now the place had reverted to a wilderness; nature had claimed her own back.

Joanna stood still for a moment, berating herself for using too much imagination. She was a police officer, here to try and solve a murder. *Ideas* weren't going to be what would solve it. And then something hit her. Why had Diana Tong suggested she come here? There must have been a reason. But, surely, there was no lesson she

could learn from here, except, perhaps, a lesson of im-
permanence. Slowly she began to walk away from the
farm, disappointed. Then she turned back. Something
had been left unharmed. It was still here. The well,
exactly as it had been recreated in front of Butterfield
Farm in the moorlands. Remembering Timony's words
she stepped towards it and forced herself to look over
the wall. The mouth of the well was clogged up with
rubbish, almost to the top. Nettles and brambles had
knotted a web which had caught passing rubbish, fallen
leaves, rusting cans. And they now formed an impen-
etrable barrier rather than a pool of water, concealing
whatever it was that lay beneath. She banged her hands
on the stone in frustration.

She stood for a while, trying to fathom out whether
there was a reason that Diana Tong had directed her
here. Or had she expected her visit to the site to help
her focus on past events rather than on the physical
property or the series?

Slowly her mind filled in empty spaces with a man
clutching at the sides of the well. No one helping him.
Fantasy? Reality? If even Timony hadn't been able to
decide how the hell could she?

She drove home in pensive mood, still convinced
that the reason for Timony's menace and ultimate murder lay somewhere in her past, but there was almost too
much of it. She was swamped by images of Timony
Weeks—the child star, the many-times bride, the child
lost to her family—except, surreptitiously, to her sister,
Timony the underage mother whose own child had been
adopted, Timony being guarded by a cynical production team, Timony who had lost her childhood at the
age of eight. There had been so much debris in front of

the truth that Joanna had found it difficult to recognize what was real and what unreal, what was significant and what not. So now the challenge was to find a path through the maze of make-believe and locate the centre. And to do that she had to reduce the story to one simple question. Why had Timony Weeks been subjected to a campaign of fear, then finally had to die?

That was the question and this was what she must concentrate on. As she headed back up the motorway towards Birmingham Joanna was a bit disappointed in herself. Usually an explanation occurred to her by instinct which fitted the facts as neatly as a handmade glove. She had always believed, with an almost superstitious conviction, that it was this that made her a good detective, this almost fey belief that her subconscious would worry at a problem until it found a solution that fitted. Detective Sergeant Mike Korpanski, as pragmatic a colleague as anyone could have, might scoff. But he and she had both benefitted from her powers of 'illumination'. Was this talent now about to abandon her? Or was it simply not ready to win through because it did not have all the relevant facts?

And yet. Something pricked her mind. When she got back she could easily look it up on the Internet. Or get Mike to do it.

She pulled into the services and connected with Korpanski. 'Mike,' she said, 'any luck with tracking down Malcolm Hadleigh?'

'Yeah. He's appearing at the New Victoria Theatre in Newcastle-under-Lyme, the theatre in the round,' Korpanski said. 'He's playing some part in Carmen.' Korpanski paused and felt he needed to add, 'It's an opera.' Joanna smothered a smile. 'Ri-ight,' she said.

'Don't ask me and Fran to go,' Korpanski growled. 'Not my cup of tea at all.'

'I wasn't. I was thinking that maybe Matthew and I should have a night out.'

'Yeah.' She could hear Korpanski's smile. 'Just don't tell him it's work,' he said. 'They're playing every night until next Tuesday.'

'Great. We should be able to get some tickets. Mike,' she hesitated, 'I want us to go together and speak to Freeman,' she said, 'but not just yet. We'll leave it till Monday. I'm heading back to Leek now.'

'Did your visit to the site inspire you?'

'Not sure,' she said, reluctant to tell him that for once her brain was totally devoid of any ideas. 'Just one thing more, Mike. Find out who owns Butterfield.'

'Timony,' he answered uncertainly.

'Not that Butterfield,' she said.

'Aaagh.' Korpanski had found enlightenment. 'See you in a bit then, Jo.'

She found the *'New Vic's'* website on her smart phone, rang and booked two tickets for the Saturday night before ringing Matthew and telling him to keep the evening free.

'OK,' he said cheerfully, not asking why. It was one of things she loved most about him. Matthew was spontaneous, game for almost anything. She could spring surprises on him and he would love it.

'I've got some tickets for the New Vic,' she partially explained.

He showed no curiosity. 'OK,' he said again.

'Carmen,' she said.

And he confirmed her opinion. 'Great. Oh, by the way,' he said. 'Your victim, Timony.'

'Yes?'

'I've got some toxicology back. She was so full of barbiturates she'd practically been anaesthetized.'

'Really?'

'Yes, really.'

She'd no sooner stopped speaking to Matthew than another call came in, from Phil Scott this time. 'We've got an address for Rolf Van Eelen and Trixy,' he said excitedly. 'I've rung him. We're on our way there now.'

'Where is he?'

'He's moved to Cardiff.'

'Cardiff? I thought he was living in Spain.'

'He left there in 2010. Reading between the lines I think his business went down the chute so he came home.'

'I'm in Worcestershire,' she said. 'I'll turn around and join you in South Wales. It'll be interesting.' And hopefully informative, she thought.

They met at the M4 services and drove in convoy into Cardiff City and Van Eelen's address. Whatever had happened in Spain he had done well for himself back here. It was a beautiful, large detached stone house at the end of a rhododendron-lined drive in a very smart area of Roath, which is, in itself, an upmarket area in the capital city of Wales. Two cars stood stationary outside: a Mercedes and a Lexus: more evidence that Van Eelen wasn't exactly strapped for cash. The door was pulled open immediately and Van Eelen strode towards them.

Joanna recognized him from the wedding photograph. He was still big and blond, slightly overweight and very confident. He eyed Joanna uncertainly, his head on one side, as though evaluating her. Joanna in-

troduced herself, WPC Bridget Anderton and DC Phil
Scott, Leek Police.

Hot on Van Eelen's heels trotted the slim brunette
from the wedding photographs: skinny black jeans and
a floppy white sweater, sleeves pushed up to the elbows
displaying stringy forearms which rattled with silver
bangles. She looked appraisingly at Joanna, obviously
a woman who sized up perceived competition without
wasting time. Having made her judgement she linked
her arm possessively into Rolf's. The gesture was so
patently obvious that Joanna couldn't help smiling.

She addressed Van Eelen. 'We're investigating the
murder of your late wife,' she said carefully. Trixy
flinched at the epithet, *wife*, but otherwise the couple
didn't react.

'Come in,' Rolf offered, 'though I don't know how
I can help you. Timony and I separated years ago.' An
anxious glance skittered across to Trixy, who stiffened.
Obviously *Timony* was still a sore subject.

'But I understand you have had some contact with
her over the years.'

Van Eelen gave a sheepish grin. 'A bit,' he said, giving Trixy a very wary glance and taking a tiny step
away from her which stretched her arm lock.

Getting out of reach?

'Mr Van Eelen,' Joanna said delicately. 'Can you
tell me whether you knew anything about your...' she
couldn't truthfully say *ex* so substituted, '*late* wife's
finances.'

Van Eelen's eyes gleamed. 'She was worth a bit.'
He remembered himself. 'Poor old Timony,' he said,
face schooled into tight grief. 'Dreadful her being shot.'

'Dreadful,' WPC Anderton echoed.

'I didn't mean how much money she was worth,' Joanna persisted. 'I meant: do you know who she's left it to?'

Van Eelen shrugged his large shoulders. 'Haven't a clue,' he said. 'A cat's home? Diana? God knows that poor woman's earned it, spending her life looking after a mad woman all these years.'

His judgement of his wife's mental state was interesting. Joanna began to wish she'd interviewed Van Eelen sooner. His take on events might have been helpful.

'If she'd died intestate,' Joanna said slowly, 'who do you think would inherit her assets?'

Van Eelen took a long time working this one out. His mouth closed. His eyes darted around the room, resting for a moment on his partner's glossy mouth, which was pressed tight with disapproval, tiny lines fluting on her upper lip. His gaze fluttered away restlessly, like a butterfly on flowers. 'I don't think she's got any close...' It was a brave effort.

'You aren't actually divorced, are you?'

'Phhrr.' He blew out his cheeks in derision. 'Never really got around to it.' Another wary glance at Trixy, who had wisely lowered her gaze to hide the fury that was flaming up in her eyes. 'Why? Is it important?'

Joanna chose her next words with great care, picking them out like chicken from bones. 'If you aren't divorced and in the absence of other claimants,' she said, deliberately avoiding mention of Renshaw, 'it's my understanding that *you* would inherit—after the government had subtracted death duties.'

'Oh,' Van Eelen said. It was hard to judge whether he was surprised or not, pleased or not.

'Just for the record, Mr Van Eelen, where *were* you in the early hours of March the fourteenth?'

The natural response to this common police question is to say that you have to think about it, consult your diary. Ask your nearest and dearest. Not, as Van Eelen did, say immediately, as though thoroughly and well-rehearsed, 'Here all night.' Another wary glance. 'With Trixy.' His arm twitched as though he was about to coil it around Trixy. But, probably wisely, he dropped it back to his side.

'Right. Thank you.'

As they left, Van Eelen made a feeble attempt at a joke. 'So,' he said, dredging up a credible American accent, 'don't leave town. Hey?'

'That would be a good rule to follow,' Joanna responded smoothly. 'And it would be very helpful if you'd let us have your phone numbers, landline and mobile in case we need you.'

Van Eelen shrank like a pricked balloon.

Saturday night, March 17, 8.45 p.m.
The new Victoria Theatre
Third row, seats fifty-six and fifty-seven

THE MUSIC WAS so well known that everyone was enjoying it. Plenty of people were swinging their feet to the rhythms, a few, irritatingly, humming along to the melodies. But hey, it was Stoke-on-Trent. It was a Saturday night and people were here to enjoy themselves. Joanna linked arms with Matthew and gave him a cheeky smile which he responded to with a grin and a brush of his lips on her cheek, muttering, 'This had better be good.'

They sat back to absorb the rich sexiness of Carmen,

flashing her legs, not in the cigar factory but in a supermarket checkout. And then in swaggered Malcolm Hadleigh, aka Sean Butterfield, to the Toreador Song. Joanna leaned forward. He was a little old to play the part of Tony Amore but with dyed black hair—or a wig—he could still swing a cape.

Matthew leaned across, found her lips this time and gave her a soft kiss, whispering, 'Didn't know you were into opera, Jo.'

She looked straight into the warm green eyes, as long and narrow as a cat's as he eyed her. 'There's plenty you don't know about me, Matthew Levin.'

'I sincerely hope so,' he said.

The theatre in Newcastle-under-Lyme is known as the New Vic, as opposed to the Old Vic which closed its doors in 1985. It is one of the few theatres-in-the-round in the UK. And once you have found the taste for this format, which is surprisingly different from the stilted stage of the more common auditorium/stage performance, you wonder how you ever enjoyed the plays so much looking up at a flat, elevated platform, rather than being amongst it all.

In the theatre-in-the-round the cast romps around a central, circular area, sometimes beetling in and out through the corridors of the audience. Added to that, for the relish of the people of Stoke-on-Trent, as well as original work penned by locals, well-known plays or operas are sometimes 'adapted', either to bring them in line with modern taste or to make them relevant to the citizens of the five towns. So in the New Vic's performance of Carmen, Tony Amore was not a toreador but a football star.

Joanna watched Malcolm Hadleigh with interest.

He was good, playing his part with relish and not a bad singing voice either. Fifty years ago, as Sean Butterfield, fourteen years old when the series had started, in his twenties by the time it folded, he must have been electric. And charismatic.

At half time they queued at the bar and as Matthew handed her a glass of wine he finally asked her, 'You seem very interested in the footballer.' Then: 'What are you up to, Joanna Piercy?'

She put her face close to his. She didn't want eavesdroppers. 'The guy who's playing the footballer,' she said very softly, 'Tony Amore, also played the part of Timony Weeks' older brother in Butterfield Farm,' she said. 'And I'm strongly suspicious that he either raped or coerced Timony into having sex with him when she was just thirteen years old. I also believe that as a result of this she had the child you found evidence of at the post-mortem.'

He pulled his face away, frowning. 'Thirteen?' he queried. 'If anyone had gone for Eloise at thirteen I would have killed him.'

She shook her head. 'But it isn't him who's dead, Matt,' she said. 'It's her.'

Matthew downed the rest of his lager and put the glass back on the counter. 'So what happened to the child?'

'I believe he was adopted by her sister.'

Matthew pulled away at that. 'I'll be watching the second half in a different spirit.'

Sunday, March 18, 10 a.m.

IT WAS POINTLESS even pretending to have a day off in the middle of a major investigation and Joanna knew she wouldn't rest until she'd cracked this one. She owed it to Timony to find her killer. She ate her breakfast, hardly saying a word. Then stood up and stretched her hands out to Matthew. 'I'm so sorry,' she said. 'I'm really sorry.'

He knew what was coming. 'It's OK, Jo.'

He'd changed since they'd been married. Tried to be more tolerant, but he continued to look at her, as though expecting her to make some commitment.

'I'll be home this evening,' she said, aware that she'd changed too. A couple of short months of marriage and they were both learning.

Next week, she'd decided, she would home in on her chief suspects. Someone had cold-bloodedly shot Timony and she was drawing closer to finding out who and why. But for today she felt she needed to focus on events from a different perspective, that of the general public. The fans. The viewers. She would call in and speak to Colclough's sister, Elizabeth Gantry again. She rang first and Mrs Gantry sounded delighted. 'Yes,' she said, 'Joanna. Lovely to hear from you again. I'd been wondering how your investigation was getting on, particularly since poor old Timony was shot. Do, please, come over.'

'Do you still have all your scrapbooks?'

'Of course. I shall never throw them away. They mean everything to me.'

'I'll be over in half an hour,' Joanna said.

She called in at the flower shop and bought a small bunch of flowers. Mrs Gantry was bound to like them. She could also give her the autographed photograph—the last autograph Timony had ever signed. Maybe that would make it worth even more.

As she handed the flowers to her the older woman blushed. 'It's a long time since anyone's bought me flowers.' Her eyes met Joanna's. 'You really shouldn't have done that, you know. There was no need.'

'Well, I'm bothering you on a Sunday.'

Elizabeth Gantry simply laughed. 'Oh, my dear girl,' she said. 'Sundays aren't quite the same when you're a widow.'

Joanna handed her the photograph too and Mrs Gantry looked at it sentimentally. 'How terrible,' she said, 'that she should meet with such an end.'

Joanna said nothing but let Mrs Gantry gaze at the photograph for a minute or two. Then she regained her native briskness. 'Here,' she said. 'I've got all my albums out as well as the cigarette cards.'

'Cigarette cards?'

'Yes. Amazing, isn't it? They used to put cards in packets of cigarettes and you collected the set.' She smiled. 'Encouraging your parents to keep puffing away just so you could acquire the entire lot. And I have, after a lot of swapping and changing,' she announced proudly, 'a whole set of Butterfield cards. Probably quite rare now,' she added. 'Maybe worth a bit since.' She swallowed. 'Since Timony's…'

'Oh, don't,' Joanna said, putting a hand on her arm, 'or I'll think you have a motive for wanting her dead and arrest you.'

Elizabeth Gantry grimaced. 'I suppose you could say that crimes have been done for less,' she said. 'But it would certainly make headlines in the *Leek Post & Times*.' She handed Joanna an album, its covers dark brown leatherette, inside thick black pages in which had been inserted coloured cards, slightly smaller than a credit card.

Joanna looked at the album. How times had changed. She flicked through them. The entire cast was here, all giving cheesy grins: Keith and David, Sean, Joab, Lily, May. The farm, even the animals: Daisy and Bluebell, Friesian cows, lambs named Springer and Jonty, cats—not posh Burmese like Tuptim but ginger and tortoise-shell. She leafed through page after page, wondering what it was she was looking for.

Elizabeth Gantry tried to be helpful. 'Was there any period in particular that you wanted to look at?'

'Yes, the years nineteen sixty-four to sixty-six.'

'Ahh.' Elizabeth tapped the side of her nose and opened the album at a page. And there it was. November 1965. Lily Butterfield in a smock. How clever.

Elizabeth Gantry was looking over her shoulder. 'Sweet, isn't she?'

If only she knew. Elizabeth Gantry, and probably every single one of *Butterfield*'s fans, had failed to understand why little, sweet Lily Butterfield was wearing a smock. And why Dariel, who was not quite sane but celebrity obsessed, had felt inclined to destroy her for losing her purity.

Monday, March 19, 9 a.m.

AND AFTER FUMBLING around in the dark the beginning of the week, at last, brought compensation. Joanna had decided to call a briefing at a civilized hour for once, giving her officers time to prepare their reports before meeting together. She knew they would not let her down. She'd turned to the list on the board and wondered whether it was complete. It might be a focus for their enquiries but... She stared at it, wondering, then faced the room.

Phil Scott was grinning at her. Obviously he had news.

'You'd better go first,' she said.

'We've tracked down Sol Brannigan,' he announced triumphantly. 'And what's better, he's not legit.'

'Go on,' Joanna prompted. Eyeing the officers she could see one or two of them had something to report. Korpanski was watching her, looking intrigued. He was wondering what she'd been up to over the weekend. She'd tell him—later. Maybe even sing him a couple of songs from *Carmen*.

Phil Scott continued, 'He's been under surveillance for money laundering. He runs a sort of property business based in Brighton but the Special Branch think it's a cover. He's been linked to organized crime—people trafficking, smuggling in cigarettes and illegal alcohol.'

Joanna frowned. 'If he's been under surveillance from Special Branch I take it he couldn't have had any link to Timony's murder?'

'Yeah,' Phil Scott said. 'They tend to keep a pretty close eye on their targets.'

'Looks like he's in the clear then.' Joanna drew a line right through Sol Brannigan's name, trying to look on the bright side. Even being able to exclude someone from their enquiries was a start. 'Do we have any news on the gun?'

WPC Dawn Critchlow supplied the information. 'A .22 semi-automatic pistol,' she said. 'Probably a Walther PP.'

'Any sign of it?'

Obviously not. Every single head in the room was shaking. 'A no, then,' she said briskly. 'Right,' she continued. 'Who's next?'

Paul Ruthin stepped forwards. 'I spoke again to Stuart Renshaw,' he said. 'He knew he was adopted but he claims he didn't know that Timony might be his real mother. He was under the impression that she was his adopted aunt. He said he was very fond of her and enjoyed hearing her stories about celebrity life.'

'Did his adopted mother *never* tell him about the blood relationship?'

Ruthin shrugged. 'No,' he said. 'He was under the impression that, like many adopted children, his adopted mother didn't know much about his blood mother.'

Joanna was incredulous. 'And he *never* tried to find anything out?'

Ruthin shook his head.

'And *never* asked for access to his original birth certificate?'

Again, Ruthin shook his head.

'And how did he respond when you told him that his dear aunt was still legally married to our friend Van Eelen, so he would be unlikely to inherit?'

Ruthin smirked. 'I got the feeling,' he said, 'that it came as a nasty shock. But he covered it up well.'

'Thanks.' She turned around. 'Right. Now we have a different list of suspects.' She added Stuart Renshaw to the bottom of the list.

'Mike,' she said, 'I want you to work alongside me. Jason, well done. You can work with Phil Scott.' Jason gave Mike a sort of resigned nod. He'd enjoyed working with the burly sergeant whom he'd hero-worshipped since his first day as a special. In his daydreams he *was* Detective Sergeant Mike Korpanski, kicking and punching his way through.

Unaware of Jason Sparks' lofty aspirations Joanna turned around to look at the whiteboard. The list was growing rather than shrinking.

James Freeman, Malcolm Hadleigh. She hesitated for a minute before studying the name *Diana Tong*. Aware that Korpanski was watching her she spoke without turning around. 'I'll want us to go back to Butterfield, Mike, and speak to Diana Tong again at some point, but not just yet. I want to press her a little more.'

Korpanski nodded. And she could tell that he was glad they were working together again, even if it did mean a break from his luxury car scam.

She smiled at him. 'I hope you're enjoying your foray into the celebrity world.'

He made a face. 'It's OK,' he said easily.

Alan King was just filing out with the others but she called him back. 'Can you give me the number of Paul Dariel's case worker?'

He fumbled for his pocket book and she copied it down.

Ruth Morgan. Community psychiatric worker.

When the room had emptied Joanna dialled the number and was lucky enough to get straight through to her. She seemed refreshingly normal, willing to help and pleasantly sympathetic, down to earth and friendly, if a little prickly and defensive of her charge. 'Paul is a pleasant man,' she said. 'He's very different from the person he was years ago.'

'Is he still dangerous?'

'He wouldn't be out if he was,' she answered sharply. 'Whatever the media say we're not in the habit of letting dangerous schizophrenics roam the streets attacking people.'

Joanna gave Mike a quick glance. 'Is that what his diagnosis is, schizophrenia?'

'Provisionally, yes.'

'Provisionally? After all this time? Does that mean you're not sure, that it could be something else?'

'Psychiatric diagnoses are a little less precise than a broken leg or a chest infection,' Ruth said briskly.

'But the reason that he gave for the original assault?'

'He claims he did it because she had defiled her body. It's very typical of the sort of reason a schizophrenic would give for an assault.'

But she had. He had not been deluded but correct.

Possibly interpreting Joanna's silence as a failure to understand, Ruth Morgan explained, 'He said she was pregnant.' She snorted. 'She was, at the time, thirteen, fourteen years old? If she was she was a bit bloody young for that. She was a famous actress, for goodness' sake. In the public eye. There was nothing in the media. Paul was mistaken. That's all. He's never even threatened anyone else.'

'Why her eyes?'

'It's where they always go for.' She said it so casually the psychiatric worker could have been saying that she shopped at Tesco's. 'Letting the devil out,' she continued, finishing lamely. 'And such.'

'He spent how long in Broadmoor?'

'He was released in nineteen seventy-five, so ten years.'

'Have you asked him whether he still harbours thoughts about her?'

'When we heard about her murder we did think to ask him some questions,' she admitted reluctantly.

Joanna wanted to bleed it out of her. *AND?* Instead she skirted around. 'Does he know where she lives?'

It was at this point that Ruth, the professional, lost confidence. 'It's a bit difficult,' she said awkwardly. 'He says she lives in Butterfield. It's what it said in the papers,' she said. 'But I wasn't sure whether he meant the house in Staffordshire or...'

Joanna gave Mike a quick anxious glance. Butterfield. It could be interpreted as a clever answer, ambiguous and smart. Or...

'How intelligent is Paul?'

'He's bright.' The answer came with a certain degree of resignation, as though she had anticipated this question. 'Of above average intelligence.'

'In your opinion, Ruth, is it possible that he could have travelled to Butterfield?'

There was no answer.

'Is he supervised all the time?'

'No.'

'Then is it, in your opinion, possible that Paul Dariel returned to Butterfield and shot Timony Weeks?'

There was the slightest of pauses and when Ruth Morgan answered Joanna knew she had picked her words out with great care. 'In my opinion, no. It isn't just Paul's current mental state,' she added quickly. 'There's the logistics. Although he's not considered a risk any more a case worker always stays at the house. For him to travel from Manchester to remote Staffordshire would be very difficult—there isn't a good public transport system. It would take all day to get there and back and although he isn't constantly supervised he does have to be present for all meals—breakfast, lunch and dinner. Added to that your officers told me that there had been a prolonged programme of small tricks being played on Mrs Weeks. Paul doesn't drive, Inspector. How on earth was he supposed to get from Manchester to the wilds of Staffordshire on numerous occasions, sometimes in the middle of the night? Someone would have had to drive him.'

'OK,' Joanna said. Ruth Morgan had presented a convincing defence case for Dariel's innocence. 'We may still need to interview him. Would that be possible?'

'We can bring him down to you if you think it's necessary.'

'Thank you for your cooperation,' she said. 'If we do want to speak to him we'll be in touch.'

'OK.'

'And now?' Mike was looking at her expectantly.

'The theatre,' she said gaily. Lunchtime rehearsals at the New Vic.

WITHOUT AN AUDIENCE the atmosphere was very different. The production seemed as amateurish as a school play, with just as much teasing and ragging, Hadleigh at close quarters looking considerably older than at Saturday's performance. They could see bags under his eyes, a line of white roots along the parting to his black hair. He greeted them warily.

The theatre had a small anteroom which they used to talk to Hadleigh. 'I suppose it's about Timony,' he said, leaning back in his chair and watching them from beneath warily lowered lids. 'I heard it on the news. Always a drama queen. Knowing her I'd almost suspect she'd done it herself.' He seemed to realize he'd overstepped the mark and, as people do, instead of retracting the statement, he plunged in deeper, looking from one to the other. 'For the attention?'

He closed his mouth to stop it from saying anything more.

Joanna made no comment but launched into the questions. 'Did you keep in touch with Timony over the years?' she asked conversationally.

'Not really. She was just a kid in the Butterfield days,' he said quickly, then chewed his bottom lip.

'Just a kid, as you say,' Joanna said. 'But twenty by the time it folded. Twenty and married.'

'Yeah, well. She was a lot younger than me.'

Joanna looked at Hadleigh for a moment without speaking. She hadn't expected someone so normal-looking. At Saturday's performance he had seemed *A toreador. A hero. A swaggering leading man*. In Butterfield he had seemed as charismatic as Elvis or Robert Redford. But close up he was very unremarkable. Shorter and smaller than she remembered. What was this thing called a screen presence that made you appear so powerful? You wouldn't have given him a second glance if you'd passed him in the street. Medium height, medium build, grey hair. Walked with a slight shuffle now, stared a little too hard and intently right into Joanna's eyes before sitting down and waiting, politely, for them to continue. Sidetracked into reflection, Joanna had lost her thread so Korpanski took over, beginning with a noisy clearing of his throat which focused Hadleigh's stare on him.

There was always only one way Korpanski was ever going to conduct this interview. Bluntly.

'You knew that Timony got pregnant in nineteen sixty-five?'

Hadleigh looked as though he was going to brazen this one out. His jaw tightened and he said nothing.

Korpanski continued smoothly. 'And gave birth to a child in nineteen sixty-six? A little boy that her sister subsequently adopted?'

Hadleigh leaned forward. 'It was nothing to do with me,' he hissed. 'Nothing. She went away for a few months. That's all I knew.'

Korpanski proceeded with the interview like a steam roller. Unstoppable, not even slowing down to Hadleigh's protestations. 'Did you have sexual relations with Timony?'

Hadleigh still brazened it out. 'You can't prove anything,' he said.

It was Joanna's turn to speak. 'We can get DNA from Stuart Renshaw,' she said, 'Timony's son.'

'And you'll find out that I am not his father. Look higher up the evolutionary scale.'

'Gerald?'

Hadleigh blinked. 'It's your job to find out,' he said, standing up. 'Now unless you're going to arrest me,' he said, with all the dignity of an ageing actor, 'I have to get on with my rehearsal.'

As they left the theatre Joanna wondered. Had she been wrong about Hadleigh? Had she misread the creepy on-screen flirtation? Had the child maybe not been his but the man Timony subsequently married?

Maybe she should find out. She might not get permission to exhume Gerald's body to see if he was wearing his Rolex watch but she had a much better chance if she needed to extract some DNA.

NINETEEN

Tuesday, March 20, 8 a.m.

TODAY SHE'D SET aside to interview Freeman again. This time in the flesh.

She had already warned him to expect a visit. So she and Mike met at Leek Police Station nice and early. They'd have to battle through the Potteries traffic to reach the M6 but then would take the Toll motorway, avoiding the M6 congestion around Birmingham and the M40. They made good time, arriving at central London in just three and a half hours, using a satnav to find their way to Sargasso Mansions. James Freeman, ex-producer of Butterfield Farm, had obviously made plenty of money. Sargasso Mansions proved to be an imposing block of 1930s apartments, eight storeys high, with bay windows all the way up. Entrance was via a radio link. Joanna eyed Korpanski, pressed the button and grinned. 'Well, here we go, Mike.'

Korpanski grinned back, his fingers crossed as Freeman's voice responded crisply to Joanna's introduction and the door was released. Inside the hallway was equally luxurious, polished black marble floor, panelled walls, a gleaming central round mahogany table on which stood a vase of lilies, two lifts doors facing—the expensive ambience furthered by the scent of the flowers and lavender wax polish.

They took the lift to the seventh floor.

Even in the flesh Freeman was still a very distinguished-looking man. Tall and thin, with a large, aquiline nose, thick white hair and shaggy eyebrows. He peered at them both, hostile eyes blazing bright blue, and scowled. 'Don't know what on earth you can possibly want with me,' he grumbled as he led them indoors, ushering them into a room elegant in pale green and *chinoiserie*. They sat on some flimsy-looking armchairs upholstered in gold and suddenly Joanna didn't quite know where to start, not even in which decade. So she chose what she thought would initially be neutral ground, to him at least. He wouldn't know what she knew. 'The original set of Butterfield,' she said. 'The real farm you used as a backdrop.'

He was instantly dismissive. 'Most of it was shot in a studio,' he said grumpily.

Joanna glanced at Korpanski. It was the response they'd anticipated. But she smothered her irritation. 'I know that,' she said. 'I mean the farm you used for the backdrop of your outside shots.'

The eyebrows drew together and Joanna mused that those same shaggy eyebrows may well have been the warning signs to the cast that the day's takes had not gone well.

'It was in Worcestershire,' Freeman finally said reluctantly, 'not too far from the main studio which was BBC Birmingham, later Pebble Mill.'

'I know,' Joanna said quietly. 'I've been there.'

Freeman looked up. 'Then why…?'

Joanna shrugged, anxious to give no more away than she had to. She could play the game of secrets too. 'It was burnt down, wasn't it?'

Freeman nodded. 'I believe so,' he said.

'Deliberately?'

Freeman shrugged. 'Who knows?' He sounded uninterested.

'Do you know *who* burnt it down?'

'I believe no one was ever charged.'

Joanna nodded. She'd checked the police records. It was down as an unsolved arson.

'Do you know *when*?'

Freeman was getting irritated. 'Is there a point to these questions?'

'Just answer me, please.'

'Must have been after nineteen seventy-two,' he answered grumpily, 'when the series folded.'

'Do you know *why* it was burnt down?'

The question provoked a long, angry sigh. 'No bloody idea,' he said testily.

'Who owns it?'

'The farmer.'

Joanna shook her head, 'No he doesn't, does he, Mr Freeman?' And she laid a piece of paper in front of him.

Freeman hardly bothered to read it. He knew its contents.

'Why did you buy it?'

Freeman's face altered, became softer, almost sweet. He gave an abstracted smile. 'I don't know,' he said. 'Sentiment, I suppose.'

'You don't strike me as a sentimental man.'

He lifted his eyebrows. 'Well it *was* my most successful series, Inspector.'

'But you have done other work since.'

'Nothing that ran for twelve years.'

'Do you visit the site often?'

Freeman shook his head. 'I haven't been there in years,' he said reflectively. 'Not for years and years.' Then added: 'I hardly leave London these days.'

Joanna gave Korpanski a nod and he continued, 'When did you last see Timony?'

Joanna smiled a jam-for-tea bland grimace and let her sergeant continue. Korpanski's style of questioning was different from hers. Confrontational, blunt, straight to the jugular. And sometimes this approach earned results.

'Again. Years ago,' Freeman said, his eyes meeting Joanna's with a touch of regret, as though he would far rather have her proceed with the questions than the aggressive sergeant.

'Did you keep in touch by telephone or email?'

'A bit of both. But not for years, Sergeant.'

Something wary and deceitful sneaked into the older man's manner.

Korpanski blundered on. 'Did you know she was writing her memoirs, Mr Freeman?'

'She may have said something about it that she might, in the future, one day, perhaps. Lots of people say that and never do it. As I say, I haven't spoken to her for—now let me see—it must be three years. She invited me to revisit the past and have a holiday at the recreated Butterfield Farm. She told me that from the outside it was practically indistinguishable from the original set. I was tempted, I must confess. But I didn't go.' He made a poor attempt at humour. 'I wasn't *that* tempted.'

Somehow his attempt at offhandedness didn't quite come off but his charm shone through like old gold.

Joanna took over. 'Did the fact that she might pen her memoirs worry you?'

Freeman didn't answer straight away but looked thoughtful. Eventually he said carefully, 'It would depend what she might have put in them.'

'Such as,' she prompted casually.

'I don't know.'

The evasion was as obvious as the fact that Freeman wasn't going to make it easy for them. So Joanna decided to change tack, partly to put him off the scent. She changed her manner to conspiratorial, pretending they were on the same side. 'Tell me about Diana Tong,' she said, in a sweet, matey tone. 'Why did she stay with Timony all these years?'

Freeman gave a dry, unpleasant laugh. 'I'd have thought that was obvious,' he said, practically jeering at her naivety. 'She's in love with her. Diana's a closet lesbian.'

It gave Joanna the perfect cue. 'But Timony wasn't, was she?'

Freeman sidestepped the question as neatly as a Chinese gymnast. 'Hardly,' he said. 'All those husbands.'

'I mean, *before* all those husbands.'

Freeman stilled and something thick and dark wrapped itself around him.

'*Before* she was married,' Joanna said, locking her eyes to his. '*Before* she was sixteen.'

Freeman stared very deeply into her, trying to corkscrew out what exactly she knew.

Joanna pressed on. 'Diana was married once, wasn't she?'

It earned her a disdainful glare. 'Briefly. It didn't

last. She was soon back, dancing around Timony like a lapdog.'

'So she was, wasn't she?' Joanna agreed.

The quiet between the three of them intensified until it was a poisonous, sulphurous cloud full of accusation and finger pointing which clung to the atmosphere. Joanna let it settle for a moment before parrying again, approaching now from another angle. She knew exactly what she was doing, circling Freeman like a vigilant vulture, preparing to move in for the kill so she could peck his flesh. 'Timony had some time off the set in nineteen sixty-six, didn't she?'

Her casual tone didn't fool Freeman for a second. He eyed her warily and didn't offer any answer so Joanna produced her sequitur. 'Why?'

He didn't even think about it. 'She needed a break.'

Joanna was still in terrier mode and rapped the question out again. 'Why?'

'The assault upset her terribly.' Freeman appeared to open up. 'She couldn't adjust to the fact that her fans could be anything but adoring—even if Dariel was mad. Poor girl. She was exhausted and terrified that it would happen again.' He decided he needed to embellish the story and "confide" in the police officers. 'At one point we wondered whether she would *ever* return to Butterfield.'

Joanna gave Mike a swift nod. Now. Now. The time had come. 'Let me correct you, Mr Freeman,' she said sweetly. 'When you say "exhausted" you mean she was pregnant, don't you?'

For a moment Freeman looked stunned rather than surprised. Then he gave a brief, jerky nod.

'She was thirteen years old when she became pregnant,' Joanna said. 'Who was having underage sex with her?'

And as Freeman didn't answer but stared out of the window at the London skyline, as though he longed to escape and dance away across the rooftops, like Dick Van Dyke in Mary Poppins, Joanna pressed on. 'Shall I put it another way, Mr Freeman. Who was the father of her child?'

The producer's face changed again, to become bleak. 'We didn't know,' he said. 'No one knew.'

It wasn't the answer either of them had expected or hoped for. Joanna gave Mike a quick, worried glance. Was this to be the end of the road?

'Do I understand that you are saying that you didn't know who was seducing a thirteen-year-old? A thirteen-year-old, may I remind you, Mr Freeman, who was in your care.' Freeman hesitated and Joanna realized that the real truth was even more grotesque. She proceeded slowly along splinters of glass, her voice low. 'Are you trying to tell me that there's more than one possibility?'

By her side Joanna felt Korpanski twitch. He almost needed restraining, as would any man who has a daughter.

'Who?'

Freeman's shoulders seemed to shrink then. He morphed into his age, now looking a troubled old man easily in his eighties. 'She was precocious,' he said defensively.

Was he actually trying to defend the person or persons who were her abusers?

'I guess that's true of a lot of young actresses,' Joanna said coldly. Korpanski simply cleared his throat with a harsh and disapproving scrape.

Freeman appeared to get the message, realized that more was expected of him. 'I always thought Hadleigh.' His eyes flickered from Joanna to Mike. 'He played Sean Butterfield,' he explained.

Joanna leaned forward to give her words more weight. 'But you have no *proof*, Mr Freeman.'

He looked uneasy at that.

'What about…' The pause was deliberate, 'Gerald, the man Timony married? Surely he would have been more likely?'

Surprisingly Freeman shook his head. 'You may find it hard to believe,' he said, 'but I don't think the child was Portmann's. I think he would have told me,' he finished weakly.

'Oh?'

For the first time since they'd arrived Freeman smiled with genuine warmth and they had the sense that he had been fond of his leading man. 'Gerald was a sentimental old fellow,' he said. 'Old fashioned in the extreme. He would have owned up to the child if it had been his.'

'You know that we're in a position to check who was having sex with Timony?'

'What?' The news startled Freeman out of what little composure he'd had.

Joanna tilted forward in her chair. 'Did you never wonder what happened to the baby?'

The shutters came down. Slam. Freeman folded his arms tightly. 'She came back without it,' he said. 'That's all I knew. That's all I *needed* to know. She came back to work and there was no longer a problem.'

Joanna was astonished. 'You didn't wonder what had happened to it?'

'Not my concern.'

'So whose concern was it?' Joanna asked silkily.

Freeman appeared surprised at her ignorance. 'Diana's, of course.'

Then Freeman appeared to shrink back into his chair. 'Diana's, of course,' he said again quietly.

Joanna gave Korpanski a quick glance. *What was Freeman saying?* Mike gave her a vague shrug.

'There…'

'Go on, Mr Freeman.'

'I never thought it would come back to haunt me,' he confessed.

Joanna waited.

'I thought I would be dead before…'

He couldn't find the words. Joanna decided to press again, 'Why did you buy Butterfield?'

'I told you—sentiment.'

Joanna shook her head slowly. 'And as I told you, you don't strike me as a sentimental sort of man, Mr Freeman.'

He gave a sad smile. 'Sometimes,' he said, 'all of us are.'

'But there was a reason, wasn't there? You *had* to buy it, didn't you?'

Slowly, very slowly, James Freeman nodded his aristocratic head.

TWENTY

Tuesday, March 20, 3.30 p.m.

AND SO, ON a bright, clear day that whispered *spring is coming, spring is coming*, Joanna returned to Butterfield. Back to the very origin of it all. She had a team of officers with her but she hardly needed them. She knew why James Freeman had bought the studio and she knew exactly where to look.

The gate stood open now, the padlock forced. There were fresh tyre marks in the mud, leading towards the ruin, the tread still sharp in the damp clay soil. The house stood ahead of them, its ruin as tragic as the wrecked face of a past beauty. As they walked towards it Joanna sensed a movement and put her hand on Korpanski's arm to warn him while the team stayed back, awaiting instructions.

Diana Tong, a thick coat wrapped tightly around her, was peering down into the well. They watched her for a moment. She seemed in a trance, completely unaware of them. Joanna put her finger to her lips to silence Korpanski before approaching her. 'Mrs Tong.' The caution was on Joanna's lips but the woman who looked back at them was not quite there. She was smiling a sweet faraway smile as she looked up, a little puzzled to see Joanna and Mike. Perhaps she had been expecting another take of the series and thought Lily or Joab or Sean would enter stage right.

'Mrs Tong,' Joanna repeated gently.

Diana Tong did not answer but continued on her own line of thought. Then turned. 'She was *my* responsibility, Inspector,' she said. 'My charge.' She waited, before adding, 'I should have looked after her better.' Then her eyes drifted towards the gaping mouth of the well and Joanna focused on that.

'Who's down there, Diana, underneath all that?'

There was a sweet scent of old flowers, desiccated now, and behind that the hint of something long ago. Underlying that was the scent of a deep secret, like a dark red rose. It hinted at something that those who knew of it had believed would remain hidden for ever.

And then the older woman sank down, rested her head against the stones and began to cry, great racking, terrible sobs.

Joanna peered in. 'What is down there?' she asked again.

Diana Tong shook her head, once, twice, three times then stood up. She knew what was coming. 'Her father,' she whispered.

With a sigh, and a glance at her sergeant, Joanna began, 'Diana Tong, I am arresting you on suspicion of being involved in the murder and concealment of the body of Hugo Hook, father to Timony Weeks.'

Known to the nation as little Lily Butterfield.

'You do not have to say anything. But it may harm your defence if you do not mention, when questioned, something you later rely on in court. Anything you do say may be given in evidence.'

It is always interesting to watch how a suspect responds to being charged with a serious offence. In this case Diana Tong simply looked a little disappointed. 'Oh, Inspector,' she said, 'you've got it all wrong. It was Timony.' And the sobs returned.

DI Piercy was taken by surprise. She gave a quick, startled look at Korpanski. Had she?

They returned Diana to Leek for questioning, leaving the team with their instructions. Excavate the well.

Search the premises.

Find the evidence.

ON THE WAY BACK, Joanna called up a team to haul in their second suspect, the person she believed was behind it all. Meanwhile, they began to ask their questions, in the presence of a stony-faced solicitor who had less facial expression than the sphinx. As was her way, Joanna didn't waste time on preamble but dived straight in. 'It wasn't your idea, was it, Diana?'

'No.' Her voice was so velvety soft the word was hardly spoken. 'I would never have hurt her. I couldn't have done. But…' The word hung in the air.

'Then why?'

Diana gave an almost haughty glance at her young solicitor before turning all her attention on the two officers. 'You ask me why? You ask me that?' Hands on the table, palms uppermost in an appeal to be believed. 'Unbelievable. I tried to warn her. I wanted to protect her. But there came a point when I couldn't any more. I had no choice. No choice at all except to destroy her.' She extended her arms out on the table. The action made her vulnerable, almost pitiful. 'Before she destroyed herself. You need to understand the times, Inspector. Butterfield Farm was an iconic series in the early sixties. They weren't sophisticated times. They were naive and they were happy times. I simply wanted to preserve the memory at all cost. We both did.'

'Start at the beginning,' Joanna ordered.

Diana looked up then and Joanna realized how tortured those apparently calm grey eyes were. But they were also deeply thoughtful and intelligent.

She gave a little smile. 'You know a lot of it,' she started, 'but you've come to all the wrong conclusions. You've known but you haven't understood.'

'Then enlighten me,' Joanna invited.

The solicitor jerked and Joanna knew he was to tell his client to say nothing but Diana, who must also have anticipated this advice, put a hand on his arm to restrain him. 'It'll be a relief to unburden myself after all this time,' she said.

At her side DS Mike Korpanski was looking thoroughly confused. Joanna didn't even need to look at him to know this. Korpanski was practically snorting in frustration. His breathing was fast, his large fingers writhing and occasionally his feet scraped along the floor. Backwards and forwards. Inwardly, Joanna was smiling. DS Korpanski was crap at hiding his feelings. He was also crap at keeping still.

She turned her attention back to Diana Tong. 'Start at the beginning, Mrs Tong,' she said. 'Start with the silly little tricks that frightened her so much. What on earth did you hope to achieve by them?'

Diana's eyes searched for empathy but there was little chance she would find it. Not here, not in a police interview room. By her side the solicitor was making notes with the coolness of a teacher marking a very average essay.

Diana continued, 'I thought that if Timony was a little scared that it would work and I wouldn't need to do anything more to keep the past buried.'

Joanna reflected that there were two potential meanings to the words.

'But it didn't work like that. She kept on writing. The trouble was that she couldn't sort out what was OK to put in and what would be better left out. She couldn't even differentiate fact from fiction. She thought in storylines and dramatic cadences.'

And now Joanna was beginning to understand. 'The body in the well. She was going to write about it in the manuscript.'

Diana Tong nodded. Jerky, vigorous movements. She folded her arms and looked straight at Joanna, as though she had decided now was the time for truth. The whole truth and nothing but the truth.

'You know, I joined the work force of Butterfield in nineteen sixty-four. The show had been running for nearly four years and, I think I told you this before, I was quite a fan. To meet my idol was fantastic. Lily was my favourite.' A small laugh. 'She was everyone's favourite. She was just a sweet child then. I knew little about her past and James discouraged us from being too curious about her background. No one wanted the press to know that she came from poor stock. It might have destroyed the image the studio and particularly Freeman had built up so carefully. It was as though James wanted her past to remain a mystery.' She gave a cynical snort. 'As though he expected everyone to believe a fable, that she'd been dropped by the fairies or something.' The solicitor's eyebrows shot up and he gave his client a quick, surprised look before settling back into the bland, uninterested expression.

Diana continued without seeming to notice the movement. 'Then one day, on set, a man forced his way in. He was a vagrant. Unwashed.' A flash of distaste soured her features. 'He was wearing a badly fitting suit. He wanted money and…' Her eyes drooped with sadness. 'To cut a long story short, he threatened to tell the papers exactly who he was.'

'Her father,' Mike guessed gruffly.

She looked at him. 'Our lovely, innocent, sweet Lily,' she said. 'Her father a jailbird. It would have been catastrophic. People were a lot more snobbish and judgemental in those days.' She paused. 'However the Swinging Sixties and Free Love is bandied about I can tell you what it was like in nineteen sixty-four. It would have been the end of the series. She would have been dropped. Dumped. Abandoned. Her mother wouldn't have had her back. She had practically sold her into slavery.'

'So he was murdered and his body dumped down the well.'

She nodded.

'Who by?'

'I don't know,' Diana Tong said simply. 'Not for certain. I've always thought that Timony was probably involved, but that doesn't seem likely. When her memory returned about the well… I do know that James Freeman must have known all about it because it was *he* who bought the property and sealed it up. It might also have been *he* who torched it. I don't know.'

Joanna needed to think. 'But there is so much more, isn't there? Someone's been pulling your strings, haven't they? What I don't understand is why you've gone along with it.'

Diana's gaze was evasive.

A firm knock rapped on the door.

TWENTY-ONE

THEIR MAIN SUSPECT had arrived. Joanna switched off the recording equipment and stood up, excusing herself.

'He's here,' she said to Diana, whose response was a nibbling of her lower lip and an almost ashamed glance up into Joanna's face. She was wondering how much the detective knew. Then she stretched her arms out, put her head flat on the table and wept. It was an attitude of complete submission.

Joanna almost felt sorry for her. 'You'll be brought some tea,' she said.

She had not *met* him but she had *seen* him on a snowy, freezing morning, driving past her while she had crouched, hiding behind a rock. As she entered the room he struck her as an angry man. Angry and arrogant. She sat down opposite him, introduced herself 'for the record', asked him if he would like a solicitor present and when he said no, launched straight in without further preamble. She'd wasted enough time, doubted Timony's story for months and knew, in her heart, that she could and should have prevented her murder if she had picked up on the signs, had probed more into Timony's fantasy world. She could have stayed the finger that had pulled the trigger, held back the hand that had pointed the gun, screwed the cap of the tranquillizers back on before they were mixed, in excessive quantities, with Timony's goodnight glass of wine. She knew this so strongly that she almost felt she shared this man's guilt.

'Why did you hate her so much?' she asked. 'Why did you want her to suffer? What had she ever done to you?'

Something was niggling at the back of her mind even as she asked the questions. The administering of barbiturates didn't fit in with hatred and a desire to hurt someone.

He said nothing.

'How could you hate her so much?' she asked again. 'She was simply a faded woman, a past actress, someone who spent more than half of her life facing backwards, trying to recapture a fantasy land of Disney and childhood. How could you?' she asked again.

Stuart Renshaw practically sniggered. 'You ask that? You surely know who I am.' There was no humility and a large dollop of pomposity in his manner.

'She was just fourteen years old when you were born.'

She searched his face for two things: remorse—at least some—and a resemblance to his mother. She found neither.

Renshaw grinned. 'You still don't get it, do you?' he jeered.

Under the table Joanna felt Korpanski bunch his hands up into fists. The muscles in his neck bulged and she could see a pulse throb. He was dying to punch this guy. She could read his mind. But that wouldn't do. She met his eyes and he gave her a slight smile of reassurance. These days Korpanski was more able to keep his emotions in check.

Renshaw spoke. 'I know what you think,' he said.

'But you're wrong. Timony Weeks or Dorothy Hook wasn't my mother. It's Diana. Diana's my mother. Not Timony. Kathleen, Timony's sister, and her husband, Keith, adopted me and brought me up as their own. I've known that from the start,' he said disdainfully. 'It wasn't that I hated Timony. That wasn't it. It was Diana who owed me one.' He leaned back, pleased with himself to have *got one over* on the police.

Renshaw continued. Most killers like to boast and he was no exception. 'Timony was my adopted aunt. And I knew I would inherit, despite her being married to Van Eelen. My mother was going to make sure Timony divorced Van Eelen. I came to see them every now and then just to keep in touch. To remind them of my existence. *Auntie* Timony...' he used the epithet, *auntie*, with such disdain it made Joanna nauseous, 'was writing her memoirs. Lovely. More money for me. They were going to be worth a bob or two. But the trouble was she kept putting stuff in that she shouldn't have done, which could have proved embarrassing and led to a couple of court cases, which are expensive. On the other hand, you can't sue the dead.' His eyes crinkled. 'Always a bonus. With her out of the way the money would have been safe—even if her stories were libellous. Diana told me about the fracas between her producer and, let's say, a close family relative, which ended in tragedy. Timony's memory of it was returning, and originally I couldn't risk it being included, so I told Diana to play a few tricks. Move stuff. Play around a bit. If Timony was considered not quite the full shilling I could have had power of attorney.'

'Why shoot her?' Joanna asked simply.

'Oh, Inspector,' Renshaw said. 'You're forgetting. You need to prove that I did.'

Joanna needed to think on her feet. 'Then let's say, just for argument's sake, that I can.'

For the first time Stuart Renshaw lost some of his cockiness. 'You want me to imagine that I shot her, and to think up a reason why?'

Joanna nodded and Korpanski looked across—interested.

'I might have found the money useful, let's say,' he said coolly.

'But you won't inherit. She was still married.'

'Exactly. So why would I shoot her?' He grinned at Joanna.

SHE RETURNED TO Diana Tong, who was sitting with a wooden expression on her face. As before Joanna launched straight in. 'So Stuart is *your* son?'

Diana nodded. 'A twisted being.'

'Who was his father?'

Diana drew in a deep breath and folded her arms tightly around her. She was reluctant to tell so Joanna replaced the question.

'And Timony's child?'

'The baby had something wrong with her. She died. I did wonder whether Dariel's attack had something to do with it—damaged it in some way. I don't know.'

'Whose baby was it?'

Diana gave a mirthless chuckle. 'He was just a nobody,' she said disdainfully. 'One of the technicians. A lad. Blond and pretty. He and Timony had the odd fumble but we never thought it had gone so far. He was sacked and Timony fell pregnant, losing the baby—a little girl—while my own child flourished like a twisted tree inside me.'

'And your child's father was?' Perhaps this time Diana would tell.

'Bloody Gerald,' she said bitterly. 'And then he goes and marries Timony. Bloody pervert. Naturally I never told Timony who the father of my child was. She never knew. In fact, she never referred to it.'

'You had Stuart adopted.'

'I couldn't have returned to the set, unmarried and with a child. Kathleen was desperate for a baby and she had a husband who would support her. It was the obvious solution.'

She leaned back in her chair, at ease with herself now. 'As Timony and I were pregnant at around the same time we were sent away, the pair of us, like naughty schoolgirls. I'd thought Gerald would visit, and that he would eventually marry me. He was such a gentleman. But he kept away and on the telephone, only to marry Timony years later.' Joanna was beginning to understand where Diana's hate must have come from in their love/hate relationship. 'When I mentioned the fact that Timony's sister was desperate for a child of her own, it was he who suggested I had the child adopted.' She gave a half smile. 'Notice the word "I". Not "we". *I* had the child adopted. Gerald wanted nothing to do with it. With him,' she corrected. 'Timony and I were sent away together, the shame of Butterfield, to be hidden in a farmhouse in South Wales, under false names and registered with the local midwife. Neither of us was married. No one knew who we were. We hardly left the property. James organized everything. Absolutely everything for us. No,' she said, not without a sense of warped pride, 'Stuart was not Timony's. He is my son.'

And when Joanna said nothing she continued, fiercely defensive, 'Under the circumstances it was the best solution.'

'But you did get married. You could have—'

Diana nodded and smiled. 'Much later. Too late to have reclaimed the child I had signed away. I was married to Colin, one of the scriptwriters. It didn't last. To be honest it never was going to last.' She went quiet. 'I'm not built that way.'

'Who shot Timony, Diana?'

The grey eyes met hers with a hint of mockery. *'Not I, said the fly,'* she said, before the veneer of humour lifted from her face. She sobered up and looked upset. 'I couldn't have hurt her. I was far too fond of her.'

'But the little psychological tricks?'

Diana smiled, again caught between two emotions. 'Those, yes. I admit that. Stuart's an accountant. He could have had charge of her money—particularly if her memoirs fetched real money. One publisher had said he might pay a good price *if they were interesting enough*. The trouble was that to Timony the word 'interesting' meant that she was going to put lots of sensational stuff in, some real and some pure fantasy. The body in the well was one such example. Timony blocked out a lot of her past—it was obviously very traumatic for her.' A look of sadness suddenly crept into Diana's eyes. 'Being on the show quickly turned her into a star, and she had everything she wanted—adoration, money, status, marriage. She suppressed all the bad things, and over time it was as though they hadn't happened at all. It got to a point where she genuinely seemed unable to recall a lot of her past, she'd hidden it so well. But, as I told you, she lost a lot of her money, and the memoirs seemed a good idea. I thought she'd just make up some events, but unfortunately, writing them seemed to re-awaken the past—more than I could have anticipated. I tried to discourage her but it didn't work. The body in the well was real, and exposing that would have had repercussions. And as for the pregnancy, it reflected badly on all of us who should have taken care of her. I don't know if she wrote about them—as I say, I haven't read all of it—but Stuart wanted the book to come out. Or at least, he wanted the money. He wasn't too happy at the prospect of Timony being taken to court. I was just managing to convince her that to go ahead, to pub-lish and be damned,' she quoted, 'was not a good idea. She was coming around to seeing things my way. It was the writing that was cathartic to her, not the money.' At that she broke down.

When she raised her head it was to say, 'I couldn't have murdered her, not after everything we've been through.'

THEY CUT THROUGH the brambles and scraped away the nettles to find their target.

Time and predation degrade a body in an interest-ing but predictable way. While soft tissue and flesh are consumed, bones, hair, clothes and objects remain. All is not obliterated.

Whatever he had been in life Hugo Hook was dread-ful in death, a collection of bones, rags and a canvas bag which contained a little money—a ten-shilling note and half a crown, a rotted leather wallet and precious little else.

'Meet Hugo Hook,' Joanna said slowly to the assembled officers and police surgeon. 'Father to the most famous child actress of her time: Little Lily Butterfield.' She continued, 'He was released from prison in nineteen sixty-five. Visited his daughter on set, hoping for some help from his own little girl now she was such a famous actress. But Timony, Freeman, everyone, wanted him out of the way. He was killed and his body pushed into the well.'

'Who by?' It was Jason (bright) Spark who'd asked the question. Joanna drew in a deep breath. She needed to explain a few things to this young man. Plea bargaining, lesser charges, statements. She smiled at him. He may as well learn right now.

'We don't know,' she said simply.

TWENTY-TWO

One week later

THREE INTERVIEW ROOMS. Two major crimes. Three suspects. A thousand questions.

As she had suspected, the remains of Hugo Hook had not revealed many secrets, even under Matthew Levin's competent hands. The bones showed signs of injury, sure, but it was perfectly possible that they had been sustained purely by falling down the well. If no one had found him he would have died from a broken neck. It was unlikely—the film set would have been buzzing with people on the days they were filming but maybe, just maybe, the person who'd pushed him got lucky and they'd all gone home. Matthew had held up a cracked vertebra almost as a trophy. 'Broken neck,' he'd said, holding it aloft. 'But not necessarily murder, Joanna. Nothing conclusive here.' He'd given a mischievous grin and added, 'Sorry, darling.'

She couldn't quite conceal her smirk. He really did practically pull off the penitent look. But not quite. 'Hmm,' she'd responded, not pleased but not really surprised either. She'd left the mortuary planning their next move. She could bluff it through, sure. She'd like to see James Freeman squirm—just a bit—for an hour or so. But she knew the CPS was not going to swallow this big fish. She might have Freeman in custody but she'd never get a confession out of him. And likewise, Diana Tong would be unlikely to testify against him because she couldn't incriminate him without involving herself. Getting in *right up to the neck*. But as Joanna approached the door to Interview Room 3, where Freeman was being held, she suddenly surprised Mike Korpanski by banging her forehead with the heel of her hand. 'Of course,' she said. 'Stupid. I'm stupid.' She grinned at Mike. 'How can you bear to work with me?'

He made a face. 'Don't really know, Jo,' he tried. 'With difficulty?'

'Mike,' she said, turning away from the door.

He looked to her for an explanation. And she tried one. 'It's all too easy to put money into the equation and make that your motive, but I wonder...'

Korpanski simply stared.

'Her memoirs.'

And there it was.

Chapter 7.

1965. Not a good year for Timony.

A nightmare. It was a nightmare. This horrid man came pushing and shoving his way on to the set. I can smell him now. Alcohol, dirty clothes.

Joanna closed her eyes. She could almost hear Timony's voice, speaking in that high-pitched, girly voice.

He said he was my father. He can't be. That dreadful, horrible, vile thing cannot be my father. James took him away. And that was the end of that. He never bothered me again. Another display of a fan trying to claim they were related to me.

Except that he was.

'Hmm,' Joanna thought. Freeman *took him away...* that was the end of that...*never bothered me again*. It was, at best, equivocal. No jury would convict on that. Particularly as Timony had come across as someone who fantasized, who was unreliable and had a history of repeatedly calling out the police. That stopped Joanna in her tracks. It was. It had been, she corrected, a set-up to discredit her character. The woman she had met had been excitable, yes, but lucid. The worm of this thought slid nauseatingly through her brain.

She summoned Jason Sparks and Danny Hesketh-Brown to her to her and gave them a task. Mobile phone records can be so informative. As was the information her team had found on their trip to Stuart's office. Now she was ready.

She and Korpanski would move from room to room, from question to question. From suspect to suspect, trying to play them one against another.

Hesketh-King was standing at the doorway, practically hopping from foot to foot. He had news. She listened. And took Renshaw next. He was the sort of person who deflates quickly when their lead is challenged. She and Korpanski settled themselves into their chairs. Joanna met his eyes and smiled. 'I know James Freeman was one of your clients, and that there's been an increased amount of contact between you over the last few weeks, especially around the time of the incidents at Butterfield Farm. There's only one thing I don't know,' she said casually. 'How much did he offer you?'

As she'd expected the question completely threw him. He had prepared himself for an onslaught. Not this. This had startled him. 'What?'

'We know that you were offered money to kill Timony, weren't you?'

'Why would I do that, and risk my inheritance?'

'Oh, come on, Stuart. A doting nephew set against a husband estranged for ten years? I'd say that gives you a fair old sporting chance of inheriting, plus the money you received to kill your adopted aunt. And once you had the memoirs, you could blackmail Freeman by threatening to send them to the publisher unless he paid you even more money. You'd end up being quite a rich man.'

He fell right into the trap. '*How* do you know?'

His solicitor practically swallowed his teeth.

Ye-es. And Joanna felt like giving a high five. As it was she simply turned and gave Mike a broad, triumphant smile.

DIANA TONG WAS calm now, composed to the point of regal dignity. She eyed Joanna with absolute composure.

'Two murders,' Joanna said, sitting down opposite her. 'One killer.'

It surprised Diana. She raised her eyebrows. 'Two murders?'

'Timony and her father.'

Diana Tong licked her lips. 'One killer,' she queried. 'That's not possible.'

'No? You, Mrs Tong, were nearest to the truth. You were the one,' Joanna said, holding up her index finger, 'who knew the reason Timony had to die. But you couldn't quite bring yourself to destroy her autobiography, could you?'

'I don't know what you mean,' Diana responded stiffly.

'We know about Stuart, Diana. We know he murdered Timony, and you helped him. We spoke to him just now—we've as good as got a confession. It's over, Diana.'

Suddenly Diana Tong burst into tears, her stiff facade shattered. 'I thought by persuading Timony not to go ahead and publish, Stuart would back off. But by then he was too keen to get his hands on the money. He was impatient waiting for Timony to change her will; he seemed to *need* money. He knew she was still married to Van Eelen, but thought he had a good chance of inheriting anyway.' She looked up in despair. 'He's my son and I'd callously given him away because he didn't fit in with my lifestyle. How do you think I feel about that? I didn't have much of my own, so he searched elsewhere.' Then she appeared to feel the need to justify her actions. 'Unearthing the past was too traumatic for Timony. She couldn't cope with it. She was never a strong woman and she didn't suffer, you know. I made sure of that. I slipped something into her drink. She slept right through. She would have known nothing about it.'

Joanna glanced across at Korpanski, who gave her a little nod. Her instinct had been correct. Diana Tong could not have caused her friend to suffer. While she had been unable to prevent Timony's murder she had done the next best thing: put her friend to sleep. It fitted together. There was only one more question that needed to be asked.

'Are you prepared to testify?'

FREEMAN NEXT. HE looked tired and old. Defeated. She would have taken pity on him but when she recalled Timony's small, frightened face, lying still on the bed, she hardened her heart. 'You've made a lot of money,' she said. 'You're very wealthy.'

Freeman bowed his head as an admission.

'But Butterfield Farm was your most successful project.'

Closing his eyes, Freeman nodded.

'You couldn't bear for the real story to come out, could you? All the interviews, the dirty stories, the scandal, the complete disillusionment with your apparently perfect creation, not to mention your reputation, sullied for ever. So you had to get rid of her, just like you got rid of Hugo Hook. I suppose Diana's kept you up to date over the years?'

Again Freeman nodded. Hardly raising his head again but keeping it flopped down.

'You knew the content of Timony's tome. Diana had told Stuart, who passed on the information. You knew about her dwindling finances, and best of all you knew she had a greedy adopted nephew, who was actually Diana's son. Gerald confided in you when Diana got pregnant. You knew that Diana would feel she had an obligation to help Stuart, having abandoned him when young.'

Again, Freeman nodded, a broken man.

'At first you thought you could simply discredit her, didn't you, when Stuart got Diana to play silly tricks. But it didn't quite work, did it?' Joanna examined her fingernails. 'It was never going to work, James.'

As he said nothing she continued, 'And so you decided to promise Timony's adopted nephew a very tempting sum of money if he would simply liquidate your embarrassment. The memoirs would never be published.' She leaned forward.

'We have your phone records,' she said. 'Evidence of communication between you and Stuart Renshaw. You fool,' she said. 'Didn't you ever think that Renshaw would keep the memoirs and blackmail you?'

Freeman simply stared at her.

'The weak link was always going to be Diana Tong, torn between two people she felt obligated to. She didn't destroy Timony's work. She couldn't. She wouldn't. It's not possible, anyway. Not these days, with technology. And that, Mr Freeman, means that you are undone both for the past and the recent murder.'

He found some spirit then. 'You'll never prove any of it,' he said, furious now, maybe sensing he had been tricked and had spilt too many beans. His solicitor put his hand on his arm to restrain his client. Freeman shook it off.

Again, Joanna smiled.

TWENTY-THREE

Sunday, April 1, 8 a.m.

GABRIEL RUSH WAS already in his office and as Joanna walked into the station Sergeant Alderley met her and jerked his head to the left. 'He wants to see you.'

'Hmm.' Her job already threatened to become a little less pleasant. Rush was planted behind what she would always think of as Colclough's desk and he was watching her with narrowed eyes. He looked like the sort of copper who enjoyed *filling out forms*, someone who would love *protocol* and *methodology*, and *flow charts*, *budgets* and *reports*. She felt her optimism curl up inside her like a piece of stale bread.

'I suppose I should congratulate you, Piercy?'

Don't strain yourself, she thought. *It'd be nice but unexpected.*

He just about managed it, squeezing the words out like pips from a lemon. 'Well done,' he said tightly, without a note of enthusiasm.

And she answered with the obligatory, 'Thank you, sir.'

'An unusual case.'

'Yes, sir.' She was missing Colclough already and he hadn't even had his leaving do.

'So what next?'

'We'll get Renshaw on a murder charge, Sir, and

Freeman on conspiracy, but the payoff is that I don't think we'll get much to stick on Diana Tong.'

Rush tried to make a joke out of it. 'Well,' he said, 'as the song says: Two out of three isn't bad.'

It was all she could do to stop herself from rolling her eyes.

She returned to her office even more apprehensive about the future. 'I'm going to take a few days off, she said, 'play the happy housewife and keep my husband contented.'

'Get out of Rush's way, you mean.'

'No. Strive for marital bliss.'

Korpanski eyed her. 'And how long do you think that'll last?'

She tried to make light of it. 'I make it a policy never to answer a difficult question on an empty stomach and a sober mind. I think we should celebrate with lunch at the pub dead on twelve o'clock.' She smiled. 'So we have four hours to get some work done.'

Sunday, April 1, 4 p.m.

MATTHEW WAS HOME early too. As she parked her car she could see him looking around their garden, something in his hand. She watched him for a moment. Long-legged in chinos and a grey sweater, the light bouncing off his hair, which was never quite tidy. For a moment he appeared absorbed in the bulbs which coloured the garden—daffodils, tulips, some bluebells which had blown in from the churchyard and self-planted. He looked up, saw her, smiled and, when she reached him, slipped his arm around her. 'We've a letter,' he said. 'Looks like Caro's writing. And a London postmark.'

He handed it to her. A neat blue envelope. 'I'll open it inside,' she said. 'Brr. It's a bit cold.'

'Yeah. Let's go in.'

But as they entered the front door, he spoke. And shared his thoughts. 'This place is too small for us, Jo,' he said. 'We should have more of a family home.'

Her heart sank. Right to the bottom of that deep wishing well.

'I'm taking a few days off,' she said lightly. 'Shall we go away?'

He kissed her cheek very gently. 'I have a better idea, Jo,' he said. 'Why don't I take a few days off too? We can have a stay-cation and look at properties.'

The dismay she felt was as powerful as a thump on the chest. Was Matthew thinking about starting a family? It was her nightmare.

As she walked into Waterfall Cottage, her joyful heart had been replaced with an organ of solid stone.

* * * * *